John T Greene was born in Dublin and, after his boarding education, commenced work in insurance in Dublin in 1957. Then in 1961, he emigrated to the UK to work in the city of London again in insurance and eventually moved to Birmingham and from there to the North West where he is a director in an insurance brokerage.

To my lovely wife Christine for tolerating someone who lives in his mind.

John T Greene

MIKE BLACK

Entrepreneur and Secret Operations Agent

AUSTIN MACAULEY PUBLISHERS™

LONDON * CAMBRIDGE * NEW YORK * SHARJAH

A CIP catalogue record for this title is available from the British Library.

ISBN 9781398438590 (Paperback)
ISBN 9781398438606 (ePub e-book)

www.austinmacauley.com

First Published 2022
Austin Macauley Publishers Ltd®
1 Canada Square
Canary Wharf
London
E14 5AA

Chapter 1

His earliest recollection of life was playing with some friends; God knows who they were because at three years of age, friends were transient and haphazard, whoever the grown-ups stuck in your way, but the memorable point is that he carried on playing in spite of a mighty pressure developing in his bowels. He ignored it thinking it would go away but this was a regrettable mistake quickly brought to his attention when all of a sudden he had a problem—how to walk home without squeezing this lump now declaring its birth and demanding attention. He decided to walk bow-legged and this he felt was actually quite successful at glossing over the situation but this illusion was demolished by being quickly raised off his feet and being carried to his front door by a voice which declared to his mother, "He's done it again."

The 'again' word struck home and he knew subliminally that there was a double-edged sword swinging about; not that at two and a half he would have called it that but immediately, in his underdeveloped and innocent mind, he resolved not to poo-poo himself again.

The year was 1943 and he knew there was something not right about the times he had entered, possibly due to the darkness that seemed to prevail like a cloud over life itself and some evil that got mentioned a lot. This was also the year when his first sister arrived on the planet.

The little seaside town where Michael lived on the outskirts was called Youghal in county Cork in the far south of Ireland and its one claim to fame was the manufacture of a particularly hardwearing carpet, and of course, his own existence, or so he thought.

The belief in his own importance arose from a peculiar experience he had in the early morning, well, in the middle of the night really. He had the habit of leaving his bedroom to jump into his mother's bed after his father had gone to work; it was usually still pitch black and so he carefully felt his way along so as to avoid the stairs; until one particular night when he arose believing his father had already left and misjudged the way and tumbled down the stairs, finally settling near the bottom. He wasn't hurt but these funny gargoyle faces appeared cackling and jeering at his stupidity at having fallen. He was obviously crying but suddenly knew that they couldn't hurt him, he realised that there was some kind of barrier that they couldn't cross.

His father arrived and asked if he was hurt and when the answer was no, his father then asked why he was crying upon which he pointed to where the gargoyles had been, saying in an accusatory manner, "They have been laughing at me."

The father looked around and said there was no one there. "But they have gone now you are here." Michael's reply gave his father the shivers, The experience made Michael believe that there is something outside of this existence and whilst it was weird, it was also comforting in an odd sort of way.

The next significant event in Michael's life was when his father announced that they were moving to live with the grandparents on the east coast. It would have been around 1945, he didn't know it but the war in Europe had ended. He did however notice the change in the atmosphere of everyday life; suddenly, there was light chatter and delight in the air.

They arrived in the little town of Arklow in County Wicklow by steam train, all very noisy; with great bustle and rushing around, they alighted from the train. Michael's father Tom gathered up the suitcases and travelling crates from the luggage carriage at the rear with the help of two men who seemed to appear from nowhere and who announced with an air of importance that they were there to ferry them to the family home.

The luggage was moved to a horse and cart that went ambling off down the concrete road with a steady click of the old horse's hooves. The family—mother, father, Michael and Emily—were invited to board a large and very comfortable horse-drawn carriage and were settled in by the livery men who draped travelling rugs across their laps. They trotted down the slightly declining road with the click of the hooves reverberating between the buildings giving the whole experience a surreal and pompous feel. They came to a T junction right opposite a cinema with a large and majestic Catholic church on the right-hand corner; they veered to the right with a sudden lurch and sped up mainly due to the gravitational pull of the downward slope. The livery driver struggled to hold the sprightly horse in check and eventually managed to do so, much to everyone's relief. They then gracefully turned into the driveway between the family home and the local pub.

The family home was a large commercial premises comprising shop, a large yard with numerous two-storeyed sheds and to the side and over the shop, there were large private quarters raising the building to 3 storeys in all.

Suddenly, as if by magic, there appeared at the side of the carriage his grandparents smiling broadly and gushing effervescently. The grandfather was a tall man well over 6 feet with a corpulent build and a booming voice to match. He was immaculately dressed in a grey suit and white shirt finished with a dark blue polka dot bowtie. He exuded the warm confidence of success. Then there was his grandmother, very refined, of French Huguenot descent, dressed in mauve with a flowing French navy delicate scarf. Her hair was in a beautiful raised style and again, she gave off a warm calming radiance.

After the hubbub of the initial greetings, they were all invited to enter their new home and to Michael's surprise and delight, they were introduced to the three maids who again expressed great warmth and delight at their new wards. One of the staff who seemed to be in charge was a particularly warm and kind-looking young woman called Maisy who it turned out later would have the authority to cane the children should they push the limits too far. This privilege she hardly ever exercised as it went against her nature.

During the next few weeks of that summer, Michael got acquainted with his new surroundings, the chaos and bustle settled down to actual enjoyment. He decided that he liked it here in this busy business atmosphere. It became apparent that his grandfather was a man of some importance in the town, supplying most of the people with their coal and a lot of the surrounding farmers with feed for their animals and grain for planting. On top of that, he had preserved the local coastline from erosion and had introduced fridges over the whole of the country. Even at Michael's age, he was impressed.

On the third floor, where the maids lived, there was also a storeroom which contained all sorts of treasures. There were some duelling pistols, lots of books, an organ powered by foot bellows and some alabaster casts of Queen Victoria and Prince Albert, doubtless stored there in a hurry after independence was gained. Although the Protestants in the south republic were accepted immediately by the majority of the Irish, they nevertheless deemed it prudent to minimise their previous closeness to Great Britain. At that time, Michael was of course oblivious to this necessity.

Soon Michael's life was to take on a strict format not imposed by his parents but by the local primary school. It was a protestant school run by the Church of

Ireland and was soon to impress upon Michael the difference between him and the Roman Catholic children who in turn were also taught the difference. This mystical difference always seemed of great importance to some people and of no importance to the people he and his parents liked. It always was in the air and noticed but never spoken about. In later life, he recalled that it was almost like a class barrier that no one had the bad manners to mention outside of one's own group.

The primary school was a doddle after the initial hiccups concerning the use of the wrong hand when writing. After various attempts by the very kind-hearted Mrs Jacobs, who ran the junior school on her own and lived on the premises, to change him over, she surrendered to the obvious and he was labelled a Ciotog. Eventually, he moved to the senior boy's primary school just at the other side of the play yard but what a difference!

The master of the senior boys was a Mr Samuel Jones—a no nonsense, rule them by fear merchant—who strongly believed in corporal punishment and dished it out regularly. The punishment or medicine applied to the boys only. On several occasions, Michael got called out for not knowing the answer to some homework that had been set the previous day or even the day before.

"Boy, it's not the first time I've had to cane you for this, up to the front you go," whereupon Michael would walk to the front of the class to await his fate. It might be 6 of the best. "If you flinch, it will not count and you simply increase the amount of caning you will get," said Mr Samuel Jones. He expected the boys not to wince or show pain or they would suffer a kind of dismissive ridicule. No, you had to take your medicine like a man, not a mouse. He checked to see if you complained to your parents about the caning and if guilty, which Michael never was due to various distractions, you would pay a price.

Michael always took his punishment without flinching, the only precaution he took was to ensure that his thumb was flat with the rest of his hand thereby avoiding a considerable increase in the amount of pain and the possibility of it being broken for Samuel Jones took a certain pleasure in the sound of the swishing cane. Michael hardened his mind into a kind of defiance and determined that he would not show the slightest reaction which gave him the feeling of resistance in the face of what could only be described as bullying. Unknowingly, this mental approach was to be excellent training for his boarding school days.

Life between the ages of 5 and 11 for Michael was very pleasant in the little seaside town of Arklow in the county of Wicklow called the Garden of Ireland. In the summer, it was especially a child's paradise and then there were the two girls next door, a bubbly pair of sisters whose parents ran a pub and a kind of mini farm in the big yard at the rear. The girls went by the names of Margaret and Pauline and many a time, Michael was invited in by the girls to have a bowl of corn flakes smothered in the thick cream skimmed off a large bowl of milk stored in the cool pantry—absolute heaven. Of course, if you got caught, there would be hell to pay but they never were.

In the late 1940s, life in Ireland ran at an easy pace, the milk was delivered by horse and cart and the townspeople came out with various size jugs to fill up with fresh unpasteurised milk and buttermilk for cooking. There were all kinds of carts pulled by horses or donkeys. Michael was particularly fascinated by one such visitor to the pub next door. A hardened, smallholding farm woman who always arrived at the back end of the day as the sun was going down. She created a lot of hearty noise, greeting various bystanders as she and her horse and cart, which she rode sitting on the side with her booted legs dangling over the side, stopped at the pub next door. Her salutations finished always the same way with a loud greeting to Michael's father and the lifting of her trilby hat: "Grand evening Tom, you're looking well", and then she dismounted holding the reins in her large fist which she slung around the lamp post with a flourish and a big grin as it whisked itself so tightly that the horse couldn't or wouldn't move for the duration of her stay—usually 5 or 6 pints of porter, according to reports, after which she drove back to the farm in the country or rather, the horse took her home. Michael tried to work out if she was that way as a result of a hard life or did she kick with the other foot as he had heard about such things although didn't really believe them.

Two dogs also owned the premises and strolled in and out at will. The smaller one became a close friend to Michael who even shared his sweets with him on an equal basis. They strolled together all over the little town and they joined a gang or rather, the gang joined Michael. The gang particularly loved the riverbank and the large area of unspoiled land that separated the river from the town's edge. Although the river's edge was a dangerous area, none of the adults seemed to worry and nobody seemed to drown in the river.

Michael did have a close encounter or rather, his sister Emily did. As she was playing by the water's edge one day, she dropped something in the water and waded out to retrieve it but as the river was swollen from the previous few days of heavy rainfall, she got dragged in by the current and then fell over. Everyone laughed, Michael included, who reached out to help her up but she got pulled out a bit more until Michael was up to his waist in his effort to grab her and then suddenly, he realised that this was serious, very serious. He shouted to his sister that he was going to get help as he himself could not swim. He turned to wade out of the river only to find that the gang had disappeared.

Nobody to be seen anywhere; he assumed they had gone to get help but then again, maybe they had run away in fear. He charged up the lane to the main street and up a couple of hundred yards to the shop and as luck would have it his father was there and realised immediately the seriousness of the situation and ran with Michael to the river. His father immediately dived in and in his panic started to swim upstream until Michael shouted, "No, the other way."

Swimming downstream with the tide was quick and his father within a few minutes had caught up with Emily who was floating on her back. Luckily, she had been dressed in a heavy duty overcoat which saved her life. The relief was so uplifting that no accusations or reprimands were made. This episode taught Michael about relationships and people; he was dismayed that all his friends had run away and not to get help as he discovered later but just to get away. He learned from this scary episode and moved on to new friends later. He also learned to be independent and to know that there are very few people that one can truly rely upon when the chips are down; and he decided to learn to swim.

One day Michael's grandmother took him to the window overlooking the main street and asked him to choose which of the two men walking down the footpath on the other side he would like to be like when he became an adult. Michael replied, "Why, the smart one in the suit, of course."

His grandmother smiled and said, "Well then, you had better start studying hard and pass the exam that is coming up and get yourself a scholarship. If you pass your exam, you can go off to college and make something of yourself." The conversation went on and it was made clear that the Master at the primary school did not think it was worthwhile him sitting the exam as he would fail. This apparently enraged his grandmother who he supposed regarded it as an insult as did he himself. Between them, they decided that Michael would stay in an hour or so after school in the drawing room and study and his grandmother would check if it had gone into his head or disappeared into the heavens. This worked fine and the checking was intensive but the end result was he got a full scholarship and booked his place in one of the most prestigious boarding schools in the country, namely —Kilgarry College.

The elation in the household was palpable. It was as if he had won the greatest prize on earth. He walked on air for several days and began to feel special. This was the moment that ambition was born and the feeling would drive him for the rest of his life.

This also turned out to be the last summer of innocence, of lazy carefree days meeting his friends and chatting to each other about their ambitions and expectations while they strolled to the beach with towels enclosing swimwear under their arms. Some days bike rides were arranged to nearby villages or simply around the harbour either watching the fishermen unload their catch and perhaps scrounging a few fish to take home but more likely surveying the multiple array of yachts and the young attractive females sunbathing on the decks.

That particular summer held one more pleasant surprise for Michael in that he had to go and live with his aunt Gertrude for a couple of months as she had fallen and badly sprained her ankle to such an extent that she was unable to walk even to the local shops. At first glance, this appeared to be a kind of restriction on Michael's freedom but it turned out to be a very pleasant sojourn with a delightful lady who, although Irish, had worked and lived in England and now possessed the most beautiful "posh" accent.

Aunt Gertrude lived in a large end terraced house right next to the beach with a long back garden full of flowers and vegetables. Michael's aunt arranged that he would do the chores in the morning and prepare the vegetables and then would be free to join his friends to roam the wild grass shore that separated civilisation from the aggressive waves that tried relentlessly to erode the coast and were only prevented from doing so by the rows of timber pylons acting as a breakwater. Dinner was at 6 pm sharp which his Aunt managed to cook in spite of her injury but Michael's help was required to set the table. After dining, his aunt invariably gave Michael an elocution lesson including the pronouncing of the English 'th' sound, requiring the tongue to travel all the way to the back of the front teeth; a most exaggerated and affected contortion. Nevertheless, Michael obliged his aunt and then forgot about it until later in life, when it loomed large again.

Then suddenly, the summer was over and preparations for college were upon the family. Aunt Gertrude came to the rescue by organising a trip to Dublin to purchase the clothes and standard suits to comply with the college's regulations.

Michael found this an eye-opening experience. The amount of clothes; the cost seemed enormous and this opinion was reinforced by the attitude of the shop's salesmen who seemed in awe of the rich English lady. In retrospect, much later in life, Michael realised his aunt relished the feeling of power as she hesitated then chose; only to change her mind for something more expensive. The bigger the bill got, and the more she treated the experience casually as something one has to endure, the more obsequious the shop staff became. It was after all an unusually good day for them.

They finished off the day by having lunch at the Savoy which of course had been reserved so upon announcing her name, they were ushered by the maître d'hôtel to their table and were served by elderly waitresses in black dresses with white aprons. The food was unpretentious but wholesome and left Michael with a nice warm glow. He looked around the busy dining room at the immaculate tables and the hustle and bustle of the head waiter pirouetting like a ballet dancer, signalling his underlings in every direction, creating the impression that this was the place to be. The glitter, the sparkle, the activity was electric and indeed, it was the place to be.

When they left the hotel, Michael felt that one day, he would be important like his aunt.

At last the day of departure on the voyage to his education came and he was just 12 years old, full of trepidation but determined not to show it; after all, he had worked hard to have this opportunity, hadn't he? He knew life would not be a bed of roses as he would only see his parents once during term if they were able to get away. It did take half a day to get to Kilgarry so he couldn't expect any more from them.

At about 10 am, both parents and Michael piled into the Wolseley 4/44 saloon and headed off to Kilgarry College where they arrived safely after 4 and a bit hours; they were too early for induction so they headed off to a café just 100 yards from the college entrance where the owner of the café/shop was known to Michael's father. A pleasant hour was passed and then back to the college where they were greeted by some of the masters in their very impressive black gowns. The masters made reassuring pleasantries and greeted Michael like a young man emphasising how wonderful the college was and how he would soon fit in and feel at home as it was that kind of homely caring place. Michael soon discovered that it wasn't completely so for many.

The college building was old and internally harsh; no doubt designed to make a man of every inhabitant. The only luxury was adequate heating throughout, with the main community hall having a pipe stove in the middle of one of the long walls thus dividing the room into two halves. The new entrants, which included Michael, were forbidden to cross the line of nails imbedded in the old floorboards running from the stove to the opposite side of the hall. This of course was a rule brought in by those who were on their second year or more and was purely for the dubious pleasure of punishing the new boy unlucky enough to inadvertently put a foot or just a toe on the line of nails. The punishment was to have one's head held between the hip of the punisher and the fist of their hand with the thumb knuckle driven in a screwing movement into the soft part of the temple at the side of the head. This made the recipient holler in agony with arms flailing about.

There was worse for those boys with soft or over-smooth complexions where they were given female names and periodically had to suffer some lout jumping on their back and pretending to simulate having sex; utterly degrading. This didn't happen to Michael as he didn't qualify, which was probably fortunate as he was not the type to suffer such behaviour and would undoubtably have reacted so violently that matters might have come to the notice of the staff with obvious consequences. Every so often, boys were expelled, and not always deservedly.

The next downside that Michael discovered was that the senior boys picked one or two of the newcomers to be their fag. A fag was someone who ran around after the senior as and when required—to go to the tuck shop or to collect his evening coffee and biscuits and of course, to polish his shoes and clean his rugby kit, etc. The selection was supposed to be haphazard as the new boys were dispatched one dark night to the playing field where they hid until someone found them. If it was one of the decent seniors, you were lucky in that you were baptised with water from the river that ran alongside the field; whereas if you were caught by one of the nasties, you were thrown into the river completely, much to the hyena baying amusement of the bastards whom God had wired up incorrectly in a moment of distraction.

As Michael had worked this out, he cleverly engineered to be caught by one of the decent guys and whilst he had to do his duties, he nevertheless was treated with respect and got through the toughest part of his four years at the college without too much misfortune.

During the second year, life got much better and he was enjoying the academic side as well as the rugby and hockey in winter and the athletics and tennis in summer, not to mention the cricket. During testing for cricket, he hit a magnificent six and then got taken to one side and shown how to hold the bat, and never did anything good thereafter. The one thing he was good at was athletics and he broke a 9-year-old record in the 440 yards. This only happened by chance as the unspoken rule was that in any race, the fastest runner was placed in the inside track but on this occasion, whether by chance or a clever move by the master in charge, he was positioned in the second lane.

This so angered Michael that he decided to show them how wrong they were and abandoned his usual tactic of waiting for the last minute to suddenly increase the speed so displaying how easy it was to win; very arrogant but this he knew. On this humiliating occasion, all the more so because of the crowd attending for the end of summer term, he decided to go from the start at a cracking speed which he was able to maintain due mainly to a mixture of anger and humiliation. At the end, he was 110 yards in front of the second-place runner and satisfied with himself. Then came the icing on the cake as he was informed he had broken the record which had stood for 9 years. This was almost irrelevant to him as he was unaware of the record and in any case, he simply wanted to prove his superiority in the matter.

However, it was the academic side that he was really interested in and in that he excelled, coming near the top in most subjects. He found the absorption of knowledge empowering in a way that was unexpected. Somehow he was aware of how lucky he was to have such a good education in that it gave a reasonably intelligible mind an advantage in the outside world of being treated as being more intelligent than one really was. This was an advantage he would one day be able to use. When the four years were up, he passed his exams and went on to a further college in Dublin.

Dublin turned out to be an unexpected pleasure; not the college so much as the city with its charm, its diversity and the sheer hustle and bustle of life in a hurry to be lived. Michael loved it and was determined to make the best possible use of his time there. He managed to wrangle, by one means or another, plenty of time out to visit an aunt who lived in Howth, a beautiful outcrop to the north of the city, or otherwise just to visit the city itself with its beautiful restaurants, cafes and shops; vibrancy was in the air and Michael was determined to absorb it all. He knew then the turn his life would take.

He was not yet 17 years old but tall and slim with dark hair and a firm jawline; he knew that the girls were attracted to him and this he liked although still with absolutely no experience.

He passed out of college with good exam results and went home for the last carefree summer holidays.

Chapter 2

Michael and his friends knew that life would soon get serious and they would have to start being adults who earned a living. This last long summer passed too quickly and his father got him a job. One evening, leaving to live with his aunt Beatrice in Dublin, Mike's father tried to warn Michael about girls; wayward ones in particular. They had never had this kind of discussion and his father was not comfortable with the whole experience so Michael interrupted him with: "It's OK Dad, I know all about it so don't worry."

"Oh you do; well, that's good then," his father replied with obvious relief.

The job was with the Irish Insurance Company, a very nice company, and the particular department he worked in had extremely friendly people there. His department was on the ground floor with large mahogany desks and a stout broad counter surrounding and framing the department from public intrusion. A row of kiosks to one side of the department contained dictation booths where one went to speak into a black cylinder with a paper marker incorporated to enable one to mark off the length of the various letters. You were trained to order your copies up front and failure to do so meant the typist had to do the work all over again and this brought the head typist down from the heavens to make her complaint to the chief clerk and humiliate the offender.

Michael experienced this once and learned his lesson. At the side of these booths was the entrance to the policy registers. These ledgers measured 18 inches across by 24 inches long and 6 inches deep; well-bound monsters not to be dropped. The juniors, of which Michael was one for a short period, had to paste up pieces of paper called endorsements into the correct policy details and it was a soul-destroying chore; fortunately, he was soon relieved of this task.

The chief clerk, a Mr O'Byrne, had a pastime in that he liked painting watercolours of landscapes; when Michael discovered this, they were able to have long conversations as Michael loved painting in either water or oils. This made life in the otherwise very strict atmosphere more pleasant and had the added benefit that his letters with tiny mistakes such as commas missing were passed after having the comma inserted in pen. This was a concession not given to many. Michael stayed with his Aunt Beatrice, a beautiful fun-loving lady who was very kind to Michael and treated him like the son she never had. She was 5 feet and 5 inches tall, slim with dark hair and she laughed at intelligent jokes— usually made by her. Her husband, a man of doubtful orientation or, as Michael would eventually find out, not doubtful at all. He batted the approach away with great dexterity feigning complete ignorance of the not so subtle suggestion by declaring that he didn't understand people with these desires but supposed they were born that way. Michael did debate with himself as to whether he ought to bring this matter to his aunt's attention and decided not to as it would only destroy her happiness and of course, she may have been aware of her husband's inclinations and tolerated them as they otherwise had so much in common.

They both played the organ in two different churches and liked the same highbrow music and visited the opera and ballet. In fact, they took Michael to his first ballet; he enjoyed it and it opened his eyes to the pleasure of appreciating something that was different.

One summer evening, Michael left the office with his friend Rory, a particularly good-looking specimen who was admired by most of the young women in the office; of course, he ended up with the most beautiful and the nicest girl who absolutely adored him. He had a shock of very dark hair and a broad smile which he could manipulate to be warm and inviting or sardonic according to his whim and his hand movements were mesmeric when used to pick up a pen or any object and seemed to hypnotise the females around him.

That evening, as he and Michael went through the front door into Dame Street in Dublin, they noticed a small group of colleagues from another department gathered together in a group and approached them to see if they were going for a drink. As they were a step or two away, one named O'Connor turned to Michael and said, "This is not for your ears, you fucking English spy."

Michael was astounded and open-mouthed and could hardly believe his ears. Rory stepped into the conversation, "Come on, Michael, I can't stand these kind of people and we don't want anything to do with this nonsense. Let's go for that drink." They did and after discussing the matter for a while, had a great evening. In Michael's mind, Rory was a good friend and had probably avoided a nasty fight which would have got everyone sacked.

That was the first time the fact that Michael was a protestant was brought to his attention like a bolt from the blue. O'Connor could not have thought that Michael was a spy; it was just his way of maliciously pointing out "you are not one of us; you are not really Irish". It served to confirm the way Michel felt about himself, his family and his ancestors. He had often wondered which king or which English politician had made the conditions seductive enough for a lot of English people to emigrate to Ireland. He was aware of course that Ireland was for a long time part of Britain and assumed that period was when it happened. Hence, the feeling of not quite belonging. He knew one day he would emigrate to his roots.

In the meantime, he resolved to find another job as apart from this incident, the pay was pretty miserable. After a month or so, he answered an advert for a position at another insurance company called The Northern Counties Company Ltd. On arriving for the interview, he noticed as he walked through the front office to the manager's private office that there—waving at him—were a bunch of his school friends from Kilgarry College. He had often wondered what had become of them and now he knew and smiled back at them but not too much as he was slightly nervous. Upon entering the branch manager's office, he was asked to take a seat and the first question was "when can you start?" Seeing Michael's surprise, the manager, a Mr Taylor who was English, explained, "You probably noticed a lot of your Kilgarry College companions outside; well, they are all great workers and I have never had a problem with any of them so I assume you will be the same," he said with the slightest increase in his voice at the end of the sentence.

Michael relaxed and gushed his confirmation and exclaimed how happy he was to see them. It was agreed he would start after his obligatory one month's notice to his present employers. Michael thought this must be the fastest interview of all time and felt quite elated at the privilege his education had given him, and also, of course, his colleagues.

He settled into his new job in this Irish branch of the English company where all seemed more normal to him. It had a less antiquated atmosphere and while almost all of the employees were Irish, there was no suggestion of nationalism but there were a few senior guys who had returned from the war and were reinstated into their former positions. They never talked about the war but they were quietly respected for having done their bit.

Having negotiated a 50% increase in salary, he was now able to have a few perks such as buying a bicycle to enable him to move freely around the city. He also decided to move out from his aunt's home, which although very comfortable was nevertheless somewhat restrictive for a young man wanting to experience the thrills of the opposite sex, wine and song—in that order of preference.

To facilitate this transformation he managed to get a bed in the local YMCA. The only downside was that the place was half full of religious zealots and would-be preachers who believed without question the bible in all its details, including the world being made in 7 days by God. The upside was the other half were what Michael considered normal just like him; well, perhaps not just like him; after all there can't be two of him.

The deal consisted of a warm room albeit shared with a zealot, a good breakfast and a large evening meal all for a pittance. He made some good friends and had many a night drinking to excess and chatting up the girls but to no avail; however, he was not bothered for when you are drunk, everyone seems to be your friend whether they are or not.

Around this time, Michael decided to shorten his name to Mike as that to him reflected the new image of a man determined to make his way in the world and Michael seemed too intimate and altogether too personal and so he decided to keep it for personal close friends or lovers. Not that the latter was likely in a country that banned contraception. The girls were too afraid and the men were also afraid of making some girl pregnant and having to marry her to save her from a life of shame regardless of whether or not she was the love of your life.

One day, Tony—a friend also living in the YMCA—suggested getting a flat together and in fact knew of one in a block of flats just opposite that was immediately available. Mike thought about it for a whole minute and agreed to go and have a look. Calling it a flat was a slight exaggeration but nevertheless it was a two-bedroom with an attached kitchen area and relatively new in good condition so they decided to take it. They were obliged to give one week's notice to the YMCA and then they moved in. The other tenants were mostly students or young people starting out in life and it wasn't long before the pair made several friends.

Within a year, Mike asked Tony if he would like to go to England. They discussed it for a week or so going over the problems, the biggest of which was money—or the lack of it. They hit upon an ingenious solution in that they would go to London for a week having first of all answered adverts or having written to various prospective employers and arranged interviews. They both had a few lined up but Mike had the most, with 13 interviews in a week. He subsequently got 12 offers which set his mind alight and reinforced his desire to go to what he regarded as the centre of the world—London.

In January 1961, Mike and Tony set off on the adventure of a lifetime but one that was stressful and quite frightening. Catching the boat to Holyhead was the easy bit, the train to London a different matter—daunting. The fog and dirt invaded one's clothes, not to mention one's nose. The carriage was well worn and dirty and not really warm enough for a cold damp January night. The night air and the noise conspired to add a further layer of unease. The journey to London seemed to take forever in spite of sleeping in short fits from time to time, always woken by clanging and banging to realise that it was really cold but as dawn approached, they finally arrived in the enormous awe-inspiring capital.

Leaving the train in a flood of people, the noise increased as did the excitement and the hustle and bustle of hurried activity. People were walking and then breaking into a run or a trot across the station chasing some timetable or hoping to catch a taxi before someone else. It was all go. Mike and Tony strolled, stopping to gawp at this and that and trying to work out in which direction they would find a taxi. Eventually, they succeeded and set off for their hotel in Bayswater. The hotel was enormous. "God, it must have hundreds of rooms," said Tony.

"Looks OK to me," replied Mike, "better than the one down the road. Did you see the sign 'no blacks, no dogs and no Irish'?"

"Didn't know some people didn't like us, did you, Mike?" said Tony.

"Yeah, it's the labourers; they like to drink till they're blotto and then they fight and wreck things; a great example I don't think, just another hill for us to climb."

"Anyway, let's go in and see what's what."

The man on reception was tall, slim, very polite, brown and French, or at least had a French accent, and was wearing a smart suit, very dapper. Mike liked him instantly. They mentioned to the tall receptionist that they had booked a room on a semi-permanent basis. "Ah oui," he said and smiled. "Je sais, we get a lot of people starting out in life staying until they get a flat or perhaps students staying until the end of their course. So that's fine," and he allocated the room which he and Tony would share. "You will be fine here," he smiled. "Voila! Your keys." Mike took the keys and shook his hand warmly. Later, they were to become good friends and Mike learned he came from Mauritius, a small island once occupied for a while by the French.

Halls Hotel was different and encompassed perhaps 100 rooms with a maze of corridors and non-soundproof rooms. The occupants were returnees from the empire with beautiful manners and even more beautiful accents who displayed an over-cheerful outer personality while they strode from the card room to the television room to the lounge on carpets that were once magnificently opulent but had been worn and faded by years of overuse but the illusion must be maintained, at least until one retired for the night.

Those starting out on life's path and the students would eventually hear the sad truth of the one-time rulers of plantations across the empire whose lives had gone from a rich life of plenty with servants to a tired hotel room in Bayswater living on pensions that had not kept up with the times and with little or no chance of getting the retirement cottage in the countryside they so justly deserved. This became evident from the arguments and tears coming from the rooms as one walked along the corridors. Michael found this upsetting but not as much as the realisation of how the government of one of the greatest countries in the world had abandoned its own.

A deeply disturbing wake-up call on how believing in a large enterprise such as a government or perhaps also a company or large corporation can end in crushed dreams and a feeling of being trapped in desolation for the last few years of one's life. The accusations from your wife of being naïve and not taking her advice when she pointed out years ago that you should have been more aggressive in your dealings with the powers that be. "And you should have been more like Charles Parsons, crooked he may be but his wife doesn't have to put up with nothing for retirement, he made sure to get his slice of the pie but you, oh no, you played it straight, Mr Nice guy, and now look where we are."

All this aside, Michael, or Mike as he now was called, revelled in working in the city. His job in the Legal & Merchant Insurance Co Ltd involved him in preparing enquiries for quotation and necessitated drawing on his exam studies. These he had recently finished and was therefore qualified but still needed experience.

He was once again in the Material Damage Department surrounded by colleagues who all appeared to speak with the same posh accent; it was only 6 months later he discovered that the girl who sat next to him was a cockney as broad as they come. Time allows the ear to discriminate, which is a shame in some ways. The chap at the front, Charles, maintained his status which he obtained by standing up to make the occasional "funny" with his thumbs entrenched in his yellow waistcoat and finishing his tale with a guffaw that was repeated at least three times, much to the polite amusement of those within earshot.

One morning Mike was called over by Mr Taylor Cummings, head of the section, to discuss a recent enquiry and told to prepare a proposal that gave the required cover with the suggested wording. He took the file and very quickly resolved the situation with his ability to recall information from his studies and gave the file back. He expected some recognition of his efforts but instead heard Mr Taylor "Fucking" Cummings put his resolutions over the phone to a superior upstairs as if they were his own ideas and finishing with "Yes Sir, my thoughts exactly."

Mike decided to give the creep a bum steer next time. The man had no shame stealing his ideas in full voice and within his hearing.

A few days later, a broker came to the office to discuss a problem on a contract that he had just arranged. Most of the staff were doing their best to pretend that they were too busy to notice him so Mike decided to approach him. After some discussion, the problem was resolved to the broker's satisfaction. The broker then asked if he would like to join him for lunch. Mike immediately accepted without checking the protocol.

While putting on his suit jacket, he noticed some looks of disapproval amid murmurings which he decided to ignore. The broker was James Cotteridge, a well turned out dapper chap full of self-confidence but nevertheless with an overtly charming and easy personality who was pleased to pass on certain bits of information as they walked down Fenchurch Street, in effect "marking Mike's cards". They arrived at Mario's Ristorante, a quaint crowded warm place, to a large area of seating broken up with individual alcoves to provide a measure of privacy as most if not all of the clientele were business people. This was all new to Mike but he got the picture immediately and determined that one of these days he must become a regular.

James walked straight up to the counter and was immediately greeted by a well-endowed blonde with a bubbly personality who asked him what he would like in an overtly suggestive way. James grabbed the inside of the bar counter, leaving his hand there and she managed during the serving process to somehow rub her ample bust up against his hand. They both laughed quietly but without embarrassment at the openly outrageous act. He then realised that James had the 'it' factor which not only worked on the female side of the population but also on the male side if the number of credit cards was any indication of his ability to climb the corporate ladder.

Mike however listened to what James was willing to impart and absorbed it all. He liked James and they both hit it off. It was at this time that Mike got a vision of the way to proceed if he was to succeed in this business and it was not to get stuck in his present position but it would suffice while he learned and brushed up his act and particularly mastered the numerous 'th' sounds that abounded everywhere it seemed. He spotted them at the beginning of words without any trouble and then at the end of words but it was the bloody ones in the middle that took a bit longer to discover. He eventually mastered it by seeing sentences in his mind as if on a movie screen and when a lot of words with the letter 't' scattered around appeared, he would slow the speech down to ensure he put the 'h' in where it was required and not where it wasn't required—this latter error in his mind being equally embarrassing if not more so. But this mess had to be conquered and it more or less was in the end.

James and Mike had reason to meet up from time to time and eventually, Mike was introduced to quite a few of the movers. Mike decided to play it cool and just glided into a collection of wholesale brokers who, over time, painted the full picture in Mike's mind. He knew that the success he wanted was to be had in the wholesale broking market with its access to most of the major insurers and to Lloyds of London.

The business that they placed is called broking and comes from all around the UK as any case where there is a real risk has to be placed in London because that is where the capacity exists to cope with high risk enterprises. The main players were Lloyds of London and those insurers that operated around the Lloyds market are referred to as fringe insurers; not in a derogatory way but simply because they were located on the fringe of Lloyds.

Chapter 3

One day James introduced Mike to Malcolm Westbrook with the words, "Mike here is looking to get into broking. Have you got anything in your company at the moment?"

To Mike's surprise, the answer was, "Well actually, yes; we are looking for a junior broker as due to a reshuffle in the internal ladder, we find ourselves a little thin on the ground." The job consisted of taking files into Lloyds and the fringe market companies; the object being to get underwriters to accept the risk or at least indicate a lead line so as to get other insurers to offer to follow thus getting the whole risk covered. It involved a lot of queuing up in corridors waiting for your turn to make your presentation and suffering the odd insult at times, especially if you were not on top of the information required.

Mike thought about it for a day or so and then phoned Mr Westbrook to say he would like to go in for an interview. Mr Westbrook bade him to call him Malcolm and agreed on a date and time. Needless to say, he got the job partly due to James's introduction as that is always helpful. The city likes to know that you are a likeable sort; they don't like surprises.

The job went well from the outset and his new colleagues were very helpful, altogether more human than those at Legal and Merchant. The atmosphere here at Greenacre Commercial was light and uplifting, something to do with the feeling of success in getting risks placed at the right rates and the commissions and/or charges that could be earned, giving a constant feeling of a job well worth doing. Lunch hours were short unless you were out on business but normally, the time was used to bone up on the afternoon's presentations. After hours, usually after 5:30 pm, was different.

A group from the office would go to their favourite haunt and drink and discuss the day's trials and tribulations for an hour or two. Two of his colleagues knew their way around and varied the drinking hole to meet up with underwriters on a personal level as getting to know underwriters paid dividends. On a daily basis, the underwriters were God to the brokers and they used their power to lord it over the mere mortals with comments such as "that broker turns them out nicely, doesn't it" quip to a colleague. Going out with the boss was a bit of an eyeopener however as suddenly the boot moved from the underwriter to Malcolm as he was noted for his very generous hospitality and underwriters were only too happy to become his friend and get invited to his villa on the Italian Riviera for a long weekend away from the hassle of work and family life.

These visits always included anything up to 10 or 12 underwriters and started with a round of golf for those interested or a day of sightseeing but finishing off with an extensive tour of the local bars imbibing pints of beer and ending with a meal for all guests at a large central table lavishly decorated in an expensive restaurant. Every care taken to make each guest feel special and important but at the same time pressing home the power and wealth of Malcolm's company. Good business. No mention of business however and no favours asked for as that would be bad form. But the whole purpose was not for a trip abroad but to ensure his staff got close to the favourite underwriters and that the underwriters got to know any new chaps, which in this instance included Mike.

A few days later, Mike called on one of the chosen with a rather large but heavy risk to place, not everyone's cup of tea from an underwriting point of view and the existing insurers were refusing to renew. The underwriter looked at it flicking through the pages, murmuring to himself and finally looking up at Mike. "Well, existing insurers kicking it out then?"

"Yes," replied Mike and went into the bullshit he had practised when Arthur the American underwriter called it to a halt.

"OK, OK I'll tell you what I'll do," and proceeded to quote a high but not exorbitant premium but there was a downside. "I want an excess of £25,000 to make these bastards improve their housekeeping and tell Malcolm only for him." Another one for the Italian Rivera then, thought Mike. It was sold to the clients on the basis they were lucky to get any cover with the present claims history. Another job well done.

Many more similar incidents arose during the year and Mike realised the importance of entertaining the underwriters and of course never asking for anything so nothing illegal and therefore no need to trouble one's conscience. It goes without saying that a few of the lesser known underwriters did go too far enriching themselves on the back of their underwriting facilities to the point of bringing down the enterprise. Great shock and horror in the media but not to those in the know who had been quietly predicting it, it was more a case of when not if as the culprits had done it before but somehow managed to persuade another money man to back them again. These companies are usually registered abroad where the criteria for approval is easier.

One day in early January 1964, Mike walked into the office early as usual to a very sombre atmosphere, the reason being the sudden and unexpected death of Malcolm. Apart from the shock everyone felt, there was panic on how this would affect the business. As well as deciding who would be allowed to attend the funeral, a conference was called to discuss the redistribution of the accounts that were managed by Malcolm for many years. The clients had to be advised of course but first of all, the business had to be divided over the various brokers.

The second in line Freddie Baker took control of the situation and called a meeting at 3 pm that afternoon. It was obvious to Mike that Freddie had been working furiously all morning as he had clear instructions for everyone concerned; all ten brokers attended and were told exactly how their jobs were to be altered. The top 3 brokers were taking the larger cases handled by Malcolm and the smaller SMEs were given to Mike and he also inherited Malcolm's secretary as all the others were already equipped with secretaries.

Mike had met Malcolm's secretary only once; a mature woman of indefinable age, he could only guess at her age but she was attractive and very efficient by all accounts. Mike was told he could attend the funeral if he wished as Malcolm had taken a liking to him. He confirmed that he would attend.

Mike made his way to Malcolm's office to find that his new secretary was busy rearranging the files having given away the 3 largest cases. She stopped on seeing him saying, "I'm your new secretary subject to you agreeing of course."

He replied, "And why wouldn't I agree? I have been told you are very efficient."

She hesitated and said, "Well, I am no spring chicken and you might prefer one of the younger girls but in Malcolm's eyes, of course, I was still young."

Mike thought for a moment as he could see danger lurking just out of sight; he knew the answer had to be carefully crafted to convey sincerity without appearing to ingratiate himself or to over flatter which always sounds false. She was 5'7" tall, slim with a tiny waist and broad hips, in fact quite beautiful. "Well, you look great to me," he said, looking straight into her eyes which were an unnervingly deep blue/grey and he felt himself blushing so he turned towards his desk saying, "The real question is can you put up with a young whippersnapper like me?" He fiddled with some executive gadget saying, "This is Malcolm's desk I presume?"

"Yes," she replied laughing, "but it's now yours of course. Oh, I should introduce myself; my name is Stephanie Richmond and you can call me Stephanie, not Steph, or perhaps Miss Richmond if you prefer to be formal."

"I can be formal when the situation requires but I prefer to use your full name Stephanie as there is enough formality out there," he said waving to the ether. "Your desk is different," he said enquiringly to which the reply was, "Oh, Malcolm broke the middle panel somehow and meant to get it fixed but typical male—he never quite got around to it."

His secretary explained how the various systems worked and then said, "You will need to meet your account handlers staff outside, there are three at the moment." They then went outside to say hello to Steve, Ben and Janet. Mike made the usual pleasantries and then retired back to his office. Stephanie made a resume of the business together with a list of the various classes of insurance held by each and the premiums applicable and most importantly, the brokerages being earned. Mike spent the next 3 days studying the account and working out how busy they were in relation to their earnings and how he could find time to improve their figures.

Mike looked at this job as being the first step on his way to earning a very comfortable living but more importantly, his golden opportunity to earn power. He concentrated on running various scenarios through his mind until he reached a conclusion that seemed to point the way to success. Greenacre Commercial being Lloyds Brokers sourced their business from local brokers around the country who were unable to access Lloyds directly. Mike decided the first step was to visit the main producers and to also try and enlist other brokerages at the same time. He enlisted the help of his secretary who proceeded to compile a tour of the country packed with visits to the right people including new names. The whole of the UK would be covered in stages but in an intensive manner to get maximum boost.

Right up to this point, he had been so busy planning his strategy and imagining how it might work out that he had never actually looked over at Stephanie while she was sitting at her desk but suddenly, he was staring at her curvaceous legs up to a level far too high which made him automatically look away. It was no wonder Malcolm didn't rush to get the modesty panel replaced and he wondered if indeed it had ever been broken in the first place. He would have to get it fixed or he would never be able to concentrate but how without making the reason obvious as she did not seem to be aware of the consternation she was causing. He, so reluctantly, would have to put an end to this pleasure before he got the blame for someone else's guilty secret. It did however make him think of Stephanie in an altogether different way but that he dismissed as fanciful thinking.

On Friday, he called a meeting and explained to his three account handlers what he intended to do and what he expected from them in terms of giving extra attention especially to the new brokers to encourage them to start giving regular enquiries. If the workload got too much, they were to speak up without hesitation.

He decided to make his first visit to Birmingham where he saw over a two-day visit 5 new brokers who reacted positively to his overtures, especially the part about in-depth searching for the information that would make the difference between an average quote or a really competitive quote. He strived to make them feel that his service was adding something special to the pot and this they grasped with eagerness. To be fair, within a few days the enquiries arrived and now he had to make certain the team reacted as promised.

He then repeated the visits to the surrounding areas of Birmingham and eventually after 6 months of intensive effort, all of the major cities and their suburbs were covered.

All in his department responded with enthusiasm and seemed really delighted to be much busier than usual. It gave them the feeling that they were going places.

The new business poured in over the next 5 years which resulted in greatly increased income for the company and very welcome bonuses for Mike which he put to one side. Now he had amassed £1m and decided to put his plan into action. He visited the investment arm of his bank and also consulted with Private Equity firms specialising in raising money for sound investments. He raised with a combination of his bank and one of the private equity firms enough to purchase a 12% shareholding in Greenacre Commercial plc. A good slice but not large enough to have to show his hand which he did not want to do at this moment.

Freddie Baker and the other senior brokers were at first full of admiration for his success but lately were making negative noises and Mike knew it was not going to be long before a row became unavoidable. The old green-eyed monster was working overtime. The usual comments such as "perhaps we are concentrating too much on business from the provincial markets or from contractors or any other group that came to mind and should Mike's department be spread out over the rest to ease the congestion". Except there was no congestion.

Mike had bought the shares through a company he had set up for the purpose where he was the only director. A year later, he decided to leak a statement to the papers that his company was interested in making a takeover without, of course, revealing his identity, this was achieved through the private equity company in the hope that the subsequent rise in share value would tempt some of the other shareholders to sell. He needed to get to 35% to be the largest. The ploy worked and a week later he was at 25%—just another 10% to go. The immediate purchase of the extra shares made the price rise again and he got the last 10%. Now he declared and the storm erupted.

The next morning, Mike went to see Freddie who was already aware that there was a new entity that had acquired 35% of the shares and was now basically in charge of the firm. He was naturally quite worried about the future and jobs in particular. He had tried to get information on the purchaser but without success. Mike said, "I have something to tell you and…" he hesitated, "…not sure how you are going to take it but it's me."

Freddie looked at him quizzically wondering what Mike was saying while gradually it was dawning, or was it? Mike said again, "It's me. I have bought the shares." Freddie again could not quite believe his ears and then his face froze in an attempt to hide his shock, disbelief and horror. Mike could read all these fleeting feelings which if he had been in Freddie's shoes, he would be endeavouring to stop the same feelings from letting himself down.

Mike walked over to the window and deliberately stared out in pensive mood to give Freddie a chance to recover and said, "If it hadn't been me, it would have been someone else and possibly a lot worse for the firm whereas I will only make minor adjustments at first and the bigger ones later; the idea being to bring everyone on side before we expand." Mike continued, "I'm hoping you will have the same dreams as me particularly in the later stage when we go into Europe bit by bit." Mike turned and looked Freddie in the eye and said, "It's not a pipedream; I only got the backing by spelling out my plans which the bank and the private equity company liked."

Mike then went into some further detail and could see Freddie was coming around so he pointed out that he needed and wanted to have the support of Freddie and the guys as together, it would make things so much easier. "You all will need to forget my young age and realise I am not a threat but quite the opposite. I have removed the threat of a hostile takeover; however, it might be better if you held a meeting to discuss all this without me being there until the matter has been absorbed by one and all and you have managed to persuade them that all is going to be well." Mike left the room saying he was going to tell Stephanie as she was completely unaware of what he had done as you can't say in advance what you are doing as it might never come to pass. "I'll await your call."

He then returned to his office and Stephanie was busy with a file but he interrupted her, "Get your coat; we are going to lunch as I have something to tell you in private." He waited at the door and seeing his impatience, she grabbed her coat and they left immediately. They went to a restaurant Mike knew very well and found a table in a corner. The place was quiet as it was a bit early for lunch so they ordered some coffee.

She was anxious to know what was happening and said, "Don't keep me waiting after all that rushing out of the office. Has something serious happened and are we OK?"

"Yes we are OK, don't worry on that account," he reassured and proceeded to tell her about his acquisition of the shares and that he was now the major shareholder, basically in charge.

She was at first delighted and then frowned. "But why did you not warn me? Or did you not trust me?"

"No it's not that; it's just I did not want to say anything in case I failed and then looked like a foolish dreamer in your eyes." Then he informed her he had dropped the bombshell to Freddie and left him to tell the other senior brokers so they could get over the shock or the envy without him having to see it. "Hopefully, they will all be able to put on a happy front by the time I see them and realise it's in their best interests as no outside company can take us over in the immediate future as they would have to persuade the remaining shareholders to sell and as they were not tempted by the sudden increase in their share's values, that is unlikely. Any shares that come up, I have the money to buy them." He explained how it was all done and then surprised her by asking if she would come out tomorrow Friday night to help him celebrate, if she was free, of course. She accepted immediately. He told her he would pick her up at 7 pm and if she wanted to go early to feel free.

When he got back to the office, he had a call from Freddie telling him they were all ready for him. He replied to the effect he would be about 5 minutes as he was just finishing off a problem.

As he opened the boardroom door, they all stood up and clapped with big smiles all around, this made Mike stop in his tracks and laugh out loud. They all came up to shake his hand and exclaim how wonderful that he had made the firm safe for the foreseeable future. He then called the meeting to order and stood at the end of the table. He rattled out his plans including Freddie staying as MD and the important change in their approach to new business.

Their secretaries would be guided by Stephanie in how to arrange the visits to the new brokers in the provinces. He briefly explained he had the financial backing to acquire other firms as necessary and to grow the firm to being a major player. It will not be easy but we have the means to achieve it. One of the brokers raised his hand and Mike said, "Yes Steve", and Steve asked if they had to have Stephanie to which Mike replied yes and why.

"The secretaries find her to be a bit of a battle axe."

Mike was surprised and amused and said, "Well, it's only for the setup; shouldn't take more than 15 to 20 minutes so tell them to brace themselves. Well, if that's all, I have to leave now; see you all tomorrow bright and breezy ready for the battle."

Mike had to see the bank as he had some forms to sign and then he would call on the stockbroker in particular, a Charles Harrison who was becoming quite a friend. He was fascinated to know how he had secured the backing of the bank and the equity company as, in his eyes, Mike had pulled off the impossible.

The next day Friday there was a buzz around the office according to Stephanie as she phoned the various secretaries to explain how they should go about phoning the local brokers that they serviced and how to expand to those they did not do business with at the moment. The gossip about the expansion plans was spreading and caused a lot of excitement.

At 3 pm Stephanie asked to leave and Mike immediately agreed but wondered why so early as they were not meeting until 7 pm but wisely decided not to make a comment. She might turn into the battle axe that some others saw.

Mike got back to his hotel at 6 pm, a quick bath and a change into casual clothes and he was off to pick up Stephanie. Her apartment block was in a quiet area and surrounded by green lawns and the odd tree. Nice, he thought and noticed one of the apartments was up for sale. He caught the lift to the 3rd floor and was soon ringing the doorbell to Stephanie's apartment. He waited for a while but no answer so he assumed she had not heard the ring although he heard from outside so he pushed the bell again. The door opened immediately and she stood there before him dressed to stun but with a face like thunder. He said, "What's up; you don't look happy?"

"You know bloody well what's up!"

He pushed his way in and said with his hand on her shoulder, "I don't so tell me."

He then got the lot which amounted to him bragging that he was going to have his way with her and it would be easy. He denied this emphatically and assured her that he had not spoken to anyone about seeing her for dinner so how anyone knew was beyond him. "If I didn't mention it to anyone, how could they pass comments?" he asked and then followed with, "Did you tell anyone?"

There was a long silence and then, "Yes, I did." She had mentioned it to one of the account executive's secretaries.

"Ah," he said, "I know the answer, some of the secretaries regard you as a battle axe and didn't want you to train them in the expansion program but I insisted and told them they would just have to brace themselves. I think there has been a little bit of shit stirring going on here. Do tell me exactly what was said and by whom."

After thinking about it, Stephanie realised that the person who told her had been very clever about it with devious comments and innuendoes and repeated hearsay. It was vague but nevertheless insulting. She assured Mike she had not shown any reaction to the comments and to this he voiced his approval. "I learned at boarding school never to show any weakness to others or they will zoom in on it and crucify you relentlessly," he told her. He then said how pleased he was that she had hid her hurt so well.

They decided to plan how she would cheerfully gloss over this evening if questioned on Monday and say nothing unless it was raised when the answer must be in such a manner as to convey complete oblivion to there being a problem and if reference was made to the previous suggestions and innuendoes, it must be dismissed as "oh that; not applicable in the circumstances relating to this meeting. I think someone somewhere has been letting their imagination run loose", and then immediately revert to the business in hand.

Mike looked at his watch and decided they were now too late to make it to the restaurant and suggested to Stephanie that they change the dinner date to tomorrow same time which she accepted and he telephoned the restaurant and arranged the alteration to their booking after promising to pay for this evening's cancellation.

Mike looked at her directly and said, "How about a takeaway?" She nodded and sat down looking tired. Mike ordered the meal and sat next to her on the sofa and said, "I do have a confession to make in that I have wanted to ask you out for years actually but felt that I had to improve my position before making a move. What with me being so much younger, I thought you would not begin to entertain the idea so I determined to work like hell to change things for the better in the hope it would improve my image in your eyes. That's why I didn't give you advance warning of my plans for the business; in case I failed. I don't mean to imply that I didn't want to do what I did just for the pleasure of success because that is true also of course I did but I reckoned that it would add some gravitas to my image which might help. I think I am making a mess of this," he said wondering what to do then the doorbell rang and he got up to answer it with some relief at the distraction.

He took the pizzas to the table and started fussing around when he felt Stephanie's arms around his waist. Raising his arms, he swivelled around to see her upturned face with eyelids closed and red lips slightly opened looking irresistibly inviting. He did not hesitate to close in and brush them open with his own lips, holding her closer at the same time. Her large eyelids opened slowly, revealing dark grey eyes into which he was drawn and he knew there was no way back to reality. He lifted her up and took her to the bedroom where they made love for two hours.

They emerged satiated, exhausted and very hungry and without hesitation dived into the cold pizzas, unashamedly devouring each mouthful with a rapidity fuelled by the need to replace their energy before total collapse overcame them. Stephanie finished by saying, "Gosh, I don't usually eat like that," as she brushed the crumbs from her mouth with a smooth movement of her arm across her mouth finishing with the back of her hand flicking triumphantly upwards.

As she turned to get a drink, he stood admiring her naked body, the way her back curved inwards and her bottom jutted out. Mike thought amusingly, *I bet I could park my beer glass on top of her backside.* He then pulled out of his reverie and lifted her in the air and told her he loved her. She smothered him in kisses and he felt the sap rising again.

The next day Mike raised the question of the flat that was up for sale and Stephanie told him it was a ground floor flat which had the use of the garden area adjacent to it which was kind of private—well, almost. It was reasonably priced so he bought it. He didn't want to go overboard as he had other plans for his money at this time.

Monday saw them both at the office bright and early just after 8 am. The training of the secretaries for their skills at contacting new local brokers for support had gone well but Mike had had a report that one of the secretaries to be trained was making excuses so he decided to tackle her first thing. When she arrived, he summoned her to his office and made it clear that she had to conform or there would be regrettable consequences. She feigned innocence and agreed to accept the instructions that day. Hopefully, her immediate boss would be relieved.

Chapter 4

The next day Mike had a very important meeting with an international insurer to discuss the intention of expanding into Europe and needed to get the inside track from an insurer familiar with the idiosyncrasies of the various European markets. Some had rules demanding that certain classes of insurance must be arranged locally while others were more relaxed. The French and the Italians were among the most difficult markets. His appointment was with Mr Karlson of Deutsche Europaischen Versicherung AG based in Frankfurt but he was visiting his UK office in London.

Their London office was small based in a side street off Fenchurch Avenue in the heart of the city of London a few steps away from Lloyds of London. Mike was ushered into what purported to be a boardroom to await Herr Karlson. Herr Peter Karlson was about 5 feet 10 inches tall of stocky build with a larger than life personality. When he entered the room, it seemed as if the sun had come out and the church bells had started ringing; of course, they hadn't but the noise level certainly went up a few notches.

He shook Mike's hand vigorously with just the right amount of pressure to avoid pain, smiling broadly and confirming he had been looking forward to meeting him. Mike immediately liked him, especially when he said he was hoping to entice him to open in Deutschland as a first step. They chatted for an hour and then Herr Karlson suggested lunch at this lovely English pub just around the corner where he always went to get the English atmosphere. He said he loved the style, the politeness where time seemed to stand still and you feel you belong to a very special group. "Of course, ze staff are excellent at zis," he said, beaming broadly.

During the lunch washed down with copious amounts of dark red wine—he preferred Bordeaux—Peter invited him to come to Frankfurt and he would show him around and introduce him to the right people to make his expansion to Germany as easy as possible. They fixed a definite date after Peter consulted his diary—a beautiful leather-covered slimline pocket-sized company issue—and wrote in 24 June 1970: English Mike here. That was flattery enough for Mike. They parted company with several handshakes and Mike knew that if he didn't do anything else that day, he had nevertheless done a good day's work.

Over the next few weeks, the training of the secretaries began to bear fruit and the office started to show signs of ambition. Competition between the various sectors became intense. The overall effect was stimulating in that the figures improved, showing what Mike had hoped for and what would impress the investors. As long as the money men could see progress, they were happy and then so was Mike. The proposed trip to Frankfurt also excited the bankers and immediately insisted on a meeting to be held upon his return to the UK. They were well aware that breaking into the German market would be a very important step and every angle had to be closely planned or the expense could escalate alarmingly.

Three weeks later he sent a letter to Peter confirming 24th June for his visit and the very next week back came the reply saying he had set up several meetings with the main players and that he had also booked him into a hotel in the middle of the financial centre. This looked promising and in spite of himself, he felt excited.

On 24 June 1970, Mike arrived at Frankfurt Flughafen and as he walked out into the open area, he espied a large poster with his name written in bold letters held up by a tall slim man dressed smartly with a chauffeur's cap. Mike approached him and introduced himself. The chauffeur smiled politely and said, "Herr Karlson wishes me to take you to your hotel and I am to wait until you are ready to join him at his club in Berliner Strasse." He then introduced himself simply as Carl.

They arrived at the Hilton and after settling himself in and unpacking, he visited the bathroom for relief and the usual ablutions finishing by giving his face a quick swill, as they say in Ireland. He smiled to himself at the word 'swill', checked his tie was straight and left to join the chauffeur.

Peter Karlson's club was a very exclusive place in quiet sombre colours, thick luxurious carpets, large gold framed mirrors in baroque style interspersed by large oil paintings with similar ornate frames, sumptuous large framed chairs and sofas patrolled by obsequious elderly servants overly polite, thus creating an air of tension which somehow transformed itself into a hushed calmness that no one would dare interrupt. A raised finger brought immediate attention.

Mike was ushered to an anteroom just off the main drawing room area and upon entering the room, 5 faces sitting at a large mahogany table turned to greet him with smiles but no sound until the servant had withdrawn and closed the door upon which Peter stood up and greeted him loudly. The remaining four stood up and hurried towards him hands outstretched. Peter introduced them one by one and one of them poured the scotch while they took their seats.

Peter took control of the meeting and matters proceeded in an orderly manner and considering they were doing him a big favour, they nevertheless contributed a lot of useful information and on Peter's recommendation, they would assist in getting him registered with the authorities. Mike expressed his delight and his surprise at their willingness to give up their time. They all agreed that newcomers were needed in the German market to help it become more modern and dynamic.

Once all the details were agreed, the conversation turned to what they were going to do that evening. It was agreed that they would all start at a good restaurant and then wander into the centre of the red light area for a few beers or if Mike preferred a cider bar. Mike opted for a few beers as he had heard how potent these local ciders could be, absolute rocket juice.

They agreed to meet at 6 pm at Marlene's Restaurant in Bockenheimer Strasse. Mike went back to his hotel to check up on the office and speak to Stephanie. After an hour or so, he decided he had better make a move as time was marching on and he didn't want to be late.

When he arrived at Marlene's, he wondered if he was at the right spot as it was a rather small ordinary place but he opened the door which announced his entrance by ringing loudly and again he was mystified as he found himself in the middle of a small room with a corner counter and a very old-fashioned lamp emitting a dull orange light on to a button in the middle of the counter.

He pressed the button which let loose a loud melodic tune rising and falling in tone but so loud his inclination was to pull the button back up. He tried without success and considered bolting out of embarrassment but before his leg muscles reacted, the inner door opened revealing an overdeveloped blonde in a white blouse that was not hiding her black bra but that may have been on purpose.

"Kommen sie mit," she ordered and turned back through the inner door. He followed as ordered. She brought him into a large restaurant dining room packed full of men in business attire and only the very occasional female. She walked with hip-swinging determination to the far end of the room where Mike saw Peter and the same four as earlier that day in the club. Again, all smiles and standing as he approached. He warmed to them immediately in spite of a slight niggle forming in the back of his mind which he noted and put to one side for the moment.

Mike had memorised all of the four names—Karl, Leo, Franz and Wolfgang—so he could say their names when shaking hands. It wasn't necessary but showed he was on the ball. The meal was excellent as one would expect from a hidden jewel for the exclusive use of the financial centre. Mike decided not to ask about the blond woman in the white blouse with the black bra who was obviously in charge and made it her business to know the diners by name. Whatever her core business, she was a very successful restauranteur.

Then the niggle was activated no doubt helped by the third glass of wine. The conversation switched to business and how much the cost was likely to be in setting up. Mike told them he had sufficient funds so that would not be a problem. They suggested it could be say half a million as a start-up venture. Mike confirmed they were in the right area but he had available up to one million or as much as he needed.

"Why were they so concerned?" he asked.

"Well," said Wolfgang, "let's not beat about the bush; we would like to buy in and in return can make it very smooth for you such as easy registration and automatic agencies with us five representing the heart of the insurance industry here in Frankfurt so the rest will follow.

"However, it has to be in the name of our separate investment company, it's for our retirement," he explained with a broad smile revealing a sparkling set of teeth much better than Mike's own so he refrained from smiling back.

Wolfgang continued, "Completely confidential of course."

They wanted 9% each. Mike thought about it for a while as this was not something he had expected but should have in view of the keen interest taken by all of them and the old saying came to mind: "There is no such thing as a free lunch." Mike quickly thought about it and realised they were offering him sure-fire success and a continued interest as it lined their pockets too. He looked up at their expectant faces and with a smile said: "I should have expected this but as I will still have the majority of the shares then OK as you are basically guaranteeing me success. Do you have the funds to buy in as it will be about £25,000 each? All costings will be open to inspection." They agreed and shook hands before ordering two more bottles of wine.

The next day Mike awoke with a slight headache and was surprised he wasn't a lot worse. He took his time getting ready for the day. A day of looking for somewhere to locate his office. He decided to visit a few estate agencies suggested by his new found friends. By lunchtime, he had done the necessary and had instructed the agencies to mail the various options to his office in London; he would return to Frankfurt next week as he was determined to ensure that the office was in the right place and of a good enough standard to reflect the importance of the company. Being an outsider as well as a newcomer, it was necessary to be better than just to be equal.

His plane was not until 1900 hours so he decided to have a carefree relaxed lunch at a rather nice café named Ricci's which had a large open air section with plants to protect from the noise of the traffic. On his way, he stopped to buy Die Welt newspaper as he could read German a lot better than he could speak it. He decided on a seat under a large bright red umbrella and chose the seat on the shaded side. Ordered "ein grosses bier" and relaxed. It felt good.

Before opening his newspaper, he decided to look around at the day. A lovely hot summer's day, beautiful old-world architecture, light traffic and pavements filled with beautiful casual chatting people gesticulating and laughing lightly as if the cares of the world were lifted and might never come back. He decided to remember as much as he could and store it for whenever he needed to give himself a reminder of how beautiful life can be. His beer arrived with a chit slipped under a saucer. He took a good gulp so it hit the back of his throat and made him gasp. *God, life is good.*

Chapter 5

He arrived back at his London flat just before midnight where Stephanie was waiting and had made a good effort at moving in and making the place look homely; an art not given to many men. She greeted him warmly by throwing her arms around his neck and lifting her legs off the floor so he had to grab her by her bottom, which was a perfect end to the day.

The following day—Friday, 26 June 1970—was going to be a day of many meetings to examine the success of the various executives in their efforts to increase the number of enquiries from the various provincial brokers in their patch and to give all an update on Mike's own efforts to enter the European market.

During the board meeting, Mike got briefed on the success of the efforts to increase the number of provincial brokers supplying business to the various account executives and it was very impressive across the full range in spite of the early reluctance expressed by some of the secretaries.

Mike then turned to the European venture and decided to tell the story in the best possible light in that the German people had been very helpful and had even introduced a local firm willing to invest 45% of the capital making the risk more attractive but also mentioning the assistance coming from the German insurers as if this was a completely different body. It was not the complete truth but it was not a lie either; just the tie up not explained as in the telling it could look like cronyism. He also glossed over the fact that the German company was now his and the German Venture Company's enterprise. The other shareholders in the British Company had no stake in this expansion. Nobody questioned him so he quickly closed the meeting with a beaming smile he had learned from Wolfgang and that was that—for now anyway.

Mike's next meeting was with Charles Harrison, the stockbroker, over lunch at a place Charles said was fascinating and explained it was a pub that spread sawdust on the floor to create a certain atmosphere and only served cold food but beautifully laid out and the only alcohol was wine. As they walked to this place somewhere in Southwark, Mike wasn't sure where exactly as the conversation was flowing; they walked past an old high brick wall when suddenly Charles stopped at an inconspicuous black door and pushed it open. They stepped inside to a warm bustling pub where every corner was turned into a dining area; here and there some slightly sectioned off areas with some barrels used as tables and the floor was strewn with a light dusting of sawdust. There was a bar but not for standing; more a counter for quickfire delivery of the cold plated meals and bottles of expensive wine.

They took a seat in one of the quieter areas and ordered their food and wine. Charles was very interested to know about Mike's advance into enemy territory and fascinated when told about the investment by the 5 senior executives. "You have hit it lucky there, my boy," he exclaimed, "but you will need good lawyers to set it up securely with no mistakes. I know the very chap to help and will set up a meeting before you go back to complete matters. I will phone you tomorrow after I speak to Roger Sawyers of Wilson Sawyers and Cumberbatch LLP to see when he is free and he will explain the problems as he has done this many times before. Mind you, he is not cheap but he gets it right."

On his way back to the office with a full stomach and a warm glow from the fine Bordeaux, Mike felt he was flying high but also felt nervous that it might all be too high and he would fall into a cesspit. He would know more after speaking to this chap Roger. He decided he had better be on best form when they met as he certainly did not want to be taken advantage of or be blinded by bullshit. He would use his ears and mouth in the proportion that he had them.

On arrival at the office, he was greeted by Freddie dashing into his office clearly worried about something. After quietening him down, it transpired that a subsidiary of one of Freddie's clients had had a claim and it was not insured. A serious accident to his client's employee resulting in death and not insured was making Freddie panic. All because the local manager of the subsidiary had signed a form changing the basis of work bringing the responsibility for the employee back on the subsidiary instead of it being down to the main contractor.

Mike told him not to panic but to bring the claim's file and the underwriting file to him and he would look to see if anything could be done. Mike knew that they themselves were insured against errors and omissions but he could also see another slight glimmer of hope in that the underwriter was someone with whom they had a particularly good relationship placing many millions of business his way and he was someone Mike liked and got on with. He lifted the phone and got in touch with John Grainger and arranged to meet.

Mike walked into John's office who at once stood up to greet Mike. John was 6 feet 3 inches tall of solid build but not fat; brown hair with only the slightest hint of grey in spite of his 60 odd years. He had laughing brown eyes, a straight nose and if he liked you, a grin that turned up on one side and down on the other. After the pleasantries were done, they got down to business. John listened carefully and looked Mike in the eye saying, "We are both going to lose this case if we don't do something and that would be a shame."

John summarised, "This is all down to the error of the local manager but the client could vent his anger at you for not anticipating such a calamity and that would be unreasonable as you spelled out the exact basis of cover which saved them money. Nevertheless, they will not want to accept that it is their fault and the cost will come out of their bottom line and that, my friend, will hurt them. I propose to make a commercial decision and backdate the cover but suggest you labour the point to the group MD that this is an enormous favour and not only due to his loyalty to yourselves but also to us his Insurers. What was the man who got killed a manual worker aged 55 years, I believe. That will be £600K to £1 million at least.

"You set up the new policy from a date before the accident and wait for the documents to be issued before notifying me of the claim. Keep all this between you, me and Freddie other than the MD of the main group, of course, but tell him no bragging about how great his insurers are. It will take 3 or 4 years to claw this back and then only if it runs well."

Mike could only marvel at this man's generosity which John immediately dismissed with "ready for a beer and a pie then". They retired to John's favourite pub.

The next day when Mike got to the office, Freddie who had been kept in the loop bounded into Mike's office to express his relief, "How the hell did you manage that?" Mike had never seen Freddie so animated; he was pacing to and fro and looking larger than his 5 foot 10 inches normally allowed. Freddie was the kind of person you could easily miss as he was usually so studious and quiet. Everything about him was neat and tidy from his dark short hair to his neat clean-cut features and tidy neutral-coloured suits. Perfect material for the mechanical running of the organisation and an altogether nice guy. A gem to be kept happy. Mike particularly liked his upper-class accent.

It was left to Freddie to explain matters to the client and stress the point about complete discretion. Freddie could no doubt explain with typical English understatement that, "Of course, insurers do not want to be seen as a soft touch, you understand, old chap; we keep this between ourselves."

That afternoon, Charles Harrison phoned to say he had arranged a meeting for Mike with Roger Sawyers of Wilson Sawyers and Cumberbatch LLP at their office in Leadenhall Street for 11:30 am the next day and Roger was looking forward to meeting him. Mike expressed his gratitude and confirmed he would attend.

Chapter 6

Mike walked through the imposing large double-fronted doors of the lawyer's offices up to the reception desk and referred to his appointment whereupon the elderly, rather severe-looking lady with hair pulled back into a tight bun pushed a visitors sheet in front of him to sign so she could issue him with a visitors card to be displayed from his jacket. This interruption irritated Mike while he watched the battle axe press a buzzer to summon some underling from above to come and escort him to Roger. *Roger had better be good or it will be the shortest interview on record*, he thought.

The underling turned out to be a young beautiful female with a ready open smile which softened Mike's attitude somewhat. She knocked on Roger's door then ushered him in. Roger was not the smooth cad he expected but a mature 50-something man in a striped three-piece suit—well-worn in but not unkempt. He wore glasses to read which he took off as he stood up to offer his hand to Mike, who took it automatically. Roger's face was a well lived in face which was severe until he smiled broadly when the deep lines magically transformed his whole demeanour from a grizzly into a cuddly bear.

He opened the conversation with: "You have come for advice to make sure those Germans don't take your trousers down."

That broke the ice and Mike laughed loudly and said, "That too but as I have the majority shareholding, I should be safe unless they are really slick operators which come to think of it, they really are." Mike started thinking of Wolfgang and his perfect white teeth smile and wondered if he was a devious sod but then decided the bastard couldn't help being perfect and left it at that.

After about three hours, they had the position mapped out to Mike's satisfaction including Roger's fee which he mentioned several times during the meeting just in case Mike should get the idea that it wouldn't cost much. It was left with Roger to get in touch with his German counterpart.

Mike strolled back to his office enjoying the afternoon sun and suddenly realised he was hungry. He was passing Mario's and so stepped in and used their phone to call Stephanie and asked if she had had lunch and not surprisingly, she hadn't as per usual counting the calories. He asked her to join him at Mario's to which she readily agreed.

As Stephanie entered the restaurant, her good looks and slim figure with jutting bottom caused a stir. It was like throwing a coin into the collection boxes of those guys that pose as statues where they suddenly come into exaggerated and flamboyant motion. The Italian waiters became caricatures of themselves sycophanting and pirouetting; it was like watching a very noisy ballet. As she approached the table, Mike stood up to greet her; she kissed him briefly and sat down. Once seated, there was a temporary lull.

She said to Mike, "You were being very gallant standing up like that."

Mike replied, "I feared what it might have done to the waiters if you had to bend down to kiss me, it was like watching the Mad Hatter's party when you first came in." He added, "You get used to a bit of fuss, especially in Italian restaurants. Anyway, I have some news to tell you," and brought her up to date with today's events.

"When are you due back in Germany?" she asked.

"Well, I was going back in a few days but as I haven't had the estate agents office details yet, I will postpone for a week and then go back regardless. I think you should come as I could do with your advice on location and type of office as I want to ensure that it is appropriate and in the right area."

The waiters approached their table headed by Luigi who took their order while two others performed a plate throwing act with shouts of bravado connected to facial looks that suggest they have just saved the world from a certain catastrophe but hey! that was too easy. After Luigi had moved away, Mike said, "I wonder how they cope if they drop one of those plates; that must be embarrassing."

Stephanie replied, "They have that covered as I saw one afternoon when it happened. Someone from the kitchen comes running out broom and dustpan in hand tut tutting all the way to the mess amid even more laughter as the waiters feign embarrassment. It's infectious; everyone in the restaurant joins in with the laughter making it worthwhile to make a mistake every so often. You have to hand it to them; it makes you want to come back."

At 3 pm, they headed back to the reality of the office.

That evening after their very light evening snack of toast with Brussels pate, they settled down to relax when the phone rang. It was his brother giving him bad news from Ireland. His father had passed away peacefully after a long illness ending with a heart attack. Mike was absolutely shocked as he had no idea that things were so bad; he had expected his father to carry on 'ad infinitum' as he always had done and so it struck him badly. He immediately agreed that he would go over to Dublin the next day to support the family but he felt a great sense of guilt as he really should have been over to see his Dad and not been so wrapped up in his own career and ambitions that he neglected his family.

His mother was devastated but being a brick would carry on dutifully and cry in private. Irish women were self-reliant people who did not like to show weakness and saw weakness as an excuse to wallow in self-pity. Not always easy to keep to such high standards though.

Mike travelled on the fast ferry taking just 90 minutes and debarked at Dun Laoghaire, a nice suburb just south of the city of Dublin, a pretty touristy area with a harbour full of yachts of all sizes bobbing peacefully and showing off their lines. As he hadn't been back for years, he had to use a road map or he would have struggled. This increased his guilt but nothing for it now but to knuckle down and take whatever flak that came his way.

He arrived at his brother's house at about 2 pm. He walked up to the door and pressed the bell. A melodious chime rang out which seemed wrong in the circumstances. His brother's wife answered the door with "so it's yourself then" and a big grin before she threw her arms around his neck giving him a warm hug. He felt the tension leave him immediately and relaxed. It was a great relief not to be accused of being a selfish self-absorbed arsehole. His brother's wife was perfectly capable of resorting to the vernacular whenever necessary but obviously he was forgiven.

It had been agreed that he would stay at his brother's house which made things easy as there was so much to organise for the funeral and where to hold the wake. It wouldn't be a wake like the Catholics arranged but nevertheless, there would be a lot of people present and lavish amounts of food and drink would be consumed.

He made his way into the lounge where his brother was waiting to greet him with a broad grin and the usual pleasantries. A few words about the old man and how he had looked before the end.

He had apparently looked fine until the very last day, which Mike was pleased to know. His brother was going to see Dad in the church and asked if he would like to come as well. He declined saying he wanted to remember him the way he was when he last saw him. This was accepted.

The funeral was very sad. Mike's father was an extremely popular man with lots of friends, one of which was a vicar that Mike remembered from his youth back in Arklow. A vicar of whom it was said flirted with the girls and they in turn flirted with him all in a very light-hearted way, of course. The afters were at Rooney's Bar in Dun Laoghaire recently renovated and known for serving very good food and very good Guinness.

Mike found it hard to keep talking with many of those present due to the fact he had moved away and basically had very little in common with them anymore. It was rather strange to realise this gap between him and family and some others with whom he had been close once upon a time. The fact was that once you move away from the same arena to new pastures then this distance creates its own loss of empathy. He struggled to cross over the void but the very effort made it hard to be spontaneous and effervescent. He was relieved when his sister-in-law called him to the phone saying, "It's your office."

He apologised profusely while carefully picking his way out through the crowd. It was Freddie advising that one of his clients had had a large fire and he had better get back as soon as possible. He immediately phoned the client and got through. He advised the client after getting the full circumstances that he would call to see him tomorrow and in the meantime, he would get the adjusters appointed. This was the perfect escape route but was genuine, which always helps.

Upon returning to the crowd, he found that people were gradually leaving as many had some distance to travel and in another hour, the family were all on their way back to his brother's house and Mike made his excuses for an early departure the next morning. The remainder of the evening was easier now that his escape route had been established.

Next morning he caught the early fast ferry back to Holyhead and had breakfast on the boat. The client's address was in Birmingham which he made to just after 1 pm. After walking into the client's office, he was greeted by the MD, "I am really impressed; the adjusters have already been in touch and will be here this afternoon and you have dashed back from Ireland to assist."

Mike smiled and replied, "Well, we try our best to be there when you need us."

That afternoon, the adjuster arrived, a small slim man about 5 feet 9 inches with a very pleasant and amusing personality. He soon got the measure of the problem and explained to the client's satisfaction the way matters would proceed, all very efficient. Mike was satisfied as was the client. A few handshakes all round and Mike was on his way to London.

A few days later, Peter Karlson phoned to ask how the plans were going and Mike said he had not heard any more from the estate agents looking for a suitable office space and intended to go back next week with Stephanie as he valued her opinion. He would let him know the exact date and his itinerary and perhaps they could meet up. He did tell Peter that the legal side was well underway with discussions between his lawyer and the German authorities.

Chapter 7

Mike and Stephanie were on the plane to Frankfurt and had made plans to use their time fruitfully. The first thing they did on arrival was to phone the estate agents and good news was awaiting them in that they had lined up three offices for them to inspect. This meant they could get off to a flying start and have time to themselves.

The next day they resolved the office problem by finding just what they wanted in the heart of the financial quarter. They agreed to the contracts with the property owners and arranged to sign as soon as the contracts were drawn up. A deposit was required which Stephanie sorted as she had the foresight to bring the bank cheques with her. They decided to spend the afternoon sightseeing but first they headed to the Rathous to pick up a local map of the town centre and Mike had a chance to use his slight knowledge to request the map in German with the sights marked.

As the staff on duty didn't speak any English, they went overboard to be helpful and friendly, leaving Stephanie and Mike very impressed. They emerged into a late afternoon in July with the sun lighting up their hearts as well as the streets. It was comfortably warm and the air was light, they stopped at the first open air restaurant come bar for a coffee while they planned their route. They were just musing over the options when Mike heard a familiar voice saying, "So zis is what ze English do when abroad on business." It was Peter Karlson.

Mike greeted him warmly and introduced Stephanie. Mike could see Peter was impressed but he refrained from making any comment; after accepting the invitation to join them, he asked how long they would be in Germany. "Oh, just a few days," Mike replied, "as we have to try and get the office sorted."

Peter said, "In zat case, you must come to my house for ze weekend, we are having a party to celebrate my birthday," and added with a knowing smile, "you will know at least another 4 of ze people there." They mulled it over right there in front of Peter and he watched as they came to the conclusion that it would be a lovely break and fascinating to meet so many German people in relaxed mode and enjoy the similarities and indeed the differences from their own friends.

They both turned to Peter at the same time and said enthusiastically, "Yes, we would love to!"

Peter burst into laughter and said, "Well, I know zatwas genuine and I'm so pleased." They finished up their drinks and then said cheerio to Peter who was on his way to his office while Mike and Stephanie continued their wander around the city. They had a couple of days to continue their enjoyment of the city sights before Saturday came around and they would be making their way to the country to Peter's house in the suburbs.

On Saturday as the taxi pulled into the tree-lined drive, Mike could see the large double fronted house with impressive porch equipped with massive pillars, almost Georgian in style. The taxi slowed down with no noise except the very satisfying sound of the tyres crunching the gravel and stopped right outside the impressive large entrance with an equally large black door. The driver helped with their cases and accepted the fare and 'ein Trinkgeld fur sie' with grace.

Almost immediately, Peter and his wife came out to greet them. Peter's wife Claudia was not the usual blond Germanic type but dark-haired, almost Italian in looks but she was certainly German through and through. She smiled; spoke in perfect English with only the slightest accent and made them feel very welcome all without losing, in spite of her openness, her Germanic reserve. This is a gift granted to only a very few.

Mike decided he would study her art over the next couple of days to see if he could find the key to such an invaluable asset. However, he quickly diverted his attention back to Peter, which wasn't easy, as he really wanted to study her more. Her ability to be so friendly and yet so reserved was something he would like to incorporate into his own persona. Now he had to concentrate on Peter who, after all, was the reason they were here.

As they were being shown to their room, some helpers appeared from nowhere and grabbed their cases. Claudia called to a young girl in a maid's outfit to show them the way to their room and so they followed on dutifully. The room was large and well equipped in regal style. You could see that Peter's love of the English style had been brought back to his home. Basically, dark blue wallpaper with a touch of gold here and there with paintings being large and mounted in ornate gold frames that set the room off. A large double bed on a sturdy brass frame and a multi coloured rich carpet finished the ambiance conclusively. Mike liked it and as he studied the room, he was learning. Stephanie on the other hand thought it was all a bit too much.

An hour later, having changed, they wandered down to the three reception rooms which were beginning to fill up with the expected guests. Peter approached them during a lull and handed them some champagne which unlike the usual rubbish did not bore a hole through the middle of his chest. They chatted for a while and Peter said he had some old English friends arriving soon. By old, he explained friends he had known for years. Claudia came by to say she had seen Harry and Joan arrive in their sporty Ford Granada.

"I always know it by the noise and the fact that it is a yellowy cream colour. They obviously like to be noticed," she whispered.

Then Harry and Joan arrived or rather, Joan with Harry in tow arrived. Joan walked in, feet in a ten to two configuration, with her head held high which was fine in these circumstances but Mike suspected that on entering a café or restaurant, it would give the impression she was inspecting the premises to ensure it was safe to eat there and wondered how many times she had had a frosty reception from the owners.

Harry on the other hand was a cheerful Mr Pickwick type with a corpulent body that suited his booming voice and exuberant laughter prompted by the hesitant "eh eh" to ensure everyone had time to recognise the amusing titbit. They were however quite normal once the initial hoo-ha died down. They held strong views on everything of course but Stephanie knew how to change the subject without appearing to do so thereby keeping the threatening fury contained. Claudia came to the rescue and Mike used the opportunity to escape.

He had seen Wolfgang enter and he cajoled Stephanie to move in that direction so he could introduce her to him who was now joined by Karl, Leo and Franz the co-conspirators who muscled into his company but in spite of that lent a certain comfort to the venture.

They had all arrived with their wives except Wolfgang who was apparently going through a divorce. The wives had disappeared into the restroom. The men all greeted Stephanie enthusiastically and showed great interest in how things were progressing. They approved the choice for the office saying that it was as central as it could be. They wandered into one of the other rooms which had a bar set up which suited Mike better as he preferred a pint of German lager to champagne.

They chatted freely until the wives returned when gradually the group thinned out until Mike and Stephanie were left with Wolfgang. Eventually, he spotted a lonely maiden looking lost and excused himself. Mike said he needed to visit the toilet and wandered back into the hall at which point he got cornered by Peter who insisted on holding him up by introducing him to Johann Zagerman who was very interested in how Mike was doing with his venture into Deutschland. Johann was a swarthy man 5 feet 8 inches tall with well-worn features, dark suntan and a stout build.

Mike explained his progress so far. After listening to the full rollout of the adventure, Johann then asked if he had any ambitions to expand further into other territories and said he would be very interested in helping as he had interests himself in most of western Europe. Mike decided to sidestep the offer by blandly saying all that was way down the line and would depend on how things went here. Mike felt this was all a bit too sudden and besides, he didn't know what business interests this guy had and there was something about him he couldn't quite put his finger on.

After his greatly appreciated toilet visit, Mike made his way back to where he had left Stephanie and found her in deep conversation with Leo's wife called Anne so he sidled off to the bar and got himself another beer and as he approached the girls, they beckoned him to hurry up and started telling him a piece of gossip. It turned out that the swarthy Johann Zagerman had a dubious background. He was extremely wealthy, a billionaire by all accounts, who had emanated from Ukraine but always travelled with at least five minders.

Mike feigned surprised interest and discovered he and Peter were close friends with mutual interests. This was a worry for Mike but decided to put it to one side for now but would ensure that he did not gain entry into his German company by any back door. He decided to phone his solicitor on Monday morning to put him on special watch and to insist that any shareholder that wished to sell had to offer their shares in the first instance to him. This had probably already been done.

Later on that evening, a quite sizeable orchestra arrived and set themselves up in the largest of the reception rooms large enough to be called a hall. At 1800 hours, they started playing Viennese waltzes which lasted for about 1 hour before degenerating into rock and roll and all the latest pop songs. Stephanie and Mike decided to wander into the garden where they could smell burgers being grilled on charcoal. There was a small group waiting to be served and they joined in.

On hearing their voices, the couple in front turned around and spoke to them. They announced they were William and Aneka. Will said, "You must be the English friends of Peter that he speaks of so fondly." "Peter is great, one of the nicest people you could ever meet but can't say the same about that Johann. He drops in unannounced and leaves without a word in a convoy of identical black Mercedes cars so you never know which one he is in, the whole thing quite strange," he quipped.

"Maybe he is in the secret service," ventured Mike with a grin.

"Oh Ja," said Aneka, "very secret."

"He said he had business in most of western Europe," Mike tested, hoping for a revealing comment but nothing further was said on the subject.

Then it was their turn to collect the burgers which Stephanie did with great dexterity in spite of the two large plates being full of all sorts.

They looked around for somewhere to eat and saw there were quite a few tables and chairs set out across the adjacent lawn and so made their way to the nearest vacant table and sat down with relief. They didn't know how hungry they had become until they started to eat but of course, time had marched on and it was now 7 in the evening; still light, of course, which made it feel early. The burgers were homemade and were devoured in record time. The fried potato mixed with small pieces of bacon was a nice touch to finish off the dish.

They were just about to get up having polished everything off when they were joined by Wolfgang minus the maiden in distress. "Did you see the row that erupted between Peter and Johann?" he asked.

"No," answered Mike and Stephanie in unison.

"Well, you missed a serious fallout, they ended up shouting at each other. I thought it would come to blows."

"What was it about?"

"I don't know exactly but Johann started it; something about Peter not having the right to agree to a deal without his approval?"

"Do you think it could be our arrangement with the brokerage?"

"Hardly, why would Johann be interested in our arrangement? He knows nothing about insurance. All he ever talks about is money, money and more money."

"That's why I asked could it be the brokerage as it will end up making money if I have anything to do with it."

"Oh ja, well, we had better find out but not at the moment as Peter will need to calm down."

"I'm here for the weekend so I will approach the subject tomorrow with Peter," said Mike.

At that, they all stood up and Mike and Stephanie made their way back to the house. The orchestra was still in full swing and a lot of people were dancing so Mike pulled Stephanie on to the floor and they danced the rest of the evening away to banish the stress that had creeped in following the news of Peter's altercation.

Chapter 8

The next morning, Mike and Stephanie went down to breakfast for 9am and Peter was already there, albeit in his dressing gown. He looked a bit distraught and hadn't shaved. Peter started the conversation, "I suppose you have heard about my altercation with Johann last evening which got out of hand and rather noisy and to be fair somewhat unseemly."

Stephanie looked down at her plate but Mike looked him straight in the eye and said, "Yes and I wondered if it was about our deal."

"No," replied Peter, "I'm afraid that I bought rather a lot of tin and made a profit of $1.2M. It was a spur of the moment decision and I had very little time to decide and did not even think of Johann. He is livid with me and feels that I have betrayed him as I should have included him automatically. What is a worry is that he has some very dangerous associates and he might be tempted to set them loose."

"Didn't you explain it was all done so quickly that you didn't have time to do anything other than go ahead?"

"He wasn't listening."

"Has he made you money in the past?"

"Oh lots, I'm afraid."

"Well, then, there is only one way out of it. You must say that with all the shouting you didn't think last evening but you are quite happy to include him in the deal minus his half of the deposit and you will share the profit with him and add that if the deal had gone at a slower pace, you would have consulted with him and he would no doubt have come in. Don't forget to say you don't want to fall out as you value his friendship more than money."

"That might work as he doesn't have many friends."

"Well, you don't say," said Mike grinning.

They were joined by Peter's daughter and younger son at the table. Peter introduced them to Mike and Stephanie, "This is my daughter Melanie and my son Thomas; they are both a handful but I love them very much and unfortunately they know it." Gentle laughter all around subsided into polite questions about what everyone was going to do that day.

Then Thomas suggested that Mike and Stephanie might like to visit the festival that was being held in the town centre. Peter chirped in, "I didn't think there was one on in July. July is the only quiet month in Frankfurt but I could be wrong as someone somewhere will have dreamt an extra one up."

"Yes," Thomas said, "it's celebrating cheese and some foods and of course, wine."

"Well, we are happy to go and have a look," Mike replied looking at Stephanie for approval.

It was decided they would all go and see what it was like especially as the weather was lovely and warm.

That evening, they arrived back tired but happy with their visit to the city centre.

Chapter 9

They arrived back in London Sunday afternoon and made straight for the flat, talking incessantly about their visit to Peter's home and all the things that had happened. Mike resolved to phone Peter on Monday to find out if Johann had responded to his offer. He did not have good expectations for the outcome as Johann was to his mind a bad egg. He had an unpleasant atmosphere about him.

Mike arrived back in the office on Monday morning circa 8:30 am to find Freddie already beavering away feverishly as one of the clients had a serious fire over the weekend, running into many millions of pounds as half the factory had gone up. All the basic work was being done: advising the insurers and appointing loss adjusters, etc. Just needed to advise the client and call down to give moral support but that wasn't Freddie's bag; he wasn't comfortable on the front line so he was sending the account executive—a very personable chap called Clive in his late forties. Mike agreed he would do what was required in a very competent manner and report back if there were any problems to be looked at.

Upon retiring to his office, the phone was ringing and it was Peter who was in a bit of a state as he could not get through to Johann. He kept getting told that Johann was too busy to talk to him. He reckoned that he was being given the cold shoulder and was nervous about what Johann might do next. Mike said he would try ringing him on his behalf and took a note of the telephone number.

He said to Peter, "What kind of business arrangement have you got with Johann? Is there a contract between you or is it a loose arrangement whereby you occasionally do a deal together?"

Peter confirmed it was the latter but to be fair, Johann had been very helpful and they had made a lot of money together.

Mike left it where he would phone him back. He then phoned Johann but couldn't get through so left a message for Johann to phone him. Just then Stephanie walked in with two coffees, handed Mike one and sat down at her desk. He brought her up to date and had barely finished when the phone rang which Mike picked up with his usual snappy: "Mike speaking."

"Johann here, Mike; I believe you might be wanting to speak about Peter?"

"Yes, that's correct."

"Well, I am really, how you say, pissed off with Peter. I mean, when I make someone a lot of money, I expect complete loyalty not to be cut out of his deals."

"Didn't Peter explain that he saw the deal with the tin and knew it was good so got carried away and just did it without thinking of you at the time and didn't think he had to share it anyway?"

"I put 6 or 7 deals his way and shared them so he should have done the same back; now I will have to make an example of him."

"As I understand it, there is no contract between you and it is in fact a loose business arrangement where you share deals from time to time or have I got that wrong and anyway when Peter realised that you were upset he offered to share the profits with you."

"That's as may be but only because I caught him out."

"I thought you two were friends."

"I don't do friends, only business."

"What can he do to make this right between you?"

"Nothing actually."

"What if he gave you all the profit?" Mike said more in testing the waters than anything else.

"Then I would consider it."

"Well, if I am going to ask him to do this then I would want it to be a done deal not just a possibility."

"Now you are pissing me off," and with that the phone went dead.

Stephanie, who had been listening in on the conversation, was horrified with Johann's attitude and asked Mike what he was going to do as that bastard could do anything.

"No matter which way I spin this, it's not good for Peter but I have to spell it out in full; after all, he knows the guy better than me,"

Mike immediately phoned Peter back and explained Johann's response. Peter went quiet and asked what Mike thought he should do.

"To start with, I would get some bodyguards and armed ones at that and pay for them out of the deal you did on tin." Mike then suggested he hire a private detective to find out where Johann lived and he knew a suitable one.

"It's always best to find out all you can about your enemy and my guess is it will be money well spent if you get any information because this bastard is a dangerous guy."

"Well, Mike, if that's what you think, I will do it and when I know where he lives; that evens up the odds somewhat but it sounds like I have gotten involved with a gangster or even the mafia."

"I will do some digging to see what info I can find out but do not delay in getting the bodyguards."

"OK."

Peter put the phone down and Mike phoned his friend Tom Bellamy in Belfast. He hadn't spoken to Tom for around 2 years but the minute he started speaking, Tom interrupted: "Is that you Michael Black and why the hell are you phoning me after all this time? What do you want from me, boyoh?"

"Yes, Tom it's me and I think I need your special help."

"It's special help, is it?"

"Yes, I'm afraid so," and spelled out Peter's problem.

"Tell your friend Peter that he better get some protection to start with as I have second-hand experience of this bastard and extreme violence is his particular speciality."

"I have already advised him to get some armed bodyguards as he threatened to make an example of him quite unnecessarily as when Peter realised the score he offered to share the profits on the deal even though he did not believe he had done anything wrong."

"You did right for as I said, violence is his particular speciality but really it's more his particular delight. Peter will need experienced guys who know what to expect. I will send over 4 one of which is a pretty little female who looks like butter wouldn't melt but she is the best and the wiliest."

"Thanks, really appreciate that as I wouldn't like to lose Peter as he is a good guy and he invests in my business."

"What is your business; you've never told me what you get up to?"

Mike explained his business to Tom who replied, "I knew it would be something highfalutin and impressive; you always were ambitious and full of it. Anyway, give me Peter's address and warn him that I am sending over a little army and he should make them comfortable and listen to their advice. In the meantime, I will find out where the Devil's pit is hidden."

"Appreciate all this and your bill will be paid promptly as Peter is not short of a bob or two."

"Good man yourself, I will be back soon." And the phone call ended without further ado.

Mike leaned back in his chair and looked over at Stephanie who had been listening with open mouth to the conversation.

"What?" said Mike.

"I can't believe what you have just arranged. How do you know these kind of people?"

"Well, by accident really but I did recognise that one day he might be very useful and in spite of his trade, he is a sound man that you can trust and for some reason he and I became friends but he never tried to push me into his area of expertise and I know that if I was in the middle of a war zone and up to my ears in shit he would protect my back to the death. That's a rare friend indeed and to be valued."

"And would you do that for him?"

"Yes of course; it goes without saying."

Stephanie then changed the conversation telling him he had a phone call from Roger Sawyer, his solicitor, referring to the overseas expansion project.

"I told him you would phone him back."

Mike lifted the phone and dialled his number and got through without too much delay. Roger informed him he had concluded his investigations and was ready to finalise the documentation but he needed him to call around tomorrow if possible. Mike said, "OK, about 11 am then."

Roger agreed and put the phone down. Mike turned to Stephanie saying, "I had better not tell him about the gangster in the middle of all this or it will never get done."

"Do you think that's wise?"

"Probably not but I've decided so I'll stick to it and anyway, his bodyguards will be there by tomorrow."

Mike walked into Roger's office after the usual rigmarole with the receptionist downstairs and commenced with a bit of banter before settling down to business. Roger had been working hard to get things tied down and finally gotten the German side to agree to signing the contract. He ran through the details and Roger agreed that it looked perfect.

"Where do I sign?" he asked.

"Not yet," said Roger, "first, your German friends need to step up and sign and send me their forms."

"I'll phone them later and get them to get a move on."

They agreed to meet again early next week. Mike got back to the office for 5 pm and decided to follow up on his promise to Roger and phone Peter in Germany. He caught him just before he was leaving the office for the airport to meet his Irish bodyguards.

"Well, I won't keep you but remind everyone to sign the contracts and get them sent off without delay as my solicitor wants to get this done."

"Sure and I will phone you back tomorrow with confirmation that it is being done but I must rush now or I will be late."

"OK. Till tomorrow," said Mike and replaced the receiver.

Chapter 10

During the next month, Mike concentrated on the London operations and how the figures were expanding following their blitz into the provinces. Stephanie visited Germany on 4 occasions to complete the setting up of the Frankfurt office and the hiring of the staff. The general manager was recommended to her by Wolfgang—a 45-year-old called Max Steifler; after meeting him, she decided he would be very successful indeed as he knew his stuff and his career path was excellent. In addition, he looked the part with his 6'2" frame, dark hair and square jawline topped by a straight nose and laughing eyes; in short, both a man's man and a woman's man.

Eventually, the Germans signed their contracts and sent them to Roger who was happy now and processed all the paperwork so the German operation was now settled.

Mike received a call from Peter basically to fill him in on the bodyguards with whom he was very impressed. He said the girl who called herself Lisa seemed to be the leader and was extremely thorough in her instructions to the 3 men. He said whenever they went out, two accompanied him; one male dressed down and the girl sometimes dressed up and sometimes as an old lady with a stick. The idea was that any attacker would think there were only 2 bodyguards as they did not even travel together but were always somewhere nearby. Peter said in an excited voice, "It's just like the movies and they are all armed."

Mike interjected, "Let's hope then when Johann sends his hit squad that it works and we send them back with a flea in their ears."

"You mean we knock hell out of them so they won't come after me again. I'll leave that to the bodyguards as they are the experts."

After a few more exchanges and pleasantries, they said their goodbyes.

A fortnight later while Mike was going through some papers with Stephanie sent by the bank who in conjunction with the equity people wanted things to speed up on the Continent, particularly in France, he received a phone call from his friend Tom Bellamy in Belfast who said in a slightly anxious voice, "You had better get your arse over to Frankfurt pronto as that bastard Johann sent three goons to get Peter and he has been shot but not fatally. He has been taken to the local hospital Rotkreuz Krankenhaus, seems it's quite a big hospital with a high reputation so he should get the best treatment."

"What about your people, are they OK?"

"Oh! they are fine not a scratch which is more than I can say for the goons— all three are dead! I'm going over to help them clean up as I have some friends in Berlin who will join us in the disposal operation," continued Tom.

"What about the risk of a further attack while Peter is in hospital?"

"Not to worry; Lisa is playing the distraught daughter so God help anyone trying again."

"Is her German good enough for that?"

"Fluent in German and several other languages as well, she is a bit of a genius but never shows it normally."

"Right. I will get over as fast as I can and I am relieved none of your people were hurt."

"See you there."

On arrival in Frankfurt, Mike went to Peter's house to see his wife Claudia and children and to see exactly what happened. It seemed that the attackers burst into the house and opened fire on Peter, wounding him in the chest just below the right shoulder. The bodyguards responded immediately by returning fire so efficiently that they killed all three of them. They then called an ambulance and got Peter safely away but they removed the dead before the ambulance arrived and spun a yarn about burglars that they had interrupted but they got away before shooting anyone else.

One of the bodyguards was with Lisa at the hospital. Lisa was apparently disguised as a nurse now so if a further attempt was made, she should be able to give whoever a nasty surprise. Nevertheless, Mike decided he would pay Peter a visit to see for himself how the protection was set up. Peter was pleased to see him and especially pleased to be alive. Mike told him they were doing their best to find out where Johann was located and they intended to pay him a return visit once they succeeded in finding him.

At that moment, Mike heard a commotion outside the door and what sounded like a struggle. He rushed to the door to see that the bodyguard had what presumably was an attacker in a grip around the neck so tight that his opponent's face was a bright crimson and it looked like he was about to die. Then Lisa appeared and said something in what sounded like Russian and the bodyguard let the attacker go. He ran off staggering from wall to wall down the corridor. Lisa then instructed Mike to follow her while they trailed him back to his base and she explained in short sentences that if it didn't lead anywhere helpful, they would have to beat the information out of him.

They kept their distance and watched him hail a cab and alight the vehicle in double-quick time. Mike thought what now but Lisa pulled him towards a motorbike parked nearby with a penalty notice attached which she immediately threw on the ground. Two helmets were pulled out of the container strapped to the rear and they both jumped on and Mike just had time to hold on to Lisa as she accelerated after the taxi. They soon caught up and had to slow down and keep their distance in case the thug was checking if he was being followed.

After half an hour of twists and turns, the taxi disgorged the thug in front of a skyscraper office block and after a quick furtive look around, he entered the building.

Lisa told Mike to go in quickly and see what floor he took the lift to and paused while checking his pockets as if looking for a note with directions on it and then when she entered to express relief at which point they would know the floor they needed. They entered the lift unchallenged and took it to the 23rd floor. The doors opened onto a corridor and opposite it was the entrance to an office labelled Zagerman Infrastructure GmbH so Mike knew they had found the right place.

They entered the office and approached a large desk behind which sat a middle-aged Frau with old-fashioned round glasses. Lisa spoke to her saying she was sent by the hospital to see Herr Zagerman as he had phoned complaining of chest pains. The frau stood up and insisted that he had not phoned but to wait here while she checked. She approached a large mahogany door and opened it and at that point, Lisa made her move following her in and pushing her to one side. Mike moved in too and Lisa turned to Mike and asked which one was Johann.

Without thinking, Mike replied, "The one on the left."

Lisa walked up to him and pulled from her bag a revolver equipped with a silencer and shot Johann between the eyes, killing him instantly. The frau opened her mouth to scream but was shot before a note escaped and the man sitting in front of the desk started to get up for whatever reason but received a kick in the nuts which brought his open mouth down on to the silencer which Lisa then fired, throwing him and his chair 3 or 4 feet across the room. She then turned to Mike still with the revolver in her hand and instructed him to leave the building on his own and get a cab back to the hospital as he was not to be seen leaving with her. He was delighted to follow her instructions as for a micro second he had thought he was next on her list.

By the time he arrived back at the hospital, it was all beginning to sink in and the upside was the relief but the downside was the absolute cold-blooded efficiency of the killings he had just witnessed. Should he feel guilty or indeed relieved that his pal and investor was now in the clear? He opted for the latter and resolved to be happy with that decision and to inform Peter he now just needed to pay the bill when it arrived.

The next day, Johann's murder was all over the front pages with Die Weld calling it an assassination. No mention of any suspects and no mention of a nurse.

When a few days later Mike got back to London, he received a call from Tom Bellamy who was back in Belfast.

"Well, me old pal, no sooner said than done, eh!"

"Bloody efficient, you lot, scary actually."

"Well, if you're going to do it, you have to do it right or not at all."

"Have you sent Peter the bill yet?"

"No bill, I'll just send him me bank details in Germany and he can transfer the money in over the next 3 months or longer if he thinks that is safer. The cost is five hundred thousand; tell him."

"I'm sure that will be no problem."

"Tell him if he gets the sniff of anything strange to call you and we will be back immediately but I'm not expecting any problems."

"Will do; and I must go over and see you for a jar or two soon."

"Look forward to that."

And the call ended.

"And when are you going to tell me what happened?" asked Stephanie.

"Tonight; but you might not like what you hear."

Chapter 11

The pressure was on from the bank and the equity people for Mike to expand further into Europe, particularly Paris and Amsterdam and Mike was happy to oblige but first he wanted to meet Max Steifler to see how he was settling into his new job in Frankfurt. He telephoned him and luckily got hold of him immediately so they arranged to meet on Thursday of next week. Mike just wanted to be sure that Frankfurt was up and running so he could concentrate on the new areas.

On arrival in Frankfurt, Mike took a taxi straight to the office and strode in and was greeted by the receptionist who recognised him immediately and had instructions from Max to take him straight to his office. The smartly dressed receptionist knocked quickly on the door paused for a second or two and then ushered Mike in. The delicacy of the procedure impressed Mike as she obviously gave Max sufficient time to compose himself before having to meet his ultimate boss.

Max was everything that Mike had been told and he liked him instantly. He looked and acted the part of an important player in the insurance broking business, immaculately turned out without overdoing it. Dressed to impress but not to humiliate.

Mike was offered a seat and was happy to sit down and relax. They chatted about all sorts of trivia for a while and then Mike got down to business and questioned Max on his intentions. At the end of the exercise, Mike was satisfied that he knew what he was doing and was likely to make a great success of the job. Mike then signalled the end of the inquest by congratulating him on getting the job and wishing him every success which he added was sure to come his way.

Max then asked him if he was going to open in France to which Mike replied in the affirmative but said it will obviously take time as they needed to go through the same procedure as for Frankfurt.

Max then said he might be able to help in that he knew someone very capable who worked for one on the large Reinsurers here in town but would love to go back to broking in Paris.

"Can you fix a meeting?" Mike asked.

"How soon?" asked Max, moving his eyebrows quizzically.

"Would he be able to meet the two of us at lunchtime today or tomorrow?"

"He is more or less his own boss so perhaps he can; I will phone him now and see."

Max did and they arranged to meet that day at 12:30 pm.

"What's his name and what age is he?" Mike asked.

"His name is Xavier Dupont and he is about 39 or 40 I think."

"Well, I like the name anyway."

"He looks a bit like me, they say."

"Oh bloody hell!" said Mike and then burst into laughter to ensure the comment was not taken seriously. "It's knocking on midday; isn't it time we were making a move?" Mike queried.

"Yes, but do not worry as we will be there first as it's only around the corner."

The restaurant was Italian called, predictably. Mario's Ristorante and was expensive which suited them as it was quiet enough to be able to talk business.

Xavier arrived after 15 minutes and was tall, about 6 foot 3 inches and typically French in that he was extremely well-dressed in a navy suit probably made to measure but one never knows these days as off the rack suits are getting better all the time.

After a brief introduction, Xavier sat down and the meal was ordered and only then did the interview commence. Mike was impressed with his record and he was eminently suited to be in charge of the running of the Paris office. One downfall he advised was that he had to give 3 months' notice but that was not a problem for Mike. Mike decided he would concentrate on the French office next as he had a suitable general manager. Mike suggested the same starting salary and perks as Max which he already knew as he and Max were very good friends and so the deal was concluded there and then.

At about 3 pm, they all departed the restaurant going their separate ways. Mike was anxious to see Peter and called his office from a public telephone and managed to get hold of him. Peter asked him to stay overnight at his home which was very welcome to Mike. He went back to his hotel and cleaned up before checking out and heading by taxi to Peter's house. He arrived there about 6 pm and Peter was already home so he received the usual robust greeting followed by hearty laughter.

A man appeared from nowhere to help with his suitcase and they made their way in to see Claudia who was her usual serene self; completely self-assured and elegant. She asked what time Stephanie was arriving and was answered by the appearance of Stephanie's taxi pulling into the drive. After more hellos and air kissing, they retired to the lounge where drinks were waiting. After half an hour of chatting, a maid arrived to inform them that dinner was ready if they would like to go to the dining room.

The dining room was sumptuous and sparkled with a high quality crystal chandelier hanging from the ceiling and on the table glistening leaded glass. The walls were adorned with dark green wallpaper relieved with traces of gold woven into an intricate design. The meal turned out to be equally impressive.

Afterwards, they returned to the lounge to talk and Claudia turned the conversation to recent events which she found traumatising and asked Mike in a hushed tone, "How did you cope with the shock of seeing three people shot dead in front of you?"

Mike thought about it for a while and then said: "I'm not sure as it was like being in a movie where everything went into slow motion and then I knew it was real and suddenly I wondered if I was next as the two extras were only killed because they could have been witnesses. Then through the fog of it all, I heard Lisa telling me to leave and to walk slowly; no rushing. I obeyed and then found that a strange self-confidence came over me and I seemed to be able to carry on as if I had a perfectly normal reason for being there. After that, it never bothered me I suppose because I didn't commit the crime. I was just a bystander or so I told myself. Perhaps sometime in the future, it will get me and I will get the shakes but I hope not."

"I sometimes feel that we should have called the police and explained everything and let them handle it all. After all, Peter had not done anything illegal."

"Claudia, it has nothing to do with it being legal or not; it was more a matter of life and death. If we had done what you suggest, Peter would be dead and you would be complaining bitterly about the useless police. Remember they tried to get Peter in the hospital and without our lot there, they would have succeeded. I am afraid when you are up against organised crime, you have to fight back viciously."

"I know you are right and I am so grateful and I don't know why I feel guilty."

"If it's any help, our lot have acted for MI6 in the past where their expertise was required so you are in good company. Just keep reminding yourself of that fact and the guilt will gradually fade away. There is no trail back to you but if by some fluke you are ever questioned about any matter connected with this then remember the old rule of thumb and use your ears and mouth in the proportion that you have them so listen a hell of a lot more that you talk. Ask questions such as why are you telling me this or are you saying that Peter is going to be attacked again. Act worried and flustered; it covers a multitude of sins."

Claudia smiled and nodded agreement.

Peter interrupted, "More wine, you two?"

Mike laughed easily and turned to Stephanie and said, "I'm game; are you?"

"Only sometimes," was the reply.

"Back to normal now I see," Peter said choking on his laughter.

The rest of the evening was very relaxing with the conversation switching from music to films and back again as the consumption of wine increased the laughter.

Around midnight, they retired.

The next day after a hearty breakfast, Mike ordered a taxi to take them to the station to catch the train to Paris to commence operations for a French office and to spend a few romantic days with Stephanie wandering around one of the most beautiful cities in the world.

Mike particularly wanted to visit Montmartre and see if they could pick up a beautiful painting but most of all to absorb the special atmosphere that hung over the area. The French have this gift of making life seem very special by exaggerating the ordinary just the way fresh bread has to be available every morning in villages throughout France and the sight of people walking back to their homes with a French stick jutting out of their shopping bag immediately triggers something in one's mind and you see the ordinary that is not so ordinary but strangely special and yet familiar and then you smile inwardly as you identify the scene before you as 'so French' with that close connection to everyday basics.

Chapter 12

The year was 1985 and Mike had set up individual companies in France, the Netherlands, Switzerland, Austria and in Milan, northern Italy, and all were trading successfully with only the occasional problem. He was happy and so were his investors and he had now decided that he would take a break and start travelling with Stephanie. It was time to relax and enjoy life more.

Mike talked it over with Stephanie and they decided to tour around Europe in a leisurely manner and the best way was to buy a good and reliable car. He decided on a BMW 7 series saloon car, a beautiful 6-cylinder vehicle which would eat the miles without fuss.

They took the ferry to Calais and disembarked into the very foreign atmosphere of France and the chore of getting used to driving on the wrong side of the road. Mike kept saying to himself, "I must be next to the footpath or the ditch at all times except when turning left and turning left is the dangerous manoeuvre." He hammered this into his brain for the first 3 days and then it became natural as if he had been doing it for years. He also understood that if you stopped in a quiet lane with no traffic, you had to think before driving off or you would revert to the English rules as that experience actually happened when he stopped to look at his map but fortunately, he remembered quickly and swerved back to the right with a quick intake of breath.

Their first stop was a little town called St Omer where they parked up in the square next to a large church. The buildings around the edges of the square were mostly bars with open air seating providing drinks and snacks and otherwise shops selling vegetables which looked magnificent and very healthy. They stopped for a drink and asked the waiter about eating places which resulted in being given what turned out to be a very good recommendation. It was lunchtime so they wandered off in the direction of the restaurant. They were warned that although the woman who owned the restaurant spoke English, she preferred to speak French unless the customer really couldn't cope.

On arrival, the owner who also served greeted them in a friendly manner but somehow managed to make you feel that you were lucky to be getting such nice attention. They were shown to their table and furnished with the menu and had the day's specials pointed out. The waitress then left to get their drinks while they decided on their choices. The starters were easy as they both chose Le Bric which was a warmed soft cheese which when first tasted made one make mmm sounds and Mike who normally ate quickly found himself eating very slowly in order to better savour the taste and texture and hopefully make it last forever. It was so wonderful that neither wanted it to end but it did.

The rest of the meal was also very good especially when washed down with some smooth red wine. The owner-waitress was very chatty and described some of the local places to visit. Very late afternoon, they made their way back to the car and Mike decided that he had not indulged sufficiently with the wine to be over any limit and he had stopped 2 hours ago as well.

The next morning after a continental breakfast, they made their way towards Brittany as Stephanie wanted to visit Mont Saint Michel. Mike had been there before but was quite happy to please her. Afterwards, they would turn around and travel east towards Germany and the Rhine where he was sure the stunning beauty would really impress her. On the way, they decided to stop at Amiens to have a look around and took so long they booked into a 3-star basic hotel for the evening. The next morning they left early and when Mike saw the sign for St Saens, he wondered if it had any connection to Camille St Saens, the famous composer, he of Carnival Des Animaux fame, and so decided to turn off for a quick look.

They entered the commune/village and parked up on the main road through. He regretted missing breakfast so as they approached a bar, he looked inside to see what presumably was the owner. He checked his watch and it was 8:30 am. The owner was a very large man dressed in a lumberjack's shirt with braces and the only occupant was a small man drinking a small cerise drink and talking to himself. Mike hesitated but then decided to take the plunge and in his best French asked if they could get le petit dejeuner here whereupon the owner jumped into action and metamorphosed into a cuddly bear making big welcoming arches with his oversized arms and showed them to a table and asked if they would like coffee with milk and with sugar and bread rolls with butter and with jam.

Mike turned to Stephanie and said, "Shall we go the whole hog then?"

She laughed an emphatic "oui." The wife then appeared with a tablecloth and chatted in a lovely friendly way, confirming the order. The old man in the corner joined in with various comments which made him laugh to himself as nobody else paid him the slightest interest. Still he was happy in his own world. The breakfast appeared by magic.

Mike asked the owner if the village was named after Camille St Saens and got the reply "Qui?"

"What did he say?" asked Stephanie as she hadn't heard.

"He said who, he obviously has never heard of him." Mike turned back to tell him and his wife who was paying great attention as Mike explained that he was one of France's greatest composers whose music was played every day on English radio and Mike emphasised "every day". The wife then disappeared and came back with a large book and opened it up at St Saens and they were still talking about it after Mike paid and they were leaving to great enthusiastic "Bon Voyages" from each. Mike enjoyed that interchange and could see they did also. Speaking a little French makes all the difference, especially when one is off the beaten track.

They arrived at Mont Saint Michel on a bright day which made it look magnificent and very imposing. They had arranged to stop at a bed and breakfast place which luckily had a vacancy and they pulled up into a parking place which bordered on to a flat lawn area in front of the guest house. As they got out of their car, the proprietor of the place greeted them with a broad welcoming smile asking them where they came from. Mike explained they were from London but then he concentrated on Mike with "And where do you come from?"

Mike replied, "London", to which the retort was "Non non non quelle nationalite?"

Mike thought to himself that this was the first time a Frenchman has been able to hear his accent and so replied, "Je suis Irelandais."

These seemed to be the magic words for he became even warmer and started telling him where he must visit and the best local restaurant for an evening meal which was just down the road and turned out to be a rather nice place called Le Petit Quin Quin.

They checked in and then wandered slowly to the restaurant enjoying the warmth of the sun on their backs as they went. After the meal, Mike asked the waiter what Le petit Quin Quin meant as he couldn't find Quin in his pocket dictionary whereupon the waiter replied it was a song from the north of France and immediately gave a full rendition of it, much to their surprise and delight. They applauded him and so did the other diners, which pleased him enormously. Stephanie continued smiling with delight and said, "You definitely would not get that at home."

"Well, there you are wrong."

"Really?"

"Yes. I was visiting some friends in Cheshire a little village called Kelsall and on about the third night as I walked in with my pal, I was approached by a rather large man who was well oiled and said, 'You're Irish, aren't you?'

"When I confirmed his suspicions, he immediately broke into a fantastic outburst of *Oh Danny Boy*. The whole pub was delighted and impressed. He was good. He changed the atmosphere from normal to special with everyone laughing and talking to each other."

"Is it because you are Irish that people do that, do you think?"

"They know we are all a bit mad so they feel it's OK to be mad back in that if anyone should object then it's all the Irishman's fault."

"And do they?"

"Not so far, I think you English are mad too but you hide it better."

They spent the next day exploring Mont St Michel and it does take a whole day as the climb to the top is quite tiring but well worth the effort to experience the vast panoramic view from the pinnacle. You feel that the vastness and the enormous skyscape are part of a special landscape painted by mother nature just to show how impressive she can be. They finished the day off by sitting on a restaurant balcony enjoying the sunset over a large coffee.

The following day they left the guest house after a full breakfast and headed east back towards Belgium on route to Germany but Stephanie suggested as they were passing close to Paris, why didn't they call to see Xavier. Mike agreed as a visit to Paris was always welcome and so near Caen, he saw the signs for Paris and soon they were on their way. Mike drove to the same hotel and booked in before giving Xavier a call. Xavier was very keen to hear him and said he had been phoning London in the hope of contacting him as they had a problem and he needed to talk to him but not over the phone.

He asked, "Where are you, are you anyway near and I'll come and meet you?"

"No need, I am in Paris at the usual hotel so we can talk here or at your office, whichever you prefer."

"In that case, the office as I don't want anyone listening to our problem."

"When then?" Mike was getting slightly worried by all the secrecy.

"Now if you are free."

"OK, see you in 15 minutes."

Mike explained what little he knew to Stephanie and suggested he would see him first and she would follow on in an hour just in case it was something very personal or embarrassing.

As Mike walked through the Paris office doors, he was greeted by the receptionist and various other staff who all seemed very relaxed and normal.

The receptionist said, "Xavier is expecting you and I am to take you straight in."

"Tres bien, apres vous, Mademoiselle."

Xavier stood up immediately and ushered Mike to the chair by the side of his desk and made a point of telling her no disturbance. Mike interrupted to say except for Stephanie who will be here in just under an hour to which Xavier nodded his agreement.

"Right then, what's the problem?" Mike asked.

"Russian money, that's the problem."

"Do continue."

"You know, when we went to the market to raise capital well, the Russian mafia invested and I have had a visit from a sleazebag telling me they want to push money through."

"Money laundering?"

"Exactly and in his words, as we need their money, we are in no position to object."

"Ah well, that's where he is wrong, we don't need money, the raising of money on the stock market was simply a convenience."

"He made a not very well veiled threat to me and my family and he is coming back tomorrow for my agreement, otherwise they will show they mean business."

"Have you involved the police?"

"Not yet as I needed to get hold of you first."

"Good, on something like this, they would simply stir the hornet's nest and what we need to do is crush it."

Xavier looked at Mike with an open mouth and could only nod agreement as Mike picked up the desk phone demanding an outside line. Mike dialled furiously and then Xavier heard Mike greet, "Tom, how the hell are you?"

Xavier realised that Tom must have answered back for Mike continued: "I need your help again and this time it might be worse as it's the bloody Russians. They have got into the company through buying shares and now threatening the general manager and family as they want to launder."

"Better get them out of the country while we sort it out to avoid collateral damage."

"You can help?"

"Of course, it will be a great pleasure to knock shit out of those bastards, I have a plan on the shelf that will do the job."

"I'll tell Xavier and I'll take over here until the problem is solved."

"I'll send over Lisa and the mob and I'll come myself as this will need very careful handling. One slip and these bastards will cause havoc. I'll give you the timings in about an hour, you staying there?"

"Yeah, here all afternoon."

Mike turned to Xavier and said, "It is all under control now and you are leaving for England for an extended holiday in the countryside which Stephanie will organise for you and your family. It's best you are all out of harm's way and then we have less to worry about."

"What are you going to do?"

"Better you don't know but you will read about it in the papers I expect."

Just then in walked Stephanie and being completely unaware of the problem smiled broadly asking Xavier how he was and how the family were until she suddenly realised something was wrong and stopped midstream while turning to Mike with a frown. Mike explained the problem and the solutions. Stephanie quickly grasped what was required and booked the flights to London and explained to Xavier they would stay with her for a day or so until she arranged a holiday in the countryside, either the Cotswolds or the Norfolk Broads. She then encouraged Xavier to make some explanation to the staff but not to mention the Russians. He came up with an English family friend who had had a very serious accident and might not survive and he needed to go immediately but Mike had kindly offered to step in and hold the fort until he got back.

Mike thought that was perfect and said so.

"Now get going and leave me to it," and he stood up and kissed Stephanie a little longer just in case. She looked quizzically and then smiled and carried on.

The phone rang and Mike picked it up. It was Xavier's secretary. "Some foreign man by the name of Kardac, I think, asking for Xavier."

"Put him through please, Yvonne."

"Monsieur Xavier Dupont?" asked a guttural voice.

"Yes Mr Kardac, can I help?"

"I want to speak to Monsieur Dupont."

"He has left and won't be back for some time."

"Who are you?"

"Me, I'm the group's managing director; can I help you?"

"My company Kardac International Investments has a large stake in your company and I would like to speak to you regarding how we can develop a close business relationship."

"How about tomorrow at 1730 hours when the office will be quiet as most of the staff will have left?"

"OK, what's your name so I know who to ask for?"

"It's Michael Black, I look forward to seeing you tomorrow."

Mike hoped that all sounded normal to the sleazebag who will be in for a surprise but first he will need to drag as much information out of him as possible. *If we are going to fight this*, he thought, *we need to know what we are up against.*

Just then the phone rang out and it was Tom advising that Lisa, Harry and a couple of the boys would be there tomorrow morning.

"Good," said Mike and filled Tom in on his conversation with the Russian.

"Hope you didn't warn him by being aggressive."

"No fear, I was politeness itself and made the appointment for 1730 and mentioned that most of the staff would have gone. I think that will make him believe I know what he wants hence the privacy. Hopefully, two or three late leavers hanging about will not seem odd."

"How have you explained Xavier's absence to the staff?"

"Close family friend in England has had a serious accident and he and the family had to rush over to see him as he might not survive."

"Perfect and I will see you tomorrow as well but I will be arriving later, about 3 pm."

Chapter 13

Mike arrived in the office early before any staff but was soon greeted by Yvonne, now his temporary secretary, who offered him a piping hot coffee and a croissant. He loved French coffee and the ubiquitous patisserie and devoured the butter enriched croissant ravenously as he had missed le petit dejeuner in his haste to get in first as he feared the Russian could pull a surprise but he needn't have worried.

Lisa and Harry arrived about 11 am and were shown in by Yvonne who arranged for someone to make them coffee. Mike greeted them warmly and they hadn't changed a bit since their help with Peter's problem.

"How have you been keeping?" asked Lisa.

"Well, but I am conscious of attracting more than my fair share of trouble."

"But it's not you but others who are doing that."

"Do you know what Tom's plans are?" he directed the question at both.

Lisa answered, "We know the bare bones of it but he will have a twist to it, no doubt."

Mike agreed and quickly explained to Lisa: "First of all, I think that I should see the Russian on his own so he feels in charge and tries to bully me into submission. I will act dumb and ask lots of questions to try and find out who and how many are behind this potential scam and when I have reached the limit I will call you in."

"That sounds good and with a bit of luck Tom will have arrived before the Russian anyway, so there will be three moving in on him. Of course, he might not come alone but we'll handle that if needs be."

They carried on discussing the proposed plan over a light lunch and got back to the office just in time to greet Tom. At 5 pm, Tom, Lisa and Harry moved out to the furthest corner away from the entrance so as not to be a noticeable threat to the Russian. It was agreed that Lisa would usher him in to see Mike and offer him a coffee if he was alone but not if he had a minder in tow.

At 1730 hours precisely, Mr Kardac was ushered into Mike's office. He looked exactly as one would expect with a large body topped with a swarthy head and sleazy black hair well-greased down. His ruddy well-lined complexion dominated by a bulbous thick nose, which flattened when he smiled as if pulled by some invisible strings, made him look decidedly dangerous. His wool suit was dark, pinstriped and oozed criminality.

Mike shook his hand and resisted the temptation to wipe his hand on his backside. He would just have to live with the germs.

"Take a seat," Mike offered.

"Thank you. I will get straight on with our request. We have invested $5 million dollars in your company or approximately 4 1/2 million euros and so long as it stays there, your share value remains strong but if we decide to panic-sell…well!"

"So what do you want to be happy to remain?" interjected Mike.

"We need to buy some insurance policies at inflated prices well…Refundable policies of course."

"How much money did you want to launder?" asked Mike pretending to be interested as he and Tom had agreed.

"About 1 million euros a year or around 80,000 euros per month up or down a bit, depending on trade."

"That sounds a bit on the high side if it is to remain unnoticeable."

"We are not giving you an option, you have to oblige," and oblige was said slowly and stretched almost interminably or what seemed so to Mike.

Mike made some notes and then looked up and said, "And who is going to foot the tax bill, for no matter which way you cut this, the turnover is going to look over-healthy."

"You will have to invent some nice losses to counter balance the profit from the increase but we will leave that to you. The alternative is we will ruin you and bring this fucking company of yours down," he snarled aggressively.

"OK, OK. I will need to think how I can do it until tomorrow. Can I have your number and I will phone you when I have worked it out?" Mike said as casually as he could muster.

The grease ball stood up and adjusted his shirt sleeves so they matched on both sides and replied, "Go fuck yourself. I will phone you and if you give us any shit, we will start selling."

"You really know how to be nice then," Mike uttered.

"I don't need to be nice to you…I have you by the balls."

And with that left the room slamming the door behind him as if to emphasise the point.

A few minutes later, in came Tom and Lisa to announce that Harry was following the toerag and once he knew which building he was going into, he would ensure that it was his business quarters and if necessary wait for him to emerge before taking him out and whoever he was with. Tom was hoping they would think it was the rival gang of Russians who were equally as vicious and it might start a bitter feud between them but if not then, as Tom said: *we do it the hard way*.

Kardac was duly disposed of by one clear shot from Harry.

"So that bastard will not be back again but I will have to be here in case a substitute turns up," Mike says.

"Yes and so will we, but this time we will rough him up a bit to get more information and dispose of him here before putting him in plastic and dropping him off on their doorstep—no messing or hesitating."

"That definitely looks like gang warfare," said Mike with a satisfactory grin.

"Extreme measures but we have to stir things up or they will just drag out."

Mike says, "Of course, they may not send another guy if they think they are being attacked by their rivals."

"Oh they will, have no fear," Tom said with certainty. "Eventually, you will need to declare to the authorities that you believe the money invested is from suspect sources and you want them to look into it but not until we weaken them by helping their rivals to succeed. On the quiet of course, neither side must realise it's us so perhaps on reflexion, we should not kill him here but follow the same routine."

"Well, we just have to sit back and wait patiently. The trick is to concentrate on other things such as real work. I'll get Xavier's PA Yvonne to bring me up to speed and see if she needs any help," said Mike.

Two days went by before the expected telephone call came in from Kardac International Investments asking for Mr Black and giving his name as Mr Ivan Romax. Mike answered the phone saying Black here and waited. Mr Romax introduced himself by saying he was taking Mr Kardac's place and wanted his response today.

"No problem," lied Mike, "but if you want this to go unnoticed, you will need to be clever but I have worked out a way. Can you call so I can explain it as it requires, apart from debits, the need to create contra entries so as to make it difficult to decipher."

It could have been the word decipher but Romax agreed instantly, in fact almost enthusiastically, and he said he would call tomorrow at 1800 hours.

At 6 pm precisely, Ivan was shown into Mike's office by Tom and the door closed behind him.

Ivan was an extremely meagre fellow with thin hair oiled flat to his skull. His face fitted his skull tightly with cheekbones protruding alarmingly which accentuated his sunken eyes all the more. The overall effect when you looked at Ivan was the rather scary effect of being aware of his skeleton rather than the live entity it enclosed. On looking into his eyes, Mike got the feeling that the soul had long ago departed.

Ivan took the seat proffered and leaned forward with a broad grin showing off his large even very white teeth which made Mike think of the scary carnival rides from his youth. He had to resist the instinct to jerk back in his seat and instead, he concentrated on the figures he had been working on to show how difficult it was to hide large amounts of cash.

Mike's figures suggested that the firm could cope with 5,000 euros a week without it showing up. This Ivan dismissed and doubled the figure with "…and that's just for starters." Mike protested for a while and then reluctantly agreed knowing full well that he would only have to accept one or two payments before they engineered the war between the two Russian sides. Ivan smiled as he stood up and offered his hand with, "Now you are getting the idea."

Mike shook the bony hand and ushered him out keeping the offending hand free of contact with anything until he had disinfected it. He got the spray he used to clean his reading glasses and sprayed his hand generously before relaxing. Tom entered after the Russian had left with, "Hey, what a creep. I'm glad you decided against roughing him up; he'd probably break into pieces."

Tom told Mike that Harry was already on the creep's tail at a respectable distance of course and hopefully will shoot him outside his office to cause the greatest amount of disruption possible.

Half an hour later, Lisa came into the office to say that Harry had shot the Russian but not fatally and had to fire two more times to finish him off. This caused panic with people running about like scalded chickens. Harry escaped by sliding down a side street, leaving the uproar behind and as he walked back, the police with their sirens blazing were roaring to the Russian's office. Two Russians killed outside their office should raise a lot of questions.

"Half the job done," said Tom, "just got to get a Russian from the other side now and that should have the desired effect. Lisa, you know where the other Russians have their office but have you identified any individuals?" asked Tom.

"Yes, I have a choice of two men and one woman," Lisa replied.

"Well, tomorrow we strike then," said Mike, Lisa looked at Mike and said she was amazed at how quickly he had gotten used to the violence required to solve the problem to which Mike said if there was any chance these people had a jot of decency lurking somewhere within their bodies then it would cause him a problem but as they are all wearing black hats, metaphorically speaking, he could pull the trigger himself without a moment's hesitation or regret.

"Ah but can you cut off afterwards and settle back into boring normality?" asked Tom.

"My normality isn't boring. I intend to indulge my love of Europe by slowly wandering from place to place enjoying the scenery, food and the people with their different languages while I have Stephanie to share it all with. I have built a great group of companies and now I am entitled to some relaxation. In the first place I will do whatever it takes to defend my businesses and feel thoroughly justified in whatever means are employed so long as we don't hurt innocent people. If that means bending with the wind then so be it; needs must."

The following day, Lisa shot two Russian males on the other side of town. It was done neatly and swiftly as one would expect from Lisa and for a while nobody knew why they had collapsed until some woman had a close look and started shouting for the police. From that moment, everybody got nervous wondering if they might get shot as well and started running in all directions, much to Lisa's amusement. Pandemonium reigned while Lisa walked slowly away.

Job done, she thought and slung her violin case over her shoulder.

The next day, Kardac International Investments phoned to cancel their meeting as Ivan had a previous appointment.

Mike replied, "Oh fine, tell him to phone when he is ready to follow up on the deal we agreed yesterday."

Mike chuckled to himself, "A previous appointment; succinctly put, I'd say."

Two days later the killings started, the media were in their element declaring it a Russian mafia gang war with 6 bodies found in various locations across the city. Questions were being asked about the ability of the police to get on top of the situation. Four more bodies turned up in the Seine and then there was a lull. It seemed to have stopped, perhaps the last few came to their senses.

Tom advised Mike that Harry and Lisa had been watching both Russian offices and saw the police make a coordinated mass raid on both places at the same time, taking away a large number of boxes full of papers. Tom realised that Mike would probably get a visit from the police any day now as no doubt the Russians had made a record of what they believed to be a deal with Mike so had better get his story straight.

Mike assured Tom it was not a problem as he had made his story up already in case he ever got challenged and it was so near the truth as be totally credible. After all, the Russians had threatened him and he had just gone along to get the proof before approaching the authorities. Tom was happy with Mike's version of events.

Chapter 14

As expected, in about a week, the office was visited by two officers of the law; one introduced himself to Mike as le Commissaire, a tall well-built man with impeccable dress sense evidenced by his French blue perfectly tailored suit over a brilliantly white shirt set off with a medium blue tie spotted with tiny red dots. He was a handsome man with a broad head and wavy dark hair neatly cropped to ensure the desired finish. His companion, a female of about 35 years of age, was also neatly turned out in a grey trouser suit; a touch too tight which didn't get missed by Mike and whilst her figure was as good as it gets, she did have unfortunately an abrupt manner, a face that was a touch too beautiful adorned by a nose a bit too perfect; all of which was accentuated by the fact she pulled her hair back in a severe tight knot, giving her a rather imposing appearance. She introduced herself as Lieutenante Bourgeot in a brisk and clipped manner. Obviously in a no-nonsense mood, thought Mike.

Le Commissaire opened the conversation with: "We are here about the Russians who have been shot in the streets of Paris in the last 2 weeks and would like to know what your involvement has been."

Mike realised that they knew about the Russians visiting his office and decided he had better face this head on and replied: "Absolutely no involvement with the shootings but what little knowledge I had of them it couldn't have happened to a more deserving bunch."

He could look at them openly with a clear conscience as of course he had not personally been involved with the shootings. Mike waited for a response but his reply had obviously knocked them off their mark somewhat so he continued: "Some of those bastards paid me a visit to inform me that as they had invested heavily in my firm; they wanted me to launder money for them, quite large sums actually. At first I refused straight off but then got threatened with them selling their shares and putting it about that I was about to fail. Their absolute distain for me made me determined to string them along with their ridiculous propositions and I pretended to reluctantly agree to go along with them which they seemed to accept. However, each time they were to arrive with a load of cash, the individual concerned was eliminated and I realised there was some kind of war between gangs going on. I have to admit I started to look forward to the next episode and then it stopped due to police action—a pity really."

La Lieutenante leaned forward and with a composed stern face said: "Et vous pensez que nous allons prendre votre histoire au pied de la lettre ?"

"And why would you not believe me, you know of course that I had to send the usual Director to England with his family as they had been threatened and on top of that, I have had to pay for special protection for them."

The commissaire intervened: "We know you have had a traumatic time of it but why did you not approach the police immediately? You can see your omission to do that creates suspicion."

"Because my information would not have been taken seriously and I would have had a slow response and once the Russians had been perhaps questioned about it that would have led to an example being made of me or perhaps one of my staff. When they started getting bumped off, I couldn't believe my luck." Mike looked at them both in turn and grinned broadly adding: "The luck of the Irish eh!"

Just at that moment, La Lieutenante dropped her pen which rolled behind her chair meaning she had to get up and bend down, presenting her rather perfect bottom to Mike who looked admiringly and then grinned again at Le Commissaire and repeated: "The luck of the Irish."

Much as Le Commissaire tried, he could not retain the laughter which burst out of him uncontrollably.

La lieutenante's "Quoi" made things even worse.

Le commissaire eventually managed among splutters to explain the joke to "La" who replied with: "Vous les homme stupides."

Mike decided the worst was over and stood up saying, "Would you like something to drink?" but La Lieutenante replied to the effect that they had to get back but they would take a wet cheque if that was ok.

"A wet cheque it is then," said Mike, smiling to hide his amusement.

They all shook hands warmly and La lieutenante's nose didn't look too thin when viewed straight on, in fact it looked perfect.

After they had left, Mike phoned Stephanie to bring her up to date and ask her to tell Xavier and family they could return now as the problem had been sorted and they would be quite safe. It was lovely hearing her voice and he told her so and how much he missed her and suggested she jump on a plane and come straight over. She apologised but said a close friend of hers called Olivia had been taken ill and she needed to help her out but would get over in a few days. She said she was sorry but couldn't do anything about it. So Mike changed tack by saying it was probably a good thing as there were some loose ends to tie up.

At 5 pm Mike left the office and walked to a little café just off Montmartre and as it was a fine evening he bought a local paper and settled down in the gentle evening sun to enjoy a large beer and occasionally admire those hurrying to and fro on their way home. It was while he became engrossed in an article relating to the commotion of the Russian warfare on the streets of Paris that he was interrupted by the now familiar voice of La Lieutenante greeting him: "Bonsoir, Monsieur Noir."

Mike looked up and smiled back with, "Mon nom, ca sonne mieux en Francais."

"I don't think so," she laughed and continued walking on with a wave culminating in a quick flick of her hand.

He watched her bottom disappearing into the crowd and then reverted to his paper.

A week later and Stephanie was still delayed in London so Mike decided to go to London himself as apart from seeing Stephanie, he wanted to check in with Freddie and see how things were going.

On arriving in London, Mike went straight to the office and found the familiarity of the surroundings a comfort after all the recent stress in Paris. He made his way to Freddie's secretary and she immediately took him through to Freddie who stood up smiling broadly.

"Stephanie gave me a brief run-through of the kind of trouble you were having but I don't know how you solved the problem."

Mike mused for a while and decided to give Freddie the same storey he gave the French police as no point in implicating him in his underhand tactics he thought.

"Well, I had several visits from the Russians and thought I was in it up to my ears and then I had a stroke of luck in that some kind of war broke out between two different gangs of Russians and they started killing each other at an alarming rate so much so the gendarmerie made a coordinated raid on both sides and arrested the remainder."

"That was pretty lucky," exclaimed Freddie incredulously.

"It's like I said to the French police who called on me afterwards as they knew I was being pressured to launder large amounts of cash, it's called the luck of the Irish."

"Did they believe you?" grinned Freddie who obviously didn't believe a word but realised it was better he didn't know everything.

"Reluctantly but were happy they came out of it looking good."

They then settled down to a serious discussion on the various statistics of all the companies with Freddie remarking that the Dutch were performing particularly well but they felt they were not getting the attention they deserved.

"Perhaps you should include them in the next part of your holiday."

"Why not; I have always wanted to visit the Netherlands in a private capacity."

Mike then stood up and took his leave as he was anxious to see Stephanie, he made a quick call before he left and Stephanie said she was on her way back to the apartment and would get there about 5 pm. Mike checked his watch; it was 3 pm so decided to take the tube and call into his local pub for a pint until Stephanie arrived home.

At 5:15 pm, Mike opened the apartment door and shouted: "I'm Here."

And then he saw it; 2 cases and 3 plastic covers containing his suits standing in the middle of the lounge. Mike's stomach went into a knot and he stood open-mouthed staring at the cases trying to get his mind to accept the obvious. He couldn't think; he just remained transfixed and then Stephanie appeared suddenly from the bedroom and greeted him with: "I've had enough."

"What do you mean?" he heard himself say from somewhere in the distance.

"We don't communicate anymore unless it's about business and I want out. I've met someone who treats me like a person; like an individual with personal feelings not some kind of personal assistant or some futuristic automaton. You are not capable of being personal. Oh! you put on a good act but that's what it is—an act."

"I'm not false if that is what you are saying; just because I don't gush doesn't mean I don't feel. I've never been any good at soppiness that always seems false or going over the top."

"That says it all!" she retorted.

"Well, if you have met someone else, there is no point in trying to persuade you to change your mind so I'll take my things and phone you in a day or so when I've calmed down to discuss the financial arrangements; at the moment, I can't even think."

With that he left and went to book into the Savoy for the night. By the time Mike went for his evening meal, he had calmed down and started thinking clearly again. He analysed the situation and decided that it was definitely over as Stephanie had found someone else and was confident enough to pack his bags. No discussions, no warnings, just finito and piss off. He was surprised how quickly he accepted the situation and immediately realised that was because there was no hesitation in Stephanie's decision, so she had been cruel to be kind, he thought.

He realised at the same time he was being very analytical. He asked himself if perhaps he had not been in love with her but had admired her and found her sexually attractive but most of all, had appreciated her steadfast support but was that all too clinical and what she complained about? And here he was not feeling the pain one supposedly felt in such circumstances. He did wonder.

He decided he would go back to Paris and from there phone Steph; he smiled at the abbreviation of her name which she hated and made up his mind that when discussing the financial arrangements, he would finish by calling her Steph just as he put the phone down knowing how it would irk her. He had already decided to be generous with the separation arrangements as after all she had been a great help and friend up until the last few weeks.

Mike therefore could settle down to a good meal and a read of the evening papers as the problem was indeed solved.

Mike waited until the end of the week and on the Friday decided to take the bull by the horns and phone Steph; he smiled and then decided he was being too silly for words and he would revert to calling her Stephanie. When she answered, he started: "Hi Stephanie, are you free to discuss the financial arrangements for the separation?"

"I am free and on my own but I don't have any expectations as we were not legally married. I am not entitled to anything."

"That's as may be legally; but morally, you are entitled as you have been a great help to me along the way and I would not have found it as easy had I not had you around and for that, you should be compensated so what do you say to you keeping both apartments and the car plus say £2 million cash? I will ask the solicitor to spell it out and will add a codicil that should you suffer a financial setback or disaster in the future, you are to contact me and I will endeavour to assist."

"Why are you being so kind?"

"Not kind actually, just trying to do the right thing hence the codicil as I would hate to hear some disaster had befallen you and I didn't know. Are we agreed then?"

"Yes of course."

"Good; we must try and keep in touch from time to time."

"Yes of course."

Mike knew that was not going to happen but it felt right to say it. He stood up and drew a quick breath and said to himself, *Now I can relax and think about what to do next.*

Chapter 15

Mike was sitting at his favourite table at the front of Café Royale enjoying the warm sunshine and people watching. Some were strolling aimlessly, obviously just passing time while others walked briskly, smartly dressed with an air of importance resulting in a mesmerising profusion of colour sparkling like an extravagance of modern art. So French, he thought and then pulled himself back to reality.

He picked up his Le Monde and at the same time took a sip from his large coffee before reading the headlines. He was protected from the strength of the sun by the canopy of the giant yellow umbrella. He got engrossed in an insurance article when he was interrupted by La Lieutenante. She was standing right in front of his table smiling down at him. He resisted the temptation to linger over her curvaceous lines and instead looked her straight in the eyes. "Not working today then?"

"No, I've taken 3 days off plus the weekend."

"Are you joining me?"

"Yes, thank you and you can buy me an ice cream. You not in the office today?"

"No, I've resolved the problems there so now I go to the Netherlands or les Pays-Bas as you call it. I'll be there for one day and an evening on business, the rest just sightseeing."

"I've never been to Holland as you would call it."

"Come with me as you have time off; I would enjoy your company. By the way, what is your name; you never let it slip, did you?"

"It's Helen but I'm not sure about going away with you as we hardly know each other; personally I mean."

"That's OK; as it's business, no expense spared and you will have your own room. I would not want to compromise you."

"Compromise me? I think I know what you mean but my English is not excellent."

"It is excellent and you understand me. Do say yes, it will be fun. I call on the manager the first day and we go for lunch and then he invites you and me for dinner in the evening or I invite him and his wife either way we all have dinner on the first night or perhaps the second. The rest of the time is ours. What do you say?"

"I say yes; sounds great and when do we leave?"

"Tomorrow morning first thing."

They caught the train to Amsterdam at 9:25 am travelling first class as Mike preferred the comfort and the lack of noise. Mike decided to use the time in finding out more about his companion and her likes and dislikes and was pleasantly surprised that they had similar taste across a lot of subjects. He thought this just might be very enjoyable.

As they alighted from the train struggling with their suitcases, Mike found they were still babbling away like excited teenagers all the way to the hotel. They had booked two rooms but Helen had decided they should share which pleased Mike but what to say to the receptionist.

In the event, it suddenly came to him to say, "We will not be needing the other room we booked as we have just gotten engaged."

"That will be fine, Sir, enjoy your stay."

On the way to the lift, Helen asked laughing: "Why did you say we have just got engaged?"

"What did you want me to say, perhaps I don't need the extra room as I'm just going to compromise this woman?"

A young woman just getting out of the lift on the first floor burst out laughing and muttered: "I've never heard it called that before."

Helen covered her mouth laughing embarrassingly and punched Mike on the shoulder quite hard. He feigned hurt.

The room was very pleasant, overlooking a canal which had a touristy looking café on the opposite bank.

"That looks nice so after you have compromised me, we can go there for lunch," said Helen putting one arm around Mike's neck and the other undoing his belt. He didn't need to be told twice.

That evening after a strenuous day, they were happy to replenish their strength over dinner at the hotel and Mike explained that tomorrow he would call in to see the office and get an update from the manager, Steven Van Dijk, and no doubt they would go to lunch and unless there was something unusual happening, he would see her back at the hotel about 3:30 pm. They would of course have an evening with both Steven and his wife but not sure which evening yet. Helen was quite happy with the chance to have a relaxing morning and maybe have a gentle walk around the city.

Mike strolled into the offices of Kaloon Verzekeringsmakelaar BV and was greeted by a well turned out young lady that unsurprisingly spoke perfect English. She asked him to take a seat while she went to speak to the manager. All very perfect, thought Mike. Steven came rushing out and welcomed Mike with great gusto, beaming from ear to ear and explaining to everyone in the office exactly who he was; presumably so he was not greeted like a stranger next time but as he had not visited since shortly after it was set up, he did not expect them to recognise him. As they were entering Steven's office, the young lady asked whether he would like tea or coffee. He elected to have coffee as it was more likely to be good.

Mike could see that Steven was nervous so he set about making him feel comfortable and complimenting him on his performance and letting him know that London was very impressed and then started asking him the kind of questions that would allow him to expand upon what they had achieved and hoped to achieve going forward. Soon Steven relaxed and the conversation started to flow naturally and in a productive manner giving Mike a feeling for the Dutch market. It turned out to be quite similar to London with the same sense of importance, urgency and pride in getting the right solution no matter how difficult the circumstances might be.

Just after 12:30, Mike asked: "Are you free for lunch?"

"Yes; we are spoiled for choice in Amsterdam," was the immediate reply.

"Right, I'm dying for a pint of lager; let's go."

Steven took them on a quiet stroll only a couple of streets away and then into a rather large double-fronted bar with an abundance of gold lettering on the door and windows and pulled open the door to allow Mike to enter first. After the bright sunshine outside it took Mike's eyes time to adjust but he was very pleasantly impressed upon looking down the long bar to see a lot of his favourite beers were available but also the elaborate layout and appearance of the multicoloured bar area and the comfortable plush seating said to Mike that he could quickly settle in here.

Mike ordered the first round and they chose a table in the corner to sit where they could talk privately. Steven did explain that they could either eat here for a quick lunch or if Mike preferred they could go into the restaurant at the rear for something more elaborate.

"No, here will be fine for a pub lunch but I would like to invite you and your wife out to dinner somewhere really good either tonight or tomorrow night if that isn't too difficult for your wife to organise at such short notice. I will understand if it's not convenient. I am here with a new girlfriend by the way so I hope you can suggest somewhere appropriate. I expect your wife would be a better judge, women usually are."

The conversation continued talking about fairly normal things such as hobbies and places to visit and by the end of the lunch time 2 hours in total, Mike felt he had gotten a good feel for the place. They shook hands outside the bar and Steven was to speak to his wife and let Mike know what could be arranged.

As Mike's taxi pulled up outside the Hotel, he saw Helen strolling back to the hotel and guessed she had decided to get some fresh air and enjoy the sun. He alighted and called out to her and she quickened her stride to greet him enthusiastically. She kissed him on both cheeks and asked if he was free for the rest of the day. He replied smiling broadly by saying that he was all hers and asked if she had seen anything she liked.

"Oh not to buy but somewhere I would like to show you."

"Let me go in and change into something more casual, it's a bit hot in this suit."

Ten minutes later, they set off to explore, starting with Rembrandt Square—a small square housing many restaurants and cafes and a large statue of Rembrandt himself.

"Is that not impressive?" she asked.

"Yes, very; I wonder where the museum displaying his paintings is."

"Just a short walk away and it's magnificent, come on, I'll show you," she said pulling him along.

They spent an hour browsing around the museum and left feeling elated with a pocket full of brochures.

As they got back to the hotel, Mike's room phone rang; it was Steven ringing to say his wife had already organised an evening meal on one of the canal boats noted for its excellent food and a small orchestra on board to add some atmosphere. "What do you think?"

After quickly explaining to Helen, they made their minds up to accept without hesitation.

"We would love to accept, I'll phone you later for details of where to meet."

A few hours later they were getting changed to meet up with Steven and his wife at the canal boat.

When they arrived, they were immediately greeted by Steven and Ann. After the greetings were settled, they made their way on board and were taken to their table which was beautifully laid out with a white linen cloth and a sparkling array of cutlery and glasses. The whole effect was quite dazzling and that, together with a 6-piece orchestra playing a melodic violin concerto, drew one into a gradually enveloping atmosphere that said you are all special here and this is your reward; a beautiful evening.

"My God, this is fantastic regardless of the food!" said Mike.

"Oh the food is supposed to be wonderful according to some friends of ours who told us about this event and they have excellent taste," said Ann enthusiastically.

"Well, let's look at the menu then," said Mike, "and if the food is as good as the artwork on this menu, we are in for a real treat."

The food was wonderful, the music sublime and after a couple of glasses of wine, the atmosphere between all four was extremely relaxed until Ann interjected with: "I hear you are a man of action and not one to be crossed?"

"Oh I'm very easy-going so I don't know what you could have heard," Mike replied enquiringly.

"All good actually. It seems you saved your German friend Peter's life by getting him protection."

Mike thought this could get hairy with Helen suddenly picking up interest so sought to make little of the whole incident by half ridiculing his efforts. "Well, great effort that; he got shot after the protection was set up."

The minute he said 'shot', he knew he had blown any chance of skirting over things and a complicated near truth story would have to be constructed on the hoof so to speak because now with a pretend casual interest disguised with an amused grin and enquiring eyebrow movements. Helen made it extremely difficult for Mike to keep up his casual detached stance.

As there was no question of saying Abracadabra and everyone would forget what they were discussing, he had to brace himself for the inevitable shafting but then his mind went into overdrive and he was able to casually continue with: "It was all very worrying as Peter was seriously injured and all we could do was keep the wound covered and wait for the ambulance which arrived within 5 minutes but seemed a lot longer at the time. The three protection people were running in a zig zag movement towards the boundary walls but to no avail as the assailant didn't hang around. We immediately followed to the hospital as the protection people were worried that another attempt might be made at the hospital where security is never great. A few days later, some suspicious blokes were seen but they turned away when they saw the protection."

"How did they know that there was protection there?" asked Helen.

"They weren't too discreet with hiding their weapons."

"But surely the hospital would not tolerate that?" queried Ann.

"Well, Peter is well known and rich so it was expected I think but anyway, nobody said anything all the time they were there. Perhaps they thought it was better than having a murder on their hands," Mike offered and waited hoping there would be no follow up but he should have known better.

"So what happened then?"

"After Peter got out, the leader of the protection group went off somewhere for a day and returned saying he knew where the elusive bastard, who was trying to kill Peter, was living. The guy apparently moved around a lot to avoid detection as he was a known killer and an outright bastard noted for extreme cruelty. They set off to track him down."

Mike left out the part where he went along too and finished with: "And it seems he was shot but they never found the perpetrators. Our lot said somebody got there before us, he must have gotten careless. I'm not altogether sure that I believe them but they didn't need to be coy because it was clear they would have killed him if they had had the chance."

"Do you feel any guilt about his death?" asked Helen.

"No, my friend would have been killed unless someone got him first."

"Couldn't your friend have gotten police protection without the need to hire thugs?" asked Helen.

"OK, let's say it was you or someone you dearly love that the bastard was after and now you consider police protection. No crime committed, just a threat so the police either stick someone outside your door for a week if you are lucky and/or also ask a patrol car to call by from time to time. After a month, the police decide that the threat has gone away and pull the protection. On the other hand, you could copy Peter's mode of protection. Following scenario one, you are dead

96

but following scenario two, you are alive and the killer is dead and you are riddled with guilt, or are you?" Mike grinned with eyebrows in a quizzical position.

"I'd go for the second option without hesitation," said Ann, looking at Helen.

"Well, uncomfortable as it is, so would I," Helen reluctantly agreed.

Mike decided he had to make this right and immediately interjected with: "It's your reluctance that makes you who you are which means I can always rely on you to make the right choice."

"I wouldn't be so sure," she joked.

"I had better keep on the right side of you then," he said laughing.

Mike then drew attention to a boat going in the opposite direction which looked equally enchanting, hoping this would change the subject.

The evening soon came to a close and after saying extended goodbyes, they got back to the hotel about 2 am. Mike started to elaborate on the episodes in Germany and Paris but got stopped in his tracks by Helen who interrupted him with a smile saying: "We at the station knew about the episode in Germany and we also knew that you were somehow involved but not sure how and we therefore guessed you intervened in some way in the Russian debacle. This was emphasised by the disappearance of the local Director and his family without trace and when all was over, they turn up safe and sound having supposedly been on holiday. We decided that as the end results had been for the benefit of the people caught up in the middle and as they were safe, it was not worth our while hounding you and in any event, we had no proof."

"That's a very French solution and I have to say very sensible; I say that reluctantly," he said, ducking the pillow catching the back of his head.

Helen jumped at him, knocking him back on to the settee with her on top beaming down at him and saying: "When you explained it as if it was happening to me personally, I could see that I should be very safe with you and I now love you more."

Mike knew he was going to be very tired in the morning but thought, *Hey! C'est la vie.*

On the Monday, Helen went back to her place as she was back at work first thing and not altogether looking forward to it.

Mike on the other hand had a call from Austria telling him they were after a very large account and could do with his input. He telephoned Gabriel and agreed to catch the train on Tuesday to Vienna—a city of beauty and fabulous music. He was looking forward to attending a few concerts while there.

Chapter 16

At 4 pm, he checked into his hotel in the centre of Vienna just around the corner from the office and called Gabriel to tell him he would see him in the morning but Gabriel asked him if he fancied a drink and a meal or was he tired. Never wanting to admit to tiredness, he said what a pleasant surprise and Gabriel said, "I will pick you up in half an hour." Mike agreed without hesitation.

Mike saw Gabriel entering the hotel and went forward to meet him. They shook hands warmly, each pleased to see the other after such a long time. They chatted easily as they walked to the restaurant. As you entered through heavily decorated swing doors, you were faced with a large room with many ornate mirrors on the walls amongst the paintings and pictures some in black and white all framed to taste and set off by numerous gold ornaments but the finishing touch was a hanging row of chandeliers each containing a mountainous array of glass diamonds reflecting all the colours and the movements of the room. A truly magical place to eat and drink.

Seeing the surprise in Mike's eyes, Gabriel said, "I'm pleased you like it, even Mozart did; he came here often so we are in the right place, wouldn't you agree?"

Mike smiled like a child in a chocolate factory and then pulled himself together. "What are you having then?" as he walked to the bar.

As they were served their drinks, Gabriel suggested they sit and decide what they wanted to eat. "Once we have ordered, I have lot to tell you."

Soon a young waitress dressed in a traditional costume with a low neckline, to please the "gentlemen" no doubt, took their order with a cheerful and bubbly manner.

Gabriel became serious immediately, explaining the case they were trying to secure. It was a pharmaceutical company called Optocreux Pharmaceuticals Europe GmbH with a turnover of £30 million, not bad for a relatively new company.

"Are you sure you are in at the right level, for as you know personal relations are very important otherwise we will end up doing an enormous amount of work for nothing," asked Mike.

"We are talking to the MD and the Financial Director and they have told me they are unhappy with the service they are getting at the moment."

"Who is their broker?"

"They wouldn't say at this time until we have further talks but it is one of the international ones."

"Who have you lined up to accompany us tomorrow?"

"Well, there is you, me, Harry the surveyor and Tomas from our Technical Department."

"That's enough, we don't want to overdo it; and how many of them?"

"Four, I believe," said Gabriel, smiling knowing that the balance was perfect.

"That's excellent and the names of the people we are meeting?" asked Mike.

"The MD is Herr Hauptmann; Erik Hauptmann and the FD is Frederick Wechter."

"And what time do you need me at your office in the morning or are you picking me up?"

"We will pick you up at 9:30 as it takes about 20 minutes to get to the factory and the meeting is at 10 am."

"Good, that's all sorted then and you have done your homework on the background I assume?" asked Mike enquiringly.

"I will start the meeting from our side and go through the covers needed and explain about the fact we will have to survey as the major part of the cover will have to be placed in Lloyds of London which explains why you are there as you have a close relationship with many of the main Underwriters but nevertheless London will expect full details including a plan and report on the premises. At this point, I will hand over to you."

"Good. I will enlarge on the placing side after which I will ask if they have any questions and it's from the questioning that we will get to the centre of their concerns so tell our guys to pay particular attention to this part of the meeting for if we perform well in this section we enhance our chances of picking up the account. And remember, we all must use our mouths and ears in the proportion that we have them; no one must feel that they have to make a verbal contribution unless the question falls into their area of expertise. In addition, these people may share power equally or it may only appear so but if we listen and pay attention, we should be able to see who has the power. Once this is established, we then need to see if he likes us or not; if he does, that's a winner."

The next day they arrived with 10 minutes to spare and entered the client's building 5 minutes early. The meeting went as planned except afterwards Erik Hauptmann asked to speak to Mike on his own. The rest were dismissed and Mike and Erik sat down again.

Erik began: "I have a serious problem and I am informed that you are the man to speak to for a solution."

Mike was intrigued as he had never heard of Erik or his company before now.

"You know Peter Karlson of Deutsche Europaischen Versicherung…well, he is also a friend of mine and he has told me how you organised some…protection to resolve his troubles and then you sorted again some trouble in Paris with the Russians I understand."

"Good God! I don't want all this becoming common knowledge but I know some people who have the ability to make problems go away."

"Well, I have a particularly nasty problem in that some Russians…well, two Russians have approached me under the pretext of doing business in Russia but actually want to buy me out and take over the company."

"You have told them no I take it?" said Mike.

"Yes but that's when it got nasty with veiled threats against my wife and children, they even know their names and lots of other details so I am going to have to sell to them unless you know how to resolve it."

Mike thought about it for a few seconds and then said, "OK, leave it with me for two days and I will come back with something. You will have to stall them for a few days." Mike's eyebrows finished the sentence with an enquiring lift on one side more than the other.

Erik arranged for Mike to be dropped off at his hotel and this allowed Mike to make an immediate call to Tom in Northern Ireland. The phone was answered by a female voice which threw Mike a bit but it was a familiar voice so he enquired: "That you Lisa?"

"Yes, who is speaking?"

"It's me; Mike Black."

"Oh, I was going to phone you as you were a good friend of Tom's."

"Were?"

"Yes, Tom died last night; a heart attack they think," said Lisa whose voice was beginning to break.

"I will be over straight away. I am in Vienna so let me find the earliest flight and I will phone you back. In the meantime, stay strong."

Arriving in Belfast, Mike was greeted by Lisa who took him straight to the office in a back street, apparently a protestant area. The entrance was through a narrow door adjacent to a small newsagents and one climbed some rickety old stairs to a further door which opened into a reasonably spacious room Harry was there making a cup of coffee and asked Mike if he would like one so he nodded agreement and took his coat off.

Mike immediately set about finding how they were going to carry on. Lisa replied saying that Tom ran the business from home and they were mere employees and did not have the finances to carry on in spite of the fact they were well paid. "So you are both out of a job now that Tom has died?" Mike asked knowing the answer but Lisa immediately came back with a definite yes.

"It's dreadful that Tom has died before his time and we will miss him but no provision was made for continuity. We will be going to the funeral as you will no doubt; but we both can't stop worrying."

Mike thought for a while and then made up his mind bearing in mind his need of their services.

"I will take over the business and set up a proper Limited Company and finance it with a paid up capital of £500,000 to start with. Then your wages can be taken each month. Lisa, you will be the MD and you Harry a director. I will be an adviser but will manage through you, Lisa. I won't be sitting here."

"That is fantastic! I just can't believe this; our worries are over just like that!"

"What I need to know is do you have or even know some of the contacts that Tom had?"

"Yes, I know a lot including the contacts at government level where a lot of our work comes from."

"Well, in that case, you had better speak to these people to inform them of the new arrangements with you taking over and confirm that you have the finances to carry on as before as you and Harry were well paid and lived a frugal life. It is better not to say you have outside help on the finances or they will want to do due diligence which could take forever. I will pay the money into your account so you can set it up and you put the money into the business account.

"If it comes out later that you must have had financial help then we will just have to come clean and anyway, I have nothing to hide. Now the reason I phoned in the first place is I have a new contract for you from a large pharmaceutical company in Austria who are being threatened by our old friends, the Russians."

"When do we start?" asked Lisa.

"Immediately, so book us all on the first flight to Vienna and a return flight in time for the funeral and we may have to fly back again on the Monday unless we have resolved the problem which I doubt."

"What fee have you charged?" enquired Lisa.

"No fee has been discussed; they just want it sorted. Get the flights done and I will tell you both everything on the way and then you can suggest the fee."

All three arrived in Vienna the following Morning at 8 am and the first thing Mike did was to phone Erik Hauptmann at his home. He answered himself and seemed flustered and informed Mike that the Russians were visiting him in his office at midday. Mike assured him that they would sort the problem and the Russians would not be bothering him after today but he needed to discuss tactics before the visit.

"We, that is, three of us will be there by 10 am and I will sit in with you as your financial advisor and my two colleagues will need to sit at a desk near your office so they can identify the Russians. Can you make sure that is arranged?"

When they were ushered into Erik's office, he was beginning to panic so all three of them set about reassuring him that it was the Russians who need to be worried, not him. Mike then suggested that Lisa and Harry sort out where they were going to sit and get themselves a bit of coffee and some paperwork so they looked busy. In the meantime, Mike ran over the scenario with Erik who seemed at last to be feeling more confident. After a while, they had agreed on their manoeuvres and Mike got him to relax and even enjoy the wait.

At midday precisely, the two Russians were shown into Erik's office and the surprise on their faces made it obvious they did not expect to see someone else there. The smarter of the two stopped and asked rather abruptly, "Who are you?" looking straight at Mike in a menacing manner.

Mike stood up and replied: "I am the company's financial adviser and whilst I understand that Mr Hauptmann wishes to sell his shares to you, I have to ensure that all is correctly drawn up and then it has to go to our solicitors for processing. You appreciate that these affairs have to be done in an open and totally transparent way which of course takes an annoying amount of time."

"He has already agreed to sell to me," he said nodding in the direction of Erik.

Mike adopted his most seriously soft and pedantic voice to explain in meticulous detail the complexities of the actions they were about to enter and also the complicated tax issues that would arise as a consequence. He could see that the Russian was about to explode but just then he changed tack with a breezy: "But never mind about all that boring stuff; let's get our heads together and see what we can do to move this along and then I will push our solicitors to do it as quickly as possible."

"What do you mean his solicitors? All I need is his signature and our solicitors will do the rest."

"I'm afraid not," said Mike dropping back into his irritatingly serious mode and continued, "The vendors solicitors have to deal with this first as they will no doubt point out some of the pitfalls to both Mr Hauptmann and of course to yourself."

"You are beginning to piss me off, Mr…"

"Mr Sullivan," replied Mike. "Can I have your offer and I will rush it through?" he said holding out his hand for the folder being held very tightly.

Almost automatically, the Russian handed over the file which Mike took and said: "I will get back to you tomorrow; oh and your name?"

"My name is in the file," he grunted.

"OK, talk to you tomorrow."

The Russian, somewhat nonplussed, turned, hesitated and then as if remembering what he was doing made for the door with the goon of a minder in tow.

When they had left, Mike signalled to Erik not to say anything and after a minute or so went to the door and looked outside. Lisa and Harry had already left, doubtless not wanting to lose sight of their targets.

Upon returning back to Erik, he could see the relief in his face at how well the whole incident went and was unable to suppress his surprise: "How did you manage to take charge so easily?"

"We have a saying 'bullshit baffles brains'."

"What do I do now?"

"Send the file to your solicitor and ask him for his opinion of the offer as soon as possible. If he asks are you serious, say not really but I still want your answer."

"What happens now?"

"Well, I am going for a well-earned drink for, in spite of what you may believe, that was very stressful!"

They went to Erik's favourite restaurant and settled down to relax and Mike reminded Erik about the next likely event: "We have discovered that there is also a gang of Bulgarians operating in Vienna and the two gangs have had some fall outs lately so with a bit of luck the Russians are going to believe that their misfortune with the two we were talking to is due to some kind of vendetta by the Bulgarians and if that happens it will escalate into all-out war between them which will no doubt bring the police into action. Then there will be mass arrests and that will be the end of your problem."

"How long before we know?"

"About a day or two but we will wait until it runs its course and intervene again if necessary."

"Oh good, how did you ever get involved in all this kind of business?"

"I had similar trouble in my Paris office and luckily, I knew this lot; which reminds me, we will have to nip back for Tom's funeral on Monday but it should be over by then, if not we will be back."

Just then there was a phone call for Erik; it was his secretary. Mike guessed there was a problem from the tone of the conversation.

"What's up?" asked Mike.

"The police are in the office and they want to speak to me."

Mike took over the phone and told his secretary to explain that Mr Hauptmann was with his insurance advisor and was it urgent or could he phone them later?

After a few minutes Erik's secretary came back on the phone and it turned out that the police would like to speak to him about the visit of the Russians this morning. Mike relayed this to Erik and suggested that they go back and get it over with as it will be something and nothing by the sound of it.

He informed the secretary that they would return and speak to them straight away.

On the way back, Mike advised Erik to keep as close to the truth as possible with the exception that he can say that he told them that he was unlikely to want to sell but he would pass on their information to his lawyer which he has since done. Their attitude was quite aggressive and threatening and he was waiting to see what happened next before contacting the police as he was somewhat uneasy although he had nothing concrete to go on and did not want to bother the police over nothing.

"Mein Gott in Himmel, that's perfect," said Erik with a touch of admiration.

"OK but you have do it on your own but I will be outside if you need me, best not to complicate matters."

On the way to Erik's office, Mike took a detour to the toilets thus giving Erik the chance to enter alone which he did apparently with a broad smile and an enthusiastic welcome while he lead them into his office and saying: "First of all, can I offer you something to drink a coffee or soft drink perhaps?"

The male and female officers both declined at once so that was settled. Erik offered them the opportunity to sit while he occupied his usual chair behind the rather large desk. "Well, what can I help you with?" Erik began.

"We are here because we have been keeping a watch on two unsavoury Russian criminals and this morning they came to visit you. Can you tell us why they should have done that?"

"Yes, with pleasure," Erik replied and went into the story they had rehearsed on the way but paused at various points so it didn't look rehearsed.

The policewoman made notes and the male officer listened intently and nodded agreement to the part about not wanting to bother the police unless there was something more to the story. Erik remembered, just about, not to mention the unfortunate pair's precipitous exit from the planet.

"You may have heard that the two who came to see you have had an unfortunate accident?" questioned the male officer.

"No, is it serious?"

"Serious enough," smirked the officer with a knowing look to his partner.

Erik said nothing but looked on expectantly.

"Both dead, that's serious enough I guess," said the female but gave no information.

Erik realised they were teasing him to blurt out something that he shouldn't know but he was beginning to enjoy this cat and mouse game.

"Well, they were coming to a dead end with me anyway," he announced and guffawed loudly and then looked at the deadpan faces of the police and said: "I'm sorry, I'm sorry. I shouldn't joke about such things but just thought about it and said it before I could stop myself. My wife would kill me for doing that," and he laughed again as he imagined his wife's face being so horrified that the man she loved could be so crass.

The police stood up saying they had all they needed for the moment and made their way to the door, the female turned around and said: "You never asked how they died."

"I forgot in the midst of all the laughter we were having. How did they die?"

"Shot, both of them. Strange, wouldn't you say?"

"Ehm, you would know more about that side of life…or death, should I say."

She gave a look of disgust and left. Erik sat down and took a deep breath and realised he had enjoyed the whole experience.

A few minutes later, Mike knocked and entered on Erik's call grinning from ear to ear. Erik filled him in on the details including the pun that fell on deaf ears which to Erik made it all the funnier.

"You know they were trying to catch me out saying something that I shouldn't know but I suppose in their line of business they suspect everyone of wrongdoing."

"Yes well, they do. Now that the police are investigating, nothing much will happen for a good few days which is just as well because Lisa, Harry and I have to attend a funeral in Northern Ireland on Monday so I will book a flight to arrive on Monday morning and return that evening to Vienna. The Russians won't try anything on the Bulgarians until Monday at the earliest but perhaps that could be too early and if they do we don't need to do anything unless the war stalls. In the meantime I going to the office as I need to speak to Gabriel about another matter. Remember, nothing much will happen over the weekend so try and relax and we will be back Monday night. In the meantime, if anything does crop up phone me on any of these numbers."

Lisa and Harry went back to the hotel and Mike phoned Gabriel to see if he was free and he was so he made his way there by taxi.

On arrival, he was immediately ushered into Gabriel's office and supplied with coffee to his taste. He updated Gabriel who was fascinated with the details and particularly how Erik Hauptmann had stepped up to the mark so quickly and with such panache.

"Did you mention the insurance to him?"

"No, not a word; on purpose I may add. If we do a good job, we will get the business without pushing for it. As you can imagine, if all our efforts with the Russians work out, he will be a mighty grateful man and moreover, he will want to keep us close in case of a reoccurrence in the future."

"The weekend is almost on top of us; are you doing anything?" Gabriel asked.

"Don't worry about us as we have to be on call just in case anything happens and on Monday, we are going to Northern Ireland for the funeral there and back in one day. When all the fuss is over and you have the new business on your books, we will celebrate." Mike grinned assuredly.

Mike took his leave and returned to the hotel where he phoned Helen at work but could not get through so he phoned her flat and left a message asking her to phone him back and leaving the number. Then he changed and rang through to Lisa and Harry who both answered and they agreed to meet down in the bar in half an hour. Just as he was about to leave the room, the hotel phone rang; it was Helen. She complained about how hard it was to contact him and Mike replied, "Well, I did give you my hotel number and I have been out with a client and phoned the minute I was free," and then it started.

"Mike, look, I have been thinking about us and I feel we should cool things a bit and have a more casual affair where we see each other when we can and we are both free to see someone else. You know, what with you always travelling and my work with unusual hours, it's not easy so you can see why we need to be on a more casual basis."

Mike was stunned and mumbled something about having only just met and then he replied: "Well, I am not into casual open arrangements. In my mind, you were probably the one for me, even though we have only just met. I felt there was something special between us. We just needed to sort out our lives so we could ensure we were together more often. These last few days have been unusual and won't last forever. You have met someone else then?"

"No, not really but I do get asked out a lot and I needed to sort things with you before seeing someone else."

"Well, you have certainly done that. So it's goodbye then?"

"Au revoir," Helen said softly.

Mike ended the call and said to himself, *It's not au revoir but goodbye. How did I misread her so badly?* He started thinking of how well they had gotten on in Holland but perhaps that was because, in her mind, it was just friendship with some sex thrown in for good measure. I suppose with that attitude, it's just a nice interlude to punctuate the week. He grinned at the choice of the word 'punctuate' but not for long.

Mike looked at his watch; it had taken all of 10 minutes to burst his balloon and he wasn't really interested in meeting Lisa and Harry for a drink but he had better put up a brave front and face the music.

"Hi, we thought you got lost."

"I know, sorry," Mike replied without going any further but instead turned the conversation to the week's events.

Just before midnight, they all decided to call it a night and retired to their rooms. Mike had just gotten his shirt off when there was a knock on his door. Mike said yes and heard Lisa muttering something so he opened the door and she pushed herself in with an admiring look at his half-naked body. He closed the door and turned to meet her and found her standing close.

She looked him in the eye and said quite brutally: "You've been dumped, haven't you? Don't lie; I've seen that look before"

"It shows then, but I'll get over it."

"You will with my help," she said putting her hand on his chest and moving it slightly.

He looked into Lisa's eyes and thought that he might as well forget the whole bloody business for a while anyway. He held her close and she smelled lovely with a fragrance that was sweet but which did not quite give enough to satisfy and this aroused his passion and they fell upon each other with a hunger that was ravenous and almost violent. They each took what they wanted before falling back exhausted and gasping for air.

"We are only doing this 2 more times," Lisa said.

"Why only two more?" he enquired.

"Because I am not having an affair with my boss even though I fancy you but after all, I am a lesbian although after that expression of pity, perhaps I am bisexual."

"Bloody hell, if that was pity, I'd hate to see the real thing."

Lisa burst out laughing and straddling him said: "You pick up on the word pity but not that I am a lesbian."

"Well, as you are limiting me to two more, it is hardly worth arguing about that matter; besides, you sure as hell enjoyed what we just had," he said, rolling over on top of her.

"This the second one then?" she queried.

"Yes but this time it will be longer."

"Promises promises," she said softly.

Chapter 17

The next morning, Saturday, Lisa left for her own room early and said she was going down for breakfast around 9 am. Mike thought, *Me too as I'm hungry.*

When Mike got down, Lisa and Harry were already in the middle of their cooked breakfast and Harry greeted him as usual. Lisa said: "I've been checking the news and thankfully nothing new on the Russian front nor with the Bulgarians but as you said, it will take a while with the police sniffing around."

"Well, perhaps we should do some sightseeing; the hotel will have some leaflets. We might as well relax for the weekend."

The hotel had nothing to entice them so they went to the town centre and ended up in a bar-cum-restaurant with live music; they ordered lunch which turned to be surprisingly good and then noticed that the entertainment had stopped and a spotlight swooped around the room and stopped at various tables when someone from the table was obliged to go on stage and sing.

Lisa said: "If that stops here, I'm off, no way am I making a fool of myself up there."

They forgot about it and listened to some awful singing and some quite good until in the middle of their conversation, the light stopped at their table and Lisa made a move to bolt but Mike said: "Don't worry, I will take care of this," and stood up.

He walked on stage and paused and then spoke in German saying, "I can't sing but I can tell you a very funny English joke." The room fell silent so Mike took that as a yes and commenced.

"Imagine an old cottage in a small village and the lady of the house is sitting by an open fire with logs burning. She is knitting and just then her husband of 85 years of age walks in and passes close to her to pull his chair forward when she notices he is whistling but his lips are not pursed so she thinks perhaps it's a log on the fire but no, it's definitely her husband and as he pulls his chair past her to the fire, she realises it is coming from his pants."

The crowd have gone quiet and are grinning broadly, hanging on to his every word so he continues. Lisa and Harry are amused by the reaction of the crowd which gets more intense as Mike continues with his story up to the point where an overlarge lady at a table near the stage gets up covering her ears unable to take any more and literally runs laughing hysterically to the entrance. This causes a loud increase in the laughter. A minute or so later, she returns to stand near the exit ready for a quick retreat. The joke finishes with a loud burst of laughter and spluttering of drinks by the men and then a standing round of applause.

Mike steps back and makes a quick retreat only to be sent on again and is forced by the enthusiasm of the crowd to tell another which he does but points out it is his last as he had not translated any more. This too was a huge success and he eventually makes his way back to his table. Shortly afterwards, free drinks start arriving until Mike tells the bar staff no more as they can't cope with so much.

A few hours later, they all head back in a merry state to their hotel and the rest of the day is a wipe-out and the Sunday was uneventful as well, a day of recovery, one might say.

On Monday morning, they left the hotel at 7 am to catch the flight to Northern Ireland; Belfast in particular. By the time they got out of the airport, it had just gone 11 am and the funeral for Tom was at 2.30 pm so just enough time to have a quick lunch before setting off for the church.

They arrived early which was just as well as the church filled up very quickly and unbeknown to Mike, it turned out that Tom was a member of the Salvation Army. A funny choice for a man who eliminated people on a regular basis albeit very bad people but still.

The Service opened with a hymn and the Salvation Army band played with great sensitivity and to be fair, the music was quite beautiful. The vicar, obviously connected in some way to Tom and the Salvation Army, gave a vigorous sermon reassuring everyone that this was not the end of Tom but the beginning and we could all look forward to meeting him again in the future. All said with such conviction in spite of the lack of evidence. Blind faith is an absolute necessity by the flock of any religion.

Mike was having none of it but he had the sneaking feeling there just might be something but if there was, we all go there and it will not be the cosy greeting that conventional religion preached with pearly gates and 'Hello Mike, we have been waiting for you and you can meet the relatives again.' Well, how many as one is related to hundreds of thousands, if not millions, of predecessors. You could of course be born as a baby into another universe to some happy couple with no recollection whatsoever of a previous life.

They all left the church surrounded by happy faces which had just wished Tom off to a new life in heaven and they would retire to have cups of tea or coffee at the reception. Mike wondered on the way if the abstinence was just for the front liners but no, there were no beers or glasses of champagne on display so they had a quick word and decided that after an hour, they would make their excuses and leave.

Lisa and Harry discussed where they would go and decided that Mike might like the Crown and Garter. They settled in and Mike was surprised to see they served Guinness so ordered a pint. After having a chat about business and then wandering on to the Austrian episode where he had to tell a joke when their conversation was interrupted by an over-tattooed foul-mouthed lout asking Mike if he was a fucking papist from the south. "I'm from the south but I'm not a papist, I'm an agnostic."

"What the fuck is that?"

"Well, that is also your answer."

"Are you trying to be clever?"

"Not really trying."

At this point Lisa stood up and told him to leave it as…he—pointing at Mike—was with her.

"And what the fuck will you do about it?"

Before Lisa could reply, Mike interrupted: "You don't want to know what she can do but when her high heel has punctured your neck or some other part of you, they will have to call an ambulance so no more drinking for a good few days so why don't you do what the French do and shrug your shoulders and wander back to your friends and tell them I not a fucking papist."

He shrugged his shoulders and walked away.

Lisa could not believe her eyes and said: "How the hell did you manage that?"

"I think it was the thought of no more drinks for a good few days that swung it and the get out of shrugging his shoulders and besides, I wasn't a fucking papist."

Harry uncharacteristically burst out laughing saying: "No! No, he hadn't noticed Lisa until she stood up and then he shit himself."

Lisa gave him a punch on his shoulder that nearly knocked him off his chair while still laughing. They stayed for a few more and then it was time to head for the airport.

On arriving in Vienna, Mike phoned Erik to see if there had been any developments and was pleased to hear that nothing new had occurred. They went back to the hotel for a few more drinks and early to bed in readiness for their visit to the factory in the morning.

On Tuesday morning at 8 am, Mike was awakened by the telephone and it was Erik so he knew instantly something serious was happening. Erik explained he had been phoned by the factory to be told the police were there in some strength and had a warrant to search the place for weapons. Erik stressed he was going in immediately to try and take charge and Mike was not to come in until further notice.

"They are not going to find any weapons and that will not please them if I know anything and I will of course pour scorn on their stupidity in trying to make a connection with a perfectly respectable company such as ours and the killing of two criminals who were chancing their arm visiting here to make me an offer which they must have known would not be accepted. They will of course say that they probably threatened me and I or someone on my behalf decided to take matters into our own hands."

Mike decided that there was only one way out of this and that was to act against the Bulgarians while the police were busy searching the factory. He called Harry and Lisa who were both on the brink of going down for breakfast and explained why they must act now.

"Breakfast can wait then we will go straight into town and hope the Bulgarians are early risers," said Lisa They left straight away each with their viola or violin cases over their shoulder looking every bit the serious musicians heading for an early morning session.

Mike went into breakfast and made sure the waiter would remember him by asking him a few questions about where to go in the evening for entertainment. The waiter was happy to oblige at some length which suited Mike. After breakfast, Mike bought a paper and settled in the lounge reading and occasionally looking at the TV but nothing showed on the morning program. He then decided to phone Gabriel and arrange to see him in person to update him on the situation and warn him not to visit today. They met in the coffee bar where Gabriel had taken him before. Gabriel was somewhat worried by the turn of events particularly as the police had interpreted the situation so accurately. Mike assured him that would all change and very quickly and explained what Lisa and Harry were doing probably at this very minute.

"Will that work?" asked Gabriel somewhat anxiously.

"Well, it will tell the police while they are on a futile search of a perfectly respectable enterprise, there is a turf war going on behind their backs."

"Ja vielleicht hast du recht," replied Gabriel.

"I know I'm bloody right so stop worrying, all hell will break lose soon." Mike had no sooner said the words when all of a sudden several police vehicles passed at high speed, sirens blazing creating a lot of curiosity. Mike looked at Gabriel and grinned.

"I am going back to the hotel and I suggest you return to your office. When Erik asks you to visit, let me know and do not discuss anything to do with the problem, just discuss the insurance. Cut him short if you have to as I will explain when I talk to him. I will bring with us an expert in bugging to ensure that the police have not planted listening devices during their visit."

On reflection, Mike decided he had better speak to Erik sooner rather than later to ensure he understood the importance of not referring to the problem in any conversation, especially over the phone. He dialled his number from his room phone and got through easily.

"Hi Erik, fancy a drink on the way home?"

"Yes my friend, the usual place OK for you?"

"Yes, about 17:30 then?"

"Perfect."

Mike put the phone down and took a deep breath. Just then a tap on the door followed by Lisa's voice saying: "It's me."

Mike opened the door and Lisa and Harry stood there grinning. Mike stood back to let them in. "How did it go?"

"Like a dream, three of them were standing outside their building chatting and we were close enough to take them out in quick succession. Some passers-by started screaming and people running for cover, again shouting and screaming a right panic which attracted those inside the building who came out to investigate so I took another shot and deliberately missed."

"Sounds perfect. Now, this morning I hired a car which is down in the carpark; here are the keys. Dump your weapons in Austria before you get to the border. Here are the keys to my apartment. Stay there until I join you which will be in a few days as I will first need to go to Zurich to arrange for the invoice to be issued in 2 weeks' time for payment over the following 6 months."

"Why so much credit?"

"To avoid suspicion as the accountant might think that some tax evasion was being perpetrated and could decide he had a duty to report it. By breaking the bill up, Erik can come up with a plausible explanation for any part that comes under question and no doubt he will be asking me for invoices from various different companies."

"Thanks for that, so we can take what we need to live on in the meantime."

"Yes of course, and when I get to Paris, we need to discuss money matters more fully now we are up and running. So think about what salaries you both need to live comfortably. Now you need to get a move on and you have travellers' cheques still?"

"Yes. We are OK for money."

"See you in Paris."

Mike looked at his watch; it was 3 pm so he had two and a half hours to kill before meeting Erik. He emerged from the hotel into bright sunlight on a lovely warm summer afternoon and the air had a sweet smell from the lime trees shading the footpath on the opposite side of the street. He crossed over carefully to enjoy some more of the fragrance and to walk in the relative cool. About 10 yards in front, the railings gave away to an alcove with open gates leading into a park. Mike strolled in, enjoying this brief moment of nothingness the sheer enjoyment of aimlessly wandering without purpose or intent. The nothingness spread like a wave caressing a sandy beach, each wave smoothing out some more wrinkles as the tide came in reaching further and further easing away more and more furrows until a smooth clean surface remained.

What seemed like a few moments later, Mike's mind decided to refocus and he looked around to see he had at some time decided to sit on this particular bench and on the shady side. Like a switch being activated, the noise of the day came rushing back and Mike jerked upright. He wondered if he had been asleep or just in a relaxing trance. He looked at his watch; it was 4:30 pm so he knew he had fallen into a soporiferous sleep no doubt caused by recent stress.

Now, time to pull himself back to reality. What he needed was a quick coffee and then with alertness and brain back in the groove, he would proceed to meet Erik.

He got to the meeting before Erik and after picking up the evening paper, he chose a quiet corner where they might talk undisturbed. The headlines were all about the violence between the two criminal factions and how the police now need to take decisive action against these consistent disturbers of the peace and their illegal trades. Then a diatribe of abuse against these foreigners and their gall at feeling they can act like the mafia here in beautiful Vienna.

Erik arrived and he too picked up a copy of the evening paper and looked around for Mike which he quickly spotted. As he sat down, he said to Mike: "Have you read the headlines? What a day it's been. More excitement in one day than I have had in all my life to date. What about you? You must be exhausted with so much to organise."

Mike leaned forward and stuck a note under Erik's nose telling him to go to the toilet and check his coat for a bug while Mike would order the drinks and follow him in as he knew what to look for.

Just like an army manoeuvre, they completed the task and fortunately no bugs were present so they could now talk freely.

Mike explained that Erik should ask Gabriel to call to discuss the insurances and ask for Mike to accompany him. "Meanwhile, I will bring along an expert in bug detection to check out your office in case the police have planted something in your general office as they may have done that more easily without your suspicious eye watching them."

Mike then explained the terms of credit on the invoice for the problem resolution and the further help he could have for specific invoices should the need arise. Erik sighed a sigh of relief as he had been worrying about that; not the size of the bill but how to get it past prying eyes as nobody in the company knew that he was being threatened. "I can't even reveal that now as it would open up a whole can of worms as you English say."

Mike smiled at the fact he passed for English and just nodded.

Erik suddenly leaned forward and said: "It goes without saying you will get the insurance business but try and show a saving please."

"It's all done and he has I believe got a saving. The two things are not connected but I do appreciate you having made up your mind in our favour and I would like to think that we could become good friends after all we have been through. After tomorrow, I will be making my way back to Paris but if ever the problem comes back, just phone and say I have a serious problem with a clause in your policy and I need it clarified. I will ask which clause and you say the contribution clause. I will be on the first flight and if it's the same lot, no further charge will be made."

"How did you get here?" Erik asked with a twinkle in his eye.

"By taxi."

"Get them in then," said Erik laughing robustly.

And so it was close to midnight when their taxis home finally arrived.

The next morning Mike and Gabriel turned up at the factory and were taken straight in to see Erik. Gabriel made his presentation which Erik was impressed with and straight away gave instructions to Gabriel to arrange the covers with effect from the expiry date of the existing insurances. Gabriel was delighted and Erik appreciated the saving which went some way towards paying for the extra-curricular activities.

Chapter 18

That afternoon Mike was on the train to his financial office in Zurich and was impressed with the tunnel going through the Alps, which is a phenomenal piece of engineering judged by any standards. After emerging from the tunnel, it seemed a very short journey to the station.

Mike took a taxi to his office and entered the building with a quick nod to the concierge who by now was familiar with Mike and waved him straight through. He took the lift to the 3rd floor straight to Jean Jacques' office; as he opened the main door, Jean Jacques' secretary stood up to greet Mike and asked after his well-being in a very tidy specific way which could have grated but as she was extremely good-looking, he started to smile in a docile manner and then realised what he was doing and cut off abruptly.

As the door opened, Jean Jacques stood up smiling broadly and the sincerity of his manner made Mike relax and grab his extended hand shaking it warmly.

"You haven't gotten into the continental way of kissing cheeks yet?"

"No, not completely but I have on occasions managed it with women so you could say I am slowly working my way up to it. Anyway, I have a few things I need to tell you which may well stretch your ingenuity but hopefully, you will come up with the answers."

Mike then brought him up to date with his new acquisition including the financial ramifications attached to the last weeks activities and how the Viennese police suspected what was going on but could not prove it and eventually dismissed their suspicions as being too fanciful.

Jean Jacques mulled over what he had been told for some time before venturing an answer, "You are right; this does stretch my imagination not so much the financial entries as they are, as you would say, a piece of shit but the setting up of this new venture is a different ballgame. I will ask you to fill out a form giving me the details of the three of you involved but when you come to the bit about the activities of the Company, I would ask you to use your creativity and imagination to present me with the most convincing sweet-smelling basket of goodies that is disguising the actuality but nevertheless expressing the ability of your company to offer protection from insidious and harmful interferences be they from internal or external sources without of course dwelling on the details."

"I think you have just done my thinking for me and it's beautiful."

Mike moved to the little desk up against the wall and tried to remember Jean Jacques' words which seemed so eloquent and yet so beautifully ambiguous at the same time. A lesson in bureaucratic brilliance.

After completing the form, Mike sat down again opposite Jean Jacques to continue their conversation and to get a full update on the finances of the various companies. It transpires that all is in order and the profits are in an upward trend.

Jean Jacques made one observation though in that Mike had not visited Milano for some time and ought not to leave it too long as Vito had made a cryptic note on one of his returns. "I think he is feeling a bit neglected."

"I have to go to Paris for a few days and then I was going to Frankfurt but I could go see Vito first. I will phone him from Paris and fix a time."

They shook hands and agreed to meet again in a month's time.

Chapter 19

Mike arrived back in Paris and went straight to his apartment to have a meeting with Lisa and Harry about where they go from here as the work will no doubt have to be generated from some of Tom's connections and both of them need to work on that side to see what they can get. Lisa was confident that work would come their way. Harry didn't get involved in this side of things.

They parted for the airport leaving the hired car for Mike to return and promised to keep in touch on a regular basis of a least once a month.

After they had left, Mike decided to go for a coffee as it was a nice day and he fancied sitting outside watching the people going about their daily business some rushing some strolling lazily, just enjoying the atmosphere of Montmartre. On the way to his favourite café, he purchased a daily paper; he liked Le Monde. On arriving at the café, he noticed his usual spot was free so gladly plonked himself down. He ordered a large black coffee and after a few minutes of people watching started to read his paper. He was quite engrossed with a particular article concerning Russian activity in Austria when a familiar voice interrupted his peace and caused his stomach to lurch into a spasm.

"Bonjour Monsieur Noir."

"Helen," he said, lowering the broadsheet and looking up at her slowly.

She seemed to be upset so he quickly asked her to take a seat which she did and blurted out: "I should never have finished with you; it's just that I was scared at how quickly things were happening but I was wrong and have been coming here and to your apartment every day hoping to see you but I suppose now you won't want to know."

He looked into her eyes which were full of tears and about to spill down her cheeks and said: "No, I mean yes, I do want to know. Do you want to start again?"

"Yes."

"I never got over you and I did try and besides all that, I got caught up in a serious debacle in Austria but none of it could erase the pain."

"I was hoping against hope you would say something like that," she said with very obvious relief.

"Have you got any holidays you can take?" Mike asked.

"Yes, why?"

"I have to go to Italy…Milano no less."

"I have summer holidays of 2 weeks to take but have to take them all at once."

"How soon can you take them? I was going to Italy tomorrow but I can delay until Monday. Could you get away by then?"

"Yes, things are quiet at this time of the year so yes."

"Good, what time do you finish today?"

"In about 30 minutes."

He leaned forward and took hold of her hand and looked straight into her eyes and said: "It's great that we are back together and we will have a lovely time in Milan, the business side will be similar to Amsterdam in that it is very pleasant and won't interrupt our time there too much. Vito, as you would expect, is a good-looking bastard but he's married so keep your eyes off."

"You mean I can't even look at the menu?" she replied laughing.

"I'll wait here for you," Mike said grinning and shaking his head.

As she walked off with a spring in her step, she made that captivating wave of her arm finishing with a flick of the wrist and her long fingers curving back, the whole appearance giving the tapered effect of some exotic dance. So mesmerising that a guy walking in the opposite direction stopped in his tracks to follow the movement of her hand as if caught in a hypnotic trance.

Mike smiled to himself as he still loved that movement even though he had seen it several times. He picked up his paper and found such was his mind that he could only tolerate reading the headlines; the effort required to read into the detail was just too much. After a while, he folded the paper and laid it down on the table and sipped his coffee which by now was getting cool but that didn't matter. His thoughts were interrupted by a gentleman sitting at the next table who asked if he had finished with his paper to which he mumbled "oui" and handed it over. He then realised the man must have thought that it was supplied by the café. Still, that didn't matter either.

After what seemed an eternity, Mike spotted Helen on her way back having changed out of uniform into tight-fitting pale blue jeans with a navy top with long sleeves turned up. Again, she was waving but this time more enthusiastically. Mike quickly got up, grabbing his chit and approaching the waitress and paying over the top in order to be able to leave quickly. He emerged from the café area just in time to be greeted by a hug and air kisses in the French manner.

"We will go to the apartment now and then we will catch our breath," Mike suggested and Helen nodded and entwined her arm through his in a way Mike was not used to but decided after a moment or two that he liked it and squeezed her arm gently to show it.

Once in the apartment and the door was closed, they looked at each other and knew the first thing that had to be done and so Helen ran as if running away but laughing and gentle screaming in anticipation of the imminent delights. An hour later, they were both naked and having a shower together, perfectly comfortable with each other's unashamed defenceless nakedness.

Once dressed again, they decided they would go out for the evening meal and Mike knew just the place but first Helen had to be brought up to date on recent events and also on what she was about to let herself become part of.

"First of all, you need to know my financial situation," and so he explained about the 7 different companies that he owned but insofar as London was concerned, only a major shareholder but that gave him control. Switzerland was explained as the main controller of the group of companies and where all the finances were coordinated. In short he told her he was worth £10 million in cash and approximately £200 million in assets but stressed he did not live up to that kind of lifestyle and didn't want to, for the moment it becomes obvious you are wealthy then you are under attack from all corners and so is your family. He anyway believed that one should not be judged on one's wealth but on one's character. He said to Helen with a seriousness that surprised her slightly, "In Ireland, we have a saying which qualifies a person: 'He is a sound man', which means he keeps his word and can be relied upon in a crisis."

"Sound man?" Helen queries.

"OK but in that context, man means person…satisfied?"

"Of course," she said smiling.

"Now we come to how this affects us personally and in the immediate question of the engagement ring."

"Yes, are you not agreeable?"

"Oh! Yes but you haven't asked me."

"Damn, I forgot in all the rush to tell you everything. Are you willing to get engaged?"

"Yes I am."

"Great, now where was I; oh yes, about the ring. I don't want it to be so expensive that it shouts it out but good enough say £2,500. Good enough to show I must have saved up for it or have it on easy payments. If I got you one for £12,000 or more, every crook who spots it will be working out how to get it from you and not necessarily by simply asking…and I do not want that to happen to you but you will know from looking at your bank account you could have it if you wanted it."

"Well, that's different and it works because I knew you were not poor but had no idea of how wealthy you actually are. In fact it might have put me off as you could have thought I was just after your money instead of your body." She grinned.

"My attitude means we can sit in open air cafés and walk casually through the streets enjoying the life that surrounds us without fear of being targeted. One of course at night has to be more careful but generally the freedom is very precious. We can of course still have a nice house in the country; I don't mean we have to live like Scrooge."

"Good. I am with you every step of the way in that flashy jewellery is like saying I have loads of money if you want to have a go at taking it."

Mike looked at his watch and said: "We had better get a move on and when there, I will tell you about Vienna. It will make your eyes pop."

They rushed out to catch the taxi and were soon on their way to Il Tropicano Bello where the Italians make every woman feel special by their antics bordering on the outlandish but always done with great kindness and enormous amounts of laughter. The result is a great evening where the good humour stays even after you have left.

They arrived at the Ristorante and were immediately made welcome by the maître d'hôtel who beckoned with great aplomb one of the waiters to accompany them to their table and were informed which waiter will be serving them this evening.

Then the fun started as 3 waiters dressed in black with white aprons approached to serenade Helen which quite quickly degenerated into a mock disagreement as to who was out of tune. This got sorted and again one of them hit a wrong note and the ruckus started all over again with one throwing a string of plates from an empty table nearby which were immediately caught but only just with the help of wild acrobatics. The patrons cheered wildly and the 3 took a bow, grinning from ear to ear. They proceeded to walk off until one of them dropped the lot with an almighty clamour and in came the clean-up merchants tutting and fussing with brushes and dustpans in hand. This Mike had seen before but it was nevertheless hilarious and Helen was collapsing with laughter.

On top of this, the food was excellent.

The next day Saturday, they bought the ring and also the wedding ring to match and Mike surprised her with a beautiful watch she had been admiring by purchasing it with the wedding ring when she wasn't watching. They then went to their favourite café where Mike phoned his usual travel agent to set up the flight and hotel for their Italian visit on Monday.

Chapter 20

On arrival in Milan, the first thing Helen noticed was the increase in the noise level. Mike agreed but said he liked it as it gave a feeling of renewed life to everything. The hotel was beautiful and adorned in a very traditional manner with antique furniture and large paintings and prints of famous paintings all giving an atmosphere of casual opulence as if style and good taste happens naturally without any effort being required.

Mike phoned Vito to tell him they had arrived and he would call to see him tomorrow as he and Helen were just going to have a look around today and get their bearings. Vito immediately suggested meeting up with his wife and going for a meal. Mike mentioned this to Helen who nodded agreement and so it was settled for 8 pm. Vito said he would call and take them to one of his favourite restaurants on the north side of Milano.

Vito and his wife Sofia arrived precisely on time which was a pleasant surprise but the exuberance of their greeting and the resulting laughter gave a feeling of exhilaration to the whole experience putting Helen and Mike into a totally relaxed mood. Mike sat in the front with Mario driving and the two girls chatted easily with the enthusiasm of two long lost friends rather than just introduced acquaintances The journey passed quickly and they arrived at the Ristorante Fredrico perched on a hilltop overlooking a vast plain in all directions and the city of Milano to the south but to the north the mighty Alps stood proclaiming their presence and size with shimmering snow-capped peaks. Mike remembered driving over them in the late sixties; he must have been mad, he thought, looking at how intimidating they actually were.

The restaurant had an alpine look and was very pretty and ornate as one would expect. It was large enough for about 50 or 60 guests and as they walked in Mike could see it was almost at capacity and had a busy hum about the place which to Mike is always a good sign. Restaurants are normally only busy if they are doing something right and having a quick look at some of the plates as they walked to their table, Mike could see the quality was excellent.

The conversation ranged from music to art to general information about the great things to see in Milano and not once did it venture into insurance or the running of the business. Thus all controversy was avoided not that there was any controversy in the first place Mike hoped. The red wine was particularly pleasant, beautifully smooth and light on the palate. As he wasn't driving, Mike allowed himself to indulge but not too much as must keep up appearances at all costs.

At the end of the evening when the bill arrived, Mike made sure to grab it but Vito made a good effort at trying to insist that he should take care of it but as it would only end up as expenses anyway, he relented. It was almost midnight when they finally got away.

The next day Mike called at the office and spent the morning learning about Vito's plans for expansion and indeed the latest trends in the Italian market. At lunchtime, Helen called to the office and all three of them went for a light meal at a nearby café. After Vito took his leave, Helen and Mike wandered through the city looking at the sights and getting ideas of where to go that evening. They plumbed for a classical concert *La Boheme* by Puccini.

Chapter 21

On arrival in Zurich, Mike and Helen booked into their hotel and phoned Jean Jacques to inform him they would see him about 10 am.

"How does he feel about you coming back so soon after your last visit?" asked Helen.

"No need to worry. I explained that it was to introduce you and that we were engaged and it was appropriate for you to get to know the business as down the line if anything happened to me, you would need to take over."

"Take over! I wouldn't know where to start," she said with alarm in her eyes.

"You will soon pick it up; just wait and see and anyway, hopefully your takeover will not be in the near future," he said grinning from ear to ear.

Jean Jacques was charming and genuinely delighted to meet Helen and they both got on immediately. Jean Jacques was in his element having someone to explain the ins and outs of his work to and the thought of training Helen to be his assistant really appealed to him. The Swiss can be very warm and friendly when they put their minds to it. The number of times Mike had been thanked in Switzerland by a complete stranger just for picking something up and placing it in a bin was too numerous to be counted. Mike wandered off to leave them to it while he got to speak to other members of staff most of whom he had never met before. After about an hour, Mike returned to find that Helen and Jean Jacques had drawn up a calendar for her visits and indeed she had invited Jean Jacques to dinner with his wife Judy that very evening and the invitation had been accepted.

Mike decided they had better book into a hotel as they were going to be very late after the evening meal as apparently, Jean Jacques had booked a restaurant up in the mountains where the view and the food were terrific.

On arrival that evening at Restaurant Latvo, they all had to stop and admire the panoramic view across a deep meadow filled valley rising up to green slopes and topped with snow-capped peaks just breathtakingly beautiful. The feeling of being all powerful looking down on the Earth below where farmhouses were tiny and the cows mere specs of colour against the rolling grasslands was quite wonderfully weird and had an almost hallucinatory effect as if one could fly and enjoy even more non ending spectacular scenery. Mike had to pull himself back from the precipice and spoke in a loud cheery voice to break the mesmerising attraction.

Once inside the restaurant, the warmth was reassuring and the alpine décor—broad and brassy—made everyone smile and relax. The restaurant was full enough without being crammed and so the staff were able to enjoy creating the expected ambiance and were full of confidence by seeing their efforts being reflected in the lively chatter and laughter of their guests. The beer glasses all foaming and full with only casual attention to measurement levels didn't seem to bother anyone in fact the haphazardness probably added to the carefree atmosphere.

They all ordered and then Jean Jacques asked if they did Raclette cheese and the waiter replied in German saying yes and it was free. "It's served immediately after your main course." Jean Jacques explained to Helen that it was a large cheese in the shape of a wheel which was melted and the melted section was scraped onto your plate and you eat it with a biscuit or bread roll.

"It's delicious," he emphasised.

"Can't wait to try it," said Helen.

At the end of the evening, a small group of four came and entertained with loud thumping alpine music encouraged by equally loud and cheering guests most of whom were very merry but it all ended well and as they were departing to their vehicles Mike did wonder how many drunk drivers will be on the roads tonight. To Mike's relief, Judy took charge of the driving on the way back as she only had non-alcoholic drinks all evening as she didn't like alcohol. Mike thought that a handy asset to have but she might question his behaviour when they were alone tonight but then again Jean Jacques was pleasant even when over the limit so perhaps not.

Mike put his arm around Helen as they entered the hotel and said, "We had better get some shuteye as we are off to Frankfurt tomorrow morning."

The next morning, the Hauptbahnhof in Zurich was bristling with activity and Mike and Helen had to queue to buy their tickets which seemed to cost a small fortune. Nevertheless, they crawled their way to the required platform and only found relief because Mike always travelled first class. It costs double when you don't book in advance but at least one has a dedicated seat so a pleasant and relaxing journey is guaranteed. Their carriage was reasonably full and it wasn't long after departure that the waiter came to take their order for breakfast. This was the part Mike particularly liked whereas Helen was not great first thing but she didn't want to be left out and then find it was all sold out later.

The breakfast came fairly soon after they ordered and was accompanied by a daily newspaper offered in three languages—German, French and English. Helen took one in French and Mike opted for the English Times newspaper as he wanted to see what was happening in London. He scanned the headlines and nothing there to affect his business so folded it neatly and pushed it to one side.

The breakfast was particularly good in continental style which Mike always felt was much better for you than eating fry-ups first thing.

They were pulling into Frankfurt when Helen asked Mike what made him pick this particular city for his first European office.

"It's the financial centre of Germany so thought it might be good for our kind of business, and it was."

Chapter 22

On exiting the train, Mike and Helen decided to have a coffee and stopped at the little bar in the main area while Mike phoned Peter and got through eventually. Peter was delighted to hear from Mike and said so in very pleasing emphatic terms.

"How long are you staying?" he asked.

"I haven't quite decided but I have just finished a tour of the various offices and I am with my new fiancée Helen. Helen has decided to get involved in management and is learning the ropes from our Swiss director Jean Jacques so she needs to be back there in a week's time for further instruction. In the meantime, I thought I would see Max and then you and Claudia and introduce you to Helen."

"You must come and stay with us, Claudia and I were just talking about you the other day and we were wondering when we would meet up again."

"That's very kind of you but we don't want to be a burden to you."

"A burden, never, my friend; we both cherish your friendship."

"I would love to accept then and will call on Claudia at about 5 this afternoon if that is OK."

"Better than that, just let me know when you have finished with Max and I will come and pick you both up and save you getting a taxi and all that hassle."

"Marvellous, see you later," said Mike with the pleasure sounding in his voice he turned to Helen. "I'm so glad he insisted and also insisted that he would pick us up as I was worried that he might have been glad to have seen the back of me."

"Why? Isn't he the one whose life you saved?"

"That's why I thought he might not want to see me as he might not want to be reminded of all that happened. Thankfully, he is bigger than that as I really like him and his wife; they are both charming and interesting as you will see."

"What now?" queried Helen, brushing a hair away from his eye.

"We had better get a taxi to the office to see Max and I am ashamed to say I can't remember whether he is married or not. I will ask him what he does in his spare time and he may drop it out in conversation."

"Crafty," she replied smiling.

They caught a taxi at the rank outside the station to take them to the office and they lugged their cases up to the main office where they were able to store them out of sight with the help of Max's secretary; she was new and introduced herself as Mimi.

"Max is expecting you so I will take you straight in. What would you like to drink, tea or coffee? Oh and I have learned how the English take their tea if you would like to chance that," she said smiling broadly.

"OK, as you have gone to that trouble but squeeze the teabag and only put in enough cold milk so it stays slightly dark; the colour of coffee with 2 heaped spoons of sugar; see how fussy we are," he said laughing.

Helen interjected, "And mine is a black coffee no sugar."

Mike thought Mimi had gotten on the wrong side of Helen there, pandering too much to him but why wouldn't she as he was after all the big boss, not that he thought like that but others did.

As they entered Max's office, he stood up to greet Mike and Helen and then turned to Mimi asking if she had offered drinks to which of course the answer was yes but Mimi then turned to Helen and asked if the chair she was going to use was OK or she could get another one from the main office. Helen thanked her but said it was OK. Mike thought, *Clever girl, she picked up on the undertone. Well done.*

"Well, Max, this is Helen, my fiancée, who will be spending some time in Switzerland on the financial side of things. She has had a quick look around and likes it as she has a penchant for figures."

"You have met Jean Jacques then, a lovely man."

"Yes, he spent a day showing me the ropes and then we had the most wonderful meal with him and his wife way up in the mountains. Stunning scenery, fascinating restaurant and the food was delicious," she replied easily.

"That sounds wonderful," added Max.

"Well, how are things with you workwise and personally?" interrupted Mike.

"Just fine; workwise we are growing at a reasonable rate as per usual. I have been informed by one or two Insurers that they are very impressed with the support they get from us and we have been offered some overriding commissions; which is just great," said Max excitedly.

"Have you had any more thoughts on opening a sub office in Bavaria; In fact do you get much business from that region as I understand they like to think of themselves as separate from the rest of Germany."

"You are right of course and funnily enough, I interviewed somebody last week who seems to be just what we need and he originates from Bavaria as well. I was going to ask you to see him once he confirms that he wants to accept the position."

"Well, Helen and I are staying with Peter Karlson for the next day or so if you want to chase him for an answer, we can get on with it."

"Will do."

"Your private life…is that going well?"

"Do I have a partner, do you mean? Yes, I do but it's a male partner. Is that a problem?"

Mike's jaw dropped and he stuttered: "I didn't expect that. I just realised that I had never asked whether you had a wife or not. It's not a problem so don't worry on that account but there will be a lot of women who will feel what a waste."

Then looking at Helen, he continued: "Isn't it peculiar how so many extremely good-looking men go wandering off on the wrong path, it's almost as if being too good-looking defines their inclination."

Helen burst out in indignant laughter saying: "You can't go around saying things like that, for heaven's sake."

"Like what?" asked Mike surprised.

"The wrong path; what's wrong, there is no right or wrong path involved, just the path each individual must follow."

"OK; OK. If I had had some warning, I wouldn't have broached the subject in the first place. It's just a shock. I don't mean to offend. I know that this sort of thing exists but I've never come across it before."

Helen laughed again and continued: "I don't believe you—this sort of thing—good God, I am going to have to bring you up to scratch on everyday life, you have been so involved in business that you have cut off from reality."

"I'm sorry Max, I apologise so let's just carry on as normal and fix up the interview with this chap you have seen and he knows of course that it will be a sub office of Frankfurt so you can keep an eye on things?"

"Yes I have explained that to him."

"Good, are you free for lunch?"

"Yes, I would suggest where we went before but perhaps you might want to give it a miss."

"Why, what's wrong with it?"

"Oh my God, you never noticed," said Helen who guessed and laughingly said to Max that that would be fine.

All three left the office laughing which made Mimi look up enquiringly but she would have to wait until much later for the answer.

On arrival at the restaurant, they were shown to their table by a young wide-eyed thin male in trousers far too tight who minced all the full 5 metres to the point where he turned with an extravagant wave of his arm to indicate, he would have you believe, the most important table in the restaurant.

After taking their seats, Mike started to look around and noticed a few things that were different; in addition some of the females were on the butch side and some were delicately feminine. *So they cater for all here*, he thought.

Max and Helen were having some good fun watching Mike take in the surroundings as if for the first time in his life and eventually, Helen had to interrupt his observations: "The women are all gay as well."

"Well, some of them anyway," replied Mike.

Helen looked at him seriously with a straight face and paused for a few seconds and then collapsed in laughter with tears running down her cheeks. Max could not stop himself from laughing and said to Helen: "You are going to get me the sack."

This just increased the laughter as Helen pointed out not some of them but all of them.

"Yes I realise they can be pretty as well but there are quite a few so I thought that…well, some must be …well, you know."

Helen tried to get the word "normal" out but with laughing that was impossible but eventually, she said to Max: "I've not had so much fun in years, this will stay in my mind until the day I die."

Mike joined in the laughter even though it was at his expense as he could see the funny side of all that occurred. They were still laughing when the meals arrived.

They had a pleasant lunch and the conversation changed to other subjects and to work as Max wanted to impress upon Mike how seriously he took his work and how he was constantly trying to improve the figures. Mike reassured him that he knew and his devious inclinations made no difference. He looked at their faces…and then collapsed in laughter.

"Your faces were a picture."

They wandered back to the office with Max in the middle and when they arrived, Mike asked if they could both be introduced to the staff. This was done and Mike made a point of getting interested in what they did and what they thought about the company. Most seemed to be happy. They finished in Max's office so Mike could call Peter to come and collect them.

It was not long before Peter arrived and came right up to the office and walked in with his usual loud bluster so they all knew he was there. Mike said to Peter that he didn't need to come all the way up but he had decided to see where Max worked. He knew Max quite well, of course.

"Where have you parked?" Mike asked.

"Down below on the street."

"But you will get a ticket."

"No, they don't put tickets on a Rolls Royce."

Peter helped with the baggage and sure enough, there was no sign of a ticket even though Mike could see a warden had just passed by.

They arrived at Peter's home and Helen was impressed. As they pulled up to the front entrance, Peter honked the horn and two servants came running out to assist with the luggage while Peter issued instructions on which room they should deposit the cases. All very efficient, as one would expect from Peter.

Almost immediately, Claudia arrived at the entrance to welcome them with her usual charm and warmth and lead the way to one of the reception rooms where coffee was waiting to be served by a young girl dressed in white with a blue apron—all very smart but yet suitable for a warm summer's day.

Claudia made Helen feel at home and they chatted easily, breaking into laughter from time to time which made Mike relax. After they had finished their coffee, Claudia suggested that perhaps they would like to freshen up and unpack a few things, adding: "You are going to stay a few days I hope as I understand you have holidays?" she ventured looking at Helen who nodded agreement.

"Great and then come and join us on the veranda at the rear for a couple of drinks while dinner is being prepared; you remember the way, Mike? Your room is top of the stairs, turn right and it's the third on the right," said Peter, adding cheerfully, "See you soon."

After a quick change into more casual attire, they were ready to descend when Mike stopped Helen at the door, looking into her eyes and asked: "Are you happy with this?"

"Yes, totally happy; they are both lovely and as Claudia is so nice, we will have a great time in their company."

Mike was relieved and opened the door, waving her through with a big smile. He remembered the way to the veranda and they soon joined their hosts where they were welcomed with a glass of red or white wine. Helen opted for white while Mike chose a red Bordeaux. The veranda looked out over a large well-manicured garden with large bushes and trees interspersed with beds packed with bright foliage and large blooms. The garden showed how the impetuous exuberance of wild nature could be controlled to give a stunningly beautiful and calming effect.

Mike raised his glass to Peter and Claudia saying how nice it was to see them both looking so well. Helen interrupted: "Mike told me about your awful experience. That must have been a very frightening time for you both."

"Yes, very frightening; it took me ages to get over it," said Claudia.

"Let's talk about something more cheerful," said Mike adding, "What are we going to do over the next couple of days; like are there any restaurants with beautiful scenery or great food served in a typically traditional German atmosphere?"

"There is a beer festival in a village not far from here; I can't remember the name of it but I know where it is. A friend told me about it as they are going to go themselves; It's a bit wild and raucous but good fun perhaps we could join up with them as that type of evening is better if there are a few of us all together," ventured Claudia in a questioning manner which brought immediate acceptance from Helen and Mike in a chorus of approvals. So it was agreed and Claudia went to phone her friend.

Peter then said he would give the matter further thought and search the local papers to see what was going on. "We like visiting your Alt Stadts as it is wonderful to see how beautiful the towns were in the past. I know it's a bit touristy but that's what we are tourists who are walking around open mouthed at the beauty of this country."

"Yes, parts are very beautiful, especially here in the West but look at the East and it is depressing how drab everywhere looks. There is always talk of reunification but I can't see Russia letting go, can you?"

"Not really but one never knows; time they say cures everything."

Claudia came back out beaming with delight as her friends had agreed to get extra tickets for the 4 and they could settle up on the night which was tomorrow.

"I know it's on a Tuesday but at this time of the year with so many on holiday, one day is as busy as the next."

Just then the young girl in the blue apron came out to tell them that dinner was served. They all finished their drinks and rose to follow the blue apron into the dining room dazzling as per usual with a table to impress a presidential entourage. The starter was soup which was beautiful although of unidentifiable origins accompanied by a mini hot roll. The main course was duck a l'orange and Mike was glad of the orange sauce as duck was not his favourite but the sauce made it palatable and saved Mike from any embarrassment.

Helen watched Mike to see how he would cope and smiled inwardly as she saw he finished the meal. The sweet was an Italian coffee based delicacy called Affogato which was sumptuous. Helen thought the meal was absolutely marvellous including the duck. Such appreciation pleased the hosts and so they retired to the drawing room for brandy or whatever took their fancy.

Peter announced that he had taken a few days holiday in order to take full advantage of their visit and they would have a lovely time showing them around.

About midnight, they retired which suited Mike and Helen as it had been a long day. In fact, a few long days when the travelling was included.

The next morning was warm and sunny and breakfast was served on the veranda during which they chatted about the Alt Stadt and the fact that while most of it had been destroyed during the war it has been reconstructed and put back the way it was as far as possible.

"The authorities like to rebuild these damaged old towns so as to perhaps make it like the war never happened but of course it could be to attract the tourists," Peter mused.

"Well, whatever the reason, I love to visit them and it really gives one a marvellous feeling of what it was like and at the same time you are surprised how advanced they were in construction way back as far as the 12th century in some places. I remember when visiting the old town in Brussels the guide pointing to one of the buildings saying that was a brewery in the 12th century and that I found astonishing," said Mike.

"I just love the old world atmosphere realising of course that I may have a glamorised picture of it. I know that today's world is much better and cleaner," Helen added.

"A lot kinder and a lot fairer," added Claudia.

"Yes but let's not be too analytical or it takes all the fun away," said Peter.

"I agree and so I prefer to think of the times in between all the wars and plagues to the odd twenty year gaps when there was peace and prosperity and they felt it was good to be alive and they could marvel at how ingenious they were in building such beautiful towns. I'm sure they had these times when commerce, self-importance and pomposity reigned supreme," said Mike with an inquisitive air.

"Well, on that balanced and sympathetic view, I think we will enjoy our tour today," said Claudia smiling broadly.

When they arrived, it was a craft demonstration day when various specialists showed off their skills at joinery, glass blowing, doll making, etc.

Having walked around for 2 hours, they opted to go for a pub lunch at a very enticing old-world restaurant. On entering, it was half full but quite busy nevertheless. Peter asked if they had garden facilities to which the reply was yes of course and the very amenable waitress in traditional costume led the way to an outside table placed in a beautiful garden high enough to have a view over the rest of the old town. Mike and Helen were beaming with delight.

"I suppose you have been here on numerous occasions," said Helen.

"No, I have never been before actually," said Claudia adding: "It's a case of never visiting the beauty spots on one's own doorstep, I suppose."

"Yes I suppose it is but I have really enjoyed our visit and will come back again. See Mike, you have opened our eyes. By the way eat well because it will be late eating tonight at the beer festival, probably about 8 pm," Peter said adding: "Better look at the menu before the waitress comes back."

The food was good wholesome food provided one picked sensibly and in that frame, Mike steered Helen away from her first choice and watched what Peter and Claudia were ordering which resulted in everyone being satisfied. Helen asked why he had suggested she change her first choice and so he explained, "When you are somewhere where food is being prepared on mass every few minutes, it's best to go for the obvious as that is what they are good at and if you go for the unusual, it can get under or overcooked just because it requires someone to give it special attention but in the rush and bustle of a time-consuming activity, there is no time to spare for a delicacy but it would be different on a Monday night at 9 pm when hardly any customers are in."

They all looked at Mike and Peter said what they were thinking with: "Smart arse" and they all burst out laughing and Mike caught the waitress's eye and ordered another bottle of wine.

When they were leaving, Mike insisted on paying and they agreed to return to the house and rest up before tonight's entertainment which would undoubtedly test their stamina if their friend's reputation was anything to go by.

At 6:30 the friends arrived in a taxi big enough for all. The friends, Stefan and Emma, were both outgoing. Stefan of average height and stocky build with short brown hair, so short it did not need to be combed, and his wife Emma a bubbly blond with a ready smile and laughing eyes were both in their late forties but fit and healthy which was evidenced by the way they bounced out of the taxi determined to get the introductions completed so the action could commence. The laughter, the air kissing, the busy handshakes continued at whirlwind speed until Stefan suddenly announced: "Right then, let's go." And they all piled in with Mike opting for the front seat with the driver as he did not like travelling backwards.

The driver was a small man of slight build very polite and he and Mike chatted easily on the 30 minute journey to the next village which they drove straight through following the bright banners bedecked with the local crest announcing the annual beer festival. "This is not as big as the Oktoberfest in Bavaria and as it is just a little village fest it is held much earlier to avoid 'ze clashing'," Mike was informed by the driver in very precise phraseology.

The tents were absolutely enormous circus like monsters which Mike and Helen approached with great expectations. Mike suddenly remembered to ask Stefan how much he owed him for the tickets and was told nothing as they were not expensive. Their tickets were displayed and they were all waved through. Stefan led the way holding Emma's hand and they entered. Before them were arranged rows and rows of countless wooden tables all laid out with place mats cutlery and side plates. Stefan weaved his way towards the centre and found a gap in one of the crowded tables big enough for six people to occupy with three on each side which was a lot better than all in a row as the interaction is better. Most of the people on the table were already drinking and very merry and quite unusually in Mike's experience they were all encouraged to join in and made to feel welcome to the table which created a warm and friendly atmosphere. No sooner had they sat down when a waitress arrived armed with a trayful of large steins which were plonked down in front of them.

Peter explained: "The first drinks are free and now we need to order what we want and pay each time. If you give a good… what do you call 'ein Trinkgeld'…ah yes, a good tip, she will remember you and look out for you all evening."

Mike ordered the first round after a quick check with everyone and then quickly calculated that if everyone gave the equivalent of twenty pounds for a tip, that would or should be good enough; he checked with Peter who thought that would be very generous indeed.

Mike turned to the waitress and paid for the drinks and then said: "Und for sie ein Trinkgeld" and gave her 250 marks, "und mehr am Ende des Abends."

She smiled broadly and protested but Mike insisted and the deal was done.

Peter asked Mike if he was always so generous but Mike said that was only when something had to be done otherwise he acted normally.

Peter was right as about 8 pm, the food arrived—a Wiener Schnitzel with lemon tomato and pommes frites and in case you had a big appetite, a large German pork sausage. On the table was tomato sauce and mayonnaise as Germans like to have both on their chips. Mike and Helen looked at each other and smiled. Helen forked the sausage and offered it to Mike who declined and she then offered it around but no takers except a bloke two people away offered his plate and Helen obliged with an approving laugh at his good appetite. He nodded and raised his glass in appreciation, laughing broadly.

The entertainment commenced about 10 pm with various batches of singers and comedians but difficult to hear the comedians but one stood out not for what he was saying but for one action alone. Mike could not follow his joke as too far away and too much noise but he was dressed in lederhosen short trousers and the usual braces and socks to the knee. He stood there with two beer bottles in his hand which he raised using them as binoculars and in a crouched position started shouting *Achtung…Achtung* which brought a great roar of approval from the crowd. Mike laughed as well just because he looked so funny but he was certain he had probably missed the real point. His party had not been listening so no clarification there then.

As the evening went on, the bawdiness increased to a ridiculous level with the waitresses having to avoid being groped and one man a few places away and on the opposite side to Mike grabbed his wife's breast quite openly who responded by pulling a surprised smile obviously feigned as he presumably did it quite often.

At midnight Stefan announced that the taxi had arrived and they slowly made their way to the exit with drunken hands trying to grab the women as they passed and by the time they reached the exit, it was relief all around. Peter said what everyone thought: "Um Gottes willen es is dort ein verrucktes Haus."

Helen looked at Mike wondering what he had said so he explained that Peter thought it was a madhouse in there.

"I agree."

"Yes, but tomorrow it will be back to normal for everyone and no reference made to the previous night's bad behaviour."

Stefan and Emma dropped Peter and all off around 12.30 in the morning and everyone said either a loud goodbye or auf wiedersehen and Helen chipped in with au revoir and then the four walked into the house absolutely shattered and semi drunk. It was agreed they would retire and talk about the evening in the morning.

It was 10 am when Mike and Helen ventured down to greet the day, both feeling a bit fragile but not too bad. Peter and Claudia were tucking into breakfast and asked whether they could face eating but both replied immediately with yes as they didn't feel as bad as they had expected and they wondered if it was down to the German purity laws for Beer. Claudia got up walked to the side unit and rang a bell. They will bring your breakfast in shortly, she informed them.

"Would you like a coffee?" she asked holding up the large coffeepot.

Mike and Helen both accepted and the smell of the ground coffee awakened their appetites almost instantly.

"Have you gotten over last night's madness?" enquired Claudia as she finished pouring.

"Yes, it was a good experience and I for one would not have missed it. It was mad; it was fun; it was warm; it was hilarious; it was even slightly dangerous but above all, the determination of everyone to enter into the spirit of the evening was obvious, which made the experience really special," said Mike as he tucked into his breakfast of freshly baked bread rolls and a selection of delicately sliced cold meats and a croissant to follow with a small jar of spicy apricot jam—he just loved it.

They talked over the evening and what had appealed about it. Then the blue apron walked in and announced a phone call for Herr Black from Max at the office.

"I had better take it if that is alright."

"Of course you must," insisted Peter.

Max had had a call from the chap he had interviewed who would like to take up the offer and Max would like Mike to meet him. Mike thought about it and decided he would phone him back when he looked at his plans for the next few days and told him he would call him back later.

Mike returned to join Helen and Peter, Claudia having disappeared somewhere, and brought them up to date.

"I do not want to interrupt our holiday but was thinking that if I suggested Friday morning to interview this chap, that might be the least inconvenient. what do you think?"

"When are you due to be in Zurich?" Peter asked Helen.

"Monday morning."

"Then that would suit but you must stay with us until Sunday. This will give you a long rest don't you think. Otherwise you have to plan where to go to fill the time."

"I am OK with that," said Helen.

"So am I but how will Claudia feel? She may have other plans," said Mike.

"What's that?" said Claudia who had just returned.

Peter explained what he had offered and she immediately expressed agreement with such delight that it was obviously sincere so everyone relaxed and Mike decided to phone Max and make the arrangements.

It was agreed with Max for Friday morning at 10:30 am and the applicant's name was Oscar Schmidt. After finishing his call, Mike returned to the others in time to hear Peter suggesting a trip to Rudesheim am Rhein, a local beauty spot right on the Rhine and one can travel up or down from there with many beautiful villages along the way. Peter pointed out that there was an Alt Stadt there which was quite beautiful and restaurants that had live music in the afternoon and even dancing.

"I have to warn you though that in the one with dancing, any woman can walk up to a group of people at another table and indicate to one of the men she wants to dance and he is obliged to agree unless he has an injury of some sort. When you are there, it all seems quite natural and the dances don't last for long."

Helen was keen and Mike thought it would be rather special too and so it was agreed they would leave within the hour.

They all piled into the Rolls and off they set. On arriving at the Rhine it was just as Peter had described. Every village was lovely with beautiful shops displaying their wares arranged to catch your eye and the flowers were just magnificent and large unbelievably so. At Rudesheim the first thing one notices is that the train comes down the main street with no separation just like a tram and the next is how difficult it is to park. Peter, being a positive chap, just squeezed the Rolls in to a tight spot and then they followed him through what looked quite normal until the upper level when they stepped through an alleyway into pure magnificence. The street widens displaying a square of ancient baroque architecture beautifully preserved and being used sympathetically. It's stunning and you are forced to stop and stare and drink it in with your eyes; to hold it in your memory for ever; you just need to keep it.

There are restaurants, shops of all types, a museum giving internal tours in at least three different languages and then la piecè de résistance a narrow alley down which Peter led the way and halfway down there, there were three restaurants all with live music, all bustling with energy and friendly noise. They chose the second one on the right which was open air and had a group of about 7 musicians who could have been plucked from a full-size orchestra except for the keyboard player. They were all dressed immaculately in dark trousers white shirt dickie bow and finished with black mini waistcoat.

Mostly violin players fronted by a mature female singer of quite good looks with a pleasing and amusing personality and when they played it was heavenly. Melodic violin strains rising and falling in volume with sudden drops to a lower key which were fortunately repeated more than once and made the whole performance so satisfying. They could have served any old food and it would have gone unnoticed except when the music stopped, a kind of reality returned and you knew then that the food was excellent too.

After about 3 hours, it was time to move on and then they noticed the overhead lift and decided to take it to the summit. Mike found it a hair raising experience hanging there in the middle of nowhere and rising up to a dizzying height amid the odd shudder as the capsule went over the stanchions. He thought, *If it's this bad on the way up, it will be worse on the way down* and was beginning to regret the whole exercise. However, on arrival, they walked a short distance to the viewing point and there before them way down below the river Rhine so wide at this point it even had quite a long island in its middle. After absorbing the beauty of the river, they made their way back to the lift which after take-off rocked for a few moments, not doing Mike's inners any favours at all but he survived without showing himself up and he did appreciate that riding over the vast array of vines was impressive.

On arrival back at the Rolls, Peter handed the keys to Claudia and Mike thought that very sensible and they all settled in. Claudia opened the sunroof to let the heat escape and suggested going back the slightly longer route as it was more scenic, and everyone agreed.

Thursday was spent visiting Heidelberg, a beautiful university town.

Friday morning, Mike made his way to the office in the financial centre to interview the applicant for the job as director of a new office to be opened in Munich in Bavaria. He arrived at 10 am and agreed to their interview technique, which basically was that Max would lead the interview and pass over to Mike when he was satisfied. At 10:30 precisely, Oscar Schmidt arrived for the interview. He was in his mid-thirties, about 2 metres tall and of slim build, dark hair neatly trimmed and dressed as expected in a navy suit with pale blue shirt and blue striped tie with a trace of pink—just the correct touch about him. Mike liked the first impression which reflected the image that Mike himself always tried to portray. Max satisfied himself that he would fit in and his connections with the area were likely to help but they would do an advertising campaign in the area when the new office opened.

Max then acceded to Mike who was happy to discuss various aspects of where the office should be based and the kind of expenditure involved and stressed that in the beginning at any rate it would be a sub office to Frankfurt but as it grew, that would change because even in the beginning, all finances were controlled by Zurich administration office. "Max's main determination is to help you get to a size where you are an independent office so he will be happy to visit you to talk prospects and problems over to make your growth as smooth as possible."

Mike then asked when he would be free to take up the position but in the meantime, would he be free on a Saturday to help Mike choose the most appropriate spot to position the office. It had to be in the financial centre near to the main players so we get noticed as a serious broker not just a newcomer on the block. He informed them he had to give one month's notice but he would be free not tomorrow but next Saturday if that would suit. Mike agreed and they would meet up somewhere suitable or perhaps at the main station.

Chapter 23

On the Friday about midday, just as Mike got back, Peter announced that Stefan and Emma would like to join them on Saturday for a trip down the Rhine from Rudesheim to Strasbourg and wondered what they thought about it. "Have either of you ever been to Strasbourg?" he asked.

"That might be nice. I have seen lots of pictures of Strasbourg but have never been. What do you think?" Helen said turning to Mike.

"Yes, why not and then perhaps we can rest up on the Sunday in readiness for Zurich on Monday. Is that OK with you, and Peter and Claudia, with you of course?"

Peter and Claudia were both in agreement and Claudia immediately went to call her friend to give her the good news.

"In the meantime, let's go to lunch nearby say in the city where we can get a taxi so Claudia doesn't have to drive back. You must know somewhere suitable?" he said looking at Peter.

Mike knew it would not be the place with the bossy blonde with the black bra under the white blouse but hopefully, he would know somewhere suitable.

"I know the very place steeped in old-world charm and you will both love it and the food isn't bad either," he said grinning.

The taxi duly arrived and having changed for city dining, they all climbed in with Mike in the front as per usual. The taxi pulled up outside a 4- or 5-storey building of brick with an ornate porch and two concrete pillars in white with touches of gold at the fussy bits. Basically saying, I am important.

They entered the building with the porter holding the door wide open to usher them into a large hallway bedecked with gold-framed artwork and various swords and shields interspersed at suitable points. A discreet waist-high wooden sign pointed to the bar area while another pointed to the dining area. They elected to enter the bar area and no doubt would order their meal from there.

The bar was reasonably large with beautifully polished mahogany tables which reminded one of a past glorious period. They chose a table and Mike went to the bar, again made of highly polished mahogany with extremely complicated inlaid designs which must have cost an absolute fortune in its day and maybe even still does. The drinks were ordered and the barman said he would take it to the table so Mike retreated with an uneasy feeling.

The drinks were delivered and the barman hesitated which Peter noticed immediately and produced the required tip instantly. Menus were produced and the meals ordered which meant they had time for further drinks which Peter ordered and refused the delivery service saying that that was just a ridiculous game he was not playing.

The main dining room was a relief from the artificially pompous atmosphere of the bar and was splendidly laid out with white tablecloths, silver cutlery and sparkling wine glasses. The place was busy yet not quite full but the quiet hum of conversation seemed to fill the room adequately creating a cosy ambiance. The waitress serving them wore a traditional dress and had an outgoing pleasant attitude. The food was excellent washed down with expensive but high-quality wine.

Mike and Peter chose red while the girls decided on a White German wine—very light and fruity. Liqueurs were offered but refused on the grounds that they invariably ruined the evening. They carried on drinking and nibbling at the cheeseboard until about 5 pm when they decided they should get a taxi back while they were still upright. Mike made sure he picked up the bill.

That evening they watched a concert on TV, a mixture of Johann Strauss, Lehar and Wagner, the latter serving to wake everyone up in time to retire to a very welcome bed.

The following morning, Stefan and Emma arrived at 9:30 and Peter got the Rolls Royce out. They all piled in with their rucksacks ready to do battle with the elements if necessary. The boats started their journeys at various points along the river and the one they stopped at was just before Rudesheim.

They settled in and after about half an hour, off they went. It was quite a long journey to Strasbourg and took the whole morning before they arrived. They grabbed a taxi into the city centre to Petite France with its cobblestone streets, canals and half-timbered homes built centuries ago—all beautiful remnants of bygone eras. They were spoiled for choice with eateries and cafes and many places giving panoramic views of the surrounding countryside.

There were so many places to visit that the whole day passed by quickly, far too quickly for all of them but that meant they had a good time and would return, no doubt. On the boat back, they relaxed with a few beers and Claudia offered to drive from Rudesheim so Peter can join in as well.

When they arrived back at Peter's home, Stefan and Emma decided to stay for drinks and leave the car overnight and take a taxi home so a long night was expected. Mike made a note to remember to always have an appointment that required him to leave after a day or two at the outside when he was next visiting friends. This he explained to Helen when they were in their room freshening up for the evening and she nodded in agreement while washing her teeth. Mike watched her and thought, *She always looks so damn cute*.

"Don't forget, we must not get dragged into anything tomorrow as we need to detox before Zurich and Jean Jacques."

"I know, otherwise I will struggle to keep up with Jean Jacques as he can be quite intense."

They need not have worried as Stefan and Emma already had other plans and left early.

After relaxing all day on Sunday, Mike and Helen were up early and had said their goodbyes by 7 am and arrived at the station by 7:30 to board their train to Zurich. Helen was quite looking forward to her new role and Mike was very happy to have her deeply involved as he needed the comfort of being able to double-check any time a problem arose.

They checked into their hotel and then made their way to the office where Jean Jacques was pleased to see them and immediately suggested that Helen would need a few days to take it all in and Mike confirmed that that would not be a problem. He then continued with: "Lisa wants you to call her as they have a new contract which she needs to discuss with you."

Mike turned to Helen and said: "I will see you later and I had better see what mischief Lisa and Harry have gotten up to."

Mike phoned Lisa and surprisingly got through straightaway. She explained that a new contract to stop an assassination in Bohn had been given to them by one of the usual culprits, this was Lisa's way of avoiding the name just in case the line was tapped.

"Have you been given any dates on this?" Mike asked.

"Nothing exact but expected to be in 2 weeks approximately."

"Well, keep me informed and I think we should get there a week before the target does."

"OK, will do. Did you have a good time with Peter and his wife?"

"Peter and Claudia, yes marvellous hosts and did things I wouldn't normally do but it was great and perhaps I should make more time to relax."

"Good. I will phone you in about a week's time but hopefully, you won't be in Switzerland as the connection is difficult."

"Cheerio then and regards to Harry."

Later that evening when they were back at their hotel, Mike told Helen about the upcoming contract given to them by one of the security services and her mouth fell open, saying eventually: "I can't believe it; you mean it has been farmed out?"

"Yes, that's it. If so, there is no coming back if it goes wrong."

"What if it does?"

"It won't; not when we are dealing with it."

"What do you have to do?"

"Don't know yet as haven't got any details other than what I've told you."

"When will you know?"

In about a week's time... Lisa reckons.

"Does it worry you?"

"No, not really as we have some good contacts that Tom used last time and they know the ropes."

Mike put his arm around Helen and asked how the induction went with Herr Hitler.

"Why do you call him that?" she asked indignantly.

"Just a joke as he is so demanding and bullies me into submission, but he is lovely really and no malice intended."

"Well, don't let anyone else hear that, especially not him or he will be upset."

"OK. I consider myself told off and I won't do it again, Miss," he replied smirking.

"If you would like to know, it was very interesting and it is extremely clever the way he manages it all and the way he knows exactly when to move money around; he makes you a lot the way he operates. Oh and he has indicated my salary," she added looking for a reaction but Mike just told her not to sell herself cheaply.

"I thought I would rent a car so we could get out and about and see the beautiful mountain scenery while we are here."

"That's a good idea; we can have some time, just the two of us."

"When does Herr...I mean, Jean Jacques want you back for another session?"

"He is busy until Thursday so we have two days to wander around."

"Right. I will make the arrangements and book a hotel up in the mountains."

Chapter 24

A week later Lisa phoned Mike at his apartment in Paris and they agreed to meet the next day as she and Harry would fly over and arrive at his apartment about midday.

After their arrival, they got straight down to discussing the assignment in Germany and they had just over a week to prepare as the assassination of the Chancellor of West Germany, Helmut Kohl, was planned for Monday, 12 September 1988, as he returned to Bohn from a meeting in Bremen. Lisa had been given quite explicit details of the exact spot where the ambush would take place. It was at a particular corner where there was a sharp righthand bend and the vehicles would have to slow down.

This would not be an easy plot to disrupt as doubtless there would be a large number involved in the assassination group due to the size of the Chancellor's convoy which would have 6 armed police on the motor cycles and 3 armed drivers plus at least 6 armed plainclothes police spread over three vehicles—a total of 15 armed men protecting the chancellor. To counteract that lot, the assassination mob would be at least 15 possible more to ensure they had an advantage.

Mike and Lisa pondered over the problem without Harry's input as he didn't get involved in details; he just killed whoever he was told to kill. He liked the simple life.

The more Mike thought about it, the less he liked it and said to Lisa: "I wonder why they don't just warn the Chancellor."

"I wondered too but perhaps it's too difficult or the information comes from a dubious source so they are not sure if it's genuine and don't want to look foolish. Who knows."

"Well, we are going to need some serious firepower and we will have to arrive after their lot or way before. I favour being early. Right, I have figured out the plan of attack. We get there early, pick spots right on the corner and see how many turn up. As the convoy approaches, Harry takes out two tyres which makes the convoy stop. They will think one of their own has gotten trigger happy and jumped the gun; excuse the pun and no, I am not a poet. This will force them to attack early or give up. I suspect the former at which point they are going to have to break cover and run towards the convoy and Harry will have a backup in the form of an AK whatever the number is and as he mows them down, the remainder will realise the game's up and will run away. What do you think?"

"Brilliant; only problem is then there are three of us and most of the convoy still alive who might think we are the enemy. We will have a serious problem," answered Lisa.

Mike stroked his chin and after reflecting for a few minutes replied: "We go tomorrow and study the layout so we position ourselves where we can just quietly withdraw while the convoy is still waiting to see if it's over or not. We will all be on the one side of the road to make withdrawal easier. Let's hope there is plenty of cover there. On the map, it looks like thick forest which is why the assassinators picked that spot in the first place."

Lisa turned to Harry and asked him if he had ever used a machine gun before to which he replied: "Yea, no problem and I know where to get one too; Tom had contacts all over Europe."

"Good and now we can relax before our trip to Germany tomorrow. I'll see what Helen is doing and maybe we can go somewhere nice for lunch, unless you have something else to do?" enquired Mike, not wanting to dominate their private lives but they both smiled and said they would love to… Mike called Helen and she was happy to join them.

Over lunch, Lisa asked Helen if Mike had told her about their plans and Helen replied: "No, and I don't want to know either."

"Why?" asked Lisa.

"If I don't know, I can't tell, not even under torture."

"If anyone ever tortures you, warn them of what I am like—lovely to my friends but a nasty piece of shit to my enemies. However, you might read about it eventually in the papers."

After that they settled down to a quiet lunch with a few glasses of wine and a lot of laughter and convivial conversation. It was agreed that Harry and Lisa would stay overnight in Mike's apartment and Helen was happy with that but was surprised when she discovered that they didn't share the same bed. Helen explained to Mike that Lisa had said that she kicks with the other foot. "What did she mean?" she asked.

"She would rather sleep with you than with a man."

"Oh you can't tell, can you?"

"Only if they cut their hair short and wear loose baggy jeans with hobnail boots and have a big bulky wristwatch on tattooed arms so you are right; you never know."

"As Peter would say…smart arse."

The next day they headed off early to reconnoitre the area of the suspected attack to plan their getaway. The terrain wasn't as helpful as Mike had hoped in that it was not heavily wooded having been picked instead for a place where the convoy would be exposed. Mike worried then if some of the attackers were to attack from the rear of the convoy, how would they counter it; then it came to him: a grenade launcher to fire past the convoy at whoever attacked from the rear. He turned to Harry and Lisa and expressed his fears and the solution. Harry agreed and Lisa asked whether it was powerful enough to throw the grenade that far to which Harry advised he thought so but that he would fire it wide on the first shot which would give him the answer.

"Right then, let's get the equipment tomorrow and then we can relax until the 12th. It might be an idea to test the launcher in advance because if it does what we expect then that is a load off my mind. I will hire a van for you tomorrow, Harry."

The next day Harry returned late in the afternoon having got and paid with the company card for the equipment. Mike asked Harry to write in the details of the address for future use and while he was at it, he asked him to fill in every other supplier he knew just so they all knew where to go in an emergency.

At dusk, they all headed off into the countryside to find a deserted area to test the grenade launcher and were very impressed with the result.

"Bloody hell, that is just fantastic and will do the job perfectly. God help those bastards that come up from the rear."

Lisa agreed but added a note of caution to Harry to remember that both sides will regard him as a target if they wise up so no bravado please if you have a good strike.

Business carried on as usual for Mike, and Helen travelled on her own to Zurich to increase her knowledge and understanding and to enjoy the company of Jean Jacques and Judy in the evening at some exotic and charming bistro. She liked the feeling of independence and also particularly liked the Swiss. She wondered what it was like to purchase a property in Switzerland and made up her mind to investigate. She would do that on her next visit.

Chapter 25

12th September was upon them and on the evening before, they headed off to Germany to get ensconced in place before the assassins arrived. Harry was settled in at the earliest possible position so he could blow the tyres and stop the convoy driving into a massacre. He arranged his equipment so it would be easy to switch from rifle to grenade launcher and finally to his AK47 Kalashnikov assault rifle.

They settled in for the night in their sleeping bags and woke up at 5 am to get organised and to drink some coffee and eat a bread roll filled with ham or cheese according to their taste. They then had a long wait until approximately 1200 hours when the mob arrived and stood around debating where to settle in for the attack. This took about half an hour and then all went quiet. Mike and Lisa had three of the gang hiding just underneath them so had to be very cautious. Soon one could be heard on the radio obviously being informed of the approach of the Convoy. After 15 minutes or so the convoy appeared causing a stir among the mob and as it got nearer Harry fired two shots in quick succession which took out two tyres causing the convoy to screech to a halt.

The mob got the order to rush the convoy while Harry could see two vans approaching the rear of the convoy and disgorging about a dozen armed men. Harry fired the grenade launcher with catastrophic effect in that it took out most of the armed men and one of the vans and he almost immediately let loose with a second shot thereby killing those retreating and destroying the second van. At this point, Harry switched his attention to the mob attacking from the front which by now had just reached his position and opened fire with the AK47 Kalashnikov. Mike and Lisa joined in the mayhem leaving all but two dead and scattered along the road. The two will no doubt tell their masters that they were betrayed which of course was true. It would have been better, Mike thought, if none had escaped but you can't always have 100% success.

Mike and Lisa rushed over to Harry to help him carry the weapons and to make sure he kept his head down as those in the convoy might think he was part of the attacking force. They scarpered away as quickly as possible down to their van and as Mike inserted the key, he prayed that the engine would fire straight away without stalling, which it did to everyone's relief and they were away.

Back at the apartment, Mike reminded Lisa and Harry that they must get a lockup and quickly as he might get a visit from the Gendarmerie and the assault weapons would be a dead giveaway. "So tomorrow, take my car and find somewhere quickly and return the vehicle to me without a trace of weapons." Remarkably, this they managed to do.

Two days later, as Mike was reflecting on the whole experience the phone rang and it was the commissaire de police who very politely asked him to visit the station tomorrow morning at 1000 hours or otherwise they could call to pick him up i.e. arrest him. He immediately complied with the request and didn't bother to ask what it was about. He walked to the spare bedroom knocking of course and entered when Lisa responded. He told her about the call and asked if she could phone her contact and ask him to sort out the problem before it became official. She did it straight away and her contact said they would sort it but Mike was to carry on as normal and not make any waves but be completely polite at all times.

Mike arrived at the police station just before 1000 hours to ensure he was not late. He was asked to take a seat and wait which he did and very quickly a young police officer came to escort him to the commissaire's office. The officer knocked on the door and entered when requested showing Mike in. He was greeted by the commissaire in a polite manner if not altogether friendly. The commissaire pointed to a chair which Mike accepted and sat down.

The commissaire looked at Mike and without flinching said: "I was going to interrogate you but on high have told me to drop it and unfortunately I am obliged to do so but I am not happy about it.

"Were you going to ask me about an incident in Germany?"

"I am unable to say anything."

"Perhaps I can say something that will put your mind at ease. If you were going to interrogate me over some recent event then I can assure you that I would only act in the interest of the countries involved or some such and I am not some bastard who thinks that he can ride roughshod over the law."

"Changing the subject, I believe you are seeing one of our officers."

155

"Yes Helen, La Lieutenant."

Le commissaire smiled remembering a previous occasion particularly when Helen had dropped the pen.

"You broke through the ice then."

"Eventually and now I am hoping to persuade her to marry me."

"Well, the best of luck."

Mike stood up offered his hand and the commissaire accepted it saying: "Do take care; life can be extremely dangerous."

"I will."

Mike then left feeling somewhat relieved that the commissaire was half acquainted or possibly even fully aware of the circumstances of 12th September.

Chapter 26

On Thursday, 15 September 1988, Mike had a call from Freddie in London asking if he could come and see him as he had a problem which was getting serious. Mike asked what it was about but Freddie as usual preferred to do it face to face. Mike then asked if it could wait until Monday but Freddie insisted: "Tomorrow would be better and you will need to be able to get hold of Jean Jacques tomorrow also. We really need to sort this before the weekend or it could get out of hand."

"OK Freddie. I will be there tomorrow without fail."

Friday at 10:30 am, Mike walked through the main doors of the office and was relieved to see all looked normal. He made his way to Freddie's office who rose to greet him and made a point of closing the door behind Mike. Mike took his jacket off and sat down and waited.

"Several of our top brokers have been approached by other firms offering them much larger salaries than they presently earn and they have asked me to bring it to your attention as they really do not want to move but they are being offered 50% more and that has to be considered."

"I have taken my eye off the ball insofar as salaries for London are concerned and I know that they haven't been revised for some considerable time. All they have had are cost of living increases. Can I use your phone to talk to Jean Jacques?"

"Certainly and I will leave you in peace as I have some things I need to attend to."

When the door closed, Mike made his call to Zurich and luckily got through fairly quickly. "Jean Jacques speaking."

"Hi Jean Jacques, it's Mike here. We have a problem in London as some of the top staff are being poached with 50% increases in salaries being offered and I know we should have done something on this before but now it's serious."

"The income of the London office has shot up dramatically and yes, we should bring salaries up to date. You could double the salaries and offer a £50,000 bonus to your top men. How many are we talking about?"

"It's 6, including Freddie."

"You can afford to put the top brokers up to £100K with a £30K bonus and Freddie up to £200K and the same bonus. You can explain that the bonus is not related to earnings but just to the overall success of the company finances. If the top salaries are out of date then the rest will be too so you need to offer a 20% increase across the board and an individual bonus of £2,500 to each employee. They will then be paid more than they can get elsewhere and that is right for such a successful brokerage in the centre of London."

"That's perfect and will kill off the attack."

"Do you always have to talk in fighting terms?"

"I'm aggressive because I realise this is all my fault. I should have done something earlier."

"Look at it this way—a big increase and a big bonus means they will feel on top of the world so by waiting, they will be ahead of the game now. It's as if they have been saving."

"OK. I will talk to Freddie now."

Just then the office door opened and Freddie put his head around to test the reception only to be called in cheerfully. Mike then explained what the offer would be and Freddie was left flabbergasted with mouth open as the new offer would put them well above the market level.

"I will leave you to break the news to all and could you call a board meeting afterwards as I would like to say a few words?"

In the meantime, Mike phoned Helen who was still on holiday from the Gendarmerie to give her an update and to tell her he would be back later that evening. She was able to tell Mike he would be going to Austria again as Gabriel had had a recommendation from Erik Hauptmann into another pharmaceutical manufacturer and he says it is all very encouraging.

"That sounds great but let's hope there are no Russians involved this time but why does Gabriel want me along?"

"It seems the MD is a good friend of Erik and wants to meet you."

"Oh well, it's nice to be wanted I suppose; talking of which, the boardroom is now free so must go and will see you soon."

Mike followed Freddie's secretary to the boardroom and entered to be greeted by smiles and handshakes all around. He walked to the end of the table and then turned around and waited for everyone to settle down.

"First of all, I have to say that it was not by chance that I came here today but on Freddie's insistence and I have him to thank for stressing the urgency of the situation. I also have to apologise to you all for taking my eye off the ball due to other problems in Europe but that is no excuse. I should have realised that the salaries had slipped behind and done something earlier. However, that is why, with the help of Jean Jacques in Zurich, we have taken the steps to correct matters and to enhance the salaries over our competitors so you should now be among the highest paid in our industry and we intend to keep it that way so long as the figures warrant it.

"In an effort to show that we are really sorry for overlooking the matter, we have offered a bonus to everyone which is not based on salary but on the profitability of the company. In addition to your forgiveness, I ask that you continue to carry on as you have and to always strive to be the best. If the growth continues then so will the rewards. Right, I hope you all have a nice weekend and don't forget to tell the staff of their increases and bonus so they have something to feel good about too."

With that, Mike took his leave saying he had to get to the airport and rushed off. When Mike got through customs, the first thing he saw was Helen waving enthusiastically at him which lifted his spirits and made him laugh out loud with sheer pleasure. He walked up to her and held her tightly for a few moments just treasuring how nice it felt and how lovely she smelled.

"To what do I owe the pleasure?" he asked.

"I just missed you and then I thought on seeing you that we might go to a swanky restaurant, Mr Businessman," she said, looking him up and down.

Before he could reply, she said: "Do I look like the kind of woman you might be having an affair with?"

"It's amazing but you look exactly like her," he said laughing.

She grabbed his free arm and they walked to the taxi rank.

They settled on an in-vogue Irish bistro called Chez Moi par Seamus, a nice play on pronunciations but their speciality was Bifteck a l'Anglaise which simply melted in your mouth and as such the place was full but they just got in, being early. When hungry, the smell of chargrilled steaks makes one go from hungry to ravenous within a few minutes and when the waiter with the obligatory white apron pours the red wine so it makes that glubbing noise, you know you are in the middle of something special. Mike watched Helen take the first cut from her steak and when she saw he was watching, she exaggerated the insertion into her pouting round lips and then when the taste kicked in, her expression turned to pain and then to one of being in absolute ecstasy.

The couple on the next table were laughing in appreciation and the woman looked at Helen and said: "I know; it's orgasmic, isn't it?"

"I would have to say... not quite," giving a quick glance a Mike.

This caused more laughter which Mike joined in, well he had to if only to demonstrate that he had no hang-ups on the matter.

Mike excused himself to visit the gents and when he returned, he found Helen still chatting with the neighbouring table and she announced to Mike that they were both Swiss and they had invited them to visit when next in Zurich, which she explained was quite often. Mike warmed to them and Helen introduced them with: "This is Heidi and Carl and they live on the outskirts of Zurich. I have told them about your office and Jean Jacques but I can't remember his surname."

"I never use it but I think it's Bayer," said Mike and then nodding to confirm it.

"On Monday, you are going to Vienna and later on in the week we will be going to Zurich but exactly when depends on how long the business meeting takes," she explained.

"We can always phone you to see if you are free. Have we got their telephone number?" he asked Helen.

Helen confirmed they had and at that point, Mike grabbed his mini pile of chits and beckoned the waiter who slid over as if on wheels. Mike paid and then stood up which Helen responded to automatically and they shook hands, promising to meet again.

Once outside, Helen asked if he was upset with her suggesting they meet up when next in Zurich and Mike assured her he wasn't but said he always struggled in first meetings and it will be better in Zurich their home ground and we will be more prepared. This doesn't happen in business as we all know what to say but it can get awkward in private until you get to know something about each other. Helen said she thought it must be a man thing.

When they got back to the apartment, Mike surprised her by bringing up the question of their marriage and said he didn't want a religious one and left to him would opt for a small wedding service with just two witnesses but he expected she would want quite a large affair.

"Well, non-religious I can deal with but yes, I would like my family, your family and some of our friends to be there. Otherwise, you are making it look like you don't care about any of them which I know is not true but sometimes one has to show that you care."

"You are right, of course. It's the private part of life that I struggle with and don't like to make a fuss but I get it that one has to show that one cares."

"And it's OK to drop your guard and even be emotional."

"Now you are going too far…emotional; it's the recovery process from emotional that kills—just too embarrassing."

Helen laughed and said when they get back, they will spend an evening planning the list of guests and where they are going to have it and most importantly when…but now, she wanted to finish that orgasmic experience.

Chapter 27

Mike and Helen arrived in Vienna to be greeted by the Austrian director Gabriel who had decided to pick them up so he could tell Mike immediately about the new prospect. He took them to their hotel and waited in the lounge area for Mike to return. It turned out the new prospect came after Erik Hauptmann told his friend how Mike had helped him through very frightening times. He decided he would be more than happy to have a broker with such extra gifts. Mike laughed at that and decided he must warn them to be discreet about mentioning his name or he might find himself getting targeted, which would negate the whole exercise.

Helen decided to have a look around the shops while Mike went to visit the new prospect. Gabriel filled Mike in on the details: "The MD's name is Kurt Tauber and the name of the company is Zintenphos and our appointment with Mr Tauber is at 10:30 at the factory."

"You said they were a pharmaceutical company, I believe?" mentioned Mike.

"Yes that's right but quite big. Their insurance spend is over 20 million schillings that's over a million pounds sterling so quite a catch if we can succeed."

"I was worrying about getting my name too well known for the wrong reason but if that's the price of success then so be it."

"I believe today he just wants to meet you and the broking exercise will be done by me and my staff later. I think he believes the existing framework for his insurance will probably be as good as it can be as the international brokers he is with are no fools, or so he says."

"Who are they?"

"I don't know, he wouldn't say at this stage."

"Well, just because they are international doesn't mean they haven't missed something but we shall see and if it's just a straight transfer over on the existing basis, what could be nicer."

They pulled up to the gates of the factory and were stopped for a security check. Gabriel gave the required details and they were allowed to proceed up to the main entrance where they were met by a young man who would take the car and park it for them. A young woman in her 30s greeted them at the entrance and escorted them to the lifts which took them to the 3rd floor and opened out into a large reception area where they were handed over to a more senior lady who announced that Mr Tauber was expecting them. They were then taken to a large and imposing oak door which opened out into Mr Tauber's domain.

The office was expensive but not flashy with a large mahogany desk and as Mike walked towards Kurt, he noticed that the carpet was luxurious by the fact that he could feel the thickness with each step. Kurt stepped forward to meet Mike with hand outstretched and a beaming smile which Mike responded to immediately. Kurt spoke first: "I feel I know you already. Can I call you Mike?"

"Of course and I will call you Kurt, is that OK?"

"Good, that got the preliminaries out of the way which is always the awkward part. Erik is a close friend since we were at school together and what you did for him has impressed me and makes you a very important friend to have. I believe you and Erik are quite friendly still?"

"Yes, we will be friends now for life I hope and it was a pleasure to be of service to him; mind you, he did pay a fee but if he had been a pauper, we would have done it for nothing and I would have paid the other staff but he made it clear that the price was not a hardship so it was a benefit all around but now I have a good friend as well and that makes it special. However, the two colleagues who do the hard bit are very experienced and highly trained without them it couldn't happen. I plan the manoeuvres and they carry it out. It used to be a friend of mine who did the planning but unfortunately he died leaving the two basically unemployed so I decided to take it over and they were delighted."

"So your first call is insurance?"

"Yes, since I started to work and believe it or not, I like it."

"Have you done anything similar since helping Erik?"

"Yes but please don't ask what as I can't say and animosity is my best friend, a quiet word among friends is fine but publicity could just mean I won't be long for this planet."

"Yes I understand but if I needed you then you would help me too, especially if I am doing business with you?"

"Of course, that goes without saying. Have you got a problem?"

"Not at the moment but things might change down the line."

"Well, if you are being forced to make a decision you don't want to make, just say that you will have to refer it to your financial director and you will get back to them. Then phone me."

They chatted on freely for almost an hour ending with Kurt signing a transfer of agency saying to Gabriel, "When you get all the files, you can go through it thoroughly and let me know if there are any faults or omissions."

"Certainly, I didn't expect you to transfer your business over so easily," Gabriel said with a surprised expression.

"Well, I was going to do it sooner or later so might just as well get it done."

They all stood up and Mike made sure to leave Kurt his card and reassured him if he needed him, he would be there as fast as possible. Kurt seemed happy and asked at the last moment how long Mike would be staying in Vienna. Probably 2 days, Mike advised him.

When they were settled back in the car, Mike said: "I suspect he will phone me before I leave. Whatever is his problem, it is imminent."

"However, we have just had the easiest piece of new business ever," said Gabriel cheerfully.

"Don't be so sure."

"Anyway, I am dropping this Letter of Transfer into the insurer on the way to our office so I know they have got it. I don't want to be left in the air."

"Left in suspenders what?" Mike quipped with a slight grin.

"Was meinst du damit."

"Hey, you have slipped back into German. It was just a play on words instead of being left in the air one might say in England I don't want to be left in suspense or change suspense to suspenders, do you see?"

"So you have some men wearing women's suspenders and not wanting to be caught in them, yes?"

Mike was crying with laughter tears running down his cheeks as he visualised what Gabriel had just said and blurted out: "Not on your birthday anyway where all your friends burst into the room singing Happy Birthday and get stopped in their tracks mouths open; all asking themselves what the fuck is going on here!"

Now it was Gabriel's turn to have tears running down his cheeks but luckily, he had just parked up outside the insurance company's offices. He got out of the car still laughing and walked towards the entrance. Halfway there, he stopped and wiped his eyes and stamped his foot several times trying to regain his composure from the control of this silly state he was in. He succeeded but only momentarily and now he was walking back to the car still wiping his eyes and unable to stop.

"I keep seeing it in my mind; you will have to do it."

"Give over, I won't be any better," but then thought we will be here all day so he got out, took the letter and went in.

When Mike got back, Gabriel had calmed down and confessed that he had not laughed so much in ages. They headed back to the office and Gabriel shared the good news with the staff who were all very pleased and excited at picking up such a good client.

Mike and Gabriel went to lunch and returned to the office about 3pm and Gabriel had a call from the insurer to phone their branch manager urgently—a Herr Carlson. Gabriel lifted the phone and was put through quite quickly. Mike could tell there was a problem from the way Gabriel was speaking and the call finished with Gabriel telling him he would call back in a few minutes.

"We have a problem with this bastard in that he is saying we are not big enough to handle an account of this size and not financially strong enough either."

"Phone him back and tell him that you have the CEO with you and he will show you that you are wrong on both counts and fix an appointment for as soon as possible. If he refuses then tell him he will lose the account because our facilities are such that no risk is too big. Tell him the name of our London office that is highly regarded by Lloyds of London."

Gabriel phoned him back and an appointment was made for 9 am the next day which was not a problem even if it was made purposefully early. They both arrived for the appointment at 8:50 am and waited to be called in, which they were at 9 precisely.

Mike let Gabriel go in first and watched with studied interest the body language of Herr Carlson; he was a fastidious little man with a desk so tidy he obviously didn't do a lot of work and causing frustration was his raison d'etre.

Mike shook his hand and sat down beside Gabriel and waited for Herr Carlson to have his say. He had obviously just looked at the Vienna office and was blissfully unaware of the full extent of the group.

When he had finished, Mike was careful to act as though he respected Herr Carlson basically to avoid any unnecessary complications and leaned forward with a brochure to show the full size of the group of companies. This Mr Carlson studied and came up with his second criticism which was that the local company did not have the financial backing to handle an account of this size.

Mike asked: "How much extra working capital do you think there should be in the company?"

"Well, I would say a quarter of a million dollars seeing as your wealth is probably counted in dollars."

"Can I use your phone please to contact our chief Financial Controller?"

"Why yes but what good will that do?"

"You will see," Mike said, dialling Jean Jacques who he had warned what would be required.

"Ah Jean Jacques, could you do me a favour and transfer $500,000 into the Vienna branch's account? The office account. And give the bank permission to speak to a Herr Carlson when he phones to check the amount of the additional monies deposited."

Mike then finished the call with a few pleasantries and replaced the receiver and looked at Herr Carlson and said: "Will that suffice or is there anything else?"

"That will be fine but there is one thing you ought to know."

"Oh what?"

"Mr Kurt Tauber's son works for the existing brokers but not for long I suspect."

Mike turned to Gabriel. "Not a problem, is it, Gabriel?"

"No, not a problem, we will inform Mr Tauber."

In the carpark, Gabriel said: "I am impressed the way you did that; not only did you put in double what he asked for but gave him permission to check it. I expect he will be too embarrassed to do it. I think you made him feel small."

"I probably did but then he was being an arschloch as you would say but you will be wrong; he will check as he will be able to talk down to the bank manager."

"I had better warn him what an arsehole he is then and don't forget to speak to Kurt Tauber about his son joining us."

When they got back to the office, there had been a call from Kurt Tauber which made it easy for Mike to call him; he got through straight away and asked: "Is everything OK? I have just been to the insurer who was demanding that I boost the local office finances so I put in double what he asked for. Your existing broker's obviously making waves. In addition, tell your son he will be joining our office here in Vienna unless he objects."

"That's two of my concerns taken care of. I have made the right decision but I have another problem. The one I said might occur…well, it has. Can we meet somewhere to talk?"

"Of course, wherever you say."

Kurt then gave Mike instructions to his club and suggested midday to meet there which gave just enough time to get there by taxi. On arrival, Mike was ushered in and taken into the lounge area where Kurt was already ensconced. Kurt stood up and said he had a room reserved where they could talk privately.

The room was like a boardroom with a shining mahogany table taken from an old passenger cruise ship perhaps. They settled down at one end and Kurt commenced: "A couple of weeks ago, I got approached by two Hungarians who wanted to purchase some chemicals; some quite dangerous chemicals such as Touline and various enhancers. As you probably know, Touline is particularly dangerous in that if it's on fire, you can't see the flame and there are various safety measures you have to take because at the first warning, you have to evacuate immediately; you do not stop to try and put it out as you will simply die and in the heat, the containers will explode spreading the fire.

"Many a factory has been burnt to the ground but it is also dangerous to human health and on top of that, the other chemicals they were asking for suggested they were making bombs. I started asking for proper paperwork and then they got nasty; at first I thought they will go somewhere else but then they came back with their order on a plain sheet of paper and said if I don't supply, they will start killing my family one by one until I give in. I laughed it off but now I am worried."

"Have you told the police?"

"Yes."

"And what did they say?"

"Let us know if they come back; it's difficult to see what we can do until a crime is committed."

"Trouble is the crime could be the murder of one of your family. I will phone my team. Can I use this phone here?"

"Yes, of course."

Mike phoned and got through to Harry who said that Lisa had just gone out but would be back in half an hour. Mike left his number and asked that she phone him the minute she returned.

"Don't worry; I will get them on a flight tonight so they will start at your premises tomorrow morning. See if you can persuade the police to visit tonight on the basis you are getting full-time protection from tomorrow morning. If they refuse, tell them you will inform the media should anything happen that you refused to protect them when asked. That usually makes them think again especially as it's only for one night in this case."

Kurt had more luck this time and as he was making private arrangements, they would cover tonight to assist. Then Lisa returned Mike's call and he explained the situation and requested she and Harry get on a flight tonight and if they forget anything, it will be replaced locally. They were to book the flights now and ring him back with the arrival time so he can pick them up.

A few minutes later, they phoned to say they will arrive at 7:30 pm but it would be 8 before they got through customs.

"Right, I will be there with the client, a Mr Kurt Tauber; see you then."

"I better phone my wife and let her know what is happening," said Kurt.

"Tell her we will eat out or perhaps here?"

"Yes, here we can eat," replied Kurt pointing at the menu.

Mike phoned Helen at their apartment to keep her up to date and she was quite happy planning the wedding to which Mike responded in his best enthusiastic voice claiming to be looking forward to seeing her plans and said to himself, *God forgive me for lying but it has to be done.*

After having a light meal, it was time to head for the airport where they arrived at a minute or two before 8 pm just in time to see Lisa and Harry arriving at the pick-up point. They threw their bags into the boot and settled in for the short journey to Kurt's house. After about 20 minutes, they were driving down a country lane with occasional large houses on each side and came to a high walled area of 7 feet tall which eventually curved into a short driveway protected by two very large wrought iron gates which recognised Kurt's number plate and opened to allow them entrance.

"That will need to change," said Lisa.

"What?" asked Kurt.

"Automatic recognition of your plate as all the criminals need to do is get a false plate with your number on it and it's open sesame."

"Got in; Himmel, you are right," said Kurt.

As they drove up the long driveway, Mike had to admire the mansion they were approaching. It was large with 10 or more bedrooms but with beautiful architecture and the drive circled a large well-manicured lawn that had a magnificently plumed peacock strutting it way across stopping only to cry out and flutter its tail showing off the sparkling flickering multicoloured circles of delight that attract and hypnotise his female partners. Looking at him, you knew he knew that he was simply the best.

"Magnificent, isn't he," said Kurt who stood beside him on the front steps.

All four of them were admiring the bird strutting when Mike encapsulated it with: "That's where the Italian gigolos get their strut from,"

Kurt's wife Maureen who had approached unnoticed burst into laughter. "He's bloody right there, Kurt."

Kurt turned around smiling broadly and introduced his wife to everyone and said to Mike: "And if you are wondering where the name Maureen came from…well, her mother was Irish."

"Well, I like the name Maureen; reminds me of someone from my youth."

"Perhaps we had better not go into that then," said Maureen.

"Not here anyway, I think we are a bit exposed in the circumstances," was Kurt's sensible interjection.

All agreed and quickly moved inside.

Unlike at Erik's place, there were no porters to carry suitcases which didn't matter to Lisa and Harry as they were fit enough to run with much heavier loads. Lisa and Harry got shown their rooms by Maureen who then returned downstairs to join Mike and Kurt in the lounge.

Mike then went over some security details and reassured Maureen that she and the children would be protected at all times by Lisa and Harry. Mike would also be in attendance for the next few days ensuring that all the precautions are put into effect. They then discussed tactics.

"These people are Hungarians, you say. How easy is it to get across the border these days as Hungary is behind the iron curtain. Is it weak down here compared to the northern end?"

"It seems to be weaker or else it's getting hard for the communists to control everywhere but every so often we become aware of Hungarian rabble."

"They are not all rabble, of course," said Mike and mentioned Zsa Gabor the actress now living in America.

"Yes but she is an actress and lucky enough to have escaped but many were not so lucky," said Maureen to nodding heads all around.

Mike turned to Kurt and explained his role in smoking these criminals out. Mike wanted him to wait until contacted and then reply in an arrogant manner and suggest what do they think they are going to do; start shooting in the streets of Vienna; how ridiculous. As if it had not occurred to him, they might come at night and he was to be dismissive and then added: "They need to be angry so they rush to get revenge, mind you, I should drive a hired vehicle so they don't recognise you just in case they do start firing in the streets of Vienna."

"What if I hire a bullet proof car?"

"Can you hire one of those here?"

"Yes with being so close to gangsters of all sorts, there is a thriving market here."

"Then do that, it's perfect and will reinforce the need for them to attack you at home. We will kill all of them except one as per usual."

Before Mike could explain why leaving one was a good idea, Kurt asked incredulously: "Why not all?"

"Because we will follow him back to his base. I mean, Lisa and Harry will follow him on the motorbike. Once their base is known, we will wait to see who comes out and then shoot them and wait some more to see if any more rush out in which case Harry does it again. Harry is a first-class sniper and has never missed so far and then they go in and mop up the rest. If there is cash there, we will take that so they believe you have hired another firm just like them. It's like with ants; no point in killing half of them, you have to kill the lot or they come back."

Kurt liked that and to his surprise so did Maureen who agreed that the tactics were brilliant. Mike thought she might be a bit on the squeamish side but not at all. Must be the Irish in her, he thought. He knew from his own town in Ireland that Irish women could be right bitches when they got going.

"Now we sit back and wait and hopefully, they will contact you tomorrow, Kurt, but if they come tonight, we have set up booby traps in the grounds. Remember to keep the kids fully informed so they know how serious the problem is. Better to be frightened than blissfully happy minutes before you are killed."

As they had missed lunch, it was decided dinner was to be served early and a young girl came to announce the fact that it was now ready. She was sedately dressed in a black two-piece and looked completely at ease in her role.

The following day, the Hungarians were stopped at the gates of the factory by armed guards with the result that an hour later Kurt received a call from a very irate Hungarian telling him it was his last chance to comply with their request or they would carry out their promise at which point they were met by an arrogant and dismissive Kurt displaying the required amount of upper class aloofness. The phone was banged down and Kurt smiled.

Mid-morning, Kurt's hired vehicle was delivered and he had to sign a form that said any damage to the vehicle had to be paid by him as they only insured it for third-party road cover. Kurt stayed at the factory for his full day's normal period to keep things looking as if he had not a care in the world about the Hungarians.

At his home however things took a different turn and the first notification was one of the booby traps going off but the traps were not set to kill and so everyone inside waited for the next step. It came within minutes as five men rushed from cover across the lawn frightening the peacock who scarpered as fast as he could. Harry took out one of them and one stopped to see what happened; the other three kept running forward and were taken out by Harry and Lisa on the entrance steps. The one that had stopped to look after his colleague started to run back as fast as he could in a zigzag swerve which amused Harry but he played along, firing about three times making sure he missed. Then both of them ran to the bike to make sure they were able to follow the bastard.

The Hungarian, as expected, took them straight back to their lair. Harry found a spot where he and his viola case could stand discreetly in an alley directly opposite the lair while Lisa stayed with the bike but about 30 yards before where Harry was standing so in an emergency she could swoop and pick him up. Eventually, the Hungarian came out with two other men and stood talking which gave Harry all the time he needed to quickly flick his viola case open and shoot all three in the blink of an eye. One could hear the shots like a triple backfire but the holes in the heads of the fallen soon made people scream and run in all directions.

Harry had now adorned a balaclava which added to the fear factor. The ruckus did have the desired effect in that two more emerged cautiously to see what was happening but never discovered anything except darkness. Harry ran across the street with his viola case flapping about on his back and his automatic rifle poised and ready while Lisa screamed up to the entrance, stood the bike and jumped into action at such speed that onlookers just stood with open mouths stuck to the ground in horror at the events unfolding at such an alarming rate. Inside the office there was one man who looked scared when Harry kicked the door open and was about to say something when the shot stopped him in his tracks. They didn't need him as he had already been trying to load more money into the safe. They quickly grabbed the cash, stuffing it in the viola case and strapping it back on to Harry's back.

Harry and Lisa emerged into a half-crowded street where the onlookers were waiting for the next instalment having lost some of their fear knowing they were not the target. Lisa was now also wearing a balaclava and as they mounted the bike in quick unison, Harry pulled a wad of cash from both pockets of his jacket and threw it at the crowd as they left. As the notes wafted down, nobody thought to take a note of the bike's registration number—not that it would have been useful to the police anyway.

On arriving back at Kurt's house, Mike had been busy hiding the bodies in the wooded area pending the return of Lisa and Harry.

Mike then phoned Kurt to give him an update but Maureen had already spoken to him in rather excitable terms.

"You would think she had just been to see the best movie ever the way she went on. I'm sorry I missed it all," said Kurt rather excitedly.

"Have you got a vehicle anywhere where we can move these bodies?" Mike asked.

"Yes, there is a van in one of the outhouses at the rear. I will be home in half an hour and I will open it up for you."

Mike went inside to get a cup of black coffee as he needed the energy after dragging the four dead bodies into the shrubbery. Maureen called him into the kitchen and he slumped into a wooden chair at the end of an enormous country style oak table not the most comfortable but nevertheless very welcome as he was shattered. Maureen was still quite excitable and strangely showed no pity for the dead criminals; it seemed to Mike that she was treating it like a movie for the moment. Perhaps that was her way of coping. In Mike's mind, these people did not deserve a second of pity as they would have killed everybody more than likely.

Maureen chatted endlessly while he slowly consumed the coffee savouring every drop. He had cut off from her just nodding when it seemed appropriate which he could just tell from the last couple of words or when her sentence ended in a high note then that was probably a question on which he just pondered but snapped out of it when she exclaimed what an exciting life Mike had.

"Oh no, most of the time I deal in insurance and visiting various branches around Europe so fairly normal generally, although I adore Europe and that to me is exciting whereas this business of protecting people is deadly serious; one slip and it can all go wrong with misery everywhere, the wrong people getting killed or maimed, not a good scenario as you can imagine but if we don't get involved then there is misery for you and your family and our refusal would be on our conscience. We do what the police should do but can't because of convention and its rules. I got into this by a desire to help someone and I've become trapped in it ever since but I'm not complaining; just don't want you to think that this is me."

Just then Kurt, Harry and Lisa all walked in together. They all wanted a coffee so Mike had another. "How much money did you get?" Mike asked and was shown the viola case stuffed to the brim and Harry saying he would count it during the night.

"Well, whatever it is, we can keep that and knock it off Kurt's bill."

Kurt came back with: "You don't need to do that; the bill will not be a problem so long as you break it up like you did for Erik so I don't get any awkward questions."

"You don't know what our bill is like."

"Yes I do. Erik told me but worth it to have one's family safe and sound."

They finished their drinks and went out to load the bodies into the van. Having discussed where to go, they decided on an abandoned quarry with a deep lake and thought that would do nicely as the bodies would not resurface for a couple of days and then the authorities would identify them which would serve as a lesson to all concerned.

The next day Mike, Lisa and Harry got up early and said their goodbyes and reassured Kurt that if the Hungarians resurfaced, they would come back at no extra charge and finish the job but hopefully, they had all been dealt with.

Mike arrived back in Paris around 3 pm and was glad to be opening the door to his apartment and settling in. Helen was not yet home so the place seemed very quiet but on the lounge table, there was a message for him telling him that she had completed the wedding plans and would tell him all about it when she got back. He smiled and thought, *I bet it's going to be much bigger than I hoped but this is where I fall down* and committed himself to paying attention and above all engaging with the process and one never knows one might enjoy it but at least you will acquit yourself with some brownie points, he told himself.

In reality, he would much rather wave a magic wand and hey presto, it's all over and they are married; but as he hadn't got a magic wand, he decided to treat it like a business venture and that way he would engage fully with all the details of the preparations and may even suggest some positive improvements which would stand him in good stead.

Having sorted the problem of his resistance, he went into the kitchen and made himself a strong coffee and took it out to the balcony where he eased himself into a cushioned wickerwork chair and finally drew a deep breath before sipping his hot steaming elixir.

He awoke suddenly to a lot of banging and Helen calling out and then she was standing over him smiling: "Have you been asleep?"

"Must have been only sat down to enjoy my coffee and obviously I dozed off."

"It will be all the dashing about and the stress of flying; not counting whatever you were up to with Kurt."

"You are right, of course."

"Well, I made a casserole with dumplings last night and only need to warm it up so after we have eaten and poured ourselves a nice glass of red, I will tell you all about my plans."

Mike was going to ask whether there were any potatoes in this casserole but decided why look for a fight when you don't have to. In the event, he needn't have worried; the casserole turned out to be a huge pan of beef, vegetables, dumplings and potatoes—absolutely what the doctor ordered. He devoured a large plateful with gusto and that replenished his energy. Helen cleared the table and laid out a screed of papers with table plans and decorations shown and the hotel already picked and booked plus the guest list which at first glance seemed enormous. Helen stood back and asked what he thought. This was where his thinking earlier came to the rescue.

"You have certainly done a lot of work and not much for me to do it seems but I'm impressed; just one question at the moment: who have you picked for my best man?"

"Nobody; that is your choice but perhaps Peter or maybe Freddie in London."

"Peter I think, as he has become a proper friend; nothing against Freddie but I only know him as a colleague but he will have to be invited and the 6 directors in Europe and we will need to include Lisa and Harry."

"They are already on the list."

"Oh well, looks like you have it all done and all I have to do is ask Peter if he will do me the honour of being my best man."

"What do you think of the hotel and the plan otherwise?"

"Excellent, it should all be great regardless of the weather; now what's the date?"

"September the 3rd 1988."

"It's about time for me at 48 years of age whereas you at 38 will probably be regarded as too young for that old bugger."

"Well, if we are having a family, I will need to get on with it."

"Are you from French farming stock by any chance?"

"There are some farming people; why?"

"Well, it will be like the women in Ireland in olden days; they just stopped working in the field for 20 minutes while they gave birth as I was told about one woman by an old-timer. He said it only took 20 minutes because she had to clean the baby off and make a sling to strap him to her breast and then she went to the horse and plough took hold of the reins with a giddy up and off she continued. She not only had a firm arse which is why she was always pregnant, old Charlie just couldn't resist, but firm arms to keep the horse under control as well."

"If you think I'm competing with that myth, you've got another thing coming."

Mike was beside himself with laughter.

"When are you due back in Zurich?" Mike asked.

"I agreed Monday with Jean Jacques, if that's OK?"

"Fine with me; we can have a quiet weekend and when we get to Zurich, I will hire a vehicle and drive to the French border and have a look around for some properties for a family home. If I see anything that is suitable, I will not do anything until you check it out."

"How big are you talking about?"

"Perhaps about 8 to 10 bedrooms and it will have to be in its own grounds, well protected so we feel safe. Not as palatial as Peter's place but big enough to be able to have friends and business acquaintances around if necessary. And it will have to have service quarters as with our busy lives we will need a housekeeper and some staff. It will all depend on what is available; once we know then we can fit the rest in."

"You are really getting into all of this which I am surprised by really; never thought you would want all that settling down business."

Monday soon came around and after dropping Helen off in the office with Jean Jacques, Mike set off towards Basel and the French border and from there to Besancon Viotte and Belford to see what the estate agents had on their books. He left a full description of what he was looking for with each place he visited and then decided to return to Zurich and got back at1:30 pm just in time he decided for a late lunch. He phoned the office from a public phone and discovered that Helen had already had a sandwich and coffee so decided to eat on his own.

Mike walked along to a café he knew and liked and on the way picked up a French and German newspaper to see what was going on in the world today. He liked to catch up every day if he could believing that it was profitable if nothing else to be on top of events. However, this Monday, all seemed much the same as last week so he put the papers down and finished his coffee and croissant and watched the Swiss hustle and bustle of activity which always seemed so refined and orderly, very like the English in fact.

Mike wandered back to the office to see how Helen was doing and was greeted with the news that Lisa had been looking for him so could you phone her and then she informed him that Jean Jacques had organised an office for her exclusive use.

"And how did the day go for you?"

"I visited a few estate agents and left the particulars of what we were looking for and they have promised to search the area and get back to me. They all seemed quite keen because it will cost a pretty penny I suppose."

At this point, Jean Jacques spoke up asking why they didn't consider Switzerland as with their wealth, they would be safer here than anywhere. Mike said he was open to that but it would really depend on Helen who might want any children to be French.

"If you are not Swiss, can you buy property here?" Helen asked.

"As you have a business here, I think you could get permission quite easily. I know a good lawyer if you are interested."

"Let me think about it for a while."

Helen then looked at Mike for his reaction and he indicated that he was easy about anywhere in western Europe so it was her choice and pointed out that where he was looking was easy to get to Zurich from; besides, he secretly liked the idea of his children calling him papa but he didn't mention that, just thought it.

176

"Can we leave now and then you can show me the area you were looking at this morning?"

"OK, no problem as I can hand the car back in Paris in the morning. I left the timing open just in case something turned up."

After a quick tour of the area, Helen decided she liked it a lot especially with the mountains in the background.

"Those mountains are called the Jura mountains but that apart, Grenoble is not far south from the area as well."

"What's so important about Grenoble?"

"It's where the Huguenots gather each year for something or other, not sure what, but my grandmother was from a Huguenot family and they had to get out of France because they were protestants and I thought one day I might look to see if there were any descendants in the area."

"There won't be if they had to get out, I wouldn't think."

"Well, some might have changed their religion."

"What would you?"

"Definitely, as there is hardly any difference between Protestantism and Catholicism after all they were once one and the same until a German nut case decided to nail his objections to the cathedral door just as the Dutch scholar Erasmus was about to publish reforms. So we have a hot headed bastard to blame for all the chaos that followed and the biggest joke is nobody has the slightest proof that God even exists apart from a few schizophrenics."

"You are just being controversial for the hell of it."

"Am I; just think about it, most of the religions are very similar with one God and then only variations on the different services. I had one Jewish chap tell me that he was not supposed to go into a Christian church even for a funeral to which I replied that if he thought that the creator of the universe in all its vastness really gave a shit which building he was in he was over estimating his importance."

"What did he say to that?"

"Nothing, we just changed the subject and carried on to the funeral."

"However, you can believe whatever you want and bring the children up as a good catholic if that is your desire."

"And you won't interfere?"

"Not until they're adults and then only if they ask my opinion…well, I might be wrong."

Helen laughed. "I still can't get over you becoming all domesticated," she said.

"I never wanted to settle down until I met you but then I knew fairly early on. It's not just your looks or the sex it's when I look at you I see a whole new world and feel that I am looking at someone special to me and for me. It's like an aura that surrounds you and although it's unusual it is somehow comforting and now we are getting married the search for the last piece of the jigsaw is over."

"I feel the same way but just didn't know how to say it but if I ever catch you eyeing up another woman, you had better hold on to your balls."

"That's enough sloppy stuff for now, let's concentrate on finding a home."

A few minutes later, they pulled into the underground carpark and caught the lift to their apartment. As they settled down to relax and watch some television, Mike suddenly remembered that he never phoned Lisa and just then the phone rang. It was Lisa.

"I have to apologise, Lisa, I got caught up in something and then driving back to Paris I forgot to phone you; awfully sorry."

Chapter 28

"We have been offered a job by you know who and it's a rather big 7 figures but I'm not sure you are going to like it and I can't talk over the phone. Are you in Paris tomorrow?"

"Yes I am; do you want to call to the apartment?"

"OK, when I book the flight, can you pick me up?"

"No problem; let me know your arrival time."

An hour later the phone rang again and it was Lisa advising that she would land at 9:30 am so she suggested getting there at 10 am. That suited Mike who liked a lie-in.

The next morning, Mike got delayed with the traffic and it was 10:45 as he pulled into the pick-up place only to see Lisa standing there with a small case over her shoulder, looking very business-like. As she climbed in, she said her return flight was at 6 pm but she thought he would need to discuss the job in front of Helen because it was in Russia.

Back at the apartment, all three of them sat at the dining table and Lisa explained that the job was to stop the assassination of Mikhail Gorbachev by a group of Russian politicians who intended to replace him with their own candidate.

"First question: why don't the security services warn him so he can protect himself?" asks Mike.

"That was my first question but the only reason they know is through the network of bugs and moles they have inside the various different special agencies and they cannot put these contacts in danger so it has to be stopped without British or American agencies being involved."

"Let's say we stop it and it then becomes apparent; are the authorities not going to think it was the western diplomats anyway?"

"That's where it gets interesting," Lisa replied with a wry smile.

"It will need to be a good plan with a good escape plot tagged on"

"Well, it's quite clever actually in that first of all, we remove all tags from our clothing so nothing advertises that it is not Russian, we use only Russian weapons and we are dropped in by helicopter just over the border where we are joined by two men so there will be 5 of us against 6 or 7 assassins. We let the assassins attack the convoy and kill the bodyguards and the secret service people and then we attack just when they believe they are about to succeed and we don't have to worry about getting shot by Gorbachev's men as most if not all are dead.

"Oh and all orders are shouted in Russian by me and I will teach you a few words that you can shout back. Any bystanders will think that some secret Russian unit came to the rescue and we then leave the scene. We go to where the British/Americans have parked a large truck containing 3 motorbikes which is enough for the 5 of us but we don't use them unless we have to. If there are roadblocks ahead, the driver will turn on a red light and we start up the bikes and get ready to leave down the ramp at the back.

"If we have to use the bikes, we continue west until we reach a forest when we turn north which will not be expected if they think we are foreigners as it's heading deep into USSR but we stop at a lake just before the village of Ostrov where we put the bikes in the lake but only after the helicopter arrives and lands and then we are off to Sweden and make our way to Stockholm from where we go our separate ways."

"Sounds good though all plans can go wrong, but I like it so I'm in. The helicopter is flying in over USSR; will that be a problem?"

"No, the pilot speaks fluent Russian and the Baltic states are not great lovers of Russia anyway."

"OK that was my last query."

"Are you not going to talk it through with Helen?"

"No she would be horrified but I will make sure she inherits my business should I get killed. In fact I will phone my solicitor now."

"Are you becoming an adrenalin junkie?"

"No, in two years I will be 50 and I will pack it in then if not sooner maybe in one year; you will have to hire someone to take my place so you had better start lining someone up."

"Right, I will tell our principals that it is on and they must ensure that the British/Americans organise the wagon with the motorbikes as they will almost certainly be needed. As the attack on Gorbachev is planned for next Friday, we will be leaving for Russia on Monday," Lisa announced while putting her papers away in her shoulder bag.

"I will take you to lunch and then to the airport."

"Great, I'm famished."

That evening, he told Helen they had another job and he would be away for a week starting Monday as it required a lot of planning. Helen didn't ask many questions as she was wrapped up in the wedding plans. Mike felt he should have turned the job down but that would have stopped any further offers so after this he will impress upon Lisa the need for her to find a replacement.

Mike spent the rest of the week checking up on all the different companies to ensure that they had everything they needed but gave no indication of his plans to anyone. On Monday, Mike picked up Lisa and Harry while Helen reported to the Gendarmerie as all hands were needed to cope with some incident to do with a horrific accident.

The outward journey had been switched to the British airport at Monchengladbach from where they would take a helicopter up to Denmark and across to Sweden; from there, the really dangerous part started in that they had to fly over one of the Baltic states but there was a kind of understanding in that these states were not over-keen on the USSR and looked forward to breaking away. It was up to the pilot to decide which route and in the event, he opted for Latvia.

Over Latvia, they were challenged but in his immaculate Russian the pilot explained that they had been looking for unauthorised boats approaching the coast line but nothing found so heading back to base. Lisa explained on the way back he will say he had been called out again.

The pilot announced 5 minutes to touch down so they all got tensed up in anticipation of trouble but they landed quickly and disembarked at double speed and the helicopter was back in the air and away. They walked north to the edge of the field and saw some lights being flashed at them so hopefully all OK and then some friendly voices speaking in broken English but absolutely welcome to their ears.

One of the men, a tall slim man of 35 years approximately, with a broad smile setting off a handsome strong face, spoke first: "We are going to my house to rest until morning. If we travel at night, we are likely to get stopped as less traffic."

They put their cases in the boot and piled in but the tall handsome chap insisted Lisa get in the front with him as it looked more normal with a woman visible.

Mike could feel the sense of intrusion into one's private life already after just a few minutes as it was obvious that this was not going to be an easy job. Perhaps in the city with more people around, it will be easier, he thought.

In the morning over breakfast, all five got to know each other and discussed the broad principals of their plan. The tall handsome chap was called Alexei and the other smaller but stockily strong chap was Dimitri who was also quite handsome and very friendly, especially to Lisa who played along.

They headed off for Moscow where they would book into a large hotel but not together. They suggested that the two of them will book in first and it would be natural for Mike, Lisa and Harry to book in together as: "…you are business people meeting some Russians to discuss business opportunities and the people you are meeting is us, of course," said Alexei with a grin.

"If you wait 30 minutes after us then we will time it to come down just as you are booking in and express our delight at your safe arrival and agree to meet for coffee after you have put your cases in your rooms. We make just enough fuss of you to get noticed and establish why you are here."

On the way with Lisa in the front to create a family image, they trundled along at an absolute maximum speed of 45 miles per hour due mainly to the state of the roads but Mike was not sure that the vehicle could go any faster anyway. The abject poverty of the people was very obvious; all dressed with no attention to care and heads bowed as if weighed down with heavy bouts of depression. Mike made a comment about depression and Alexei answered: "There is a lot of depression as most of the people have nothing and spend their time trying to earn enough to keep food on the table. There are hardly any luxuries outside of city life. The country people are forgotten as they don't count and they haven't got the ability to do anything about their plight."

"What about Gorbachev; is he doing anything to correct matters?"

"Well, he is talking about opening up the country but that is why we are called in to save him as some politicians want him gone."

"I see it all makes sense now so we need to have a good look at where the attack is going to take place so we come up with the right strategy."

They made their way through the city's broad streets to within a mile of their hotel where Mike Lisa and Harry disembarked with their luggage and strolled in the general direction of the hotel and looking in shops along the way they managed to waste the 30 minutes before arriving at the front entrance. As they were booking in, Mike heard Alexei's voice calling to him and turned around with great relief that they had all met up.

"Welcome Mr Black," said Alexei and looked inquiringly for the further introductions which Mike duly made with lots of laughter and cross chatter creating a general cacophony of noise before they retired to their rooms having agreed to meet for coffee as soon as the baggage was dumped.

Alexei and Dimitri had found a quiet corner to cater for the five of them but the conversation was kept to just general remarks and touristy type observations because, as is quite often the case, foreigners are distrusted and therefore bugged everywhere they go.

Alexei did make one comment about the plans for tomorrow in that he would take Lisa and Harry to visit the general area of the factory while Dimitri would take Mike to the site as he has wellington boots in the van as the site is very muddy especially after all this rain.

Alexei then announced that he had booked a table for 5 at a nearby restaurant and they should make their way there now and as it was close by, they could walk. Once outside, Alexei said: "This evening we don't talk business; this evening is for fun and drinking; tomorrow is for business." They all understood that nowhere around this area was safe.

The next morning after breakfast, they set off to a desolate place to check the weapons which were found to be in excellent condition.

"Where are we storing the weapons?" asked Mike.

"Here, watch this," said Dimitri who pressed something on an old rusty machine and a part of the wooden partition opened to reveal a storage area.

"Fantastic," said Lisa.

"Now let's go and look at the battle ground as I am anxious to examine the options so we have every angle covered," added Mike who never relaxed until a plan had been formed and agreed upon.

After storing the weapons, they made their way back to the city centre and parked up close to the attack area. On walking around, Mike realised that the plans he had seen were not accurate as on one side, the buildings had long gone and the area was open. So the assassins were going to attack from one side only but would use three wagons or possibly four to box the convoy in. Then he realised that the wagons would be in place from the outset with men dressed as workmen in attendance. So they would attack from both sides. This made matters more difficult but at least he knew what their plan must be and hellish clever it was too. He explained all this to everyone and the two Russians were impressed at his deductions and Alexei said to Lisa: "So that's why he does the planning but what to do now?"

Mike continued: "What happens is Harry stays back so he can see both sides of the convoy and the one that doesn't open its rear doors is the one the president is in. The secret service will jump out to retaliate not realising they are being attacked from both sides so they will get shot. Harry will be watching for anyone approaching the president's vehicle and take him out.

"Once the initial onslaught has commenced and the group starts to approach the president's vehicle with intent to place a bomb on it or underneath it, we will move in. At this point Harry will watch for those carrying anything that could be a bomb and ensure they never make it to the vehicle. We approach two on each side and if there are a lot more on one side than on the other then one of us switches sides as we get closer. At this point we have the advantage of surprise and should get them all or most of them. Afterwards, we disappear as fast as possible and remember, any orders shouted are to be in Russian."

They all nodded agreement and thought the plan was a good one.

Dimitri asked if Harry can really take a man out long distance and Mike reassured him yes he could as he was an experienced sniper.

They spent 2 tense days going over and over the methodology until it was automatic in all their minds.

Finally, after what seemed an eternity, Friday arrived and they were ready from very early on; too early actually but being late was not an option. The convoy was due to arrive at the attack site at 10:25 local time. They were there from 8 am as had to make sure they were there before the assassins arrived and well concealed. Harry was positioned up high and to one side so he could see around the front lorry in case it was a high sided one.

At 9 am, two high-sided lorries arrived and parked up on the open side of the road. There seemed to be 4 men in workmen's overalls checking that they were in the correct position and then they climbed into the backs of their vehicles to await the convoy. At 10.25 am, a lorry—fortunately, a flatback—came down the road just in front of the convoy and when it passed the two parked vehicles it slammed on its brakes skidding sideways to block the convoy's path. Just then, another flatback lorry arrived behind the convoy. All of this must have caused panic in the secret servicemen's minds as they suddenly realised they were in trouble.

The motorbike police were the first to be shot then the doors of the vehicles opened and the attachment of men jumped out and skidded underneath the vehicles as they had very quickly realised that there was no other cover to be had but it was going to be a one-sided fight as one after the other was killed in a hail of bullets.

Meanwhile, Harry had taken out two of the men from the side lorries. The assassins now started to advance on the little opposition that remained, the two who had taken up positions underneath behind the wheels of their vehicles were soon disposed of, which was the moment Mike, Lisa and the two Russians ran forward killing 4 instantly while Harry got the fifth who was carrying a bomb of some description leaving just one who decided to bolt.

Lisa shouted some orders in Russian which brought the fighting to an end and then they quickly—amid more shouting—left the scene. It would have been obvious to Gorbachev's bodyguard that they were saved by the second group of fighters but Mike, Lisa et al were not hanging around to be congratulated. They quickly dispersed and made their way to where the rescue wagon was positioned and were very glad to see it was there.

Mike approached the wagon and knocked on the cab door but got no answer so pulled the handle to open the door and saw immediately that the driver had been shot dead as there was a lot of blood and he was slumped over the wheel. Mike turned and asked Dimitri who was by him if he could drive the wagon and his no problem answer was a relief. Mike moved the body to the floor of the cab in front of the passenger seat.

"There is something seriously wrong here but for the moment, we have to get out of here so we carry on as planned but the minute we get to the forest stop then we switch to the bikes. I have an awful feeling that we have been set up," Mike ordered.

The wagon carried on and as soon as it turned North, they knew they would reach the forest without mishap and sure enough, Dimitri was braking and pulling the vehicle to a halt. Dimitri went around to the back and opened it up with a big smile.

Mike helped pull out the rear ledge to enable the bikes to be driven off. They locked the wagon and turned south the opposite of what was agreed just in case there was an ambush waiting on the agreed route.

After half an hour, they stopped to decide what to do and to check the side bags on the bikes which were supplied by the British so it may have had survival kits installed. The main items were two tents and some basic food like biscuits and tinned meats. They had a discussion as to the best way back which all agreed was going to be by boat to neutral Sweden or to Denmark but their choice of destination would depend on the type of boat they could beg steal or borrow.

They decided to turn north again but on a different route and head for Latvia which had the narrowest landmass between Russia and the Baltic sea so they could get a boat somehow and the advantage was that anyone trying to guess where they were would have worked out that they had gone south whereas they were north again. This gave the extra option of seeing if the helicopter turns up or not. After 4 hours, they arrived at the original agreed rescue destination and hid in some nearby covering from a small crop of trees.

At the expected time, the helicopter arrived and slowly descended into the field; the door was opened and a couple of men were waving. Mike agreed he would approach and if he discovered on route that something was wrong, he would dive down flat and the group was to take them out and try and get the pilot. Mike referred this last remark to Harry. As Mike approached, he watched the men in the helicopter very closely and once within earshot, shouted to them: "Where have you come from? You are late."

"Sorry about the late. We come from Germany."

With that, Mike dived and lay flat. Immediately, all hell broke loose with his four companions rushing forward as they fired and Harry in the lead running wide to get an angle on the pilot which he did with such speed and accuracy that the pilot did not even begin to commence lift off and it was all over. Lisa had had helicopter training some years earlier but not on this particular model but she took command and ordered the removal of the bodies while she familiarised herself with the controls. They all got aboard to be told to strap themselves in as it would be an erratic take-off and they all had better pray they didn't crash.

In the event, they arose in a spinning motion, sliding up then down and all the time plenty of fucks and shits and you fucking bastard and then oh right and the trajectory stabilised gradually as Lisa got the measure of the controls and then her training kicked in and they headed off in the correct direction and gained height out of harm's way they hoped. They headed west over Latvia still under USSR control but the quickest route to the Baltic Sea and Sweden. Once they reached neutral or non- aligned Sweden they would turn south along the east coast of Denmark and into Germany and make their way hopefully to Monchengladbach British airfield. Halfway across the Baltic sea, they were fired on by a much faster fighter plane.

Lisa shouted to Harry: "Get ready at port door, Harry!"

And then generally: "Whoever is closest, get ready to open the doors on my command! Harry, I'm going to dip to allow them to close up on us and then I will rise up to level with their flight path the doors will open and then you must try and get the pilot as they roar past. We will only get one shot at this so if you miss, get the fuel tank, or we are dead."

Lisa dipped the helicopter and back up again almost immediately, she ordered the doors open and Harry shot not once but twice. He got the pilot and the fuel tank and they all had the satisfaction of watching the plane dive with smoke billowing and laughed out loud with the sheer relief of being off the hook once more.

"Hopefully, we are safe now," said Mike who realised he was sweating. "You two are geniuses to have pulled that off," addressing both Harry and Lisa.

Just as they arrived over Germany, Lisa spotted planes on the starboard horizon and warned Mike with: "I bet it's the bloody Americans unless I am mistaken."

Mike pointed out some trees below, a kind of mini forest and there was a road going through it and suggested they see if they can hide there but added: "When we land, get out and close the doors after you so it looks like we are still in it and run a 100 yards away because if they see it, they will bomb it."

They dropped down and hid the helicopter as best they could but it was still visible if they looked hard enough which they did and after several attempts blew it to pieces.

Mike, Lisa, Harry and the two Russians walked south overnight and in the morning hit a town where they caught a bus to Frankfurt and from there, Mike and Lisa went to Dulmen, the American Airbase just north of Monchengladbach. This was the base involved in the plan to stop the assassination while Harry and the two Russians went to the British base of Monchengladbach. Their plan was to visit the places where the airbase troops relaxed and listen to the gossip and see if they could pick up any unusual information particularly after too much drink had been taken.

After a week, Harry phoned Mike to say he had heard an interesting piece of gossip about an American Colonel Max Collins who visited the British base and was overheard having a serious argument about an operation in Moscow with Major Phillips and saying, "For Christ's sake, man, there is always collateral damage in these operations; just get over it."

Major Phillips replied to the effect that they were just sacrificial lambs to him and then said he would be reporting it but Colonel Collins said, "If you do, I will have your career." It seems Collins didn't care who heard him according to the soldier telling the tale.

Mike informed Harry that he had heard some gossip about Collins but nothing tying him to Moscow but now with this information, he had the proof they needed.

"I'll tell Lisa the news but first I will have to arrange somewhere to stay and we can't book into a hotel as we would have to show our passports which would alert Collins. I'll phone you back shortly."

Mike phoned Peter and explained the whole business to him and he immediately said: "Of course and I know someone who can get false papers. How many did you say, five of you?"

"Thanks Peter, false papers would be excellent."

Mike phoned Harry and told them to head for Peter's house in Frankfurt as they will be staying there for the moment. He then phoned Helen and explained the delay without saying anything further but suggested that she stay in Zurich for the time being and he would explain all in a few days. She asked if he was OK and then agreed she would stay there until he got in touch.

Mike and Lisa headed to the local bank and it was agreed between them that the less well known was Lisa so she would get the cash but he had better be with her as there will be questions like why do you need so much cash. Lisa was right; the teller asked a lot of questions and even called another man to approve the withdrawal but eventually, it was agreed.

Mike and Lisa stopped at a public phone box and Mike phoned Major Phillips and told him what he knew and particularly that it was a deliberate strategy by the Americans to allow them to be caught and when they escaped, they tried to get them killed.

"You can inform Colonel Collins that the one whose career is going to finish is not yours but his and tell him that he has picked a fight with his worst nightmare. They tried four times to kill us and failed even with vastly superior arms. Tell him to imagine the shame that is going to befall him and even worse the ridicule for failing in his shameful scheme even with all the power he possessed."

When he put the phone down, Lisa was full of admiration for the message. *If he sends it, he may kill himself,* she said.

"I hope so otherwise we will have to do it as we cannot leave it or he will get us eventually."

"What about the media?" asked Lisa.

"In normal times, I would agree but at the moment the newspapers would balk at showing up the army. We shall see what happens but I could try it before we do anything."

On arrival in Frankfurt, they took a taxi to Peter's house and Claudia came out to welcome them with her usual charm and elegance. Mike still could not help himself from studying her to try and find out the secret of her graceful and confident demeaner. She was tall but not too tall, she was slim but not too slim, she was good looking without being glamorous, her gestures were elegant but not exaggerated, her smile was reflected in her eyes and when she welcomed you, she meant it.

Suddenly, the penny dropped that she was genuine and accepted her visitor for the person he appeared to be and simply concentrated on making him feel relaxed and at home thus she had no self-awareness which made here breeze through every eventuality and made her the person everyone wanted to be like. Mike was pleased with himself for having worked it out and having done so it made him like Claudia even more, if that were possible.

Peter got home early that afternoon and was his usual welcoming self but nevertheless, Mike apologised and explained why they couldn't risk booking into a hotel until the American Colonel was sorted as otherwise he was likely to send a hit squad around.

They all very soon relaxed such was the warmth of their hosts reception and the lavish supply of drink followed by a wonderful dinner the likes of which they had not had for a while.

After dinner, they retired to the lounge where relaxation was assured by the sumptuous quality of the furniture. Mike sunk into one of the many armchairs and immediately felt like he was falling asleep but was brought back to reality when Claudia came dashing in asking for the name of the American Colonel we were talking about earlier. Mike said, "Colonel Collins; why?"

"Well, he has been on the news or rather, he was mentioned on the news as he shot himself this afternoon."

Lisa, Harry and the two Russians cheered with big smiles of relief and Mike said: "If he had not been such a bastard, we could have done a gentleman's agreement with him but such was his nature, one would have to be mad to agree anything with him."

"Now you don't have to worry." said Claudia.

"Well, let's just wait and see what comes out in the wash when the conjecture over why he shot himself starts," added Peter.

"It will be hushed up as they will not want an enquiry. It will be put down to ill health," said Mike.

"Tomorrow, we can be out of your hair," said Lisa raising her glass.

"It's been lovely having you here and hearing your hair-raising escapades but you all need to take extra care from now on, especially when getting involved with government departments as they seem to have no qualms about dropping people in the mire," said Claudia.

The next day, they all went their own ways or rather, Mike went to Zurich and the rest went to Northern Ireland. Lisa said she would send the bill for £2m to her contact for payment and he would no doubt let her know how it was to be broken up.

Chapter 29

On arrival in Zurich, Mike saw Helen waving at the end of the platform and smiled broadly at the sight of his lovely wife to be. He walked up to her and embraced her there as if he hadn't seen her for years and said: "This time, the mission was really hairy and has altered our opinion in that we will not be working with the Americans or anything they have a finger in again. I will tell you all later but hell, it's lovely to see you and especially lovely to smell your perfume. What have you been up to?"

"I've been thinking; and you know how dangerous that is but what about buying a house in Switzerland and there are so many rich people that we won't stand out. We will be able to lead a fairly normal life whereas in France the minute you start with protections and walls everywhere it creates a stir and I have been looking at some in areas where we can buy with Jean Jacques' help of course as he really does know his way around the property market. Are you agreeable?"

"Yes in a word, it has crossed my mind the same way you have been thinking in that we have to blend in otherwise life could be very difficult. Have you got some properties to show me?"

Helen grabbed his arm tightly and snuggled up to him, smiling with big doe eyes so he knew that he would be agreeing to something much more than he had anticipated but then again he thought that should have been obvious from the beginning. As they walked to the hotel, Helen explained that she had earmarked three properties for him to look at tomorrow if that was OK. He agreed.

The third property was the one that appealed to both of them instantly. A fine well-designed double-fronted property in its own grounds with 11 windows on the upper floor spread evenly across the front and on the ground floor a large entrance door with pillars approached by a staircase of broad Italian marble steps. The lot encased in a high brick wall which enclosed the 5 acres of land comprising of a well laid out garden with a wooded area at the rear. The front entrance gates opened on to a sweeping driveway which arrived at the house on the left side and exited on the right back on to the same driveway so just one entrance to control. They decided straight away to go for it.

Their offer was accepted which pleased Mike as the matter was concluded and over with quickly, which suited his attitude. Helen did voice one worry in that if they have a family, she would have preferred the children to be French rather than Swiss, not that she had anything against the Swiss; just being French, she felt awkward a feeling of betraying her heritage. Mike assured her there was no need to worry on that score because he was keeping the apartment in Paris and in the latter stage of any pregnancy, she could transfer to the apartment to ensure any child was born in France. This resolved the matter and removed any guilt she had but then asked him how he felt about his children's nationality but this he dismissed with the response that he was European so any child of his that was French was just fine.

The day of the wedding soon arrived and Helen had it organised perfectly. They had decided to have it in Paris and the hotel that Helen picked, the Hotel Lyonnaise, was just perfect and accommodated the 100 odd guests easily. It was a lovely sunny day so the splendid gardens were just a lovely additional space to escape to for a quick break from it all not that Mike felt the need but some of the guests did. Mike had invited around 40 guests and Helen about 60. On both sides, the guests were a mixture of family and colleagues. Mike had informed his colleagues that they should put the expense of staying over in Paris for the weekend on their expenses and all hotel bills plus meals out could be included but added, tongue in cheek, that presents for friends at home would be at their own expense.

Peter was delighted to be asked to be best man and Mike did toy with the idea of asking his brother but decided that as he and his brother had not kept in touch, it would be unfair but instead ensured that his family stayed in the apartment with him and Helen and then would move to the house in Switzerland after the weekend where they could all get to know each other all over again and hopefully stay in touch. Mike knew that the fault for the drift was his preoccupation with success in business.

Mike's mother just forgave him and was delighted at his success and was determined just to enjoy the whole holiday and that, Mike thought, was extremely generous of her as he did not really deserve to be forgiven so easily. Life in the apartment was extremely hectic with seven close family members from Mike's side all living together but they managed and of course, Mike had to get out on the day before the wedding and he moved into the hotel with Peter and Claudia.

The secular wedding took place as expected and was beautiful with the music being supplied by a trio of musicians comprising a violinist, a cellist and a harpist with one of the pieces being the very moving Swan by Camille Saint Saens. The cellist seemed to make it soar to the heavens with a strong emotional sweeping movement and then fall back with a sigh. Mike could feel his Adam's apple working overtime to prevent even the slightest tear from escaping. Helen could see the struggle and it made her smile. She turned when you may kiss the bride was said and as he kissed her, she whispered in his ear, "The nightmare is over now."

"Does it show?"

"Only to me."

Mike found himself turning around to walk back down the aisle without really being aware of anything like in some sort of trance but awake enough to smile and nod as they went.

The hotel had arranged it so the reception section was right next to the wedding area so Mike and Helen were soon in the open doorway making welcoming gestures and comments to their guests as they wandered in to be seated by the staff. Soon Mike and Helen were encouraged to take their places at the top table which was a great relief. Both Mike and Helen took a quick drink of the wine that had been poured which calmed them down somewhat.

The meal was absolutely marvellous and of top quality. It was really appreciated as all the plates were clean when they were being recovered.

The speeches were started by the father of the bride and Helen leaned over to Mike and said: "I have warned him not to make any sexist or racist remarks."

"He will be hard pushed to get a laugh then."

With that comment, Helen punched him on the shoulder which made him indulge in mock pain. Helen's father picked on this immediately saying: "The fighting has started already then, this must be a record."

He then went on to make a good speech with a few laughs in spite of the restrictions.

It was Mike's turn and he first of all declared how happy he was that she accepted his proposal but it had been a bit of a rocky path and he explained their first interchange when she came to interview him about a certain incident accompanied by the Commissaire and she was introduced as La Lieutenante and that was how for weeks he referred to her—La Lieutenante.

Mike continued: "But towards the end of the interview when referring to something that suddenly went away, La Lieutenant asked how I explained that and my reply was the luck of the Irish. This so inflamed her she dropped her pen and it rolled behind her chair so she had to get up and bend over to pick it up thus presenting her bottom to me. The Commissaire was watching me so I turned to him and said the luck of the Irish and with that he burst out laughing. La Lieutenant was not amused and labelled us both stupid men as she left. It was then I was captured. And from there, it took ages to progress to the next step but it was worth it as before Helen, I always thought that I was a confirmed bachelor."

Then the usual compliments to the bridesmaids and he was able to relax properly.

Peter's speech was amazing and built Mike as some kind of hero but was also very quick to include Lisa and Harry without whom it would not have happened and then went on to explain how they became close friends over time. He of course left out the shootings.

After a few more speeches, they all moved to an adjoining room where a band was playing popular music and there was dancing. This also allowed the married couple to mingle with their friends and relations and be introduced to those they didn't know.

At about 1 am, Mike and Helen took their leave and retired to their suite in the hotel having promised to see everyone in the morning. They were not going on honeymoon until later when they would make a calm decision on where they would like to go.

In the morning, Mike and Helen had their breakfast interrupted by friends and colleagues saying their goodbyes and were just about to leave when Mike's family arrived all looking slightly worse for wear. After they had gotten themselves sorted, the conversation turned to what they would like to do that day. It was eventually decided that a boat trip along the Seine would be the best option. Mike left Helen chatting to them and retired to see what he could get. He tried the hotel reception first who were very happy to make arrangements for him; about 30 minutes later, they came into the breakfast area to give Mike the options available and he chose the one where they had the boat to themselves and it stopped along the way for lunch which could last for as long as they needed, and afterwards returned to base for about 5 pm, all depending on how long they took for lunch. Mike thought that sounded great—a nice lazy day sightseeing and being looked after—and everyone agreed.

At about 10 am, the hotel provided two limousines to take them to the embarkment area for their trip. The boat was already there and the staff were extremely helpful and Mike immediately compared this boat to the others passing by and could see that it was a superior craft. It had two areas for its passengers in that one could elect to stay out, open to the elements, or go inside a glass roofed area for drinks or simply to escape the heat as it was air conditioned. Mike knew that this boat was worth the money he was paying and was therefore happy to relax and enjoy the day.

As they made their way, the lady giving the tour spoke good English but with a strong French accent which tickled the ears of everyone listening and added a certain "Je ne sais quoi" to the pleasure. At about 1 pm, they arrived at the spot where they would leave the boat for lunch and again the tour guide led them pleasantly to the best, if the only, inn in the tiny village, more of a hamlet really, where they were welcomed by very friendly staff who fussed over everyone, making them feel special which is a lovely gift.

The food was simple country cuisine but beautiful and washed down, in Mike's case, with a red wine that was simply superb. Those who chose white were equally impressed. The hamlet consisted of one mini market which included the ubiquitous bakery for fresh rolls in the morning and a store with open sided workshop where they made saddles and sold some locally together with all kinds of livery but the tour guide lady emphasised they sold to many businesses around France as their workmanship was so appreciated.

They walked past a village area of hardened sand where a few old men were playing boules watched by even older men smoking their pipes in between their incisive remarks as to the acuteness or idiocy of the current player. As they continued back to the boat, some passing locals stared the way country folk do and Mike felt as if he had just walked through a time capsule; beautiful, precious and of historic value which should be preserved for eternity but would he want to live in this capsule. Definitely not, not with his mind knowing all the alternatives available but perhaps yes if he had been born into it and knew nothing of the outside world then maybe one is blessed with a relaxed contentment. He felt a shudder come over him and decided to snap out of it and engage with those around him.

The way back in the luxury boat was like the way up with beautiful scenery and outside the odd sound of birds and the faint chatter of humans mainly excited children and as one got nearer to the city the murmur increased to a level where one cut off and no longer noticed it but one heard the sounds one was supposed to hear like, mind the step, do take care and make your way to the cars please. Once inside the vehicle, the silence hit you again and you broke it by talking. Everything back to normal. The family absolutely adored the afternoon and felt apart from the beauty of the trip, that it was rejuvenating.

On the way back to the apartment, Helen dived into the local bakery to get some bread and a selection of cheeses in case anyone needed to top up later on in the evening.

Once ensconced comfortably in the lounge with the large French doors open to air the room and keep it cool, Mike explained that tomorrow he was taking them to his home in Switzerland and they would travel by train but in first class and with lunch so it should be a very pleasant journey.

"On arrival in Zurich, two of our cars will be there to take us on the final leg. I don't have a chauffeur but two of the staff have kindly offered to drive. I was asking them to order two taxis but instead they volunteered to drive which is nice of them so how could I refuse."

On leaving the station at Zurich Mike went ahead to see where the cars were likely to be parked and found them instantly as they were quite close on the right hand side so Mike corralled his troupe to the required positions and the staff jumped out to assist with the luggage. Mike introduced them immediately: "This is Juliette and this handsome chap is Simon," Then with handshakes all around, they were soon off weaving their way through the busy traffic and out into the quieter plush areas until they eventually turned off the main road and up a 200 meter drive with open field on the left and a heavy growth of bushes and trees on the right which obscured the house until the last minute when it opened out into a wide gravel frontage to the house.

"It's a mansion," said Mike's mother but Mike assured her that it was small compared to some in the area but that he was more than happy with it.

The staff had laid on afternoon tea with cakes so they were all glad to settle down after the long journey and relax and it was this time that Mike expressed his regret at not keeping in touch properly over the years and now intended to make it up to everyone the only way he could and went on to explain that because he concentrated on work all these years he had been lucky to have found a winning formula and indeed was very wealthy and so he added, pausing slightly: "I have here 4 envelopes one for each of my siblings and one for my mother which contains cheques (pre-paid cheques). They are all for the same amount which is approximately half a million pounds and I would like you all to use it to make life easier. In addition, I would like you all to help Mum find a house, flat or bungalow that she likes and I will pay for it. I will buy it in the company name so when Mum is finished with it, I will sell it and depending on the circumstances prevailing at the time, will divide it between you."

All their mouths were open and they obviously were not expecting this so he continued: "I know this does not make up for my self-centred and selfish behaviour over the years but that I cannot fix so the chance to help each one of you in this way is my only option. I hope you will accept it and not think I am just big-headed."

"Can you afford this?" asked his older sister, Harriet.

"Yes, and very easily. My present worth is around £200 million pounds of which 10% is in cash but I do not try to live up to that and until I met Helen, I lived like a business man who was comfortable and had an expense account but not particularly wealthy. I didn't and still don't feel the need to announce my wealth by extravagant living, this week being an exception. If anyone local makes a comment about my large house, I will make out that I had saved over the years and still needed a large mortgage so I am going to have to be careful for a long time but hey you only live once so in for a penny in for a pound. You know, I'll take a leaf from the way Irish farmers talk."

"Who were the two from Northern Ireland? She looked hard," Harriet asked, furrowing her eyebrows.

"Lisa, you mean?"

Mike was about to go on but got interrupted by Helen: "She is hard from all accounts but if she likes you she has a heart of gold according to Harry. Now would anyone like some fresh rolls or bread with a cheese board and Wine or Beer. And then we can discuss where we are going tomorrow. It's important that we give you a lovely and happy time."

Mike was glad of the interruption and also he was beginning to feel a tad hungry which is strange bearing in mind how much he ate at lunch on the train.

As the maids brought in the cheese and fresh bread cut into large chunks which always makes it look more appetising, everyone tucked in and after some alcohol was consumed Mike's siblings were able to thank him profusely without feeling embarrassed and when Mike looked at his Mum, she seemed to have warmed to the point of feeling proud of him. Mike relaxed and started to feel as if he had undone some if not most of the harm he had done over the years.

Helen watched, fascinated at the way Mike—whose self-protecting guard had been lowered—was changing into this ordinary relaxed bloke and although she was delighted to see this new man, she knew the barriers would be up again tomorrow although Mike being Mike, he would try to disguise it. However, he did stay relaxed until the end of the week and they were all saying their goodbyes and promising not to leave it so long again before meeting up.

Chapter 30

The year was 2008 and the financial crisis which started in 2007 was now in full swing and was having an effect on Mike's businesses excluding the Northern Ireland operation with Lisa, Harry and the two Russians that was carrying on as normal but now Mike at 68 still did the planning but did not accompany them on their foreign ventures. Although to be fair, these are generally smaller, simple events but Mike now felt that as the father of 3 children, he had a duty to stay alive as long as possible.

Mike's main concern now was to first of all visit the London office to discuss the problems caused by the financial crisis in that insurance brokers were finding that their income was falling due to severe competition as the insurers fought to attract more business their way which had the inevitable result in reducing premiums very welcome to the public but the reduced commissions from these lower premiums was of great concern to brokers who had to consider how to combat the trend.

On his visit to London, Mike took his daughter Celia, who at 19 was showing interest in the business, so he felt she might as well sit in and see what it was like. On arrival in London, Mike took the underground to Bank station and from there the two of them walked towards Fenchurch Street in the heart of the city. At 68 years of age, Mike looked at least 19 years younger and had a strong stride so that his daughter had to ask him to slow down every so often. As they entered Mike's office, which now occupied most of the tower block, he approached the reception area and was immediately recognised and greeted cheerfully by the middle-aged lady in charge and mentioned that the board had assembled and were awaiting his arrival.

Mike thanked her and said: "I had better not keep them waiting then," and made his way to the lift.

Having hung up their overcoats, they proceeded to the boardroom and Mike opened the door, entered first, turned to face Celia and then back again to the assembled members and said: "Gentlemen, this is my daughter Celia who has expressed an interest in becoming a broker and what better time to start than in the middle of a financial crisis!"

At that all the men immediately stood and greeted Celia and one pulled back a chair adjacent to where her father would sit, which she accepted with an open smile.

Mike sat and looked around the table and beamed, saying: "I see there are only a few older ones left now and the rest of you all look very dynamic and ready for the fight so have you come up with any ideas on how to stop the downward trend?"

Freddie, who was now 78 years old and still enjoying his extended work life, summarised their options by saying: "We only have to make up 10% to come out level pegging so we feel we should do more cross selling particularly on new lines of business such as directors and officers liability policies, legal expenses and various add-on policies like business travel and group personal accident."

"I agree with everything you have said but would add a few thoughts of my own. We keep half the commission from a case that comes through a provincial broker which is more and more these days but in addition we must start charging an admin fee of say £100 on each case and point out there is no commission on this figure. In addition, we need to start going around the market on some cases to see if it can be bettered and as we issue the documents on some of these ourselves we can increase the premium the insurer wants while still showing a reduction to the insured but we have built in an extra charge."

"Is that legal?" asked one member called Nick.

"It depends on how you do it. You would have to agree with the underwriter that we issue the documents but he would give us the leeway to increase his premium by say a maximum of 10% where we feel we can carry it and that is split equally between him and us. On those cases, he agrees to increase the commission to allow us to have half of the increase thus increasing our commission on these cases by 50%."

"That's brilliant; we all know a few who would be willing to play ball but we would have to wine and dine them," said Nick.

"Naturally, an investment will be necessary; just ensure that the investment does not negate the advantage but you have to be sure that there is no impression given of any underhand practise but instead a mutual agreement to develop his account with good business in return for which he is paying an enhanced commission and why wouldn't he in such circumstances. I suggest you try it with one underwriter first of all and then maybe add another one later if running well but you would not need more than two initially."

The meeting then went on to cover more mundane matters and was wrapped up by midday with Mike agreeing to go to lunch with Freddie and he suggested they ask Nick to join them.

They walked to Freddie's favourite basement bistro and settled into a quiet table in the corner giving a clear view of the whole area so they could see if a rival was within ear shot. Mike took the opportunity to spell out to Nick the necessity of being careful in his discussions with the underwriter he was approaching and that, "…in any event, they would not want more than two really because people talk or brag and everything gets exaggerated which could make us look like villains or at least like we are pulling some fast strokes. Even if the latter is true, if it becomes public, our advantage would soon disappear." Nick was quick to see the point Mike was making and assured him he would be very discreet.

They then relaxed and enjoyed the meal and Celia was intrigued with the way the waiters and waitresses managed to work so efficiently in such enclosed spaces but confessed later that she enjoyed the special feeling of being in the biggest financial centre in Europe if not further afield. She described the atmosphere as being electric and that everyone seemed to know that they were in the middle of somewhere really special and important.

Mike left the table to visit the men's room and when he got back, Freddie had paid the bill and Nick had asked Celia out and she had accepted.

"That's if you have no objections, Sir," said Nick.

"No, just one condition which is you make sure you get her back to the hotel tonight safe and sound; if you fail then consider yourself to be in the last hours of your life."

With that, Mike turned to Freddie and winked and they headed back to the office with Nick and Celia trailing behind.

As they were leaving, Freddie suggested that perhaps as Mike was going to be on his own tonight, he might like to come to his house and meet his wife and have a light supper. Mike thought this was very nice of Freddie and accepted gladly, following which Freddie passed him his address with: "See you about 7:30 then."

"So you will."

With that, Mike and Celia headed off to their hotel.

As usual, Mike checked exactly how long the taxi would take to get him to Freddie's house which was 30 minutes so he had a few hours to kill; as Celia was busy deciding what to wear, he started phoning the other offices he was going to visit—Paris, Amsterdam, Frankfurt, Milan, Vienna and then back home to Zurich—and he would invite Jean Jacques and his wife to dinner so he could give him a complete update on the tour.

At 7:25 pm, the taxi pulled up outside Freddie's house, a large detached house in suburbia obviously a good neighbourhood, Mike was greeted by Freddie and his wife Hilda, a pleasant lady in her seventies. After the usual introductions, they made their way into the dining room where some cold meats and a cheese board were awaiting their attention. After supper, they moved to the lounge still with wine in hand and settled down to continue their conversation which had passed beyond the usual chit chat stage and had broached the subject of the Northern Ireland outfit.

"What exactly do they do?" asked Freddie.

"Well, they offer help to companies or individuals, usually the MD or the FD of the company, who are being threatened in some way by perhaps organised crime and again usually by immigrants from countries like Bulgaria, Hungary or Russia."

"That must get dangerous," said Hilda.

"Yes it does but I don't go out on site these days as I feel I am getting too old and might put the others in danger; you have to be very quick and nimble to survive; besides, I have family now so have to be around for them."

"What was the most dangerous case you were on?"

Mike told them about the protection of Gorbachev but toned down the abject slaughter of the assassins to instead where they fled carrying their wounded and how the President was left unharmed but he and his crew had to make their escape so the Russians would never know that the west was involved as they would obviously want to know how they had such information in the first place. He then explained how the Americans tried to eliminate them to safeguard their secret and the ingenious aerial manoeuvres carried out by Lisa and about the squadron they sent to get them including how they bombed the helicopter.

Finally, how Mike threatened the American Colonel causing him to commit suicide so ending the threat to him and his crew. He ended by saying they swore never to be involved in anything to do with the Americans again because of their casual attitude to collateral damage.

Freddie and Hilda were very impressed but Mike made sure they knew he did not do this anymore and just did the planning for them.

"The planning is like a game of chess; you have to plan the attack but also more importantly, the escape and all the alternatives along the way. In effect, one has to imagine the whole operation from beginning to the end and anticipate what could go wrong."

"Sounds fascinating," said Freddie and Hilda in chorus.

"It is but there is a heavy responsibility in that if I slip up, I could lose a crew member so I sometimes go to the site well in advance of the activities, about 2 or 3 days beforehand to ensure that I have a good understanding of the actual risks on the ground."

"You may not want to tell me but what kind of fee would that operation make?"

"I will tell you but please be discreet especially avoid anyone connected to the media. It's £2 million but remember there were 5 lives on the line. Although the two Russians weren't our responsibility, we decided to employ them or they would have ended up as vagrants."

At 11 pm, Mike took his leave and told Freddie he really appreciated his invitation and had enjoyed the evening and would invite him and Hilda over to Switzerland in the spring. His taxi had arrived as he was opening the door, he looked back and they were both standing there so he waved and they waved back. Mike knew then that as they were still waiting there they were genuinely nice people.

Back at the hotel, Mike checked to see if Celia had returned but found that she was still out but he was not too concerned as he had asked her to phone him when she got back so he could stop worrying. In this day and age, it was so much easier with mobile phones as she could phone him if she felt in any danger. He made his way upstairs and settled down to read the rest of his paper and have an Irish whiskey nightcap. He was just about to fall asleep in the chair when his phone rang, waking him with a jolt. It was Celia and she was outside his door as her room was just opposite his. He opened up and asked her if everything was alright, which happily it was.

"Would you like a nightcap before you turn in?" he asked.

"Yes, why not. I didn't drink much the whole evening as we trailed from one club to another."

"That can be tiresome."

"Yes, but I think Nick just wanted me to see London's nightlife all at once in case I never came back," she laughed.

"Did you like him?"

"He seemed a nice guy but probably not for me. I didn't feel anything special."

"Good, don't look at me with surprise but any future guy has to either know nothing about you so you know it's you he wants and not the money, or he has to be rich so again you know it's you he wants."

"Did Mum know you were rich when you met?"

"No not really, she knew I was not struggling but she had no idea other than I had a business in Paris that was successful so I was what is called comfortable. However, as she was a policewoman who struck me as completely honourable, I didn't have to worry about that kind of problem."

"So you can read people?"

"Yes and you might have inherited that ability too hopefully."

"Have you thought about which one of us you want to take over the business?"

"Well, you are the eldest so it could be you if it strikes you that you want it or either of the other two so long as one of you really gets bitten by the bug. But whichever way it turns out is OK with me. All three of you could work in the business together if need be. All of you should have a charmed life thanks to dear old daddy," and he laughed.

Celia laughed too and threw her arms around his neck, kissing him on the cheek.

"We had better get some sleep as we are off to Paris in the morning which will give you a further taste of the business."

Paris was alive and beautiful as usual and the ride into the city by taxi is always part of the pleasure. They got dropped off near the apartment and walked the hundred metres to the entrance and as they entered the building the concierge rushed to help them with their luggage and greet them like they meant the world to him. True delight or practised behaviour it nevertheless made Mike feel special which he always appreciates. He accepted the help and gave a generous gratuity, which Celia noticed.

"Do you always do that?" she asked.

"Yes."

"No wonder," she commenced but saw Mike's frown and stopped.

"Did he make you feel welcome?" Mike asked.

"Yes until I saw what he was at."

"Or could it be he always gets a tip and so rushes to help so he does something to earn it?"

"I suppose."

"Well, he always cheers me up so I will take it as it looks like."

"Sorry."

"Right, let's see if Xavier is in," as he phoned him.

Mike got through and they agreed to meet at 11:30 am.

On arrival at the office, they were shown straight into Xavier's office. Mike and Xavier got straight down to the business in hand and Celia listened intently. Then about midday Mike suddenly suggested lunch where they can continue the conversation to which Xavier agreed. Xavier suggested a local restaurant which was excellent and good value and within walking distance so they all headed off.

The restaurant was typically French with white tablecloths, silver cutlery and lots of flunkies around, or so thought Celia. French waiters are very good at upping the atmosphere to the rarefied arena where the cultured reside and of course, making you feel that you must conform to this dignified and superior regime. To Mike, it was all part of what he deserved and indeed why he had worked so diligently.

Mike gave Xavier the same talk that he made in London and Xavier was definitely on the ball, Celia noticed. He had no hesitation in accepting the necessity of these steps Mike was advocating. They left the restaurant at 3:30 pm and parted company with handshakes and the promise to talk again soon.

On the way back to the apartment, Celia suggested getting something for breakfast in the morning but Mike vetoed the idea as he already had planned to go to his favourite café for breakfast and anyway, the food would just get wasted.

Mike asked Celia if she would like to go to a concert of music by Handel, Corelli and Bach. She thought for a while and agreed. In the event, to her surprise, she absolutely adored the mixture and described it as invigorating. She had of course heard of these composers before but always assumed that their music would be boring whereas of course they were the pop stars of their era.

They had a coffee on the way back to the apartment and Mike reminded her it was Amsterdam tomorrow.

In the morning Mike and Celia wandered down to his favourite café where he explained to Celia he used to sit and watch the day go by and remind himself how precious life was and that every moment should be appreciated and not taken for granted. This café, he explained, was where every four or five days he would hear her Mum pass by saying 'Bonjour Monsieur Noir' until one day, she came up while he was reading the newspaper and stood in front of his table. He lowered the paper with his heart in his mouth and asked her to sit and have a coffee, which to his surprise she did. That was the start of it all. "If she hadn't stopped, you and the boys would not exist. Strange how precarious all our existences are."

They continued on their tour and Celia really enjoyed the different locations and the people she met and said at the end that she would really like to join the business, which pleased Mike enormously.

As they entered the office in Zurich, Helen and Jean Jacques were just leaving for lunch so they all decided to join up, Just at that moment, Mike's mobile phone rang and it was Lisa. Mike answered and told the rest to carry on and he would follow.

Lisa was concerned as Major Phillips had been attacked outside his airfield in Monchengladbach and killed. They suspected it was an American purely from the boots he was wearing and his size. He was unusually tall.

"You think it might be a revenge killing for forcing Colonel Collins down the road of suicide but that was 20 years ago, wasn't it?"

"Yes, time enough for a son to grow up and decide to put right a travesty," said Lisa.

"OK but will he know about us?"

"Can't say but should we not get him before he gets us?"

"He would only possibly know about me; doubt if he would know about you," intimated Mike.

"OK but it's like the Three Musketeers—all for one and one for all, or is it the other way around? I don't want to find myself being the boss here so what are we going to do?"

"Only thing we can do is hunt him down. I will do some research on Colonel Collins and see if his children are mentioned anywhere. In the meantime, I have a job nearer to home for you."

Mike then went on to tell her about Stephanie and how her husband had left taking all the money out of her bank account leaving her in a mess but perhaps she might be able to persuade him to do the right thing.

As Mike was walking to the restaurant, he saw a very tall guy army type walking on the opposite side just a little behind and he wondered why he noticed him but decided to test the situation by nipping into a shop that he knew very well where he could nip out the back and around to the front of the block to see if it had any effect on the big guy. Sure enough, he was standing outside peering in the window and that was enough for Mike; he called Lisa and explained what had just happened and she quickly volunteered herself and Harry to be there by tomorrow.

Mike phoned Jean Jacques and explained that he had something on and would not be able to join them. He quickly jumped into a taxi and headed straight for home.

The next day about 11 am, Lisa and Harry arrived and they hatched a plan to see if they could capture the guy trailing Mike but failing that to take him out. Mike went back to the same area and stopped at a café, ordered a coffee and waited. About half an hour later, he saw the tall American and decided to make himself noticeable by standing up and calling the waiter in a loud voice to pay in a hurry. He then walked down the street and could see in the window reflections that the American was following him. He didn't seem to notice that he in turn was being followed.

After a short distance, Mike turned down a quiet back street with the American in tow. Lisa who was wearing rubber soles caught up with him and hit him hard with the butt of her revolver and down he went. She quickly slapped on some handcuffs and she and Mike just had to wait for Harry in the van to arrive. That seemed to take an eternity but in fact was about 5 minutes. It took all three of them to lift the American into the van he must have been 16 or 17 stone in weight.

Harry drove to an abandoned factory estate and they got the American out who was now coming around and moaning. They found an old wooden crate and plonked him on it. Harry went to the van and brought back a bottle of water and some headache tablets which were pushed down the American's throat. They left him for 15 minutes to allow the pills to work and to plan their interview technique.

They all walked back to face him and Lisa took the handcuffs off and he spent a while rubbing his wrists as they had bruised him quite badly. Mike started the interview, "I know who you are, Rick Collins," and waited a moment for that to sink in and continued: "You are the son of Colonel Collins who committed suicide about 20 plus years ago and you have come for vengeance on the man who you believe caused your father to take such drastic action but the problem, my friend, is you only know half the story."

"Listen motherfucker, if you are going to feed me some bullshit, don't bother. I would rather fucking die than listen to it."

"For us that's the easy option, we kill you then no more problem. Once you see that you may just get curious as to why we haven't done it already."

Lisa decided to add her bit with: "During the cold war era, spying on the Russians was big business and the belief that one could do whatever to preserve an advantage was common place albeit there were supposed to be limits but unfortunately not everyone realised that or wanted to realise that and your father was one such bastard."

Rick got angry with Lisa calling Daddy a bastard quite understandably. Mike decided to step in and enlarge on the specifics: "We three were hired, yes hired and paid to prevent the assassination of Gorbachev which the West became aware of due to their intelligence but did not want the Russians to know about their ability to infiltrate the military to such an extent which is why they did not use their own men. We had to disguise ourselves as Russians and were dropped into a deserted area where we were met by two Russians who helped us move around unnoticed unlike your good self I have to add.

"We carried out our plan and succeeded against superior odds to eliminate the assassinators and were making our way towards the escape wagon parked nearby only to discover the driver had been shot presumably because he disagreed with the last minute changes which would potentially leave us trapped and killed. Fortunately, one of the Russians was an experienced wagon driver so we solved that problem."

Lisa took over again with: "Eventually, by twists and turns, we made it to the rendezvous area where a helicopter was to take us back to Germany but fortunately, Mike suspected there might be a double cross here as well and by a ruse we discovered that was the case and Mike's signal was he would drop flat to the ground and then we opened fire, killing them all. We took over the helicopter and got away but over the Baltic sea we were chased by a twin engine

208

plane much faster than us but we managed to get the better of them too and downed their plane. We now felt we were home and safe but no as we entered Germany a squadron of American fighter planes arrived on the horizon and we had to ditch on a forest road and get away quickly. They found the helicopter and bombed it to smithereens."

Mike took over again: "We had to be very careful when we got back to civilisation as we could not book into a hotel or use a card as we would be hunted down but we managed. We eventually found by a circuitous route that the last minute changes were implemented by your father and were regarded by him as being just collateral damage, nothing to worry about. I then spoke to Major Phillips whom your dad had also threatened and asked him to inform your father that we would go to the media and expose his disgraceful behaviour and to impress on him the humiliation he would be subjected to because he could not better the small group that he had hired to carry out such an important role even with extremely superior forces. At the time, Lisa said that he would commit suicide and my comment was I hope so as otherwise, we have to kill him ourselves because he will not give up."

"Well, Rick, what's it to be; have you changed you mind now you have a fuller story, it's not the full story but we kept it short so as not to bore you. And you might as well know that if we three take a vote on it, Harry and I will vote to eliminate you as then there are no more worries," said Lisa leaning into his face.

To everyone's surprise, Rick just sat there with tears running down his cheeks. Everyone just looked and said nothing but eventually, Rick spoke: "I can't believe my father did those things but I can see he did and as a result, I killed an innocent man. How can I live with that. I killed Major Phillips."

"Well, don't get too upset about Major Phillips, yes, in those days he didn't do much wrong but today he would be accused of neglect of duty for not reporting what you father was going to do. Yes, I believe he knew in advance about the changes but is suited me at the time to pretend that he didn't so he would pass your father the message. You can now move on and live the rest of your life without guilt of any kind and we shan't be mentioning the matter of Major Phillips to anyone. I always remember in these situations an old Master at my college saying to us boys if along life's path you get into a mess for some wrong doing do not confess it to all and sundry but keep in under your hat and learn from your mistake and move on."

"Well, on that philosophical thought, let us have yours," said Harry.

"I will not try and kill you again or any of you if I am freed," he said looking at Mike.

"OK, we will drop you off in the city."

After dropping Rick off in the city, they headed for Mike's home as he wanted them to meet his children. He told Lisa that he would transfer a fee for the help and she blew her top saying she would just send it back. However, they ended up agreeing a fee for sorting Stephany out which they would start on when they got back.

As they pulled up to the front entrance, Helen and the three children came out to meet them and Helen said she had been worrying as it wasn't like him to duck out of something at the last minute unless it was serious. He explained that it was all something and nothing in the end.

He asked Lisa to explain while he went to change. When he got back half an hour later, Helen had asked them to stay overnight as they must be tired with all the running about and they were very happy to accept, they needed to relax.

Mike made sure to get the children chatting to Lisa and Harry with the intention of explaining what they did and how important it is although it's not connected to the main line of Mike's business.

Mike brought up the problem that Stephanie was having so Lisa would know it was not a forbidden subject and explained how one would normally deal with this through the courts which might take years and the lawyers' fees could take a quarter of your money for starters. Whereas Lisa and Co will probably have it sorted in a couple of weeks depending on what the two-timing cad had done with the money.

"I am glad you are going to help her as she was Mike's first girlfriend and helped quite a lot when he first started," said Helen.

"Not sure many wives would take that attitude," responded Lisa.

"Well, she must be in her eighties now as she was older than you, wasn't she?" asked Helen.

"Yes must be at least eighty-five, no time to be left penniless so I've sent her something until you sort it," Mike said grinning.

"No pressure then," said Lisa laughing.

Mike stood up and walked to the drinks cabinet near the window when there was a loud bang and the window blew in, showering the room with tiny pieces of glass and Mike collapsed on the floor. Lisa, experienced in these matters, was there first and found the bullet hole which fortunately had missed the vital organs. Helen who was hysterical came over a few seconds later and Lisa calmed her down with the news that it wasn't fatal but to call an ambulance as he would have to go to hospital.

The ambulance was there within 10 minutes and Helen got in the ambulance with Mike who was unconscious while Lisa and Harry followed in Mike's car. They discussed the matter on the way and decided it was that bloody American; like father like son, so he would have to be eliminated.

"I bet that bastard has seen the ambulance so he knows he has not finished the job so it's 24-hour guard duty. If we are lucky, he will try again tonight."

Once the operation was over, Mike was settled in a private room and Helen stayed by his bedside. Lisa and Harry donned some white coats and walked the corridors but not together. Harry then decided to walk outside so he replaced the white coat with his own mac as it had been raining. He walked some distance away from the main entrance and watched for about 20 minutes and then he spotted the American lurching up the steps towards the main entrance so he took his revolver out, took careful aim and pulled the trigger. He saw the American fall and rushed over. A crowd had gathered so he pulled out his pistol and fired it in the air that caused screaming and panic with people running in all directions. Harry closed in on Rick who was writhing in pain and leaned over and said: "Just like your shit of a Dad but you are going to die right here."

He then stamped on Rick's hand and he heard the bones breaking. Rick screamed he then shot him in the leg and again he screamed; then the other leg with the same result, at which point, he leaned over Rick and looked him in the eye before the final shot between the eyes. He then turned and walked down the street, wiping the gun with the wet leaves of a hedge and cooling it down before holstering it. He turned down a side street and took his dark raincoat off and turned it inside out and continued in a light, totally different coat. He called Lisa and explained what had happened in a kind of code just in case. He told her he would see her in the morning.

Lisa returned to the room where Helen was on bedside watch waiting for Mike to gain consciousness and told her the problem had been dealt with so no more worries. Helen looked quizzically at Lisa so she said, "You know the problem has been eliminated so you can relax but you will hear a bit of commotion in about 10 minutes from now as the police will arrive to make their enquiries. If Mike hadn't been at the interview, we would not have had this problem but he is a big softy at heart which is why we all love him."

"Do I have to keep my eye on you?" Helen jokingly asked.

"Your marriage is in no trouble from me. I'm gay," Lisa replied and added: "Unless you are too?"

Helen was about to defend herself fully until Lisa stood pointing her finger at her and said: "Got you!"

And they both ended up laughing until Helen noted how inappropriate that would look to a passing nurse or doctor and so they stopped, covering their mouths to stifle the noise.

About an hour later, Mike woke up asking how long he had been asleep and was surprised to find it was about 15 hours until he realised it was quite a big operation to save him and he was extremely lucky. Lisa said, "You have a lesson the learn here," and Mike raised his eyebrows in a questioning way so Lisa continued: "If the tree is weak then so will be the seeds that fall from it."

"Well, are you going to learn from that?" asked Helen, smiling in that knowing manner that required a slight downward tilt of the head.

"You mean, of course, I shouldn't have given the bastard's son a second chance. I know now why women are always right," and as he saw their eyebrows move to a frown he continued with: "Hind…" and started laughing before he added, "…sight is wonderful, isn't it?"

And then laughingly begged not to be punched at the moment which started both women laughing; just then the doctor entered the room saying: "This is wonderful to see."

Upon which the women explained Mike's last comment which happened to amuse the doctor but he announced he was staying out of these dangerous waters.

After a brief examination, the doctor announced that Mike would need a week in hospital and then he could go home but no strenuous exercise for a month or until the wound had completely healed to make a full recovery.

Later on that day, the police arrived to interview Mike as they heard it might be connected to him. Mike played the innocent very convincingly and asked why they thought it might be connected to him. The answer was they knew of his connection to various governments, "…not sure what you did but we got notified by the individual that you were responsible for the death of his father and he intended to kill you. Now he has been killed on the doorstep of the hospital."

"Ah, I wonder if it was him who shot me then?"

"Probably."

"As you know, I have been out of action since yesterday so I haven't given any orders and in fact I only woke up this afternoon so he must have crossed someone else. However, I can tell you his father committed suicide; he wasn't killed by me."

"He didn't say you killed him but that you were responsible for his death."

"Well, as you know so much I can give you a brief summary of the past but not a detailed one or I will be pursued by the British and American secret services which means they will probably do what he failed to do. I can tell you that during the cold war we were asked to go into Russia and perform some functions and not get identified which we managed to do and then we went to the escape area to find that the Americans had killed our driver presumably to keep their secret more secret than if we survived.

"We overcame that attack and several others including our helicopter escape being taken over by the enemy but managed to escape that as well and when we eventually entered Germany in the said helicopter the Americans sent a squadron to shoot us down but they failed. It took us ages to establish the bastard behind these attacks and it was indeed the father of the man who was shot downstairs. I reported this to the British who must have threatened to expose him is all I can think."

"Perhaps the Americans got him before the whole matter became public knowledge," said Lisa.

"You could be right and that is what I will put in my report as you certainly couldn't have done it or even ordered it," he said to Mike with a pleasant smile and then took his leave, being courteous to the ladies who obviously were not even on the register according to his mind.

"I think I will discharge myself in a day or so as can't see me being able to stand any longer in here."

Helen replied that he should wait to see what he felt like when he had to get up and walk around. Mike then tried to pull himself up and found he was not as good as he thought so agreed with Helen and he settled back to normal conversation and that included thanking Lisa and asking her to thank Harry who should relax around the house for a while as it looked like it was all going to blow away quietly.

"We have to go to Dublin soon and sort your ex out or I should say sort her husband out," Lisa mentioned.

"That will be fun for you; not as difficult as your normal jobs," said Helen.

"Yea, should be a doddle but you never know, Steph might have had bad taste in men apart from being a louse he could be a vicious bastard which we will assume anyway just in case."

"He will not be a nice guy to walk away from a woman in her eighties leaving her penniless; he has to be an evil little shit. How does he live with himself? I mean, he has to justify it somehow to himself," Mike wondered.

"When I worked as a policewoman, I started off thinking like that but I saw again and again what people can do to others without the slightest feeling of guilt and even those that claim to be decent nice people can do things when pushed that would horrify you. You have to know someone very well and over a long period before you really know them unless something intervenes that shows their worth," interjected Helen in her La Lieutenante mode.

Lisa went to Dublin and met up with Stephanie whom she liked and they discussed everything that had happened to her and how she had trusted him after so many years but gradually, he had been moving sums over to his account. She didn't notice as he had taken over the running of the household while she continued to work even into her eighties. Then one day, he announced he was leaving her so she checked her account and her savings account and both had been cleared out apart from enough to last two weeks. This she considered especially mean. She thought if someone was stealing from one's own partner, they would not actually clean them out so they could not carry on.

Lisa got the name but not the address. His name was Ernie Wynn so he should not be too difficult to find, thought Lisa. Having tried all the usual avenues, Lisa decided to go around the local estate agents with the story that Ernie had left a very valuable Rolex watch behind and she wanted to return it in person. After about the sixth agent, she came up with success in that the young woman had the address but was not prepared to hand it out due to the confidentiality owed to their clients.

Lisa leaned forward so she was uncomfortably close to the young woman's face and in a menacing voice said: "So you have the address but you are not prepared to hand it over due to some goody two shoes agreement between you and this bastard who has fleeced a client of mine out of almost two million pounds. Do you want to change your mind?"

The young women was somewhat nervous now but stuck to her guns and nodded no in the most uncertain way ever and with good cause.

"Well then, you leave me no choice," and with that Lisa pulled out her revolver and shoved it up against the young woman's face saying: "Now pretty little thing; give me the damn address or I will terminate your life here and now."

Lisa pressed the gun hard into the woman's face and she immediately complied shaking and with tears running down her pretty little face. Lisa looked at it and warned her she would be back if she called the Gardai.

She now headed to Ernie Wynn's new address. He wasn't in so she went on a pub crawl and sure enough on the third pub there he was in all his glory being the big lad entertaining his cronies and bragging about his new found wealth and how he was going to Brazil on holiday where the women are all beautiful and not shy about coming forward, 'if you know what I mean,' he added with a leer.

Lisa pondered for a while on which strategy to apply—let him get absolutely plastered or try to encourage him to pick her up. She decided the quickest way was if he fancied her, she could go back to his place and get matters resolved rather than deal with a drunken asshole.

Lisa finished her gin and tonic and went to the bar and looked in his direction and smiled. She then concentrated on ordering her drink at which point Ernie approached and started chatting and insisted on buying her drink which Lisa graciously accepted. One drink became two and so on and when Ernie thought she had had enough to bend to his suggestions; they left the pub he with his arm about her shoulder. Lisa played the compliant little thing, leaving Ernie in no doubt about his lucky day. Ernie had slight difficulty in getting the key into the lock whether from drink or anticipation will never be decided for once they entered the lounge, Lisa hit him hard with the butt of her hand gun knocking him down but not unconscious. Lisa stood over him but not straddling him in case he kicked; she shoved the gun into his face and said: "Now asshole, you are going to transfer all the money you stole from your wife back into her account in one move and if the bank refuses, I will kill you unless you persuade them to comply." And continued with:

You will now be arguing for your life.

"If you kill me, she won't get her money back."

"She will but it will take longer and the company that gave her this bonus is happy to replace it until she does. This is not just a matter of money but of principle. I know… a concept you are not familiar with. It involves honour…oh!

there I go again reeling off concepts and words that are completely alien to you; I might as well be speaking Japanese."

Lisa stepped back to allow Ernie to rise to the occasion albeit not the occasion he was anticipating and shoving the laptop into his hands ordered him to get moving. He opened into his bank account and tried to move the money in one hit but the bank objected even though it was just a transfer between accounts in the same bank. The size of the transfer—£1.5M—was the problem. It was a referral. Lisa explained to him what to say when he phoned them.

Just then Harry phoned to say he had arrived so Lisa gave him directions saying she would need his backup.

"I'll be there in 15 to 20 minutes."

"Good, see you then."

"Who was that?" Ernie asked.

"My colleague who is a sniper amongst other things so if you have to go to the bank in person and you mess around, he will take you out and make no mistake he can put a hole in your head between the eyes at over 100 yards away. You had better realise any problem and we will cut short these negotiations and your wife's money will be replaced while she goes through the courts to get it back; meanwhile, you are dead and buried."

"Some of this money is mine," Ernie whined.

"Yea about £20k but Stephanie says you can have £50k but you do not deserve it. Get on with it. I'm beginning to lose patience with you. Hurry up or I just finish it now."

"OK, OK. It's gone through as we are both with the same bank."

Lisa phoned Stephanie and asked: "Have you got it?"

"Yes, it's in."

"Phone the bank and forbid them from taking any instructions from anyone except you or better still until you arrange a new account that is more secure."

"Finished?" asked Ernie.

"Yes, you steal and you get a reward of £50K but I can't wait for you to step out of line, you little sleazebag. And if anything should happen to Stephanie, any funny business, we will be back and show you in the time it takes to turn that light switch on how quickly you will no longer be a problem. Stalin was right— No Man No Problem."

Lisa then turned to walk away, deliberately giving the impression of a careless attitude but she already knew she could see their reflections in the glass print hanging on the opposite wall. Within a stride or two, Ernie decided to try his luck and lunged at Lisa, who deftly sidestepped leaving him pawing the air. He stopped and with a sheepish grin was about to say something when Lisa smiled back and said, "Cheerio asshole," and shot him dead.

She then tidied up took the laptop and left thinking, *Yep, Stalin had the right idea even if he did strain it just a little but hey, that's an outsider's view*. As she was exiting the building, Harry arrived and said: "You had better shift as I can hear police sirens. Nice of the Gardai to warn us of their arrival, don't you think?"

"Come on, let's catch this bus back to the city centre."

They quickly crossed the road just in time to board the bus. As they sat down, their thighs were rubbing together and Harry was getting a bit hot under the collar which Lisa noticed and told him not to be silly and reminded him she was a lesbian. He said he knew but she was so damn attractive.

When they alighted from the bus and were making their way to the hotel, Lisa asked Harry if he was desperate for a shag.

"Well, I wouldn't put it like that but yes."

"OK then we get one room and just this once I will give you a treat."

Harry was astounded or in the vernacular gobsmacked and got very excited so Lisa said: "If you don't calm down, it's off. I am not walking up to the reception with you looking like a dog on heat."

"OK, OK, I will calm down," he promised.

They managed to book in without a problem and Harry had the best night of his life so far but strangely, Lisa was happy to stay in Dublin for an additional day and night.

The next day they got a call from Mike from his hospital bed to tell them that Stephanie had been arrested in connection with the death of her husband. She had not been charged as yet so he asked Lisa to phone Carroll Brennan and Christie Solicitors and ask for Eamon Flaherty to represent Stephanie or if he can't, to recommend the best there was and he stressed the urgency.

They made the call and Eamon was luckily able to take on the brief and reported to the police immediately. He persuaded them to release Stephanie into his custody which they agreed possibly in view of her age or because they had no evidence other than she had asked a firm of investigators to find her husband.

Having gotten Stephanie's release, Eamon phoned Mike for an update on the background which Mike duly gave in that Stephanie did employ some investigators and they did find the erring husband and forced him to return the money he had absconded with but that was all they were required to do. They may for some reason have killed Ernie but they were not asked to do that. Eamon came back with: "I am going to need proof of that as it might be hard to convince a jury but if I get it soon enough then the prosecutor may decide not to proceed."

"They are not going to turn up to either a court or direct to the police but I may be able to persuade them to go and make a statement under oath to a firm of solicitors in Northern Ireland or in the UK and that can be presented to you. Would that do?"

"Probably but get it sooner rather than later."

As it happened, Lisa knew someone very well in the North who could take the statement without causing a problem and adjust the timing to ensure that Lisa and Harry had already left the country. Of course, it would make return visits to the country a little awkward but that could be resolved in time with make-up and false passports.

In due course, the case against Stephanie was dropped and her life went back to normal but she claimed better than normal. No asshole pissing in her footsteps now. Mike felt relieved as she should have a clear run to the end now.

The week in hospital seemed to Mike to last forever and when he finally got out, it was such a relief. He felt they were being over cautious as he had been walking around the wards for the last two days without any problem but that's doctors always worrying.

On the departure day, Mike made sure to thank everyone involved in his recovery with presents of several chocolates and two cases of wine. The new chauffeur had been asked to pick them up and turned up exactly on time as was expected. They got into the rear seats and waved goodbye to the nurse standing by the door. The journey home was unexpectedly dramatic due to several bullets piercing the bodywork of the Bentley. Fortunately, nobody was injured.

Chapter 31

When they got home, Harry and Lisa were there having settled themselves in and were very surprised to hear of the new developments.

"He must have had close colleagues or relatives willing to avenge him, I expect," said Harry.

"Yes, let's see if the Colonel had more than one son."

Lisa was busy searching the connections and came up with the answer within minutes; he did have more than one offspring she announced with triumph. "A daughter called Joanne and guess what, she works in Germany as a liaison solicitor for the American army."

"Tomorrow, you and Harry should go to Germany and pay her a visit but if she is a solicitor, she will not be carrying out the dirty work herself but will have employed someone. If not, she may know some of her brother's friends willing to avenge him in what they see as a miscarriage of justice."

"OK, we will be off after breakfast."

"Where are the Russians?" asked Mike.

"On holiday in Mexico of all places," replied Harry with a surprised look on his face.

In the morning when Mike got down to breakfast, Lisa and Harry had already left and Helen announced to Mike that they were now sharing the one room.

"Did you know?" She asked.

"No, that is a surprise so quiet Harry has changed her preferences then. Good luck to them; they are well suited. I shall have to rib them when they get back."

"No you don't, you will only embarrass them," Helen replied alarmed at the prospect.

Laughing, Mike agreed not to say anything and leave it to them to announce something if they wanted to. Later on that evening, Mike got a call from Lisa saying they had traced the sister and would call on her tomorrow.

That evening Mike also had the pleasure of Jean Jacques and Judy for dinner which turned out to be a very relaxing evening with plenty of good conversation and good wine to help the flow.

Mike felt at the end of the evening when the guests were leaving that it was a shame that it all had to end as he had not been so calm and had not enjoyed such civilised conversation with friends for ages. They all agreed to do it again soon. Helen would of course be seeing Jean Jacques on Monday morning in the office.

Lisa and Harry made an appointment to meet Joanne Collins in her office to discuss her brother and were surprised to hear she did not know he had been shot as nobody had contacted her. They agreed to give her the full story when they arrived.

Joanne's office was on the 10th floor of a multistorey skyscraper and had a great view over the Berlin cityscape. Lisa and Harry were ushered into Joanne's office situated on a corner which gave magnificent views even if somewhat unsettling as the windows went down to the floor giving one the feeling of being balanced out on a concrete ledge with no protection to prevent one plunging down 10 storeys. Lisa and Harry stood next to the door glued to the spot and Joanne looked up at them with a broad smile saying: "You suffer from vertigo, I see."

"Didn't know I did until just now," said Lisa.

"How the hell did you get used to this?" asked Harry.

"I've never experienced anything like it. I'm weak-kneed," said Lisa.

Joanne got up from her desk walking close to the window which didn't help but then walked towards them saying: "Follow me to the boardroom which has no windows at all."

They all made their way with Joanne in the lead and entered a plush comfortingly secure room with as Joanne said no windows.

"I know I am going to shudder in a minute or so after that experience," said Harry.

This made Joanne laugh out loud and Lisa joined in which relieved her tension and jokingly said, "If you were questioning anyone in that room, they would agree to anything just to escape."

This tickled Joanne even more. Then Joanne got serious. "You told me that my brother Rick had been shot; can you elaborate more for me as this is the first time I heard of it."

Lisa gave Joanne the background including the Russian escapade and the suicide of her father and when she had finished, Joanne spoke very candidly: "I knew about my father's suicide and to be honest I was very happy with that as he was an abusive husband to my Mom. He beat her to within an inch of her life on several occasions and as soon as I moved out I took Mom with me and told him if he didn't leave her alone I would spill the beans to the newspapers. He had just been made a colonel so he couldn't have stood any bad publicity. I told him I hated his guts and if I was a man I would beat the shit out of him, such a coward. I'm afraid Rick took after my father and was an equally nasty piece of work who started off beating animals and then people smaller than him so if he has gone too, so much the better."

"Did he have any close friends?"

"Only one that I know of, a redneck called Billy Joe Barnes, a right sycophantic little creep who worshipped Rick and did his dirty work for him. No matter how Rick spoke to him, he creeped up Rick's backside. It was sickening to watch."

"What does he look like?" asked Lisa.

"He's tall, skinny but wide shouldered and has a slight stoop. He has a bony face with creepy narrow lips always in a sneer and he has untidy short mousey hair with a piece sticking up at the front like the peak of a cap but looks like the cap has slipped a bit to the back which gives him a kind of village idiot appearance. The minute you see the gawky shyster, you will know it's him. He should have been put down at birth and I know that's awful but wait until you see him; he will make your skin crawl, just don't turn your back on him."

Lisa and Harry left Joanne's office with their heads spinning and didn't speak for a good half hour as they walked back to their hotel. Harry broke the silence: "It's like coming across that snake with multiple heads."

"You referring to the Hydra in Greek mythology?" asked Lisa.

"Am I, oh yeah…Yeah, the very thing," he said while staring straight ahead.

Now Lisa was suppressing the desire to burst out laughing but was doing her best not to give in as she didn't want to hurt Harry but was saved by a man walking towards them who slipped on something which almost made him fall but he righted himself just in time but lost his hat in the process so as they passed, Lisa could let rip with the suppressed laughter.

"It wasn't that funny, Lisa."

"Wasn't it?" She could barely say the two words such was the desire to collapse again into full-blown laughter. She decided to run up the steps of the hotel and the effort seemed to help. Finally, she was over the hump and could regain control that is so long as nothing further happened to remind her of that look on Harry's face as he pretended to be worldly wise. Then the receptionist asked him if they were eating in this evening and there it was, that look back again as Harry struggled to make a decision; he turned to look at Lisa but she had already bolted to the toilettes down the corridor and was inside hanging from one of the door handles as she gave in and roared with laughter, wiping her eyes with the back of her hand as another woman walked in and found the infection taking her over too so she ended up laughing and spluttering "why am I laughing", which only made the situation worse.

Eventually, they both calmed down and Lisa explained about Harry being unable to make a decision but refused to realise it and instead went into this look like a deer caught in headlights and explained that she knew that he would turn to her for help so she bolted. This made the woman start again as the image crossed her mind but not so intensely as she was almost worn out. The two women introduced themselves and agreed as they were both eating in to meet up with their spouses, having agreed not to spill a word.

The next day, Lisa and Harry caught the train to Zurich and called Mike on the way to explain the attitude of the daughter and how she had no time for either the father or the brother but did give them a very good description of Rick's friend who it turns out in not the full shilling so no negotiation would be possible.

Lisa asked Mike to get on the computer and try and find out where Rick had been staying as that may be where this Billy Joe Barnes might be living.

"Don't you just know that with a name like Billy Joe, he is going to be a halfwit redneck and nasty as hell; mind you, I am prejudiced by the write-up Rick's sister gave. We should arrive in an hour so call me if you have any success with the address."

Lisa picked up *Die Welt* and caught up on the news while Harry admired the passing countryside but after half an hour, Lisa put the paper down and asked Harry if he was happy.

"Yes, I am always happy when I am around you but I don't know what you see in me as I am not the brightest."

"You may not be the brightest but you are one of the kindest men I have ever met."

"Kinder than Mike?"

"Yes, Mike is a pragmatist."

"One of those, is he?"

"Harry, you don't know what a pragmatist is, do you?"

"No."

"It's someone who makes decisions on practical grounds rather than on ideals or beliefs. It's OK not to know things if you haven't come across them before just ask the person to explain and funnily enough sometimes they struggle to clarify what they mean."

"But you, Mike or Helen don't, do you?"

"Sometimes we do but we can't do what you can do. So it's each to his own."

Just then Lisa's mobile rang and it was Mike; he had found the address and said he would text it to her. It turned out to be in Bavaria so they would have to stay in Zurich for the night and return to Germany tomorrow.

Mike then realised that they would have to rest up before going back to Germany so suggested they come and stay with him and after this job they had better find themselves somewhere to live as going back to Belfast was out for now and what about the Russians, Mike wondered, but Lisa said they could talk about that tonight.

Lisa and Harry were exhausted after all the travelling and were happy to relax and enjoy being waited on by Mike and Helen's household. They got up late and had a slow breakfast and then discussed the day's plans with Mike. When that was sorted, Mike asked: "Have you decided where you want to live?"

"Yes, just across the border in southern Germany which will give easy access to you when needed."

"And the Russians?"

"They can be nearby but not living with us or next door. Their style of living does not suit me," she explained.

"I will ask Jean Jacques to investigate the possibilities as he is brilliant at that kind of work. Regarding this Billy Joe Barnes, you do realise he could be here in Switzerland rather than at home?" Mike clarified.

"Yes, so keep out of public view until we get back."

Lisa and Harry left about 10:30 am for the main station in Zurich city centre and tried to enjoy the train journey to Munich. When they arrived, the sun was shining and it was a pleasant day. They left the station and walked to the UBahn and reading the map, quickly found what they wanted and bought the ticket which they then had to cancel or get punched. On arriving at their suburb, they walked to the street where Billy Joe was supposedly staying and Lisa went up to the door while Harry looked around the back.

Lisa rang the bell long and persistently but no answer so she went around the back where Harry had already broken the rear door and opened it so they entered slowly, listening to every sound. Nothing on the ground floor so went upstairs cautiously and heard some music playing behind a closed door. They approached the door and burst it open suddenly which awakened Billy Joe from his drunken stupor.

Billy Joe jumped out of bed bollock naked searching for his gun but unable to find it and turned to face his assailants with: "Who the fuck are you and what do you want?"

Now he was standing Lisa could see he was exactly as Joanne had described and she was right—he made her skin crawl and not because he was naked; that somehow was irrelevant. The fixed leer, the staring eyes and the pure malevolence was obvious to all.

"Are you Billy Joe Barnes?" asked Lisa in as sweet a voice as she could muster.

"I might be, who the fuck is asking?"

"Me, I'm asking but I already know that you are Billy Joe Barnes because Rick's sister described you to a tee."

"That bitch, she hated Rick. What the fuck do you want breaking into my place?"

"To wish you Bon Voyage."

"What the…"

"Cheerio asshole," and she shot him in the head so it was quick.

"Neat, he turned this lovely house into a slum," said Harry as he studied the filth and clothes strewn across the floor.

"I've done him a favour really; he was on the slow slippery slope to hell; I just reduced his agony."

"Let's go; some of the neighbours may have heard the shot," said Harry.

"Right and now we can sort out where we are going to live. I fancy Freiburg in the black forest a beautify city where we can slide in unnoticed much better than a small village where everybody knows your business."

"We have plenty of time; let's go and have a look," enthused Harry.

By the time they got back to Zurich that evening, they were convinced that Freiburg was the place for them and were anxious to see what Jean Jacques would have to say when it was put to him. Mike thought it was a good idea and agreed that a city was best especially when they would be disappearing on jobs for days on end.

Jean Jacques was delighted to help and had the appropriate connections in Freiburg to smooth the transactions when they settled on a purchase but the Russians were not so straight forward in that he advised Lisa that she would have to buy their property and hire it to them at whatever rent she wanted; i.e., as low as she needed it to be.

"The Russians are back from their trip to Mexico at the weekend so we will have a chat with them and all go to Freiburg next week and see what we can find," Helen informed Jean Jacques.

On the Monday, they all headed off to Freiburg and along the way, Helen spelled out the fact that she did not want them living near her or close enough for anyone to connect them to her as she didn't want the notoriety which would come from their heavy drinking and partying until the small hours. This they seemed to understand, saying they liked vodka and whores and that was it but that they would keep the house clean and tidy so that whores liked visiting.

Lisa was going to ask whether they really meant whores or just easy women but decided against it. The Russians disappeared and said they would phone when they were ready to join up again. This suited Lisa and Harry who did a tour of estate agents and went to look at what they liked. They fell in love with a four-bedroom detached house with a couple of buildings at the rear which would suit Harry as he liked motorbikes and this was just the ticket.

As for Lisa, it was an impressive house not on the scale of Mike's but she didn't want that; she wanted a good quality house in an area where they could slide in and not make friends with the neighbours or a least only one or two of them. This was a long way from where she came from and the same for Harry who came from the backstreet slums of Belfast. This was not too far up the scale as to be uncomfortable; just what they deserved and about the equivalent of £400,000, which they could easily afford.

They returned to the estate agents and put in a cash bid for the asking price which was immediately accepted. Harry said in front of the agent, "You could probably have gotten it for less," but Lisa said, "I like it and it's perfect for us so don't want to mess around and then somebody comes in with more. I can't be doing with that; it's now done and we can get the lawyers working on it tomorrow," and then she turned to the agent and said, "Any problems and we move on. I don't like messing about."

Having offered their details and obtained the vendor's particulars, they left walking down the street to the bus stop as if on air. At the city centre they went for a meal and during it phoned Jean Jacques who was delighted that they had found something so quickly saying that they could afford two or three times the price they paid or even more. Lisa replied that she was happy with her decision and did not want to be ostentatious and Jean Jacques understood but added that they will never get through the money they have at this rate of living to which Lisa replied: "That suits me fine so I never need to worry then."

"No, you will never need to worry."

"If only you understood what that means to Harry and me."

"Fine, call in tomorrow and we will get the ball rolling."

Shortly after, the Russians came wandering down the street and stopped by their table and showed Lisa a brochure of the building they wanted. As they had finished eating and the Russians had had a burger on the go, they headed off to where the building was which was only 5 minutes away and that puzzled Lisa slightly but even more so when they arrived at the spot. They had picked a detached property standing next to a warehouse on the one side and derelict land on the other. The house looked good alright, well-maintained, and it seemed belonged to someone who held out against the developers but as the climate had changed, the developers had no further interest in the property so it was going for a song, around the equivalent of £150,000, not bad in their eyes for 4 bedrooms, etc.

"You can have much better," said Lisa.

"No, this is perfect as it's near the city centre, easy to get to for drinks and food and cheap in taxi with whores. At night nobody around so can have fun as loud as we like."

"Well, then, that's settled, good day all around so time to get back eh?"

Lisa and Harry walked in front smiling at the simple desires of the Russians; everything around pleasure and no shame about it. Harry kept shaking his head saying it shocked him the way they kept saying whores. "Do they mean whores?" he asked looking at Lisa.

"I don't know, perhaps all women who are easy are classified the same but anyway, I am not getting into a conversation about it with them."

"I think they live in a parallel universe," said Harry.

Lisa pretended to look at something across the road so Harry would not see the suppressed amusement in her eyes as she asked herself where did that come from.

Then she decided to tell him about her change of plan regarding her friend Marie in Belfast in that she was not going to invite her over but instead send her a parting gift. "By the way, I am not inviting Marie to join us so you won't be having a three in a bed."

"Why?"

"Because you are enough for me, don't be so disappointed."

"I'm relieved actually."

"Oh!"

"Well, I've never done it in front of two before and it may have put me off, I'm not a complete Neanderthal."

"No you are not, you are far too pretty," said Lisa laughing and squeezing his arm as they walked along in complete unison.

After talking to Jean Jacques, he then decided that they should buy both properties and hire the Russians their house and better to charge them something as it will make them appreciate it more. Lisa agreed. As Lisa and Harry were cash buyers, the deals would be transacted quickly and they should be able to take possession in about 4 weeks.

Lisa was happy with that.

Chapter 32

Mike decided to call a family meeting after discussing the manner of his successor with Helen and she agreed that it should be done now.

That evening, Mike, Helen and their three children—Celia, James and Pierre—sat around the dining room table and Mike started the conversation: "Have you talked among yourselves and decided who wants to take over the business?"

Celia replied immediately almost as if she was the elected spokesperson: "It has been decided with all of us agreeing on the outcome that I will take over the running of the business and James wants to be an actor and intends to take a degree in Art and Theatre Studies and Pierre intends to follow his artistic talents which as you know are quite considerable. If they don't succeed in their preferred paths, there will always be a job for them in the business but they might as well follow their dreams in the first place.

"In the event that they need to revert to the business, I will be the Managing Director and as I don't suffer from male ego problems, they will be treated fairly but will nevertheless have to pick an area that they are happy to live and work with. As I will have the majority shareholding, I will be able to ensure that the business does not get split up because of sibling rivalry or squabbling and if they cannot fit in I will ensure they are looked after as there is more than enough for all of us."

Mike looked at Helen and she was as impressed as Mike in the way Celia laid out the plans for the future but Mike asked: "Are you saying that if they fail in their fields, you at worst will allow them to sponge off you ad infinitum?"

"Yes but they will not be sponging off me but drawing down from their share of the company but in any event, they are not spongers by nature and if they are forced to go down that road for a while, it would not be forever as they are proud and have a sense of duty."

"Right then, I can say I am relieved that you have all worked it out and reached an agreement that you can stick with. Celia, you will need to start learning about the different parts of the business and what each section is worth so you need to weight your answer when a problem occurs. For example, London makes a lot of money followed by Frankfurt. In London, for example, Freddie is getting on and some day will have to be replaced which is not an easy thing to do as he has kept the peace for over 20 years. In addition, there is the section with Lisa and Harry but I will talk to you about that at a later date as it is very sensitive indeed."

The meeting then broke up and Mike phoned Lisa to give her an update and she seemed genuinely pleased with the outcome. Mike then asked her about the new name she was applying to her company. Lisa said she had thought about it long and hard and decided with: "First of all, I want it set up in Germany as I am going to be living there so the name will be BPP GmbH and its occupation will be described as Basic Physical Protection provided as a backup to Management Liability Insurance. What do you think?"

"Brilliant."

"Oh good, as I was sure you would find fault with it somehow."

"No, it's just the ticket. I am going to tell Celia about this company to see what her reaction will be. If she is OK with it then all problems are solved."

"Are you thinking of dying or something?" demanded Lisa.

"No but it will happen someday so I need to get it resolved while I still can."

"Very forward looking."

"I am going to talk to Celia now and will let you know how it goes."

Mike found Celia in the drawing room and said: "I need to talk to you in the office now."

They withdrew to Mike's office and he closed the door after she entered and sat behind his desk and told her all about BPP GmbH and the past adventures and assured her she would not need to participate in the actual down to earth fighting but she would have to plan the attacks or the defence actions. This needs to be very precise almost like a computer program with every eventuality thought of in advance so everybody survives. He ended by asking: "What do you think?"

"I'm flabbergasted, how exciting and yes I'm up for it, and hopefully, you will be around for the next few and I can see how it's done."

"I'm not thinking of going just yet but you are right; the bell tolls for everybody," replied Mike as he lifted the phone to call Lisa and give her the update. "So, let me know, Lisa, when the next one comes in as you haven't needed me much lately."

"It won't be long as I had a call from Northern Ireland's usual source saying there is a high profile case on its way to me and it carries a high price tag."

"Good, we will talk soon then."

Mike turned to Celia and explained that she was lucky as a large case was on its way to Lisa and she would be coming here to do the planning. "So you will be in on a complicated one from the start."

"I can't wait to see how it's done."

The following week, Lisa and Harry arrived with the two Russians and the plans for the next case.

"Russia again and it seems they are planning to get rid of Putin this time," said Lisa.

"And they want us to risk our necks again?"

"Yes but I have established that the Americans are not involved and I have explained if there is any attempt at double crossing us we will hunt down all the perpetrators not just the leaders and publicly kill all involved. It will not be done discreetly like last time."

"Have they understood that we are serious, as if I need to ask," said Mike.

"Yes they have assured me that there will be no betrayal this time."

"OK, on that basis, what have you got?"

"In three weeks' time, Putin will be travelling to the Kremlin from his holiday home along this wide avenue here and at this set of lights, the assassins will cause a traffic jam on Putin's side at the lights and on the other side much further back so they can attack from both sides without worrying about moving traffic. The cars are bulletproof but not bomb-proof meaning it is imperative that they get close to the vehicles. They will have to bomb all three as they cannot be sure which vehicle Putin is in."

"I wonder why they want to save him in the first place; I would have thought they would be glad to be rid of him but perhaps they fear who would replace him more. Anyway, this is a very good plan of attack and very difficult to thwart," said Mike rubbing his chin while he imagined the whole operation and after a few minutes came up with the following suggestion: "We will need a low loader plus a tank and two armoured vehicles to stop this but can we get these, legally or illegally?" Mike asked, looking at the Russians.

Dimitri answered, "There is an army camp that I worked at near Moscow where the tanks and armoured vehicles are all parked in the open, fully fuelled and ready to be used. As any set of keys operates any tank and the same with the armoured vehicles, it would be easy but a diversion would be needed to ensure everybody was concentrating on the opposite end of the enormous site while they steal the vehicles." The low loader would be used to move the tank efficiently and quietly and that he would get it first and park it near the exit so the tank did not have far to travel before it can be shut down as the noise was horrendous and would waken the dead.

"Good and then we need to store them while we decorate them to look like they are collecting for wounded and retired soldiers. So lots of bright signs and bunting needed."

"Me, Harry and the Russians will go tomorrow to Moscow to get things started. You and Celia follow in 3 days say Friday for the weekend so you can check the site to make sure you haven't overlooked anything."

Mike agreed. He then turned to Celia and pointed out that she should see the site in reality but she should not join in on the attack until she was sure she can stand the carnage and then only after severe training so she was able to defend herself but in the meantime on the next case, she can do the planning to see if she was up to it.

"You can see how it all has to be imagined and then there is the escape plan for which we will have two vehicles at the ready in case one doesn't start and both packed with changes of clothes for all of us so it matters not which one we use. We will use the BMW X5 as a preference because it is diesel and will give us longer mileage before we have to refuel but if it doesn't start the Lexus will. On Friday or Saturday, you will see the Kremlin and the beautiful buildings surrounding that area so ornate and colourful that you can hardly believe your eyes. Well worth the visit just for that."

On the Friday Mike and Celia travelled to Moscow and as expected, Celia fell in love with the beauty of the area around the Kremlin but only had time for a fleeting look as they made their way to study the spot of the expected attack. Mike examined all the side streets until he found one that was perfect. It was narrow enough to block with the tank and had a good escape route out of the city but it was quiet enough to park two vehicles marked as police vehicles which he hoped would stop them getting stolen.

Mike was done now so they retired to their hotel to book their flight back for tomorrow or Monday. If it was Monday then they could spend the day having a tour of the city and relaxing just like a tourist. As it turned out, they had a day of being a normal pair of tourists.

On the day before the attack, Mike landed at Moscow's airport and made his way to the city centre staying at the same hotel as before. He was joined that afternoon by Lisa, Harry and the two Russians for dinner to conclude some business deal of course. During the discussions, Mike learned that everything was in place and the tank and the armoured vehicles were decorated beautifully and would therefore not arouse suspicion. They would be looked at and then forgotten with perhaps the odd onlooker wondering where they were going to be stationed.

All they had to worry about was the timing of their run down the avenue as it had to be just behind Putin's convoy so they could pull out on to the opposite carriageway which would be empty due to the traffic being held up by the assassins and then pull back in again at the front to ram the blockage probably taking one or two private cars as well as the offending Wagons used by the attackers to block the way. At the same time the armoured vehicles would fire their machine guns in the air or at the assassins if they were already on the carriageway. The idea being that a path would be clear for the convoy to push or ram its way forward to escape.

On the day of the attack, they were parked up in a side street waiting for Putin's convoy to pass and as it did, they pulled out behind it about six or seven vehicles back. When they approached the lights, as expected, there was a hold up and the sound of gunshots as the police motorbike riders were taken out. Dimitri in the tank pulled out onto the opposite carriageway followed by one of the armoured cars the other remaining for a time to protect the nearside of the convoy but strangely the assassins only attacked from the offside across the empty opposite carriageway. They were hindered first of all by the tank and then by the armoured vehicle which mowed down several attackers as they moved forward.

The tank then pulled back in as planned and rammed any car or van in the way pushing them aside like toy vehicles and then continued forward to push the wagons causing the obstruction which it succeeded in doing quite easily thus there was the gap as expected for the convoy to push forward and away; blasting their horns as they passed. The second armoured vehicle was now also just behind the first and they both pushed into the space created and followed the tank to the destinated side street where their escape vehicles were parked.

They blocked the street in case the attackers followed them but there was no evidence that they intended to engage further. Dimitri jumped in the BMW and turned the key. It fired up. Great relief and just before they left, they shot the front tyres out on the Lexus. They made their way to the empty barn in the middle of nowhere so they could change out of their army gear and back into civilian clothes stored in the boot; from there, they went back into the city and to their hotels.

It took a week before they were able to leave Moscow due to the lockdown that resulted from the attack on the president which they spent pleasantly enough wandering to nearby restaurants and drinking excessively.

That little venture netted them £5 million. Lisa pushed out the idea of retiring as they had more money than they needed which, if she was serious suited Mike as he will feel a lot better if Celia didn't get sucked into this side of the business. He knew how fascinating and exciting it all seemed which it was but the cost of a mistake can be death or even worse for a female. He asked himself why he did not feel as protective towards Lisa but then realised that when they started, she was very much the expert and he was the apprentice.

He admired how she had conquered the ability to cut off afterwards from the horrors but when he got more entrenched, he realised she decided in advance that if what she was doing was good then whatever happened to the opposition was of their own doing and in her mind they were evil so no need to spill any tears. After all, this was how Mike himself came to cope with the same horrors.

A few days later, Lisa confirmed that they were all retiring as they had had a good run but could not keep pushing their luck as it just might run out one day. Mike was happy with her decision and also happy with his share of the last fee. She and Harry came to speak to Mike personally as they really appreciated everything he had done for them as before they had no chance of building up sufficient money to retire and she admitted that Tom had not been as fair as he should have been. Mike knew this but passed no comment.

When Harry walked away to look at something, Mike said to Lisa: "So Harry has made you change your choice of partner; well, more power to him."

"Harry is very kind and caring and physically when he is naked, he has very smooth skin just like a woman's skin actually so I suppose it's a bit like a woman with a dick; perfect really," she said laughing.

Mike looked around to see if anyone had heard her last remark but it seemed nobody had so he replied with: "Do you have to be so blunt?" he said laughing.

"Well! It's what you wanted to know, wasn't it?"

"I suppose but hadn't really thought that far."

"I do make him shave before he starts with the lovemaking, as he calls it."

"Enough, too much, I'm off now," laughing as he went.

"See you in the morning with Jean Jacques as I want to wind the company down," she shouted after him.

He stuck his thumb up to indicate his agreement, still laughing at her comments.

Mike couldn't wait to tell Helen and Celia about Lisa's plans for retirement and what a relief it was as he didn't really want Celia getting involved in that side of the business as it was too dangerous and one day as Lisa said their luck just might run out. Helen was delighted but Celia wasn't too sure but realised that she had a lot to cope with running such a widespread business and was looking forward to that. Mike suggested he go along with her for the next few visits until they all get used to her and then she can announce one day that Mike was going into semi-retirement and will only turn out now and then as required.

Chapter 33

The year was 2019, 3 years after the vote to leave the European Union and go it alone with the country being divided almost down the middle. The old politicians being mainly of the middle road reluctantly accepted the result of the election although they believed it had been won by the hard right pushing an avalanche of lies down the throats of the population but there had also been a shift right across Europe and the world generally towards more extreme governments sailing on a wave of populism.

In Britain, the right wing press battered the opposition Labour Party in a way that could only be described as outlandish but to be fair, the Labour Party's choice of leader and the swing to the extreme left gave the Tories and their newspapers a gift.

In the event, Boris Johnson won with a large majority of 80 seats and surrounded himself with like-minded allies having removed all the politicians that were not Brexiteers to the back benches. The government now had a free hand to negotiate with Europe but seemed to be heading for "No Deal" which many claim will not be as bad as feared but others were far from sure and feared backlogs at the ports and shortages of food. The shortages of food were of course imports which may not be delayed as they were Europe's exports and making them profit so why would they delay them and the UK needed the food so they would not delay them either. The problem, if there was a problem, will be with the UK's exports.

Fortunately for Mike, the insurance world had set up branches in Europe to ensure that they could continue to serve their European clients and that they had an existence in Europe regardless of the politicians and these were mainly in areas where Mike had his presence already, like Paris, Amsterdam, Frankfurt, etc. Therefore, if anything, it might be an advantage for Mike but he would have to wait to find out. In the meantime, he was busy coaching Celia so she could acquit herself with confidence.

Mike made his way in to the office in Zurich to see Jean Jacques and have a chat about how Celia was measuring up to the task ahead. All in all, Jean Jacques was very impressed and decided that she would be good for the company as she had come up with some improvements and one in particular he wanted to discuss with him today.

"What has she come up with now?"

"Amalgamating all the companies into one."

"Well, I would agree all the European companies but London would be a problem and with Brexit, we had better be careful," Mike replied while trying to work out the ramifications.

"I would agree with that; better to be a little cautious as it can always be done later if necessary."

"Well, you as a Swiss ought to know the problems with being outside the club."

"Yes there are quite a few but don't forget, we pay into the club but every so often there is a problem but so far we have managed to overcome them by negotiation."

"If we had done what you did at the beginning and stayed out, none of the present problems would have arisen." Said Mike stroking his chin as he pondered.

"You were determined to get in as you knocked on the door three times before it opened."

"I expect the politicians at the time thought that it would be better for the United Kingdom to be inside the biggest market in the world rather than on the outside," said Mike thoughtfully.

"Since then, the UK has been worried about the market becoming the United States of Europe and don't want any part of that saying they did not want any Federalism," added Jean Jacques.

"They did for a while until they realised a big flaw in their argument which was never said out loud but it would not have been long before someone pointed out that the country the Brexiteers admire most is the USA a federal country and the biggest economy in Europe Germany another federal country and even another one they admire Switzerland CH Confederation Helvetique. But worse to come the UK is to all intents and purposes a confederation too with 4 parliaments and one of those in charge. So they dropped that pretty damn quick," Mike said laughing.

"I get the feeling that maybe you would prefer it if the UK had stayed inside the club," said Jean Jacques.

"Well, I ask myself would the UK being one of the leaders, as they were the second largest net contributor, have more power in the world being in than they will have being on their own for make no mistake it is not about money which the public were encouraged to believe but about power in the world. And a force like the UK, France and Germany together is a formidable power and big enough to stand with the USA, China and Russia."

"But these alliances can be rebuilt relatively easily."

"No doubt in due course they can and the country will survive as the people are quite ingenious at finding solutions to adversity. Don't forget in spite of the present politicians the UK has set up businesses all over Europe so they have started already to find ways around hurdles."

At that moment Celia walked in and was somewhat surprised at seeing Mike but smiled and asked whether Mike was checking up on her.

"No, but I understand that you are really enjoying the job."

"Yes and I have a few ideas I would like to discuss with you to see what you think."

"Whenever you like."

"No time like the present," said Celia smiling.

They retired to Celia's new office which was much nicer that anything Mike had had over the years, not that that bothered him but he found it amusing; he did understand the need which would remain until he died he supposed as after which, she would be the absolute boss and not need to prove anything.

The main item on the agenda was the combining of the various companies all under one umbrella which Mike agreed with and had always meant to get around to doing it but something always got in the way. They agreed upon a plan of action and on which corporate lawyers they would appoint to carry out the process.

Mike insisted that he would hold the majority of the shares until he decided to retire and hand over to Celia and in addition his personal finances would have to be extricated from the business but in a way that did not cause problems for the business.

They had just concluded when a phone call came through for Mike. It was Peter Carlson in Frankfurt who seemed a bit stressed. His opening line was: "We have a real problem looming here in Deutschland. It's the BaFin, they have come across our little investment plan and are going to accuse me and the others of some form of impropriety and have warned us it will go to court if there has been any unfair trading by any of us with you."

"Well, you have no need to worry on that account as there never has been any unfair trading and we have kept scrupulous records of all our dealings with all of you and I am quite happy to turn up to the BaFin enquiry with chapter and verse. So tell them that."

"Oh good, that's a relief."

"You will let me know when they are holding the enquiry and when I will be expected to attend and where."

"Of course, but I am worried as it doesn't take much to ruin one's reputation."

"Yes I am well aware of that but as I said, our records will show that all trading including with you and your colleagues has been done with the clients best interests at the heart of everything which is our duty. So you have no need to worry."

"Right. OK. Talk to you later when I know what is happening."

Mike put the phone down and wondered how they came across the fact that they were involved with his company; was he perhaps being investigated because of being a newcomer or simply the fact he was foreign. One never knew.

He returned to speak to Jean Jacques to keep him updated and also to tell Celia who had just walked in. Jean Jacques postulated that they were trailing through the finances and wondered who was behind the 45% and lo and behold, it was some people from the insurance company side and immediately smelled corruption.

"They will be most disappointed when we turn up to the meeting."

"We turn up?" queried Mike.

"Yes we, as you will need my deliberate, painfully detailed input to put their brains into a kind of stupor. I will draw up graphs to show there was no particular bias towards the 45% and that all of our decisions were based on what was best for the client and not what suited any particular Insurer. When I pause you hit them with the blarney and some more facts and then as you draw breath I start up again so by the end of the day they will want to draw a line under this episode and go home. My presentation will take 4 or 5 hours. Another reason you need me is my German is better than yours."

"Well, let the battle commence," said Mike grinning from ear to ear.

All went quiet for 3 weeks then the summons to appear arrived at the Swiss office; the address obviously having been supplied no doubt by Peter and the gang which was fine and they gave just a week's notice so not messing around.

Jean Jacques and Celia had prepared the defence making sure to not leave out any argument in defence of the company's neutrality insofar as its dealings with insurers were concerned.

Mike had scrolled through the arguments and agreed that they were strong and ought to succeed in batting away any suggestion of impropriety.

On the morning of the meeting, Mike, Jean Jacques and Celia walked into a very austere building in the heart of Berlin and were directed to the 10th floor about halfway up. They were ushered into the meeting room and because they were three, it caused quite a stir.

The chairperson, an elderly lady, was surrounded by two other persons on each side and she looked up over her spectacles and said: "I see you have brought a small army with you, Herr Black."

"No, just my chief financial controller who not only controls the finances but every minute part of the business and my daughter who will inherit the business when I retire."

"That's if you have a business to pass on," uttered one of the cretins on the right-hand wing.

"You would be well advised to enjoy your brief moment of feeling superior but it would have served you better to do your homework before casting aspersions against such respectable persons assembled here at your behest for if any of your accusations should leak, you will be smiling on the other side of your faces when the writs arrive."

Such aggression surprised everyone and a silence fell upon the room which Jean Jacques took immediate advantage of by asking about the modus operandi.

This intervention restarted the meeting but the cocky upstart felt somewhat embarrassed by the attack which had too much truth in it to be immediately rebuffed. Mike sat down awaiting the eventual onslaught by Jean Jacques which will not be until afternoon by the way things were labouring.

The prosecution's case, if it can be described as such, ended at 1200 hours and was based on guesswork and supposition; the only finger of suspicion being the 45% investment issue.

The chairperson decided to break for lunch and to reconvene at 1330 hours to allow plenty of time for the response. Little did she know.

At 1330 hours precisely, the afternoon session began with Jean Jacques in command. He produced graphs to show the distribution of insurance placings over the last 10 years followed by more statistics comparing the market quotes on all major accounts and explanations on each showing the reasoning for each placing with the particular insurer and why.

This avalanche of graphs and statistics had the minds of the adjudicators racing in all directions, trying to absorb and understand the implications of what they were reading, which was where Mike stepped up to paint an overarching picture and explain exactly what all the information demonstrated. At this point, Jean Jacques interrupted Mike by coming up with more graphs and statistics but in a summarising and much simpler format concluding that all transactions were carried out in accordance with the standards expected of high quality brokers.

The chairperson suspended the meeting until the morning at 1100 hours when they would announce their findings. Mike knew that they would find in their favour given the barrage of information produced.

The following morning Mike's optimism was proven to be justified in that the chairperson announced that no impropriety had occurred at any time since trading began and the matter was now closed.

After the formalities were closed, the chairperson approached Jean Jacques and congratulated him on the detail of his report finishing with "typically Swiss." He replied with a curt "of course" and smiled. She then turned to Mike and again congratulated him on the way his business in Frankfurt was run and added, "If they are all run like that, you have a very sound business model."

Mike replied: "They are as Jean Jacques is the Financial Director in overall charge."

She then went to have a word with Peter who was there representing the other 4 co-investors and dallied but only for a few moments after which Peter came to see Mike, Celia and Jean Jacques with the first words being: "That was just brilliant!"

"Yes, he is, isn't he?" nodding at Jean Jacques.

"Well, I feel like celebrating and so will my colleagues and we owe Jean Jacques a debt of gratitude. Well, Jean Jacques, are you happy to stay over and have a nice meal and some German beer?" asked Peter.

"I think that would be great but I will have wine not beer," was the immediate reply.

Peter phoned Wolfgang and asked him to get in touch with the others and come and join them in celebrating their success. Mike turned to Celia and asked if she would like to stay or disappear rather than hang about with a gaggle of old men to which she agreed to stay for lunch but would then catch the train back to Switzerland as she felt that an evening with all of them might be stretching it a bit.

They moved to one of Peter's favourite haunts and settled in at a table big enough for 8 and almost immediately in rolled Wolfgang Leo Franz and Karl all smiling and on top form. They were delighted to meet Celia and Jean Jacques. Their obvious relief and bubbling good humour indicated that they were in for one hell of an afternoon and evening. Perhaps Celia had made the right judgement thought Mike.

After lunch Celia stood up and said she was off to catch the train and in front of everybody kissed Mike on the cheek and said remember you are the oldest here so don't try to keep up with this bunch of renegades. They all laughed and promised to look after the old codger which of course was a promise not worth anything. Nevertheless, as Peter pointed out, taking into account some of Mike's escapades, he did not need looking after.

In fact at 79 years of age, Mike knew that he could not drink as much as he did when young and always managed to keep away from any mad extravagances that the rest would indulge in without a moment's hesitation. Tonight he wanted to ensure that Jean Jacques was the centre of attention and got the glory he so deservedly earned.

At about 1700 hours, they moved to a new venue a restaurant with a difference in that as well as food there was a typical German band pumping out popular music from the past as well as the present. The noise level was simply horrendous and the food was burgers or sausages but they did serve Jean Jacques's favourite Cote du Rhone wine. He was now getting quite merry and happy. Mike knew he was not used to over indulging so would need to keep an eye on him.

Halfway through the evening, the band took a break and the noise level dropped dramatically and the food ordered earlier was served which was efficiently done as all food was either burgers or sausages full stop.

Just as Mike was beginning to tuck into his burger, a young man about 25 plus years of age came over shouting at them saying: "You lot nobbled the BaFin and got away with murder. I and my colleagues from other papers were going to

241

call you out when you left the meeting and there were about 10 of us but we all got pulled at the last minute. Some instruction from on high."

"Perhaps the authorities didn't want you shouting foul when there was no foul," said Mike.

The youth wobbled, obviously drunk and continued: "You lot can do no wrong then with friends in high places."

Wolfgang aggressive as per usual fronted up the youth and towering over him said: "The only instruction you are going to get from on high is my fist if you don't fuck off."

That did the trick because one punch from Wolfgang would do serious damage and the youth was not quite that drunk yet. Mike considered whether or not he should try convincing him that there was no foul but the drink made him say to himself, *Bollocks, do I need the hassle*? The matter fell away into an abyss.

Watching Jean Jacques slowly getting drunk was very amusing and reminded Mike of a film he had seen about a race between antique planes based in the early 1900s where the man in charge of the sites a robust German was efficiency itself on the first leg of the race; less so as each stage came and went until near the end everyone was his friend and he could barely stand up with laughing and being super affable to everyone but he doggedly slurred his way to the end. Here and now, Jean Jacques was smiling and everyone was his friend. He had to direct the wine bottle with both hands to keep it over the glass as he tried to top up the bright red elixir. He looked at Mike and waved his glass before moving it to his mouth and missing it completely but not to be outdone, he gradually worked his glass in a sideways movement until he reached the required position to take another very deliberate mouthful. The success of this operation required another gleeful smile and a lift of the glass and then it was like the battery had run down and the lights went out.

Time for bed, he announced and closed his eyes. Mike moved quickly to take hold of him and said to the group he had better get him back to the hotel and Peter immediately said he would give him a hand as he would never manage on his own. Jean Jacques was still able to smile and thank them for being his friend. At the hotel they got him into bed and he was asleep before they left the room.

"A lovely man really," said Peter.

"You're not wrong. Better get you a taxi now."

"No need. I booked in earlier as I guessed it would be a hard time. I'm on the next floor up so see you for breakfast at 0900 hours."

242

Mike set his alarm for 8 am more in hope than expectation but surprisingly, he woke up feeling fine and can only put it down to the stringent purity laws applicable to German beer where no chemicals were allowed. He was down by 9 am to find Peter had beaten him down and jokingly said to him: "Have you put your towel by the swimming pool?"

Peter roared with laughter and said: "Gott im Himmel, your brain is quick in the morning."

"I had better phone Jean Jacques to see how he is," Mike suddenly said.

"No need; he has just walked in," said Peter waving to catch his attention.

Jean Jacques walked over to join them and asked how long they had been down but on looking at the table could see Mike had not had his breakfast yet.

"Oh good, we can go up together. I am famished," he announced with a grin.

"I didn't expect to see you up until midday," said Mike.

"Wine isn't called the gentle alcohol for nothing," he replied.

They settled down to breakfast and began talking over the previous day and how the stress gave away to relief and what they wondered was that youth babbling on about orders from on high.

"I wonder if it had anything to do with that job you had in preventing the assassination of Helmut Kohl," asked Peter.

"They wouldn't know it was us, so I don't think so."

"You would be surprised how after a few years keeping it secret might not be so important anymore and the word gets out. That would earn you a lot of brownie points as you say," continued Peter.

"Well, whoever pulled the media off us gets my thanks. Once that lot starts, you have trouble; even if you prove your innocence, the finger of suspicion is still pointing at you," said Mike while pouring another cup of coffee.

After breakfast, they booked out of the hotel and Peter made his way to the office with a light heart and a spring in his step while Mike and Jean Jacques caught the train back to Zurich.

On arrival in Zurich, Mike decided to head for home while Jean Jacques opted for the office. When Mike alighted from the taxi at his front door, Helen came out to greet him smiling broadly saying: "You must be shattered after your victory."

"Yes; not from the inquest but from the celebrations afterwards; it was worth it to see Jean Jacques relax and get totally plastered but he is a very pleasant drunk all smiles and good humour. I have decided we need to have a good break from business and do a tour around Europe travelling wherever we feel like with no real plan. What do you say?"

"That's sounds very adventurist; are you sure you are up to the driving?"

"Oh! Yes as we can stop whenever we want and book into a hotel and with the Sat Nav I can even phone ahead to a town and book a hotel and then use that as the destination. All very easy. Are you up for it?"

"Yes but I will need a few days to get organised with clothes and things. Let's say we leave on Monday. I know it's the middle of August but as we are not sun worshippers, we won't be joining the throngs and should only have a marginal increase in the crowd level."

"That sounds perfect. I just feel I need to cut off completely."

Mike had now reached the stage where Celia had basically taken over and according to Jean Jacques, she would be brilliant at his role in overseeing the whole network and controlling it financially, in fact she would be better at it than Mike himself who never really got into that kind of detail hence the need for Jean Jacques but now it seems she can replace both of them so that saves money when Jean Jacques decides to retire. Of course, she can always call on Helen to assist on the financial side if required.

That was the business nicely taken care of and his son James having completed his drama course was now starting his acting career and in constant work with the likelihood of great things to come. He will be nevertheless supported by the business from time to time as necessary although he has not made any extra demands other than his allowance so far while the youngest Pierre is in Normandy enjoying himself and getting noticed by the Artworld so perhaps he too might be a success. Only time will tell in that strange world.

In his early days, Mike had wondered if he might have made a success as an artist as he had a certain talent and whilst it was miles better that anyone else he came into contact with was it good enough when compared to some of the great masters from the past. But then the exciting world of business intruded and the allure of making money and building up a business took over and he got caught up in a whirlwind of success after success. The effect was intoxicating and there was no way out until the end of the road which he had now reached or had he just got old, perhaps both.

Mike now wanted to see if he could cut off completely as if the business was no longer his concern or would the stress of that course be even greater that the stress of being involved.

He could always backtrack he told himself. He knew of so many people who died after retiring that he approached this stage with a certain trepidation. He hoped that touring around Europe would keep his mind excited enough to get over the hill of change whereby he could settle down to a slower and more enjoyable lifestyle. Well Monday will be the beginning.

Chapter 34

Monday morning, 12 August 2019, Mike and Helen set off on their adventure heading east into Austria, stopping in little villages as they went for ice cream or a coffee or just to have a look at some beautiful scenery but there is so much of it that the temptation is overwhelming. The first city they came across where they stopped to spend the evening was Innsbruck a beautiful place with a river running through and the snow-capped Alps dominating the whole area. They booked into a city centre hotel so they could walk down where all the outdoor cafes were bustling with tourists and decide which one seemed to be offering the best food by looking at what people were ordering. Eventually, they settled on one place; quite busy which was a good sign and settled down to relax.

They ordered their drinks; wine for Helen and beer for Mike which arrived quickly. While waiting for their meal, they discussed where they might go next and Mike suggested Vienna and contacting Gabriel at the office for there was a client that he promised to take out to dinner Erik Hauptmann who had had a problem and needed their special services. They succeeded in bringing his problem to a successful conclusion to the client's delight and as a thank you he transferred his business to them. Mike explained that he was a similar type to Peter in Frankfurt and very enjoyable company. Helen said why not meet him for in her opinion meeting people as they travelled simply enhanced the whole experience. That was settled then.

In the morning, Mike phoned Gabriel and explained that he would like to meet up with Erik Hauptmann as he had promised to take him to dinner and as he and Helen would be in the neighbourhood on holiday in a day or so as they wanted to see Salzburg first and then would go straight to Vienna he wondered if he and Erik plus their wives might be free in say three days. Gabriel was delighted at the idea and would speak to Erik that day to see if he was available.

Salzburg was a delightful mix of the Altstadt and the Neustadt one on each side of the river and the birthplace of Mozart was kept as a museum displaying his early musical instruments. The power of music to keep him famous for goodness knows how long is very impressive and it will continue for many more years to come possibly hundreds more.

They stayed just one day and then headed for Vienna which Mike was looking forward to particularly both from the point of view of the restaurants and hopefully the meeting with Erik. Along the way Mike received a phone call from Gabriel saying the meeting was all fixed up for the evening after next so Mike clarified it by saying Friday as he hated any vagueness and got confirmation from Gabriel:

"Right, so I will see you Friday evening and you will fix up the restaurant somewhere really nice as he apart from being a lovely chap is an important client and must be one of your biggest."

"He is the biggest and has almost doubled in size since he moved to us."

"Helen is looking forward to meeting you and your staff and of course, your wife, so we will have a great evening."

They arrived in Vienna late afternoon on Wednesday and booked into their hotel and then went for a walk around to stretch their legs and admire the beauty of the city. They had a drink in Mozart's favourite restaurant and were tempted to eat there but decided to return to the hotel so they could relax after a tiring day's driving.

Thursday they did their sightseeing and thoroughly enjoyed their day getting back to the hotel at 2100 hours just in time for a nightcap.

They had the following day to themselves until 1700 hours when they would meet up with Gabriel and his wife and then join up with Erik and his wife at the restaurant. So they decided to take a trip organised by the hotel on the river Danube. The hotel provided the transport to the boat and they and a few fellow travellers were given priority on board to first class accommodation which suited Mike who hated crowds. The journey along the river was great and the weather beautiful which made it all the more enjoyable especially the stop for lunch. They arrived back at 1530 hours which gave them plenty of time to get ready to meet their evening guests.

At 1600 hours precisely, Mike's mobile rang and it was Gabriel phoning to say all was set up to meet Erik and his wife Margot.

"Heidi and I will pick you up from the hotel at 1700 hours as we are meeting Erik at the restaurant. It's called Metropole Wien and it's supposed to be the latest thing in chiche and I'm afraid horribly expensive."

"The expense is worth it for such a good client just so long as we have a nice time. See you at 5 pm and thanks for picking us up."

Mike told Helen the timetable so she could ensure she was ready on time which to be fair, she nearly always was.

At 5 pm they wandered down to the foyer just as Gabriel and Heidi walked in which was perfect and the introductions were soon completed with Helen getting on with Gabriel and Heidi instantly, which was a relief to Mike as one can never be sure with women as they either get on famously or hate each other's guts. Heidi was a pretty dark-haired girl of slim build and open personality and talked easily, which fitted in with Helen.

On the way to the restaurant which was about 20 minutes away, Gabriel, affectionately referred to as Gabby by Heidi, filled in Mike on the latest amendments to the insurances and the revised sums insured etc which was all very impressive.

"So Optocreux are expanding quite rapidly lately. Have they any more plans, do you think?"

"Erik takes it all in his stride and acts like it is all very naturel and no big deal," said Gabriel, full of admiration for Erik.

"That's the confidence of success and money."

They pulled up in front of a very impressive edifice double fronted with large stone covered porch supported by stout pillars at the top of a 5 step entrance with flunkies guarding the doors. It made its point effortlessly.

Mike asked: "Is this place run by an Italian by any chance?"

"Yes, why?"

"Thought so," Mike replied smiling to himself which left Gabby wondering what the significance was.

They alighted and paused for a moment and then a too good looking young middle eastern Romeo arrived to park the vehicle casting a delighted look over the expensive top of the range Mercedes as he slithered into the driver's seat and whisked the vehicle with great flair, much to Gabby's consternation, somewhere around the back.

It didn't help with Helen saying: "Who's to say he doesn't take that for a spin later on?"

This made Mike roar with laughter as he saw the expression on Gabriel's face but Helen continued saying they should return the keys which made Gabby about to intervene with one of the door flunkies until Heidi stepped in to calm him down saying it was all insured so relax. He then looked at Mike and started to see the funny side and laughed as well which made the girls join in and that was how it was when they bumped into Erik and Margot who had only just arrived before them. Erik looked great for his 75 years.

Mike grabbed Erik's outstretched hand and introduced Helen and Heidi to both and Margo wanted to know what they were all laughing about so Mike explained in detail which had the same effect on them especially when Mike emphasised Gabriel's expression as the Romeo driver gave the car its first shock.

When they stopped laughing, they looked around the restaurant and it was stupendous no other word for it from the table decorations ranging from delicate splashes of red and blue with flowers to match but not so large as to obstruct one's view. Large chandeliers running along the full length of the room a full 20 metres or so. Mirrors and large paintings adorned the walls some paintings classical in style and other bold and modern but reflecting the colour scheme of the table set up. They were taken to a table with a view over a rear garden at the bottom of which was a lake lit up with ornate lights giving beautiful reflections in the calm waters.

"It is nice here," said Margot, looking around, "and the lake is particularly beautiful," with which they all murmured their agreement.

Erik said to Margot: "This is the man who sorted out my Russian problem and coached me all the way through it. You remember how worried I was?"

"Indeed I do; it was a horrific time not knowing what was going to happen as they threatened our family and knew all our names. It still gives me the shudders."

"Well, it's all over now and obviously not going to arise again. We have all retired from that side of things but we can resurrect it if any of the people we helped need our assistance again as apart from me they are all still young and I can still plan operations if need be but hopefully that will not be necessary. Anyway Erik, I understand you are going on from strength to strength," said Mike in an effort to change the subject.

"Yes, things are flying high at the moment and long may it continue," he said crossing his chest.

"How long are you going to continue working, Erik?" Mike enquired grinning.

"As long as I feel like it. It seems if you retire, you end up dying shortly afterwards. I suppose it's the sudden change in tempo that does it so I will keep motoring on and just ease off gradually; that way, I get the best of both worlds."

"I agree. I say I have retired but really I have just delegated all the hard work to my daughter and I will keep doing the easy bits like visiting the various companies and meeting people while I am on holiday all mixed up together. Like you, the best of both worlds."

"I'll drink to that," said Erik raising his glass.

Everyone joined in and that was the beginning of a relaxed evening. Helen and Margot found they had a lot in common and found they identified with each other's perspective on things in general. Helen made sure to include Heidi in the conversation as it must have been difficult for her and Gabby both being younger.

The dinner was wonderful as one would expect and as the alcohol flowed so did the conversation in all directions without hindrance due to age or nationalities. All were enjoying the evening and when it was time to depart Erik asked Mike and Helen where they were off to next and Mike replied Italy.

"Well, on your way back, you must come and stay with us at our home for a few days so we can get to know each other better."

"Oh! Yes, you must," said Margot looking at both Mike and Helen.

Mike and Helen agreed and they all made their way outside. The flunkies got Erik's car first and they all said their goodbyes accompanied by the usual air kissing.

"Heidi, tonight must have been stressful for you but you have entered into the evening and really shown how well you can mix with older people so thank you for that," said Mike and turning to Gabriel said that when they got back from Italy, they will call him and they will have another evening just the four of them and he must choose where he would like to go.

"Great, we will look forward to that and will find somewhere interesting to take you both, perhaps with music?" he asked with a raised eyebrow.

Mike and Helen both nodded agreement and then Gabriel's car arrived back all safe and sound and they piled in. Fortunately, Gabriel had been very careful with the drinking and consumed mostly non-alcoholic beer, his last pint and a half being three hours earlier. Gabriel dropped them off at their hotel and they said their au revoir until they returned from Italy.

In the morning after breakfast, they strode with their bags to the BMW and got themselves comfortable while Mike set the Sat Nav for Hotel Venezia

Mestre. He explained that when they got close to Venice, i.e., Mestre, they would book into the Hotel Venezia on the mainland with secure parking and then either go on a hotel organised trip or get a taxi to the departure point for Venice. "If I leave the car parked on the quayside while in Venice, it might not be there when we return. Venice is crammed with history and architectural beauty; in fact, so is the whole of Italy. You will see that being in Italy is like dying and waking up in heaven."

"I can't wait. How do you know so much about it?"

"I was there in the mid-sixties but never had a chance to get back so this will be interesting to see if it's still as good as I remember it."

They set off full of expectation and Mike explained that the last time he had to watch his money carefully and the car broke down which cost a small fortune but trying to get the bank in the UK to transfer the funds to a bank in Italy was a nightmare full of bureaucracy.

"This time, if anything goes wrong, we have more than enough so we can relax and now with cards, it is easy to pay for something so no stress," he said with a smile all of which amused Helen.

"I never realised you were such a worrier but on the other hand, you can get mixed up in horrendous dogfights with bullets flying all over the place and that doesn't seem to be a concern."

"That's different; on those I have thought the whole thing through where I actually see it like a video in my mind and I have planned options for every possible variation that might occur. So you see, there can be no surprises."

"What, just like a game of chess?"

"Yes but I am no good at chess because it's only a game so I can't engage with it whereas in real life chess, one slip or one omission could result in your or your friends' death so it must not happen and it never did."

The journey down was very pleasant with great scenery and then once in Italy, Mike opened the windows slightly in one of the towns to let Helen experience the noise level of Italians going about their daily business. She could not believe it. It was deafening but as Mike pointed out, the place was pulsating with life and what was more, it was infectious; absolutely wonderful. Although if you look closely at the actual activity, it is all done in slow motion probably due to the heat.

Mike pointed out the slow rate of activity apart from when there is a traffic fight then punches can be thrown much to onlookers delight and after a few minutes it all simmers down and the onlookers shrug their shoulders and laugh while they get back in their vehicles.

All of this reminded Mike of the last time when he came this way of the difference between the North, i.e., Germany, where he was visiting a zoo and standing by the enclosure of the ostriches where a worker was cleaning the bird's mess with a dustpan and brush rather like the one used in the home, only bigger; when one of the birds obviously didn't like what the worker was doing albeit he was working very efficiently with quick deft strokes until the ostrich started pecking his heel. At first the worker just turned around and shooed him away but the bird persisted so the worker put down his tools and grabbed the ostrich by the neck, pulling his head level with his own and stared into the bird's eyes while he smacked it across the face both ways.

To say the bird had a surprised look on his face was probably exaggerating but then the worker turned the bird around facing the shed at the other end and frogmarched the bird holding his neck and his backside while he strutted towards the shed and pushed the bird inside and slammed the door shut. Then he returned to his duties, carrying on in the same efficient manner. The whole incident made the onlookers giggle and shake their heads in disbelief.

They soon arrived at their hotel, a large substantial building in the town centre with secure parking, and they grabbed their cases and made their way to reception. While booking in, they sorted out their visit to Venice as the hotel did arrange daily visits at reasonable rates. A visit was arranged for the next day commencing just after breakfast at 0900 hours.

In the morning, a mini bus arrived to take three couples to the departure place for Venice proper. It was a bit basic but Mike and Helen were both used to roughing it in the past so it did not bother them. They were dropped off where the ferry was moored and told they would be collected at 1900 hours, which gave them a full day to explore.

They did Piazza San Marco and took a gondola through various back waters which was quite fascinating but one needed an umbrella to protect from the grilling sun. When they left the gondola they headed straight to the first place selling ice cream and bought large cones each and then looked for somewhere to eat. The afternoon was spent roaming around art galleries and churches. The buildings had great histories but after so many visits they were quite tired and were glad when 18.30 hours arrived and they were due back at the ferry.

That evening, they ate at the hotel as they were too tired and suffering from heat exhaustion to wander any more.

The next day, they got up late and had a leisurely continental breakfast starting with a bowlful of fruit followed with fresh rolls and sliced meats plus the usual pot of well-blended coffee. Then they checked out and made their way to Florence which they were really looking forward to seeing. Mike had been there before but it was all a bit blurred in his mind but he remembered the Cattedrale di Santa Maria del Fiore or simply the Duomo di Firenze but when he got there, he remembered standing in front of the entrance and the strict rules before entering especially applying to women such as arms above the elbow covered. The next place was the Uffizi Gallery full of magnificent renaissance paintings. These take your breath away, they are so beautifully painted with such great detail almost as if a photograph had been taken of the scene.

They had some lunch and then headed to Pisa and the leaning tower and from there to Rome and drove straight through Naples and on to Sorrento and the Amalfi Coast where they stayed for a week relaxing and swimming in the warm sea. Mike looked up at the mountainside while floating on his back like he did when young and the memory had stayed true in his mind; the pinkish-purple heat haze broken by little white dots being the luxury villas spaced out all the way to the top. He resolved to memorise it again as it was simply a perfect fantasy picture but he had no desire to live here too warm to do anything except laze about.

When the week was up, they headed back north and on the winding west coast weaving in and out with numerous blind bends; Mike kept blowing the horn as did drivers coming in the opposite direction. Helen asked him why he kept doing it and Mike explained: "I very quickly noticed in the 60s that if I did not respond to the horns coming the opposite way, they came too close. At the time, I was travelling with a girlfriend who had dozed off and with a car coming around the corner and in my lane, I shouted SHIT and braked hard, jerking the car so sharply that my friend woke up screaming with fear and swearing at me demanding to know what was happening and I remember my reply which was that bastard took a coat of paint off my bonnet as he passed. Needless to say, she didn't see the funny side.

"I started replying to the sound of a horn by blasting mine and then I knew that was the unofficial code; if no reply then it was safe to cut the corner but if you got a reply, keep to your own side. In fact I never cut the corner but still sounded the horn. They also used to sound the horn when overtaking and some still do. At first that used to irritate me but then I saw the sense, particularly when I got beeped and I waved them on and the wagon passed with a load of workmen standing and waving at me from the open back with large smiles as they roared past. Very pleasant but mad as hatters the lot of them."

"I've noticed that about Italians but they are very friendly and nice," Helen said laughing.

When they got as far north as Pisa, Mike decided to head east to get over to near Rimini and head north from there to Vienna. Mike asked Helen to phone Gabriel to see if all was OK with him and tell him they would see him tomorrow and then phone Margot to make sure it was still on to visit them for the weekend.

Mike suggested that they stay in Italy for the day and cross the border tomorrow morning so they can enjoy one more day of the Italian atmosphere and this she agreed to enthusiastically as, like Mike, she had fallen in love with the whole experience.

The first thing they noticed the following morning on crossing the border was the sudden lack of noise. It was like someone had closed the door and shut the carnival off. The sudden drop to almost complete silence was quite unnerving.

"Can we go back?"

"What now?"

"No, no, not now but sometime soon."

"Of course, I feel like that too."

Mike started thinking about Italy and what it was that made you want to always go back and decided that it was addictive the feeling of being alive, living life as it should be, laughing, shouting, squabbling and making up noisily and being placated with love and laughter all happening at once and afterwards moving on to someone else's squabble and smiling with the shrugging of shoulders as everyone realises the pointlessness of falling out but that's life; a never ending road but at least you are in the middle of it all surrounded by stunning beauty and spoiled by the most tantalising meals one could ever dream of, and to Mike, that was the full meaning of La dolce Vita.

Helen had dialled Gabriel at the office in Vienna and the ringtone brought Mike back to reality with a lurch.

"Hi Gabriel, it's Helen and you are on speaker. We are going to be there about 12 noon so see you for lunch if you are free and then we move on to Erik and Margot for the weekend."

"Yes, look forward to seeing you and Mike. Hope you had a nice holiday?"

"Yes it was lovely. Tell you all about it later."

After lunch with Gabriel, they phoned Margot to confirm that they were on their way and she gave them a few tips on what to look out for on the way. They followed the Sat Nav and were soon in the vicinity which was very obviously an upmarket area as they drove down a tree-lined avenue with high walls and imposing tall iron gates or heavy wooden ones all protected by cameras and microphones you had to speak into to attract attention. Some had cheeky messages like 'smile you are on camera'. Eventually, they came to Erik's place again with large heavy wooden double gates and Mike had to get out to speak into the console before the gates ponderously opened to reveal a long avenue leading up to a small chateau.

"Very impressive," said Helen.

"Well, I guessed it would be as he is very rich indeed."

"Not for you though."

"No, not for me. The more ostentatious you are, the more attention you attract and the more security you need but eventually, you get robbed and if you are unlucky, killed. We have gone halfway along that road and that is far enough unless you insist?" Mike asked with raised eyebrow.

"No, but it will be nice to spend the weekend in a castle and we can brag about our friends who own a castle."

"We surely can," said Mike laughing.

As they pulled up at the front entrance, Margot and two young male assistants came out to greet and to help them unpack the car. Margot was her usual self and announced that Erik would be home early as he was looking forward to their visit. The Chateau was on top of a slight hill so overlooked most of the countryside, giving a feeling of superiority all very impressive.

As they entered the main entrance, it opened up into a large hall area with an impressive mahogany front facing staircase rising up but splitting to the left and right at the top making it look massive. The deep red carpet edged with a gold design gave the hall a feeling of total opulence.

"Your cases have been placed in the blue room which is on the right and the second door on the right so you are at the front with a nice view over the countryside," Margot informed them as she ushered them in for afternoon tea, or coffee if preferred.

They all sat down and Mike decided, in spite of the pomp and ceremony, that he was going to relax and enjoy the weekend. He guessed that Margot was slightly uncomfortable being the hostess with the mostest so he broke the ice by telling her about the zoo worker and particularly emphasising the efficiency of the German keeper frogmarching the ostrich to his hut and as she started laughing, he followed up with the crazy rules on the S bends down the west coast of Italy and about the first time he discovered the unwritten rules and the old girlfriend who woke up screaming.

At this she laughed heartily and totally relaxed with tears running down her face at which point in walked Erik who was laughing due to the infectious affect. Margot insisted that he tell Erik about the crazy S bend rules which he did and threw in a few other anecdotes on reminders from Helen.

"Now you have retired from your off piste activities, do you ever get asked to do any more of these jobs?" asked Erik.

"Not so far but it's not just me that has retired; it's also Lisa and Harry who incidentally have shacked up together and live just over the border from Zurich in Germany. It would have to be something very special to entice them to come out of retirement."

"I thought she was a lesbian?" said Erik.

"She was but Harry is something special according to her so good luck to them I say."

"Oh exactly, it takes all sorts," said Margot and then continued saying, "It takes all sorts; funny expression that."

"Tonight, we eat here as you must be tired but tomorrow, I have booked us into a concert with music by Mozart in the first half and Johann Strauss in the second half. It's all very cleverly done I'm told with the first half being in a serious mood and then in the second half the backdrop is changed to a pub garden rather like a Renoir painting with revellers drinking and chatting in the foreground and in the background many dancing to the various waltzes as the music takes on a light-hearted even bawdy atmosphere. The lot done in period costumes should be good," said Erik.

"Sounds great," chorused Helen and Mike.

The weekend was everything they expected but soon came to an end and on the Monday, Mike and Helen went to the office to see Gabriel and arranged the evening dinner with him and Heidi that they had agreed to before their trip to Italy.

Tuesday morning, they left to return home and arrived in mid-afternoon. Both were glad to be able to relax and do absolutely nothing for the rest of the day, apart from emptying the car.

They talked about their adventure and decided that the holiday had been fantastic but they had crammed too many other visits in which made it a bit heavy going, so decided to play it differently on the next adventure.

After a couple of days of relaxation, they both recovered their strength and good spirits and were ready to take on the world again.

On Saturday, Mike and Helen had the house to themselves which was unusual but the staff had been given a week off on holiday and Celia was on a visit to the Amsterdam office.

Being alone seemed to change Helen's attitude towards Mike in that she was constantly flirting which made Mike adopt the same attitude, ending up with Helen teasing and running away giggling as she ran upstairs holding her floral dress up at the front, thus exaggerating her pert bottom, teasing Mike even more. He ran upstairs and at 79 years of age found it taking his breath away slightly; as he licked his lips, he wondered if he looked like some know-it-all lizard with eyes popping, chasing its target and said out loud: "This could be the end of you, Mike, old chap."

In the event, he survived the encounter but as he was getting out of the shower, he slipped and banged his head on the way down which stunned him slightly and he encountered those gargoyles again still laughing at his misadventure.

Helen was leaning over him, asking if he was alright, and he replied: "It's those bloody gargoyles again so I told them to sod off. I'm not going yet."

THE END